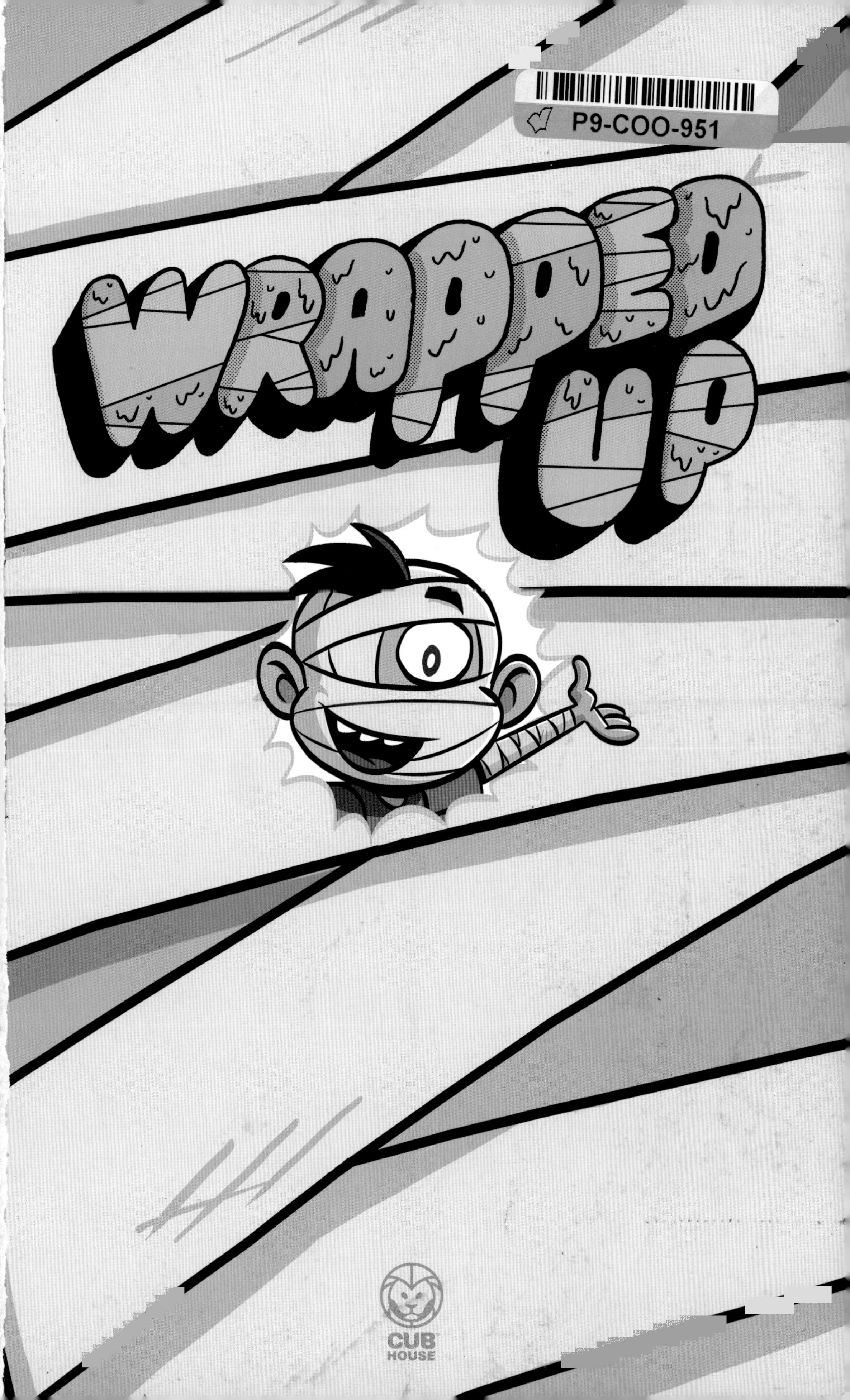
WRAPPED UP
CUB HOUSE

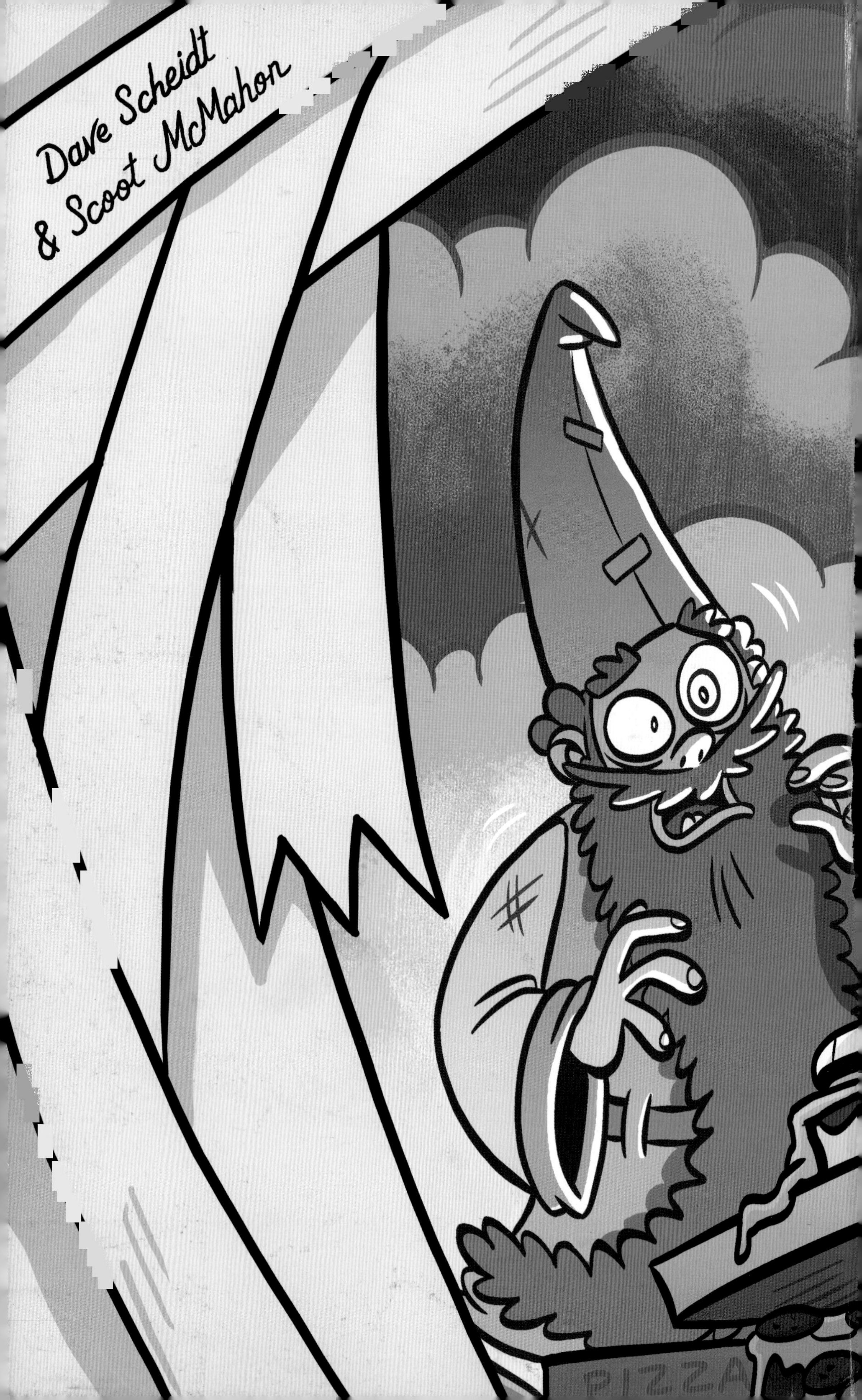
Dave Scheidt
& Scoot McMahon
PIZZA

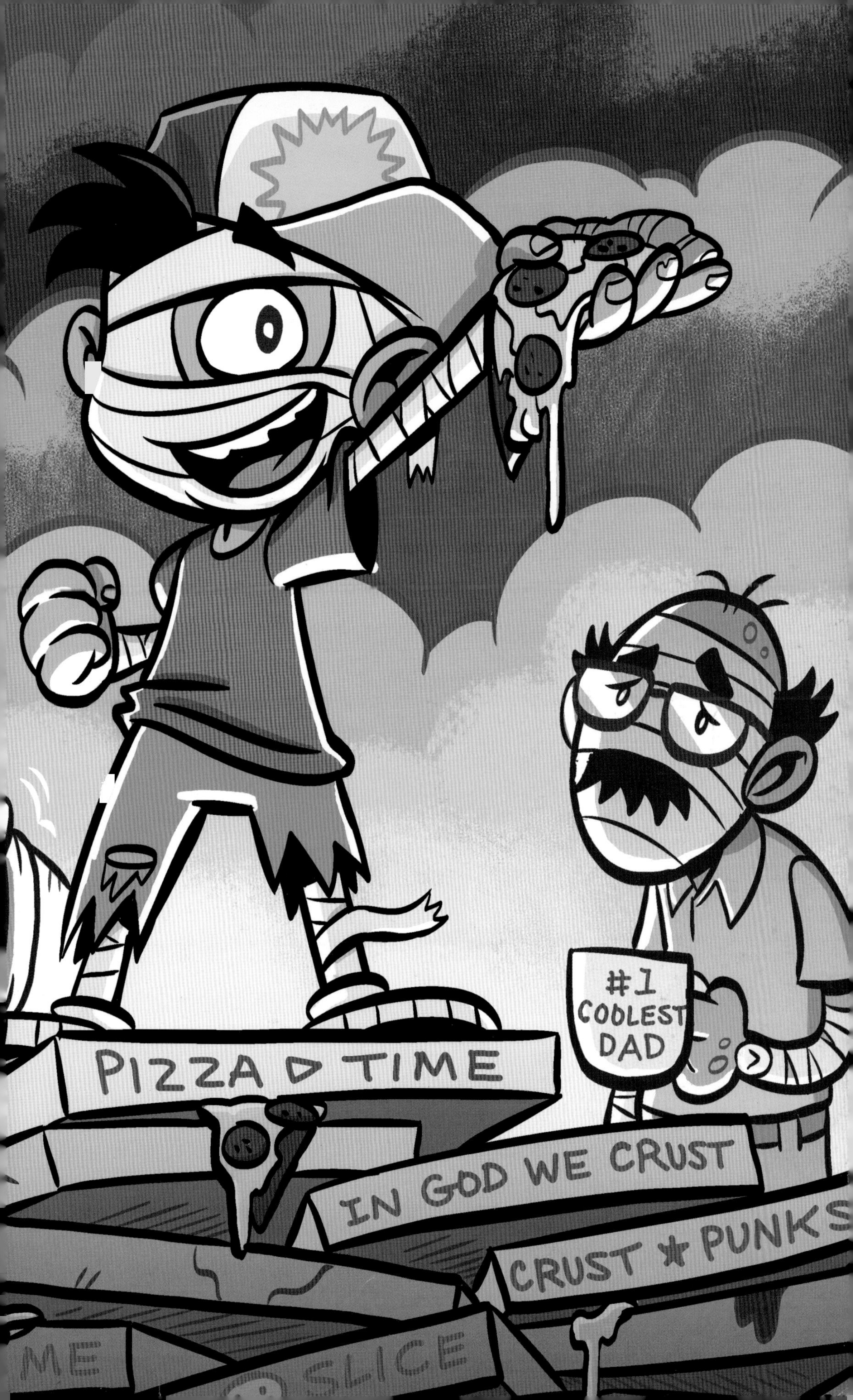
#1
COOLEST
DAD
PIZZA TIME
IN GOD WE CRUST
CRUST PUNKS
SLICE

WRITER
Dave Scheidt

ARTIST
Scoot McMahon

COLORIST
Sean Dove

BACKUP STORY ARTISTS

Jess Smart Smiley   Carolyn Nowak

Miranda Harmon   Kelsey Wroten   Coleman Engle

Editor: Hazel Newlevant

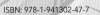

ISBN: 978-1-941302-47-7

Library of Congress Control Number: 2017955348

Wrapped Up, Vol. 1, published 2018 by The Lion Forge, LLC. Copyright 2018 The Lion Forge, LLC. Portions of this book were previously published in Wrapped Up, Issues 1-5 Copyright © 2017 - 2018 The Lion Forge, LLC. LION FORGE™, WRAPPED UP™, CUBHOUSE™, and their associated distinctive designs, as well as all characters featured in this book and the distinctive names and likenesses thereof, and all related indicia, are trademarks of The Lion Forge, LLC. All Rights Reserved. No similarity between any of the names, characters, persons, or institutions in this issue with those of any living or dead person or institution is intended, and any such similarity which may exist is purely coincidental. Printed in China.

10 9 8 7 6 5 4 3 2 1

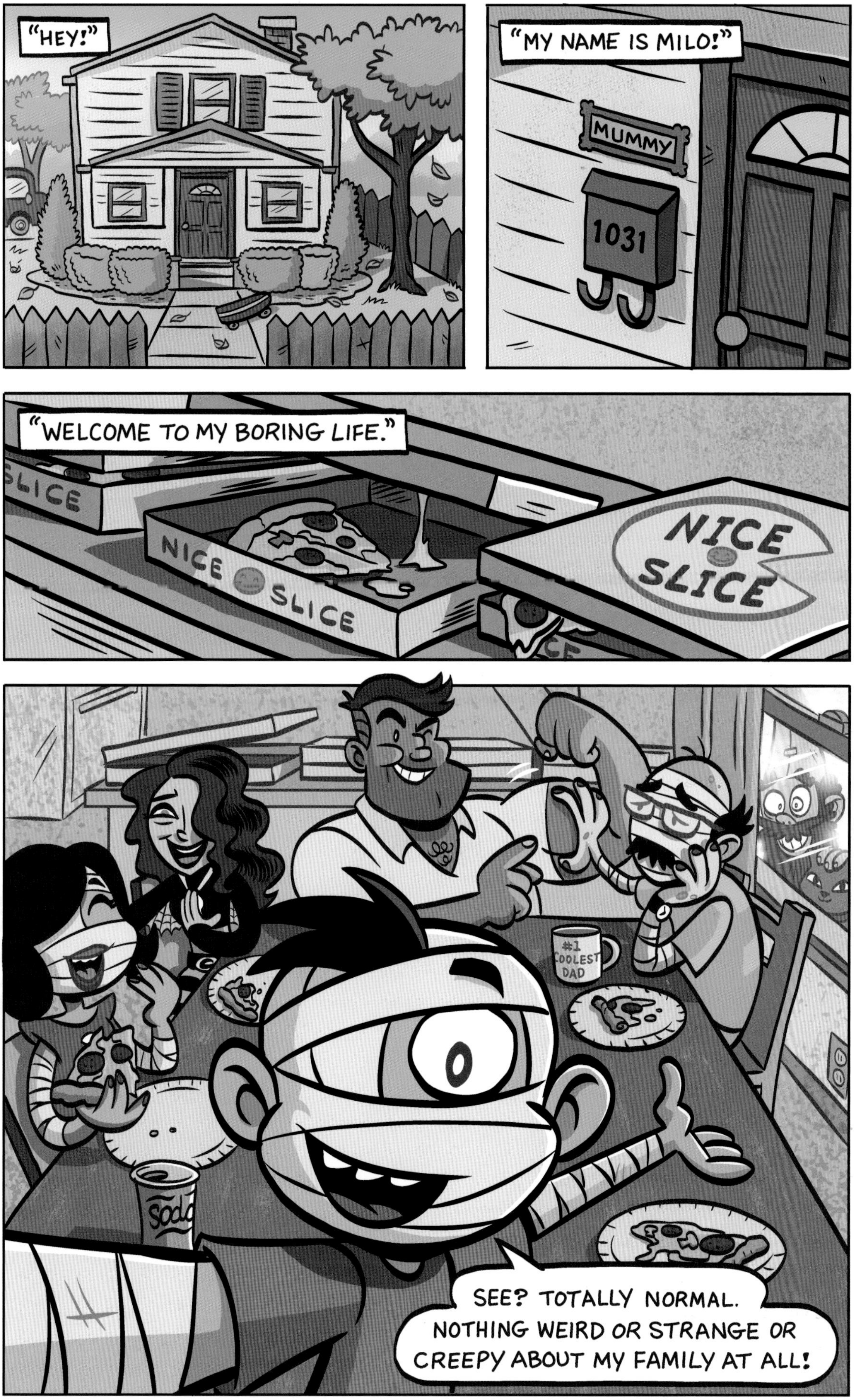
"HEY!"
"MY NAME IS MILO!"
MUMMY
1031
"WELCOME TO MY BORING LIFE."
SLICE
NICE SLICE
NICE SLICE
#1 COOLEST DAD
Soda
SEE? TOTALLY NORMAL. NOTHING WEIRD OR STRANGE OR CREEPY ABOUT MY FAMILY AT ALL!

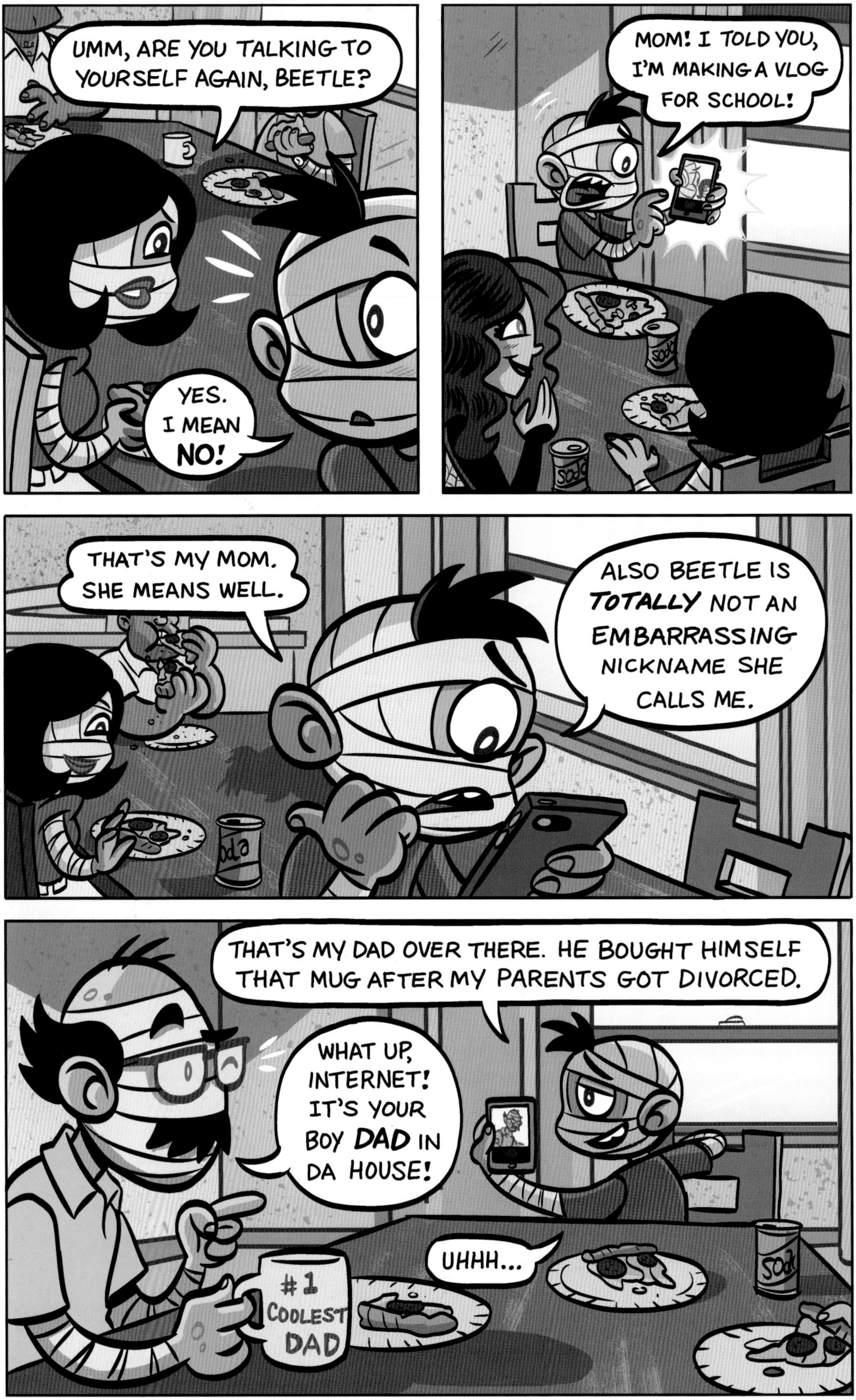
UMM, ARE YOU TALKING TO YOURSELF AGAIN, BEETLE?
YES. I MEAN NO!
MOM! I TOLD YOU, I'M MAKING A VLOG FOR SCHOOL!
SODA
SODA
THAT'S MY MOM. SHE MEANS WELL.
ALSO BEETLE IS TOTALLY NOT AN EMBARRASSING NICKNAME SHE CALLS ME.
SODA
THAT'S MY DAD OVER THERE. HE BOUGHT HIMSELF THAT MUG AFTER MY PARENTS GOT DIVORCED.
WHAT UP, INTERNET! IT'S YOUR BOY DAD IN DA HOUSE!
UHHH...
#1 COOLEST DAD
SODA

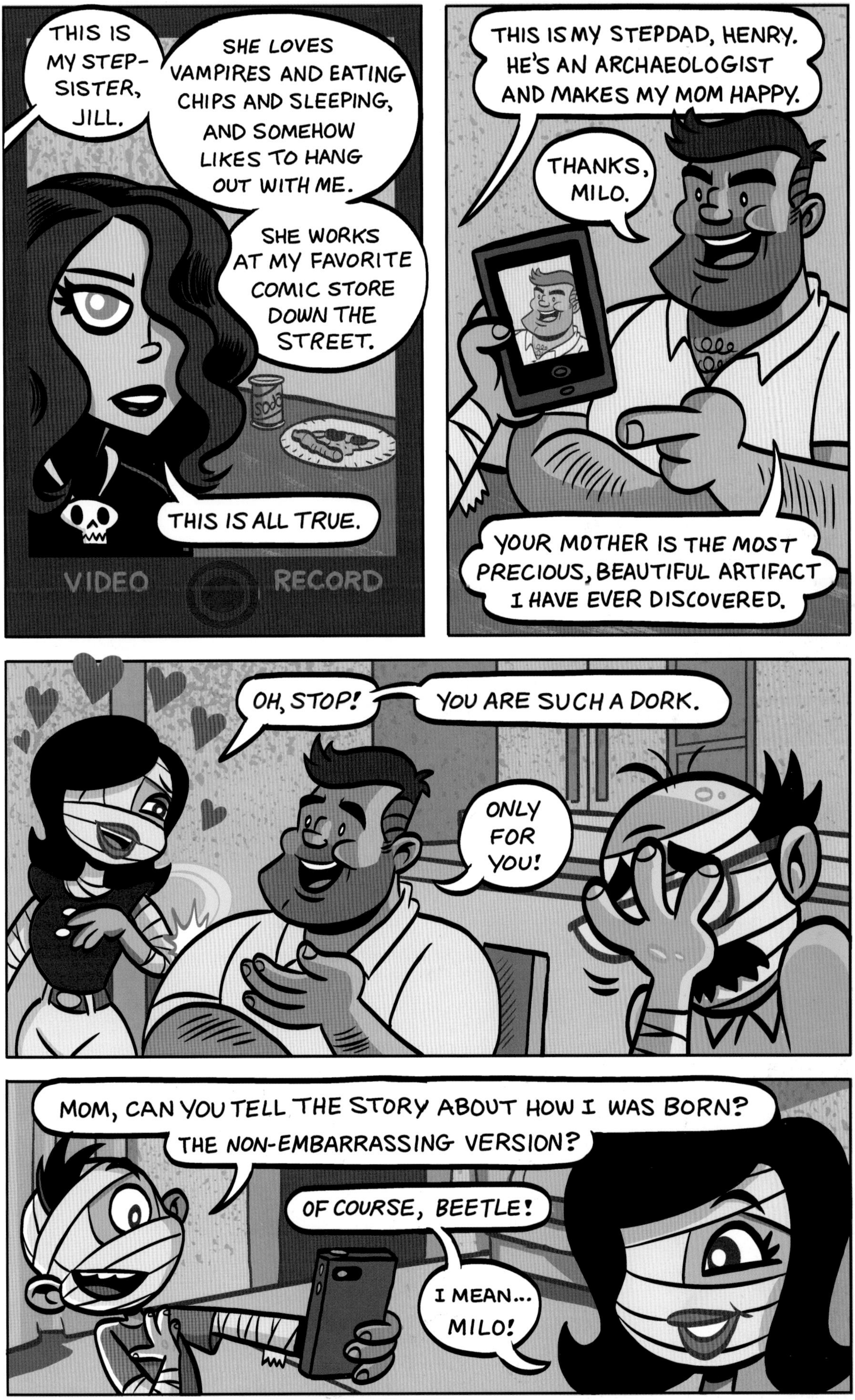
THIS IS MY STEP-SISTER, JILL.
SHE LOVES VAMPIRES AND EATING CHIPS AND SLEEPING, AND SOMEHOW LIKES TO HANG OUT WITH ME.
SHE WORKS AT MY FAVORITE COMIC STORE DOWN THE STREET.
SODA
THIS IS ALL TRUE.
VIDEO
RECORD
THIS IS MY STEPDAD, HENRY. HE'S AN ARCHAEOLOGIST AND MAKES MY MOM HAPPY.
THANKS, MILO.
YOUR MOTHER IS THE MOST PRECIOUS, BEAUTIFUL ARTIFACT I HAVE EVER DISCOVERED.
OH, STOP!
YOU ARE SUCH A DORK.
ONLY FOR YOU!
MOM, CAN YOU TELL THE STORY ABOUT HOW I WAS BORN? THE NON-EMBARRASSING VERSION?
OF COURSE, BEETLE!
I MEAN... MILO!

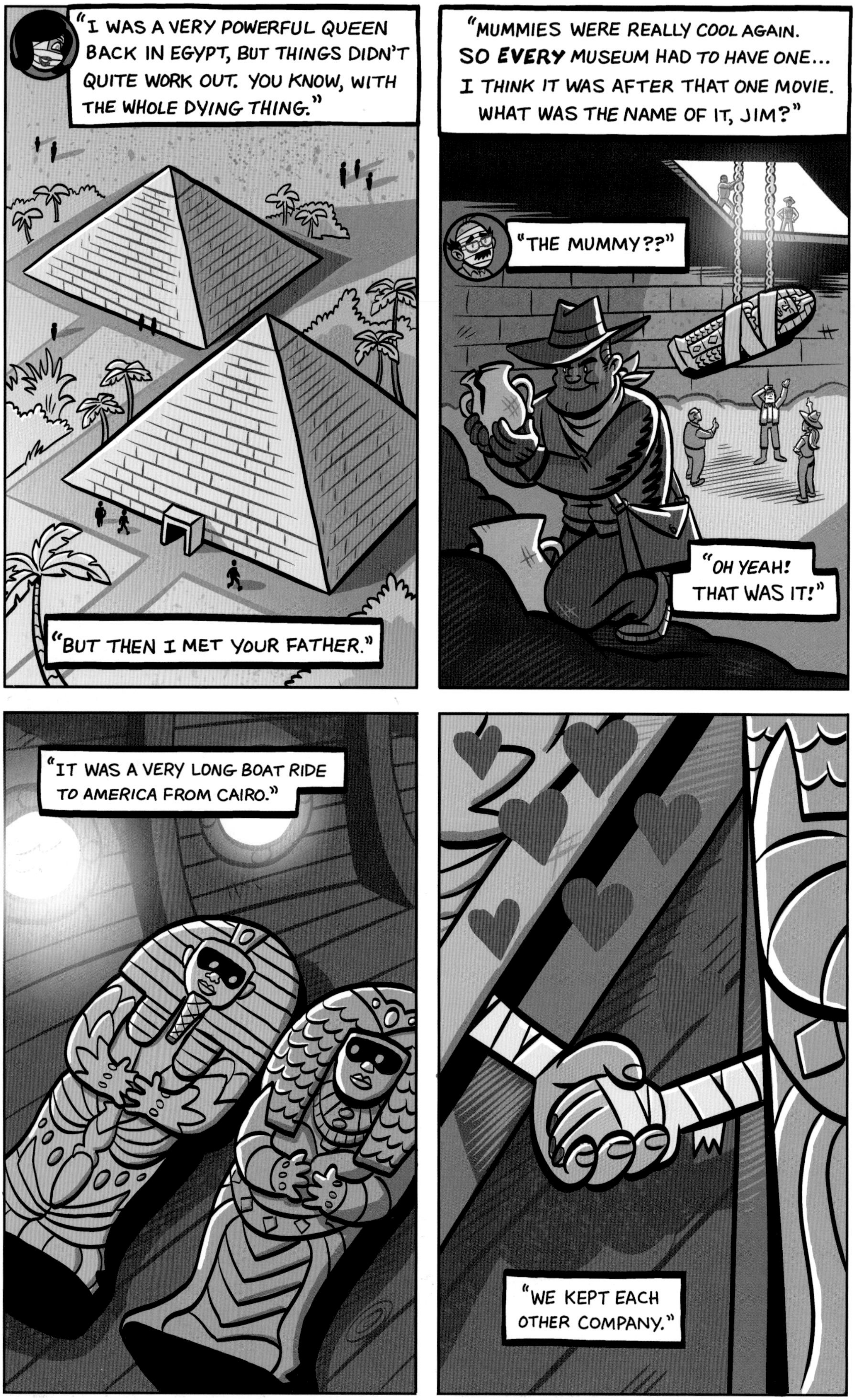
"I WAS A VERY POWERFUL QUEEN BACK IN EGYPT, BUT THINGS DIDN'T QUITE WORK OUT. YOU KNOW, WITH THE WHOLE DYING THING."
"BUT THEN I MET YOUR FATHER."
"MUMMIES WERE REALLY COOL AGAIN. SO EVERY MUSEUM HAD TO HAVE ONE... I THINK IT WAS AFTER THAT ONE MOVIE. WHAT WAS THE NAME OF IT, JIM?"
"THE MUMMY??"
"OH YEAH! THAT WAS IT!"
"IT WAS A VERY LONG BOAT RIDE TO AMERICA FROM CAIRO."
"WE KEPT EACH OTHER COMPANY."

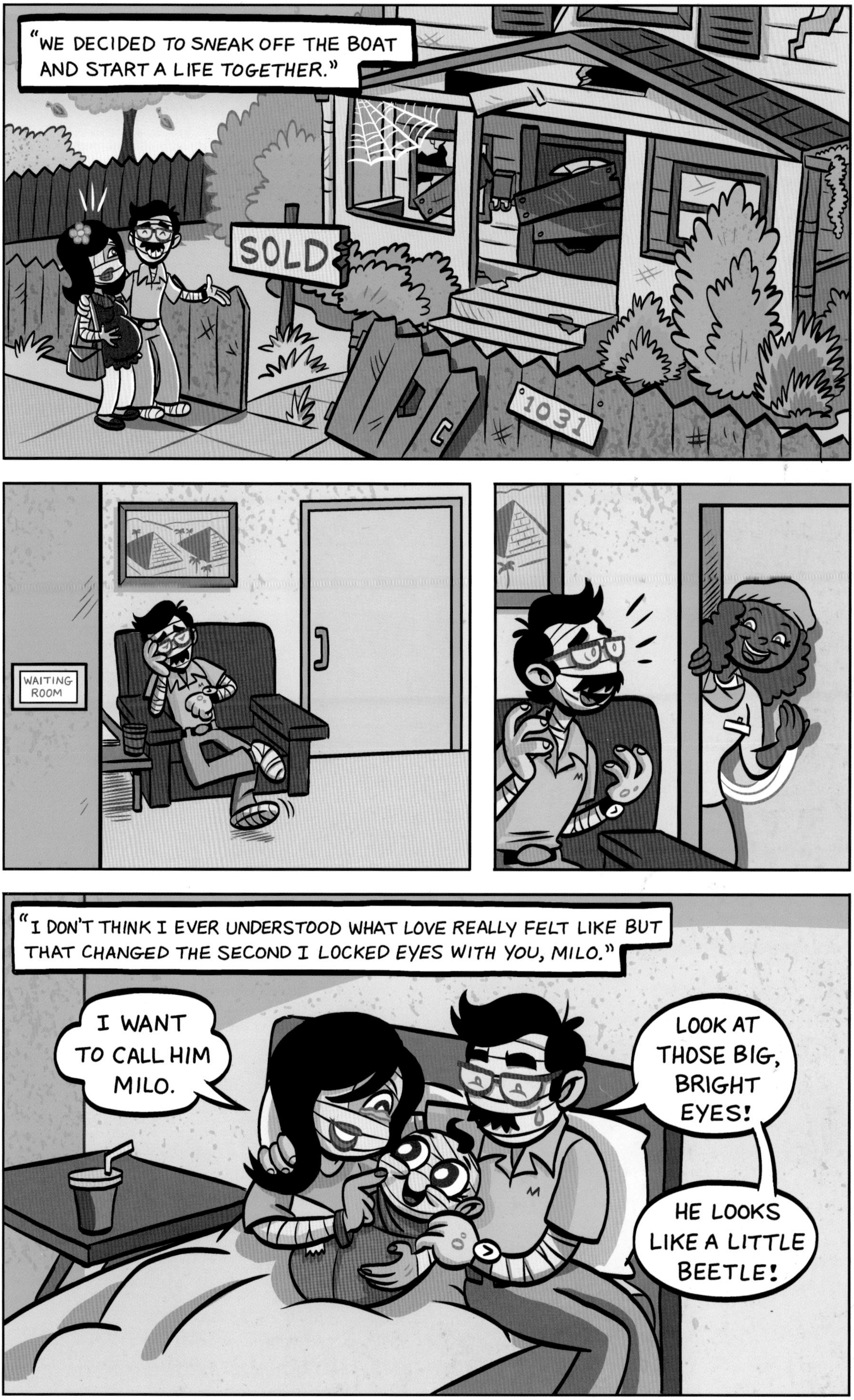
"WE DECIDED TO SNEAK OFF THE BOAT AND START A LIFE TOGETHER."
SOLD
1031
WAITING ROOM
"I DON'T THINK I EVER UNDERSTOOD WHAT LOVE REALLY FELT LIKE BUT THAT CHANGED THE SECOND I LOCKED EYES WITH YOU, MILO."
I WANT TO CALL HIM MILO.
LOOK AT THOSE BIG, BRIGHT EYES!
HE LOOKS LIKE A LITTLE BEETLE!

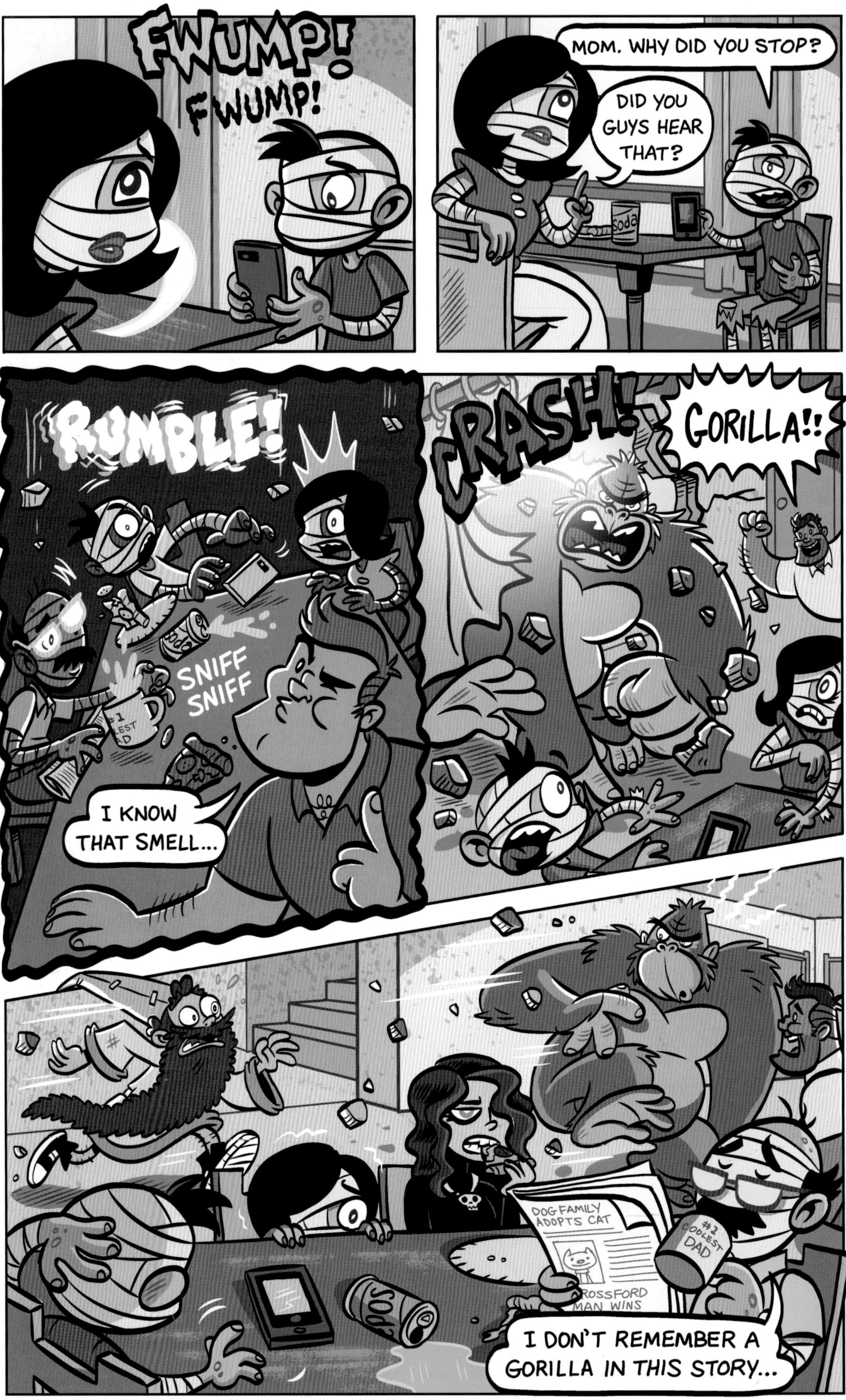
FWUMP!
FWUMP!
MOM. WHY DID YOU STOP?
DID YOU GUYS HEAR THAT?
SODA
RUMBLE!
SNIFF SNIFF
I KNOW THAT SMELL...
CRASH!
GORILLA!!
DOG FAMILY ADOPTS CAT
ROSSFORD MAN WINS
#1 COOLEST DAD
I DON'T REMEMBER A GORILLA IN THIS STORY...

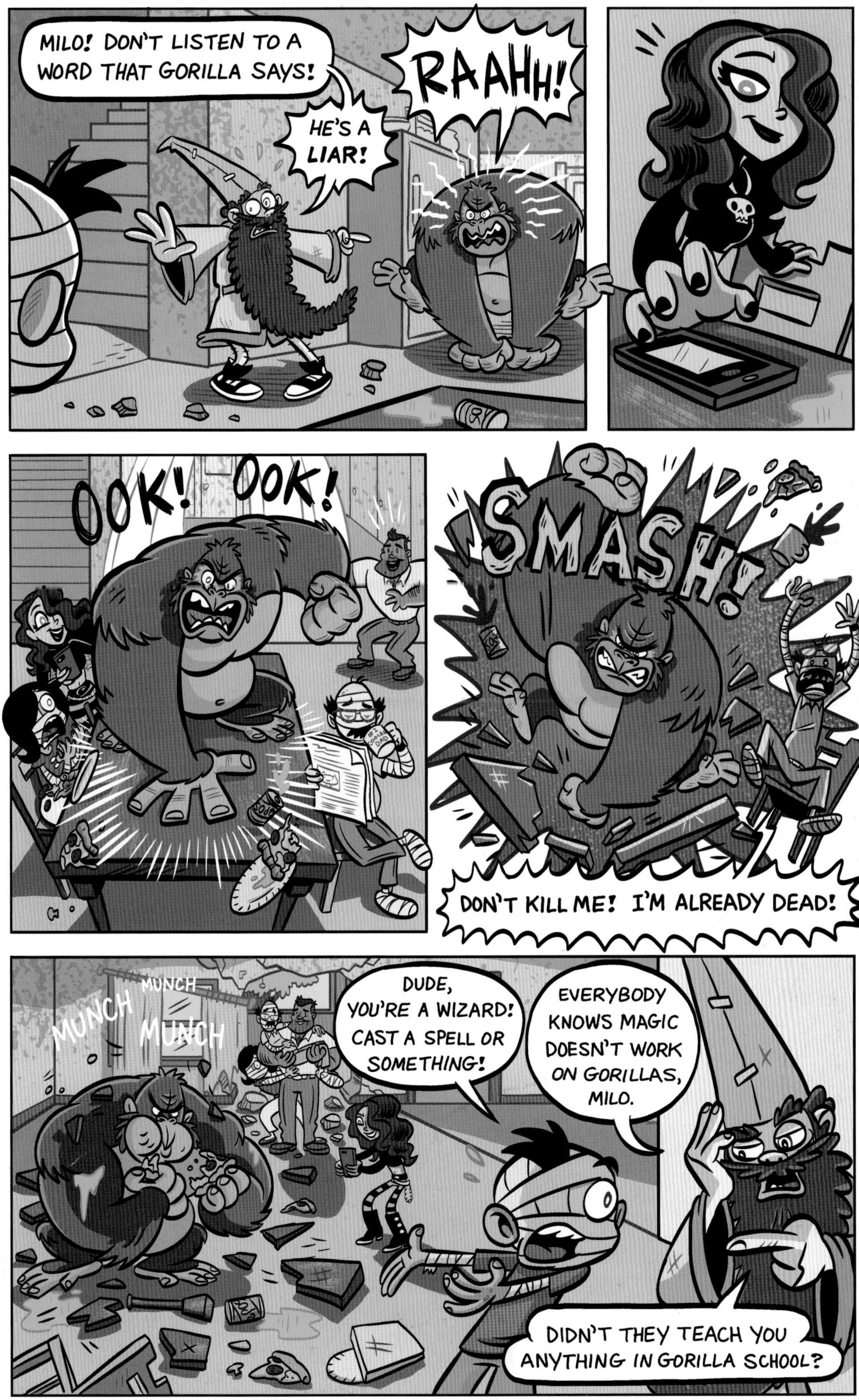
MILO! DON'T LISTEN TO A WORD THAT GORILLA SAYS!
HE'S A LIAR!
RAAHH!
OOK! OOK!
SMASH!
DON'T KILL ME! I'M ALREADY DEAD!
MUNCH MUNCH MUNCH
DUDE, YOU'RE A WIZARD! CAST A SPELL OR SOMETHING!
EVERYBODY KNOWS MAGIC DOESN'T WORK ON GORILLAS, MILO.
DIDN'T THEY TEACH YOU ANYTHING IN GORILLA SCHOOL?

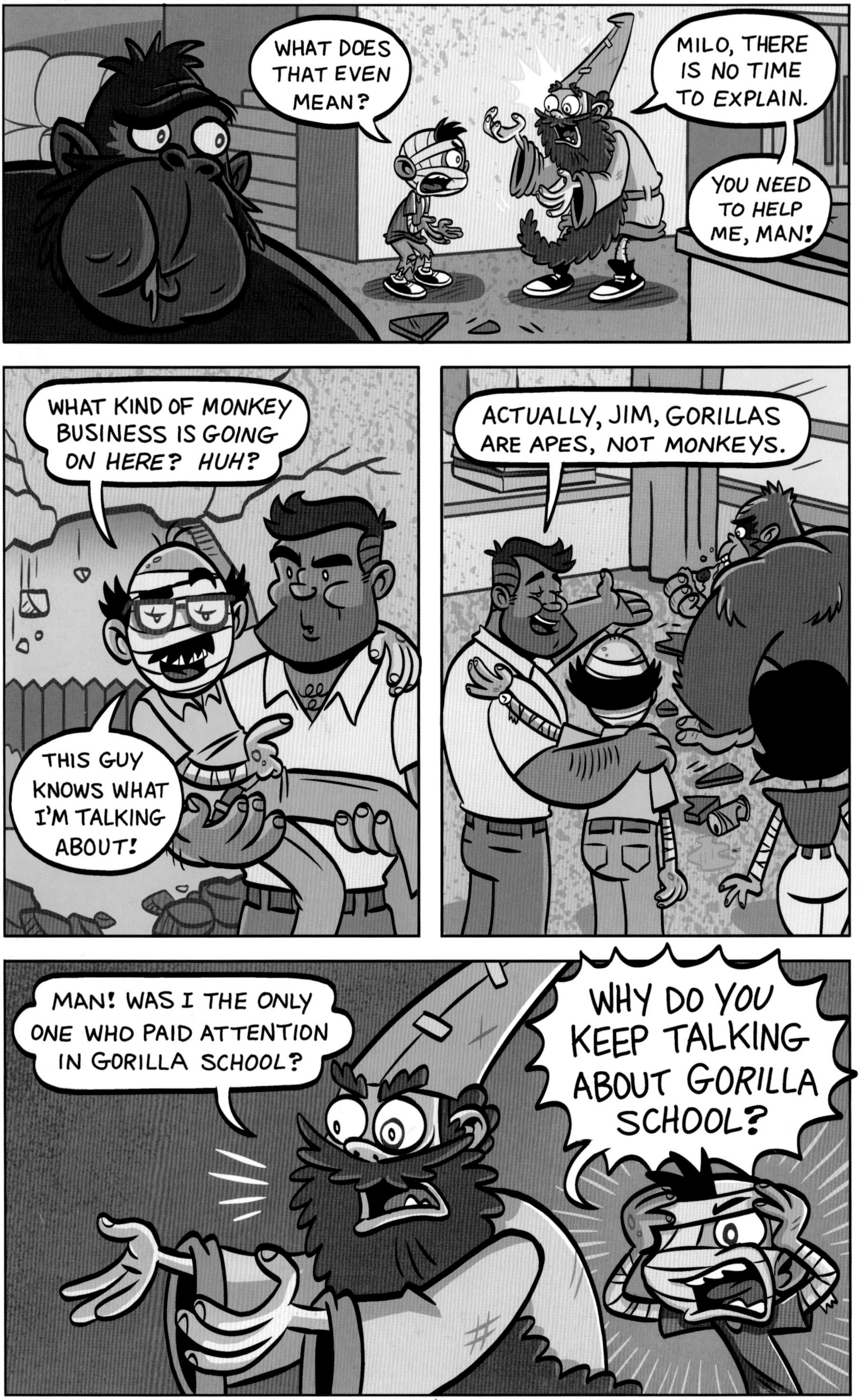
WHAT DOES THAT EVEN MEAN?
MILO, THERE IS NO TIME TO EXPLAIN.
YOU NEED TO HELP ME, MAN!
WHAT KIND OF MONKEY BUSINESS IS GOING ON HERE? HUH?
THIS GUY KNOWS WHAT I'M TALKING ABOUT!
ACTUALLY, JIM, GORILLAS ARE APES, NOT MONKEYS.
MAN! WAS I THE ONLY ONE WHO PAID ATTENTION IN GORILLA SCHOOL?
WHY DO YOU KEEP TALKING ABOUT GORILLA SCHOOL?

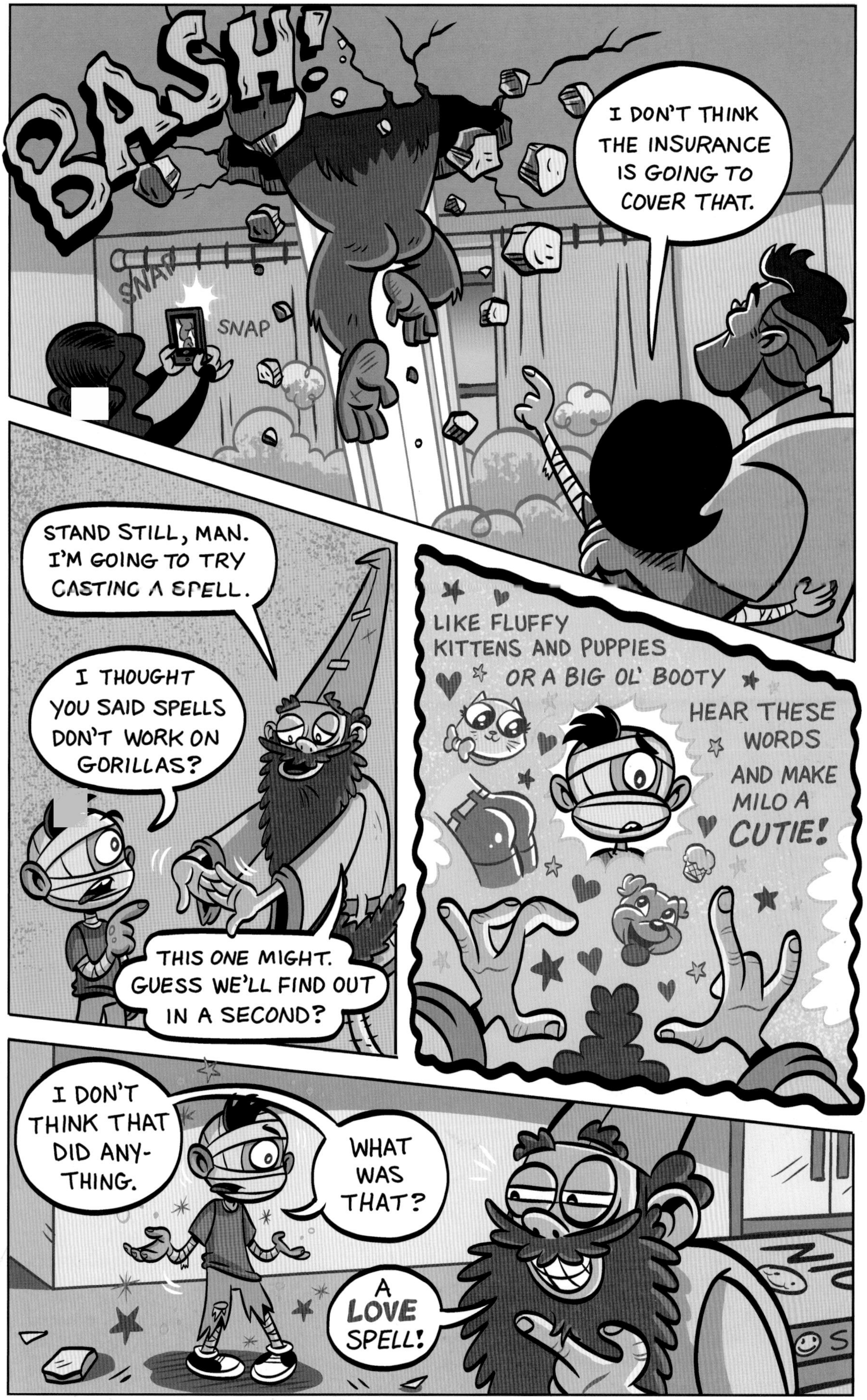
BASH!
SNAP
SNAP
I DON'T THINK THE INSURANCE IS GOING TO COVER THAT.
STAND STILL, MAN. I'M GOING TO TRY CASTING A SPELL.
I THOUGHT YOU SAID SPELLS DON'T WORK ON GORILLAS?
THIS ONE MIGHT. GUESS WE'LL FIND OUT IN A SECOND?
LIKE FLUFFY KITTENS AND PUPPIES
OR A BIG OL' BOOTY
HEAR THESE WORDS
AND MAKE MILO A CUTIE!
I DON'T THINK THAT DID ANY-THING.
WHAT WAS THAT?
A LOVE SPELL!

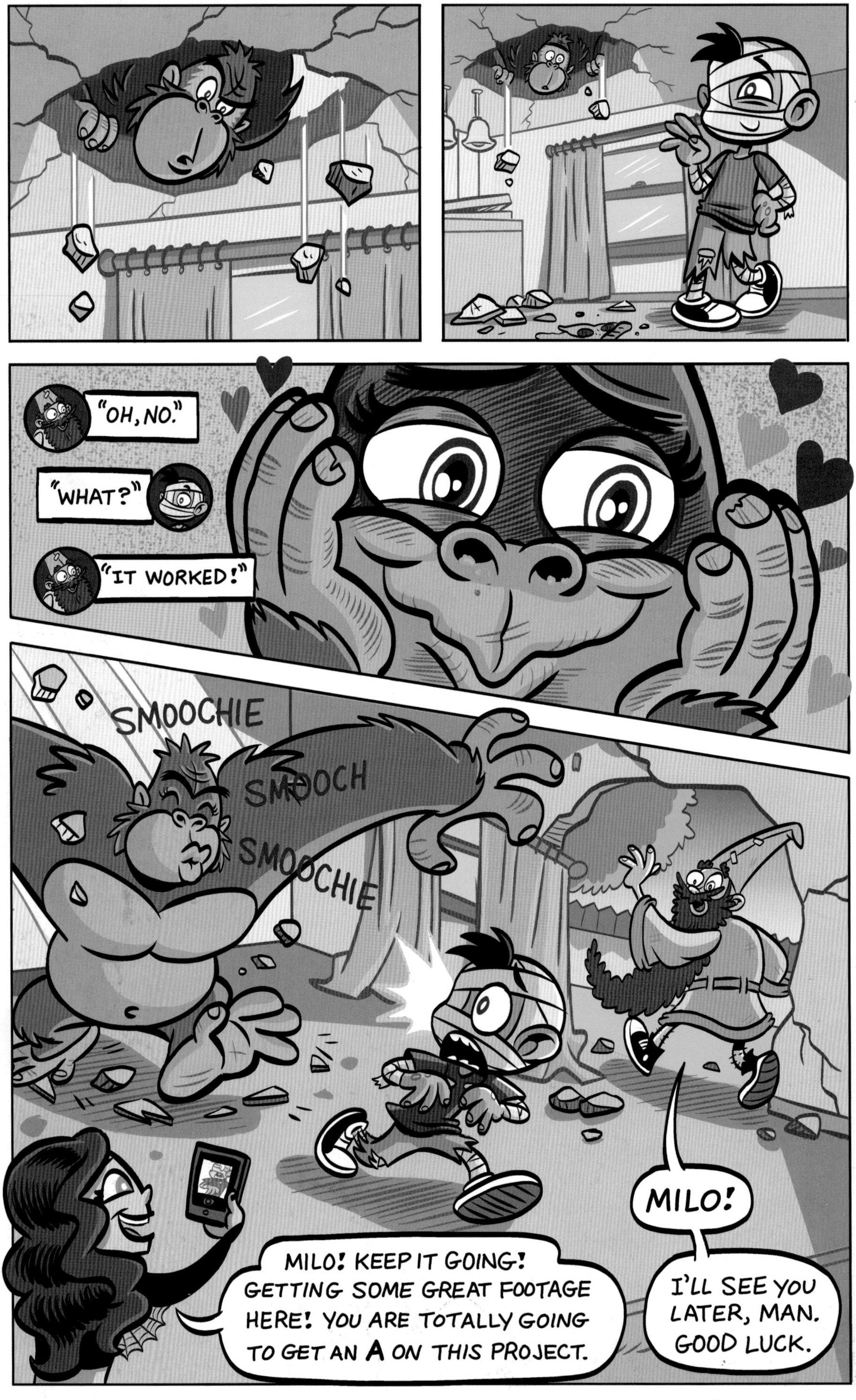
"OH, NO."
"WHAT?"
"IT WORKED!"
SMOOCHIE
SMOOCH
SMOOCHIE
MILO!
I'LL SEE YOU LATER, MAN. GOOD LUCK.
MILO! KEEP IT GOING! GETTING SOME GREAT FOOTAGE HERE! YOU ARE TOTALLY GOING TO GET AN A ON THIS PROJECT.

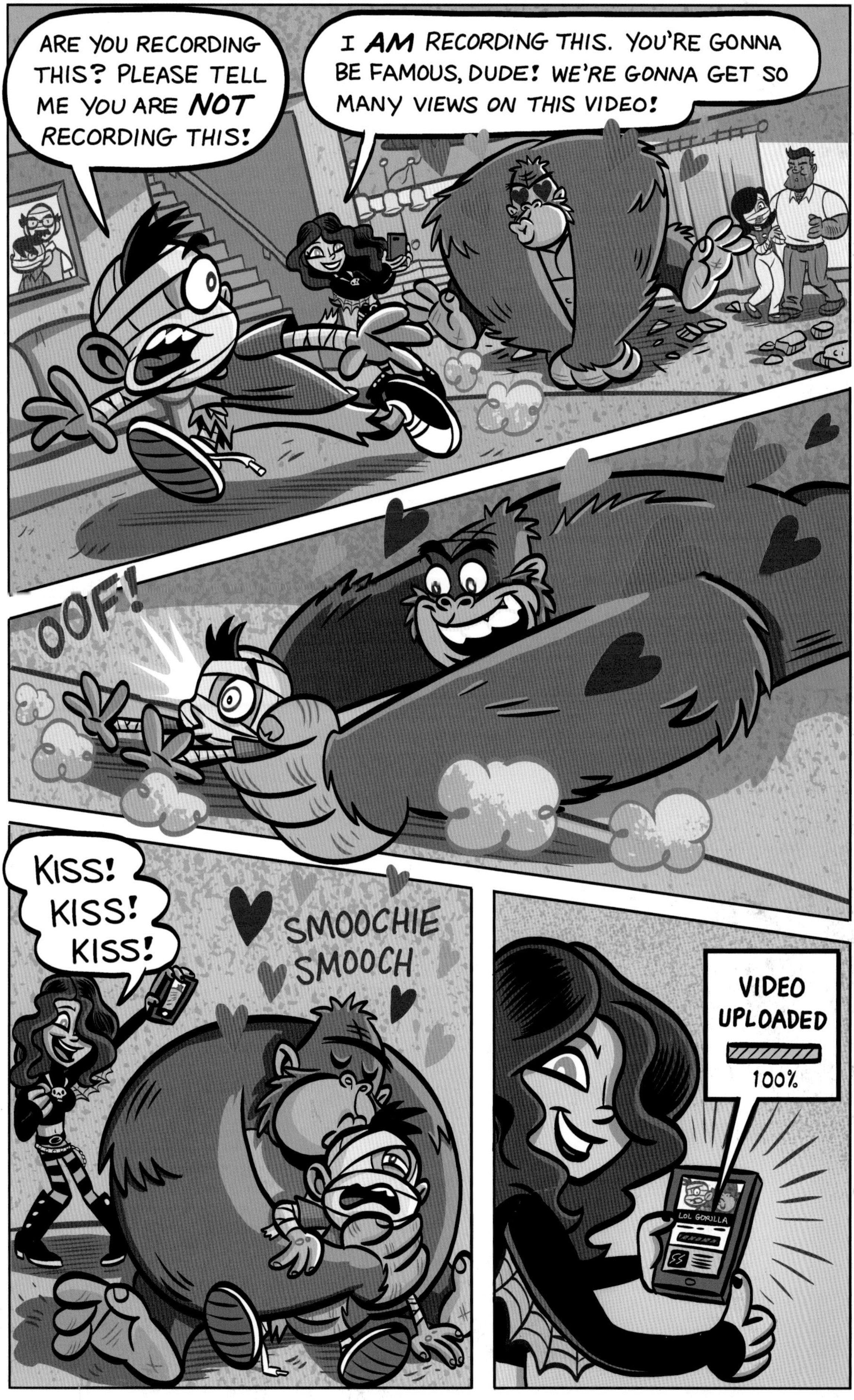
ARE YOU RECORDING THIS? PLEASE TELL ME YOU ARE NOT RECORDING THIS!
I AM RECORDING THIS. YOU'RE GONNA BE FAMOUS, DUDE! WE'RE GONNA GET SO MANY VIEWS ON THIS VIDEO!
OOF!
KISS! KISS! KISS!
SMOOCHIE SMOOCH
VIDEO UPLOADED
100%
LOL GORILLA

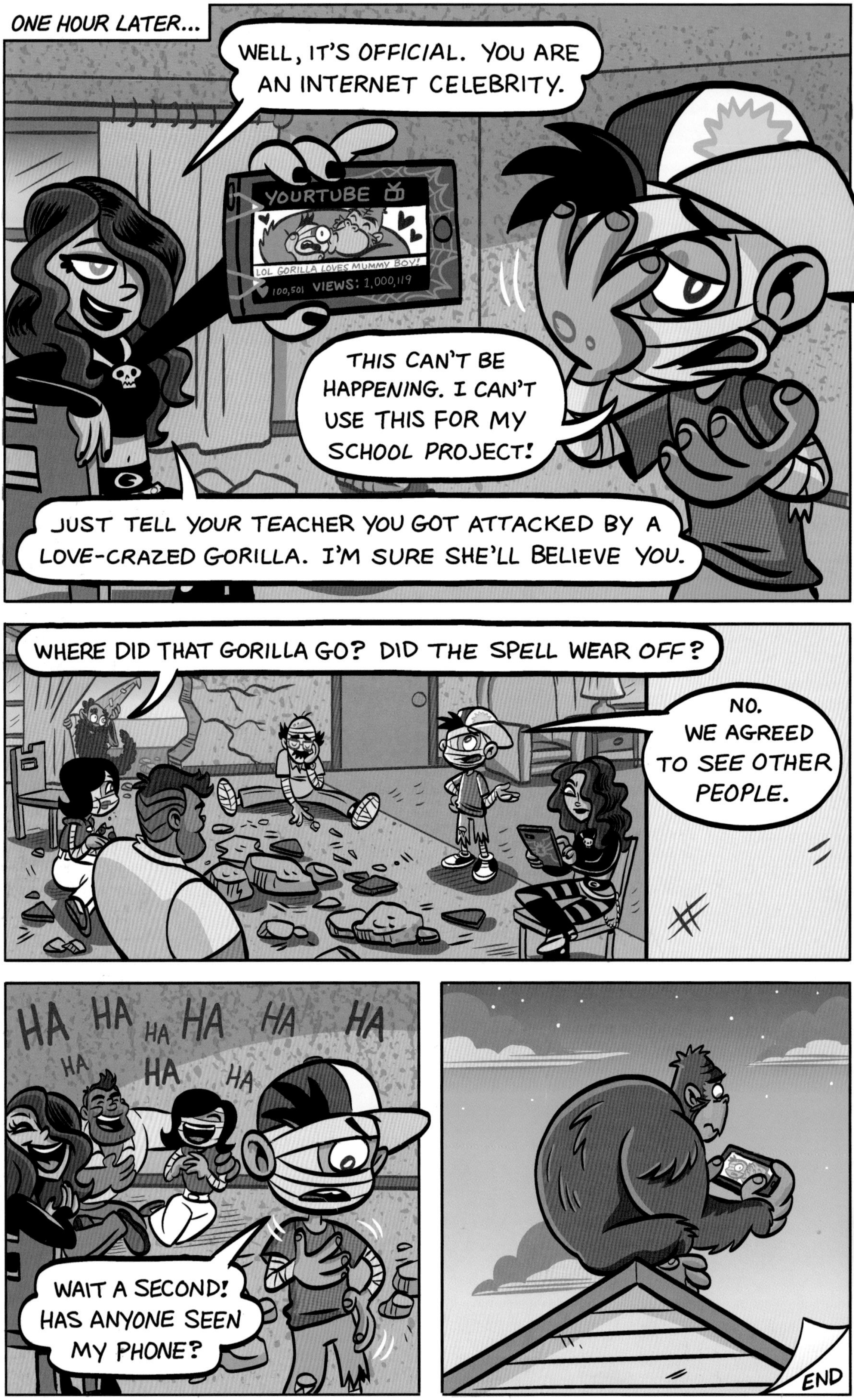

ONE HOUR LATER...
WELL, IT'S OFFICIAL. YOU ARE AN INTERNET CELEBRITY.
YOURTUBE
LOL GORILLA LOVES MUMMY BOY!
100,501 VIEWS: 1,000,119
THIS CAN'T BE HAPPENING. I CAN'T USE THIS FOR MY SCHOOL PROJECT!
JUST TELL YOUR TEACHER YOU GOT ATTACKED BY A LOVE-CRAZED GORILLA. I'M SURE SHE'LL BELIEVE YOU.
WHERE DID THAT GORILLA GO? DID THE SPELL WEAR OFF?
NO. WE AGREED TO SEE OTHER PEOPLE.
HA HA HA HA HA HA HA HA HA
WAIT A SECOND! HAS ANYONE SEEN MY PHONE?
END

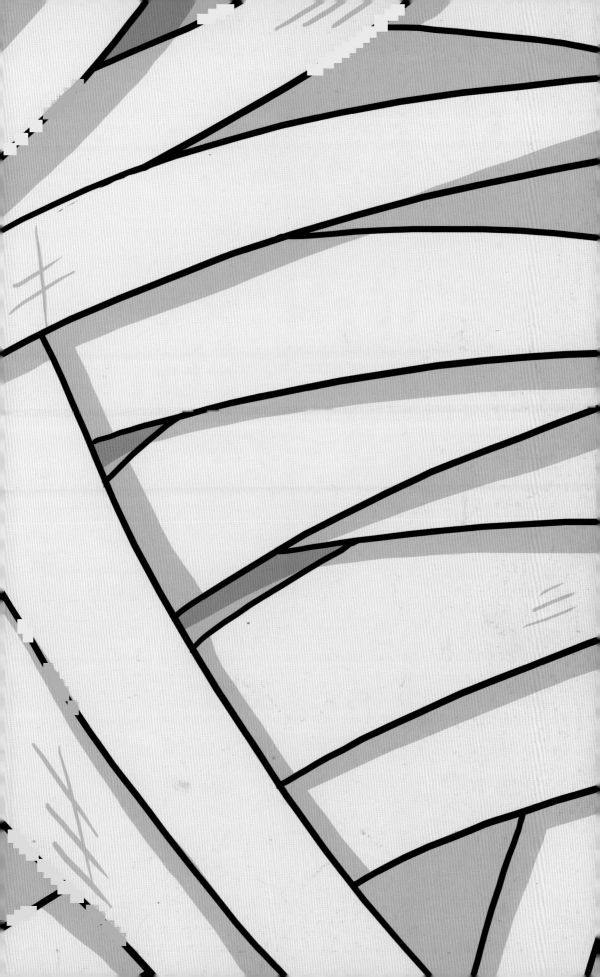

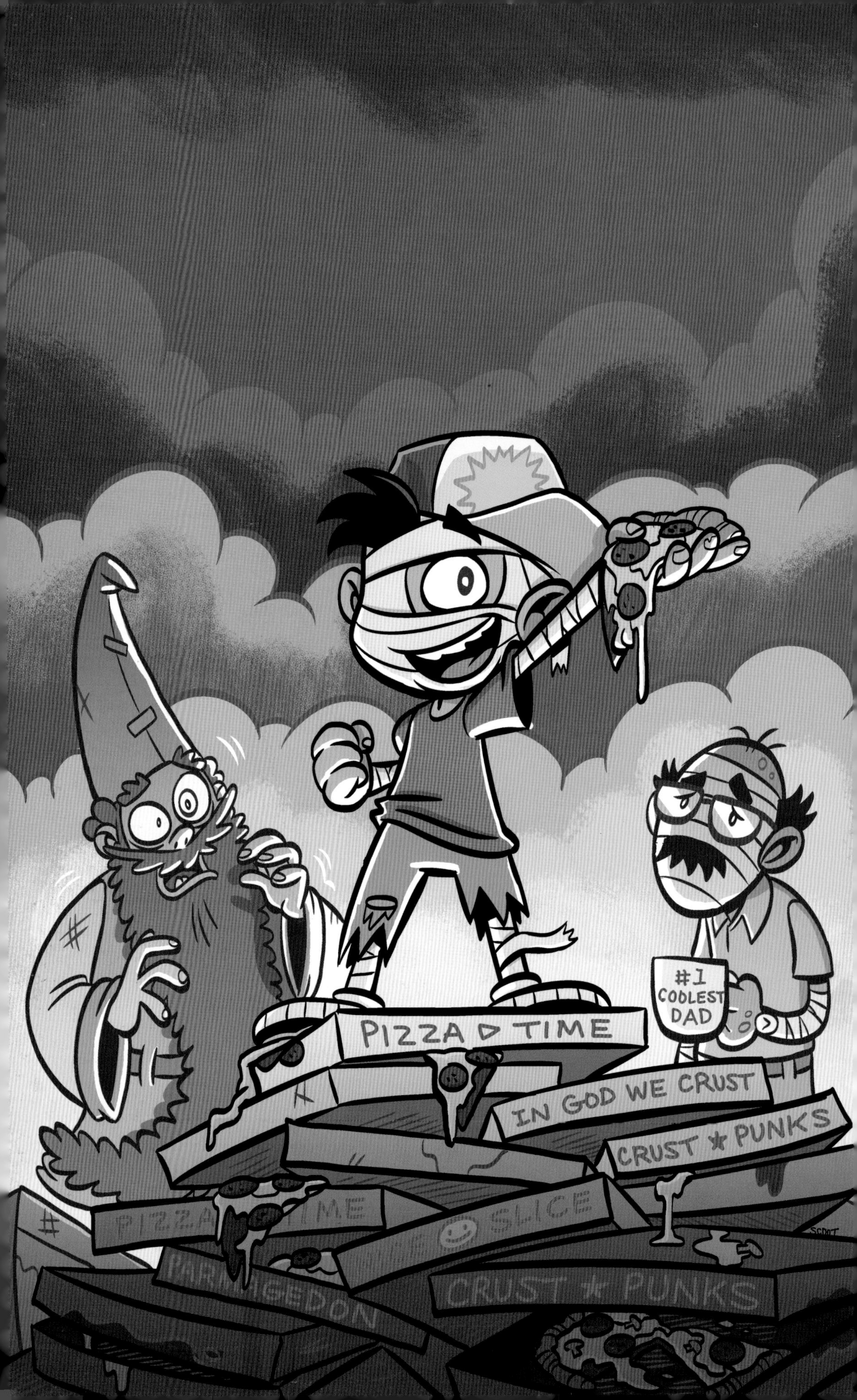
PIZZA TIME
#1 COOLEST DAD
IN GOD WE CRUST
CRUST PUNKS
SLICE
CRUST PUNKS

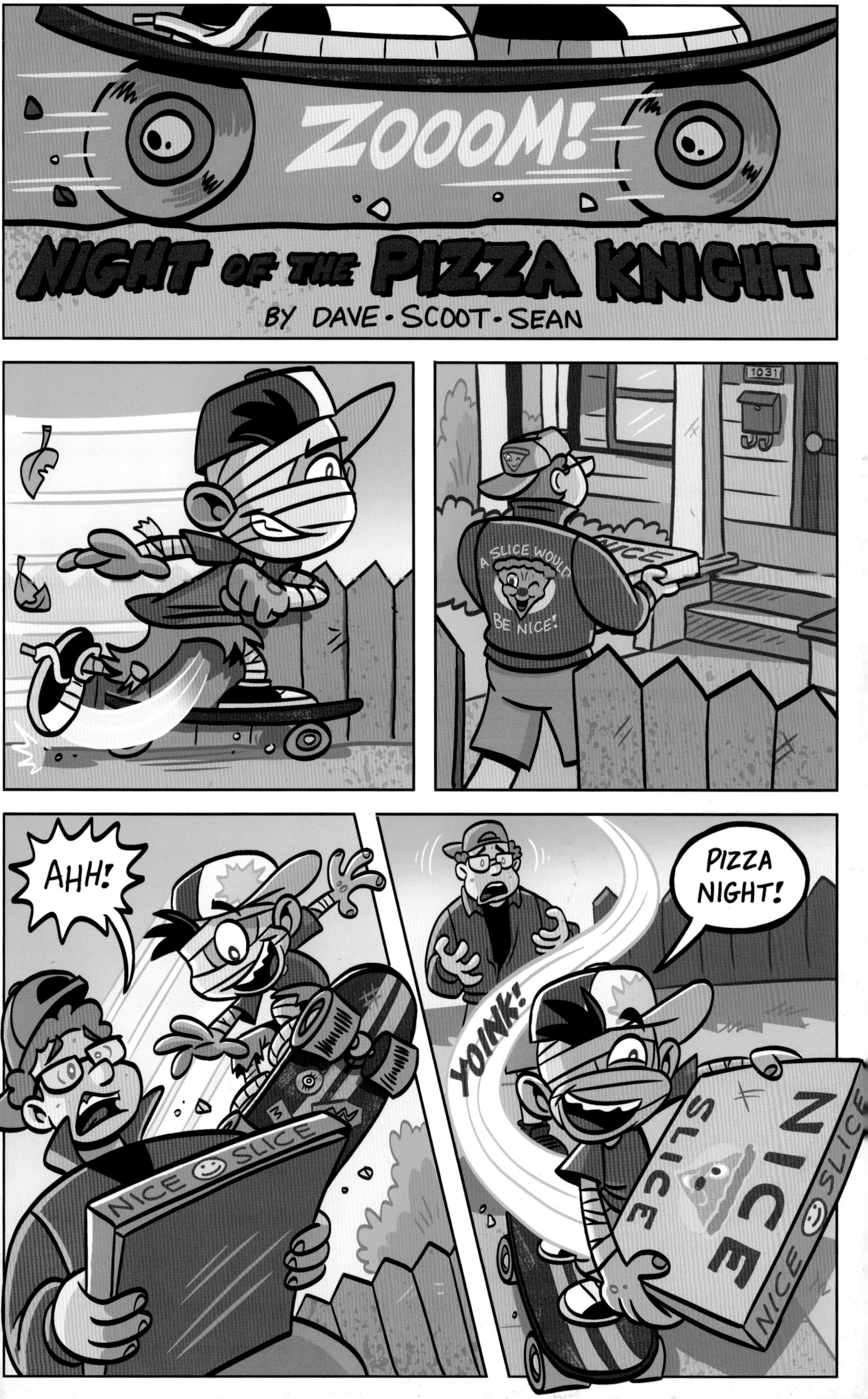
ZOOOM!
NIGHT OF THE PIZZA KNIGHT
BY DAVE • SCOOT • SEAN
1031
A SLICE WOULD BE NICE!
NICE
AHH!
NICE SLICE
PIZZA NIGHT!
YOINK!
NICE SLICE
NICE SLICE

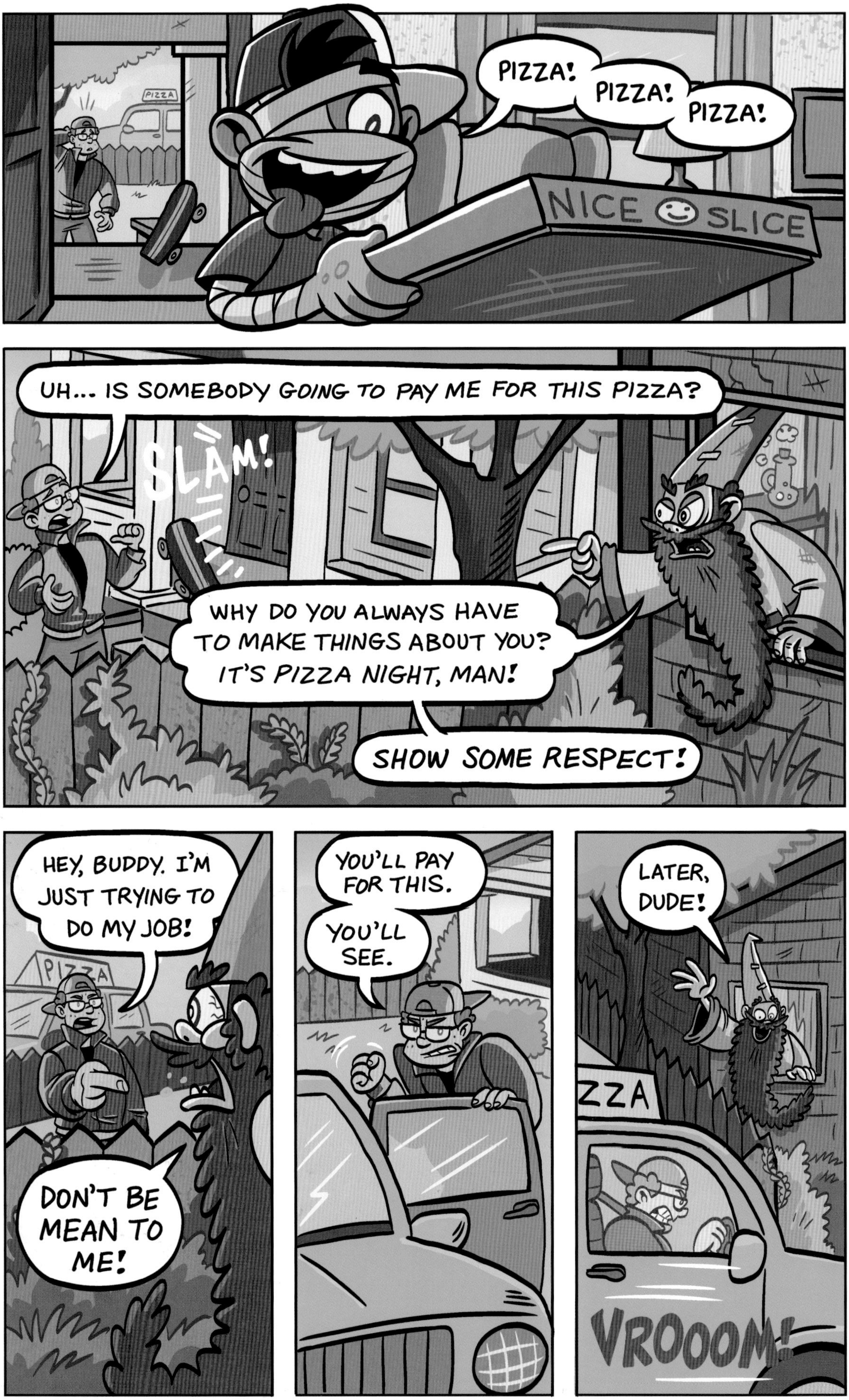
PIZZA
PIZZA! PIZZA! PIZZA!
NICE SLICE
UH... IS SOMEBODY GOING TO PAY ME FOR THIS PIZZA?
SLAM!
WHY DO YOU ALWAYS HAVE TO MAKE THINGS ABOUT YOU? IT'S PIZZA NIGHT, MAN!
SHOW SOME RESPECT!
HEY, BUDDY. I'M JUST TRYING TO DO MY JOB!
DON'T BE MEAN TO ME!
YOU'LL PAY FOR THIS.
YOU'LL SEE.
LATER, DUDE!
ZZA
VROOOM!

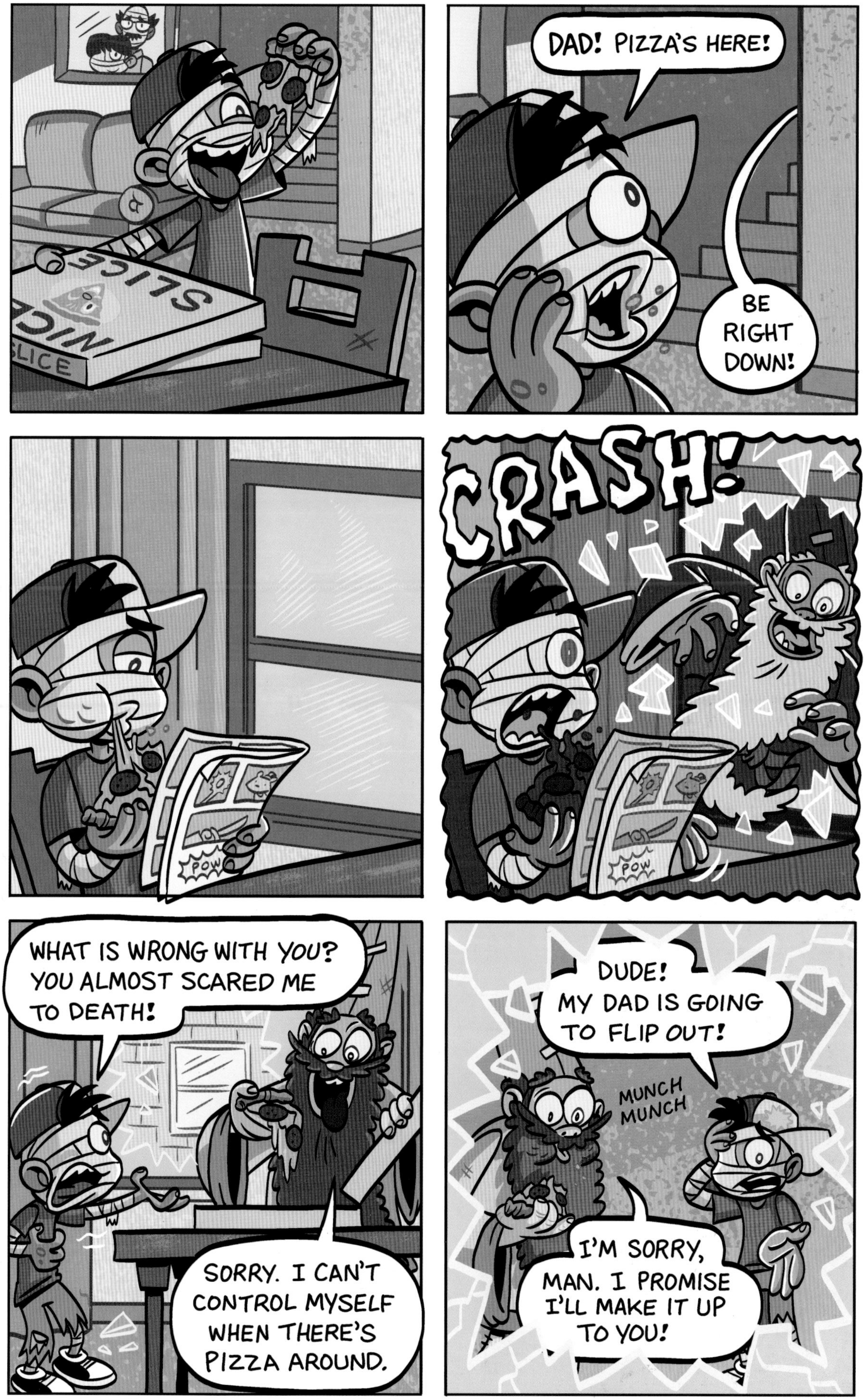
NICE SLICE
SLICE
DAD! PIZZA'S HERE!
BE RIGHT DOWN!
CRASH!
POW
POW
WHAT IS WRONG WITH YOU? YOU ALMOST SCARED ME TO DEATH!
SORRY. I CAN'T CONTROL MYSELF WHEN THERE'S PIZZA AROUND.
DUDE! MY DAD IS GOING TO FLIP OUT!
MUNCH MUNCH
I'M SORRY, MAN. I PROMISE I'LL MAKE IT UP TO YOU!

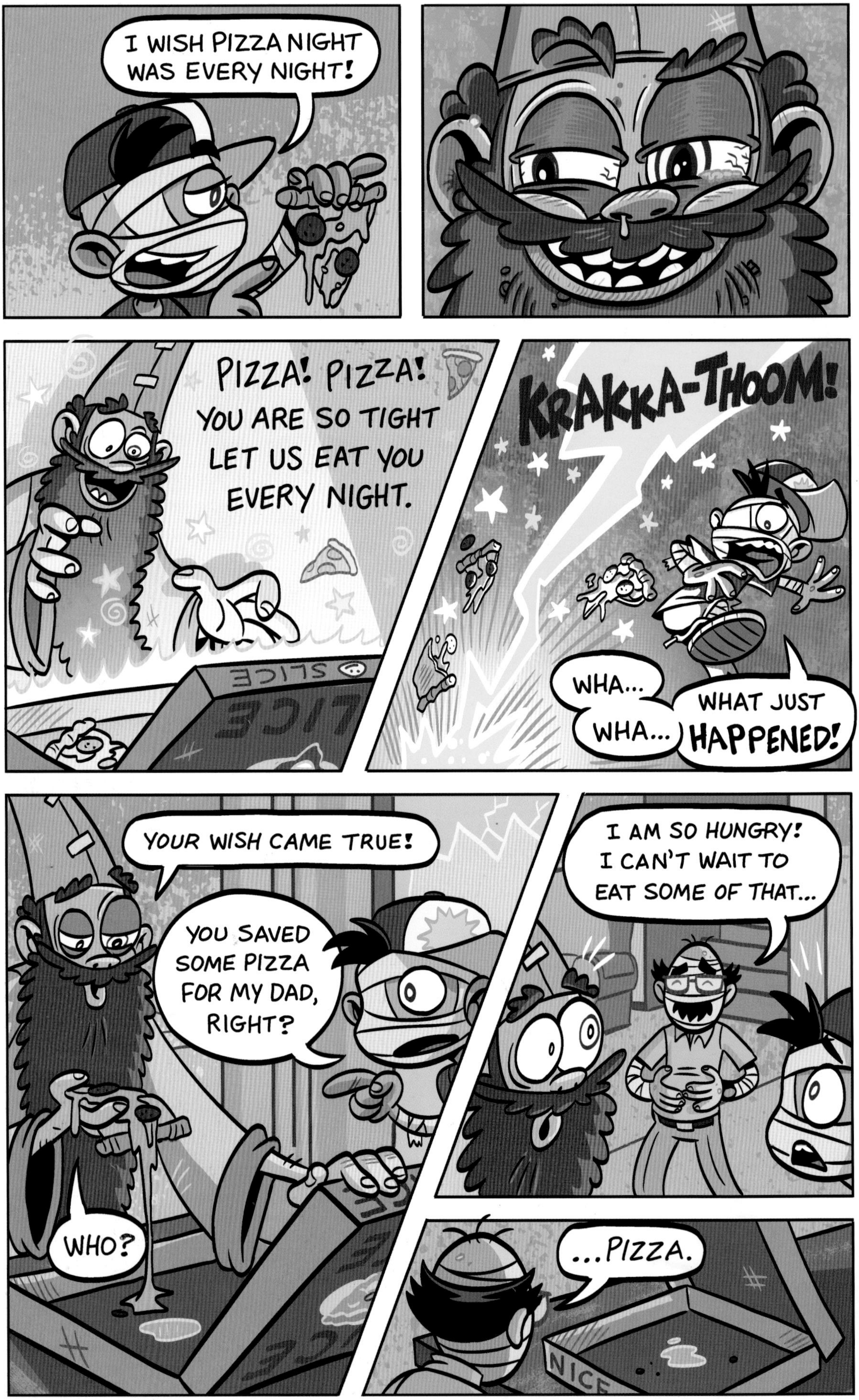

I WISH PIZZA NIGHT WAS EVERY NIGHT!
PIZZA! PIZZA! YOU ARE SO TIGHT LET US EAT YOU EVERY NIGHT.
SLICE
KRAKKA-THOOM!
WHA... WHA...
WHAT JUST HAPPENED!
YOUR WISH CAME TRUE!
YOU SAVED SOME PIZZA FOR MY DAD, RIGHT?
WHO?
I AM SO HUNGRY! I CAN'T WAIT TO EAT SOME OF THAT...
...PIZZA.
NICE

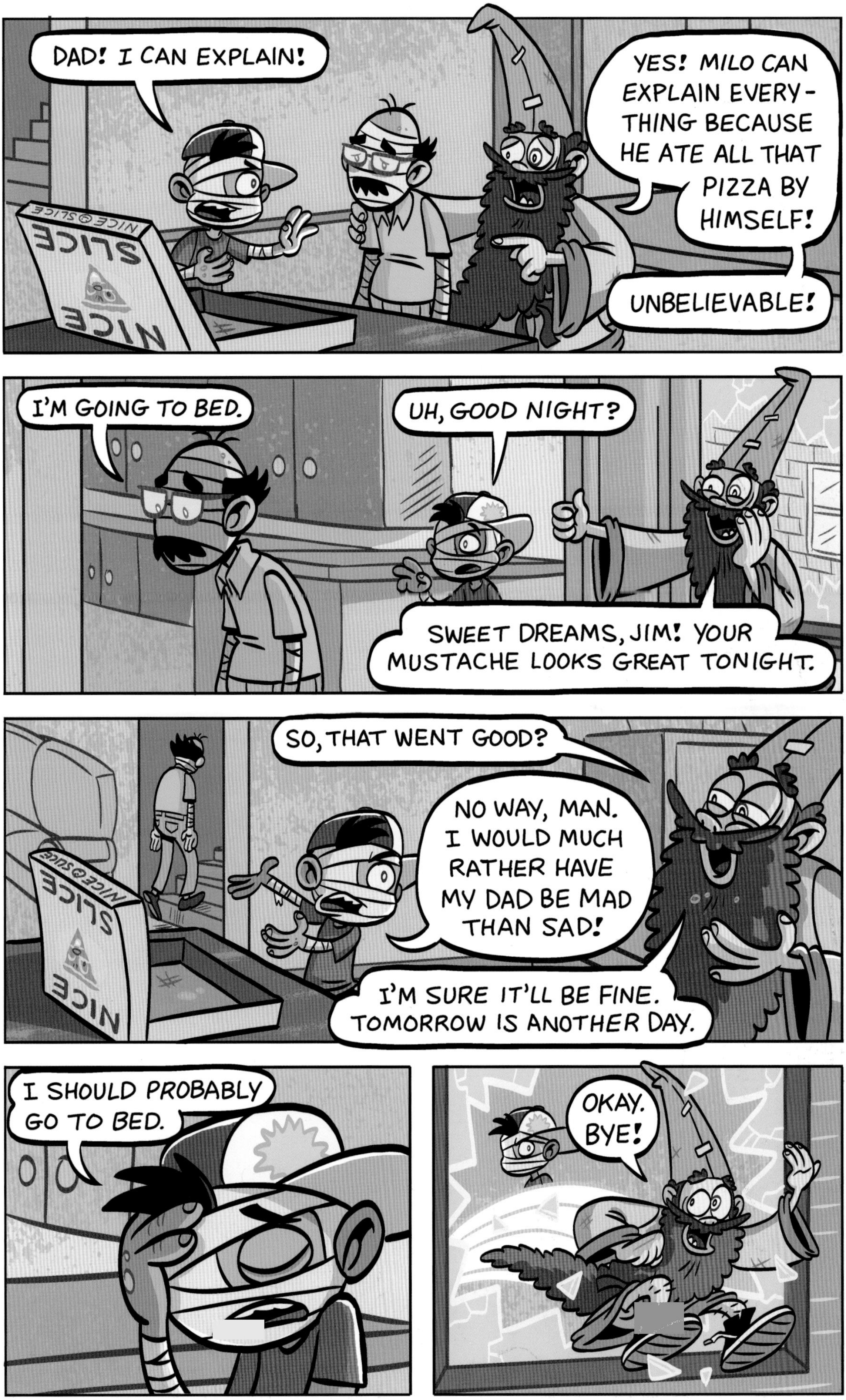
DAD! I CAN EXPLAIN!
YES! MILO CAN EXPLAIN EVERY-THING BECAUSE HE ATE ALL THAT PIZZA BY HIMSELF!
UNBELIEVABLE!
I'M GOING TO BED.
UH, GOOD NIGHT?
SWEET DREAMS, JIM! YOUR MUSTACHE LOOKS GREAT TONIGHT.
SO, THAT WENT GOOD?
NO WAY, MAN. I WOULD MUCH RATHER HAVE MY DAD BE MAD THAN SAD!
I'M SURE IT'LL BE FINE. TOMORROW IS ANOTHER DAY.
I SHOULD PROBABLY GO TO BED.
OKAY. BYE!

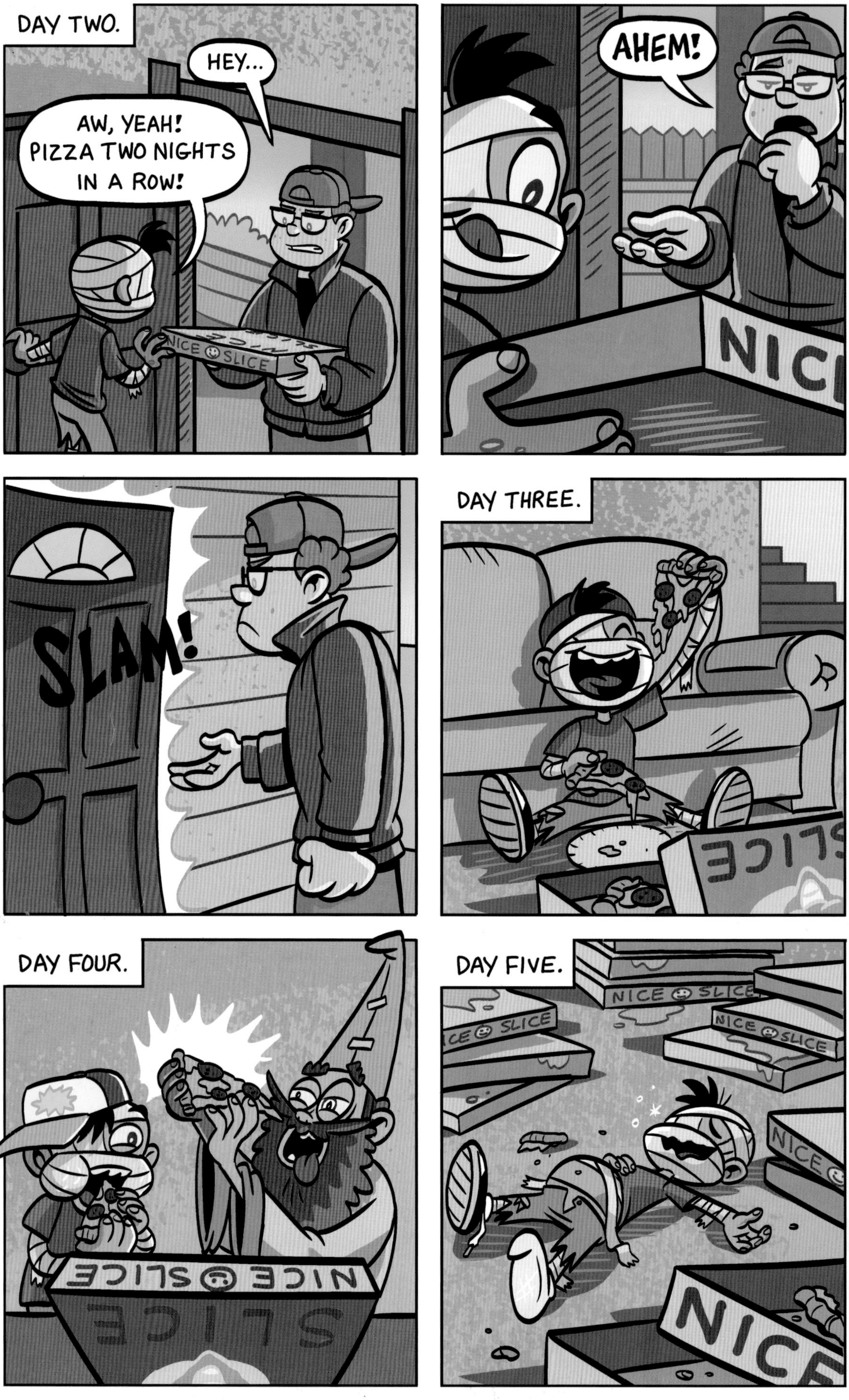
DAY TWO.
HEY...
AW, YEAH! PIZZA TWO NIGHTS IN A ROW!
NICE SLICE
AHEM!
NICE
SLAM!
DAY THREE.
SLICE
DAY FOUR.
NICE SLICE
SLICE
DAY FIVE.
NICE SLICE
CE SLICE
NICE SLICE
NICE
NICE

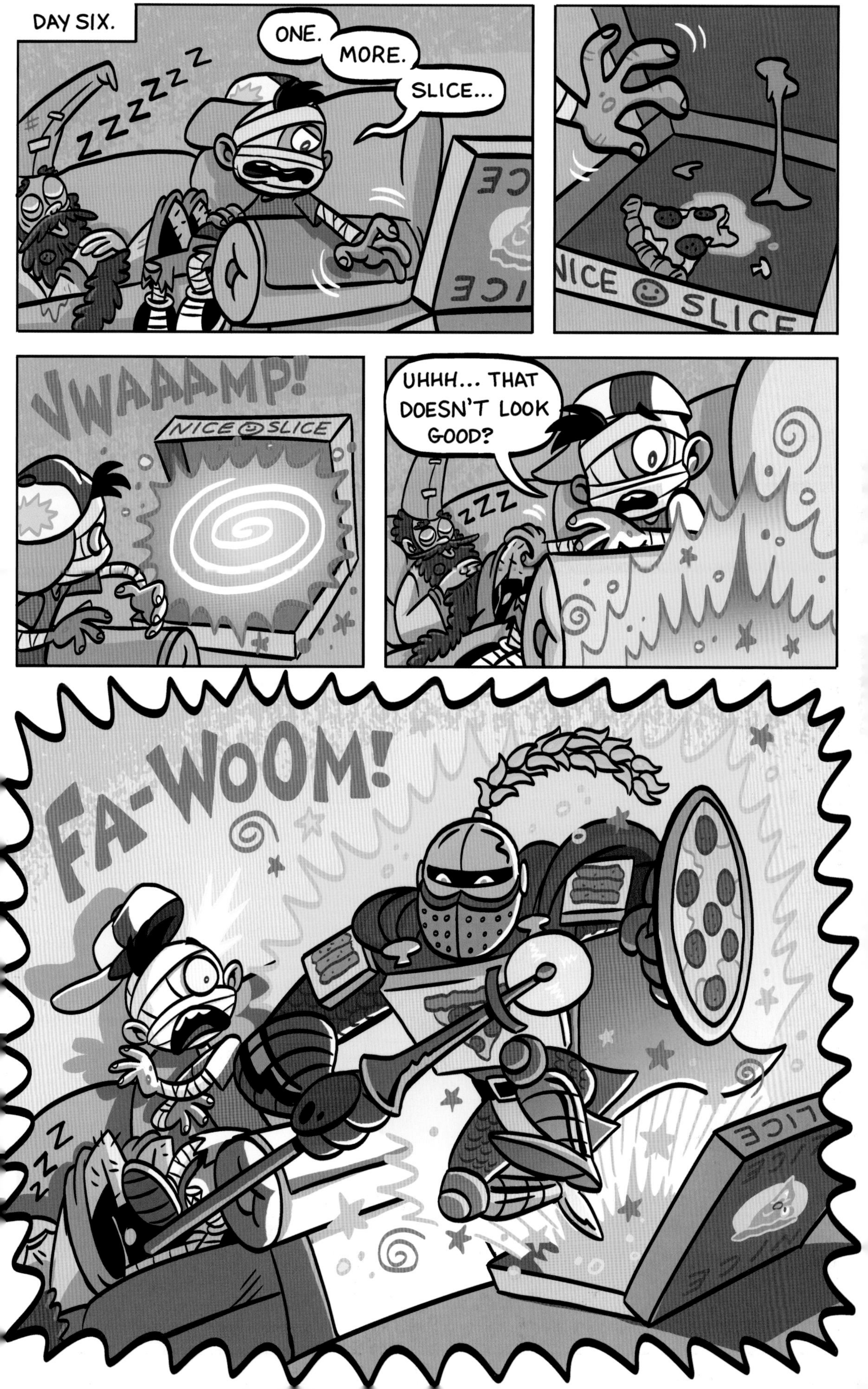
DAY SIX.
ZZZZZZZ
ONE.
MORE.
SLICE...
NICE SLICE
VWAAAMP!
NICE SLICE
UHHH... THAT DOESN'T LOOK GOOD?
ZZZ
FA-WOOM!
ZZZ
LICE

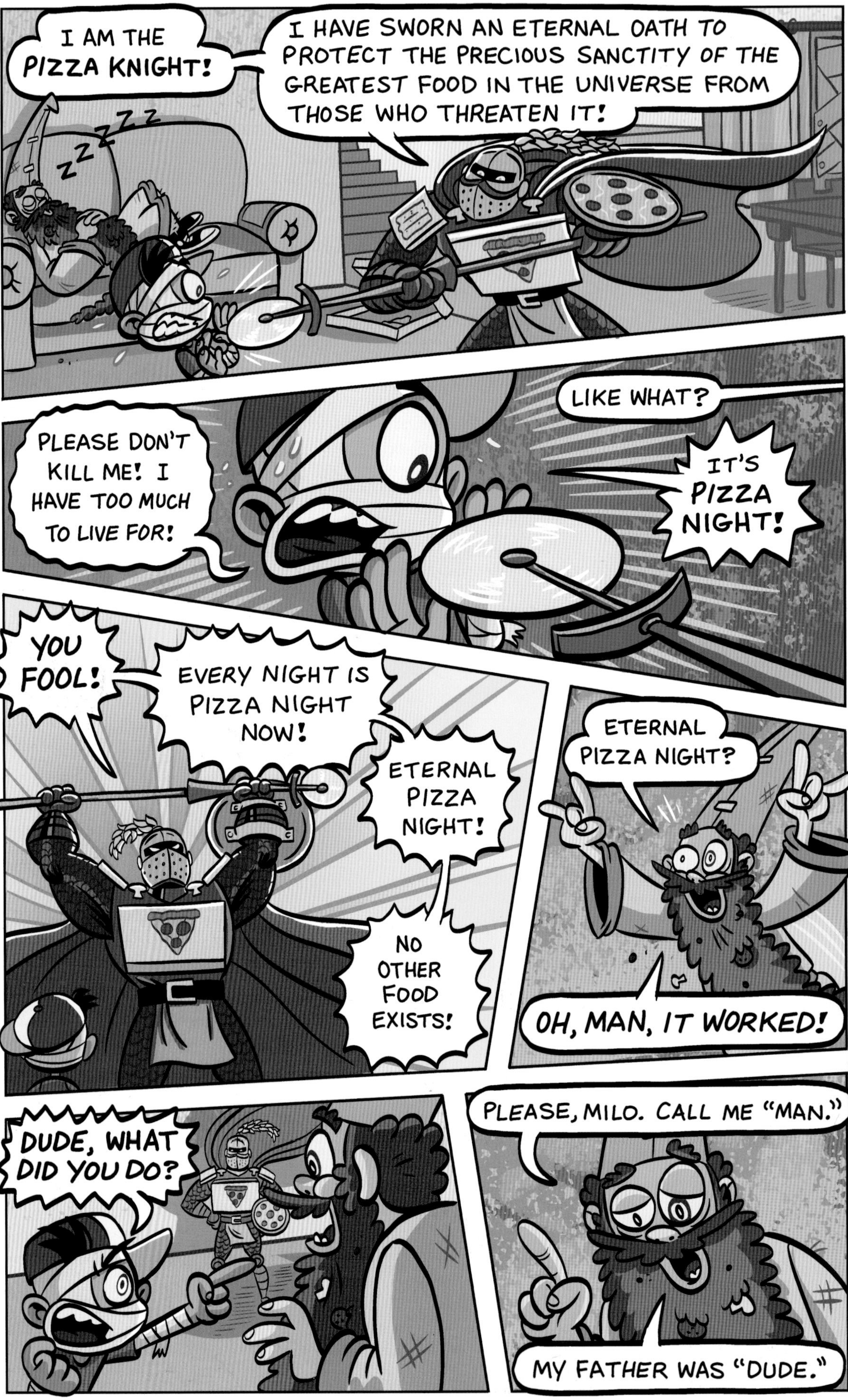
I AM THE PIZZA KNIGHT!
I HAVE SWORN AN ETERNAL OATH TO PROTECT THE PRECIOUS SANCTITY OF THE GREATEST FOOD IN THE UNIVERSE FROM THOSE WHO THREATEN IT!
PLEASE DON'T KILL ME! I HAVE TOO MUCH TO LIVE FOR!
LIKE WHAT?
IT'S PIZZA NIGHT!
YOU FOOL!
EVERY NIGHT IS PIZZA NIGHT NOW!
ETERNAL PIZZA NIGHT!
NO OTHER FOOD EXISTS!
ETERNAL PIZZA NIGHT?
OH, MAN, IT WORKED!
DUDE, WHAT DID YOU DO?
PLEASE, MILO. CALL ME "MAN."
MY FATHER WAS "DUDE."

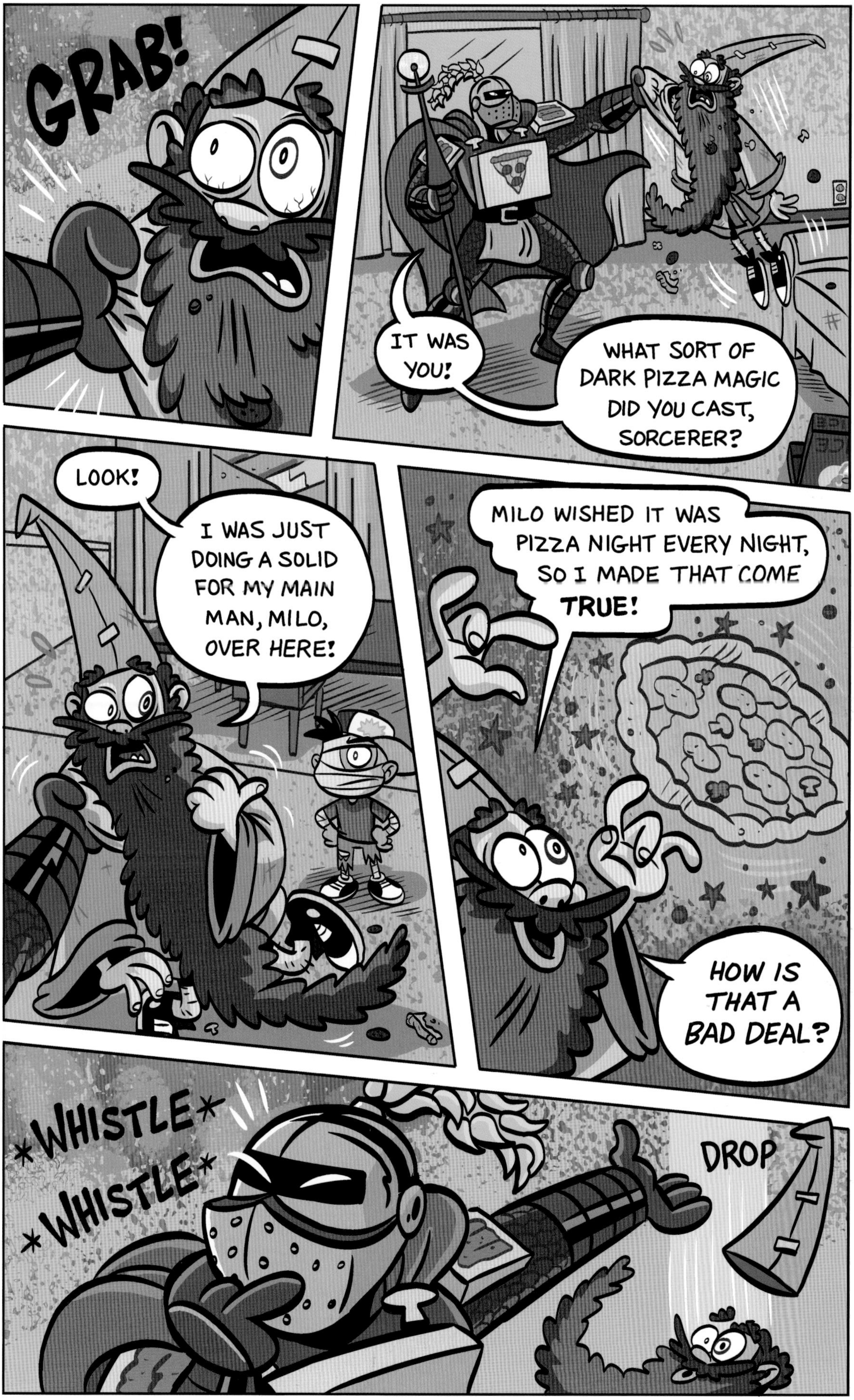
GRAB!
IT WAS YOU!
WHAT SORT OF DARK PIZZA MAGIC DID YOU CAST, SORCERER?
LOOK!
I WAS JUST DOING A SOLID FOR MY MAIN MAN, MILO, OVER HERE!
MILO WISHED IT WAS PIZZA NIGHT EVERY NIGHT, SO I MADE THAT COME TRUE!
HOW IS THAT A BAD DEAL?
WHISTLE
WHISTLE
DROP

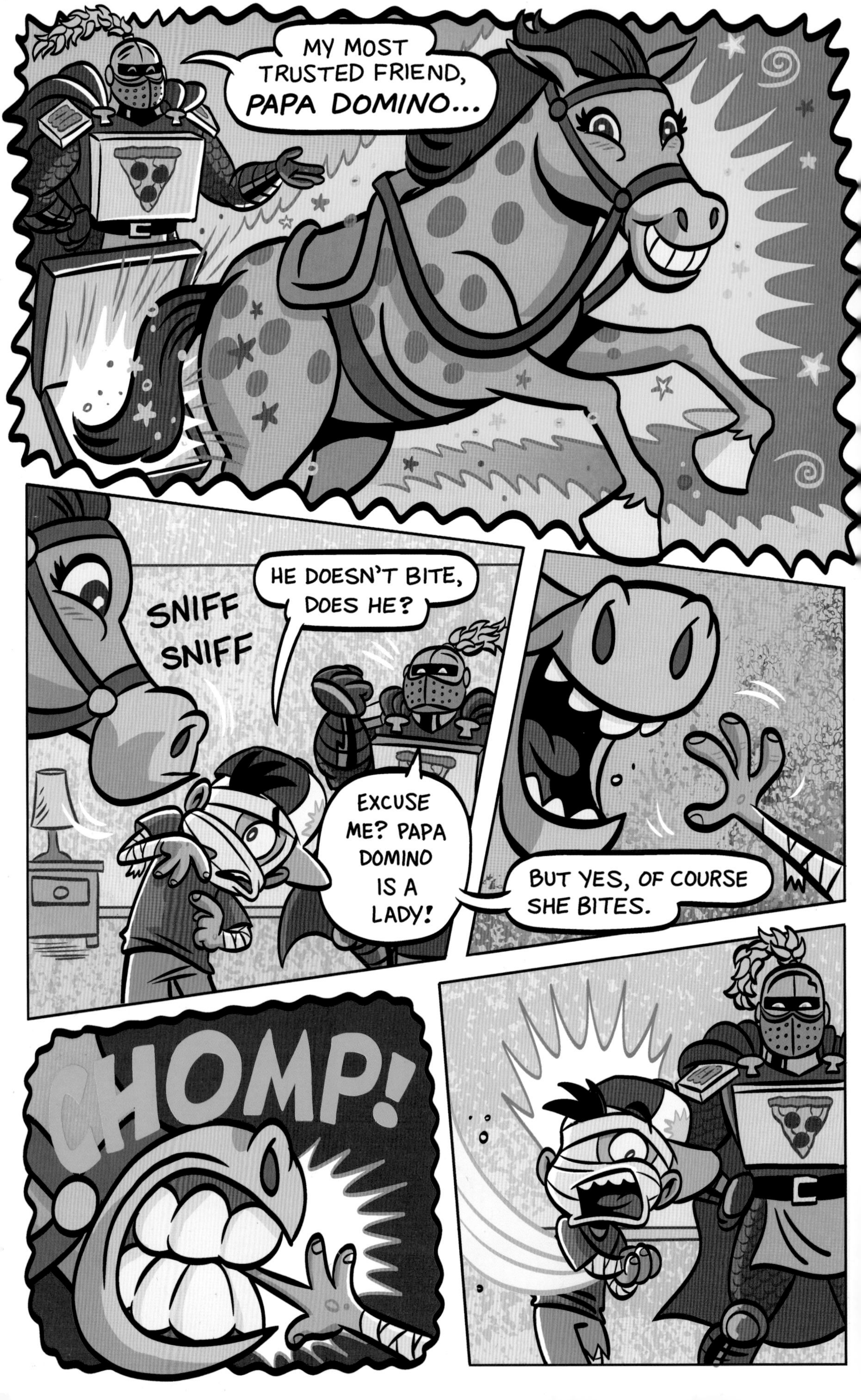
MY MOST TRUSTED FRIEND, PAPA DOMINO...
SNIFF SNIFF
HE DOESN'T BITE, DOES HE?
EXCUSE ME? PAPA DOMINO IS A LADY!
BUT YES, OF COURSE SHE BITES.
CHOMP!

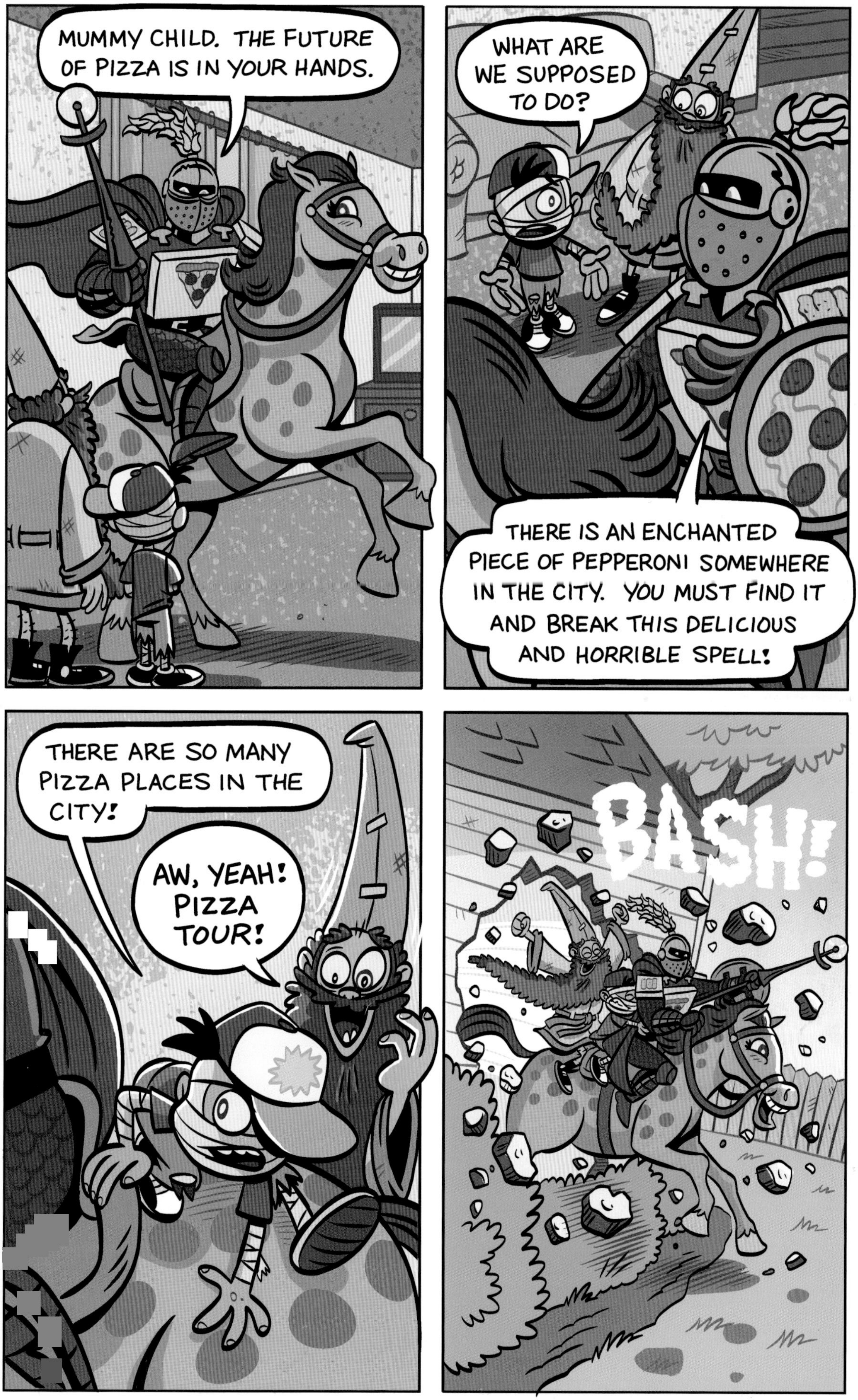
MUMMY CHILD. THE FUTURE OF PIZZA IS IN YOUR HANDS.
WHAT ARE WE SUPPOSED TO DO?
THERE IS AN ENCHANTED PIECE OF PEPPERONI SOMEWHERE IN THE CITY. YOU MUST FIND IT AND BREAK THIS DELICIOUS AND HORRIBLE SPELL!
THERE ARE SO MANY PIZZA PLACES IN THE CITY!
AW, YEAH! PIZZA TOUR!
BASH!

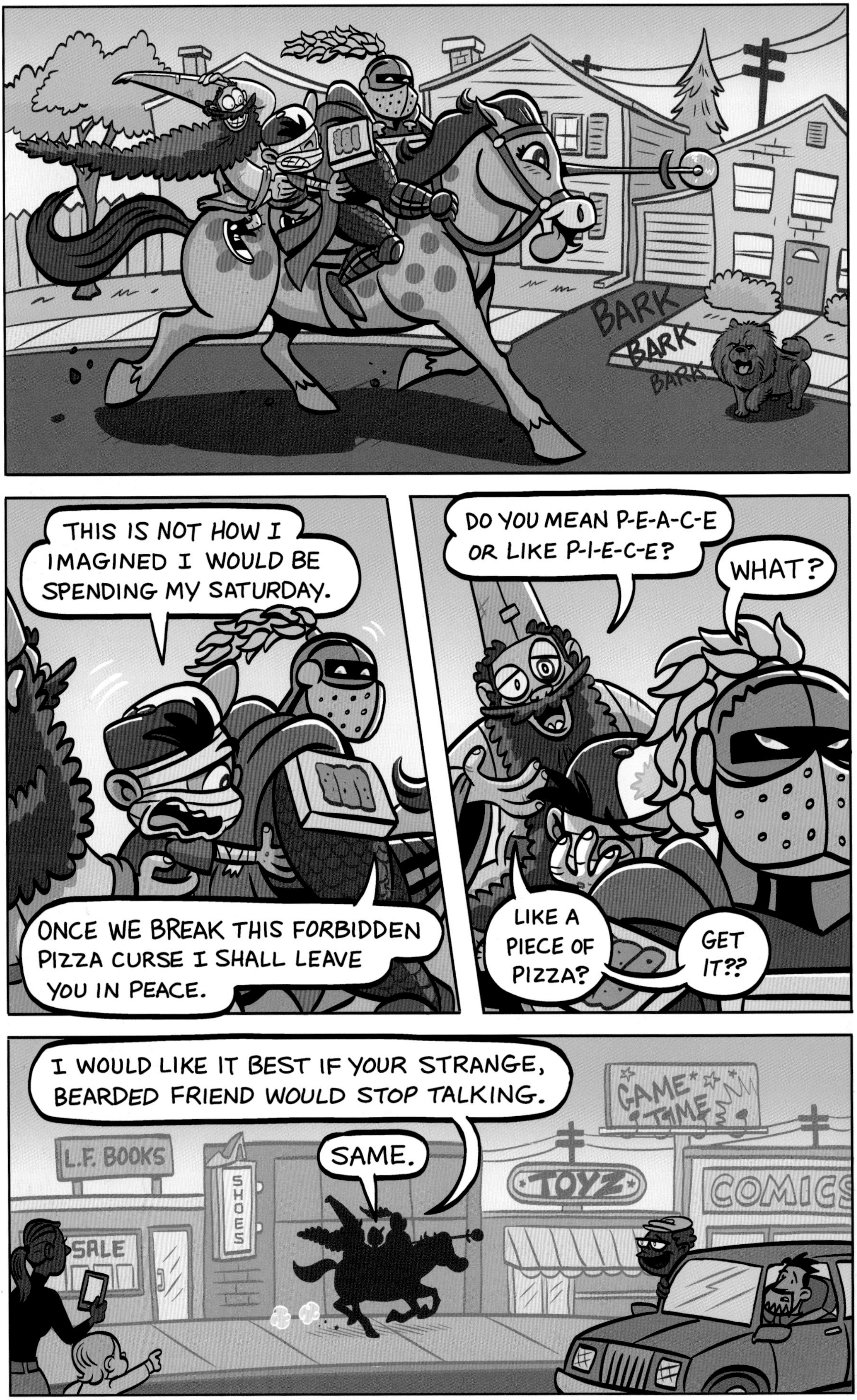
BARK
BARK
BARK
THIS IS NOT HOW I IMAGINED I WOULD BE SPENDING MY SATURDAY.
ONCE WE BREAK THIS FORBIDDEN PIZZA CURSE I SHALL LEAVE YOU IN PEACE.
DO YOU MEAN P-E-A-C-E OR LIKE P-I-E-C-E?
WHAT?
LIKE A PIECE OF PIZZA?
GET IT??
I WOULD LIKE IT BEST IF YOUR STRANGE, BEARDED FRIEND WOULD STOP TALKING.
SAME.
GAME TIME
L.F. BOOKS
SHOES
SALE
TOYZ
COMICS

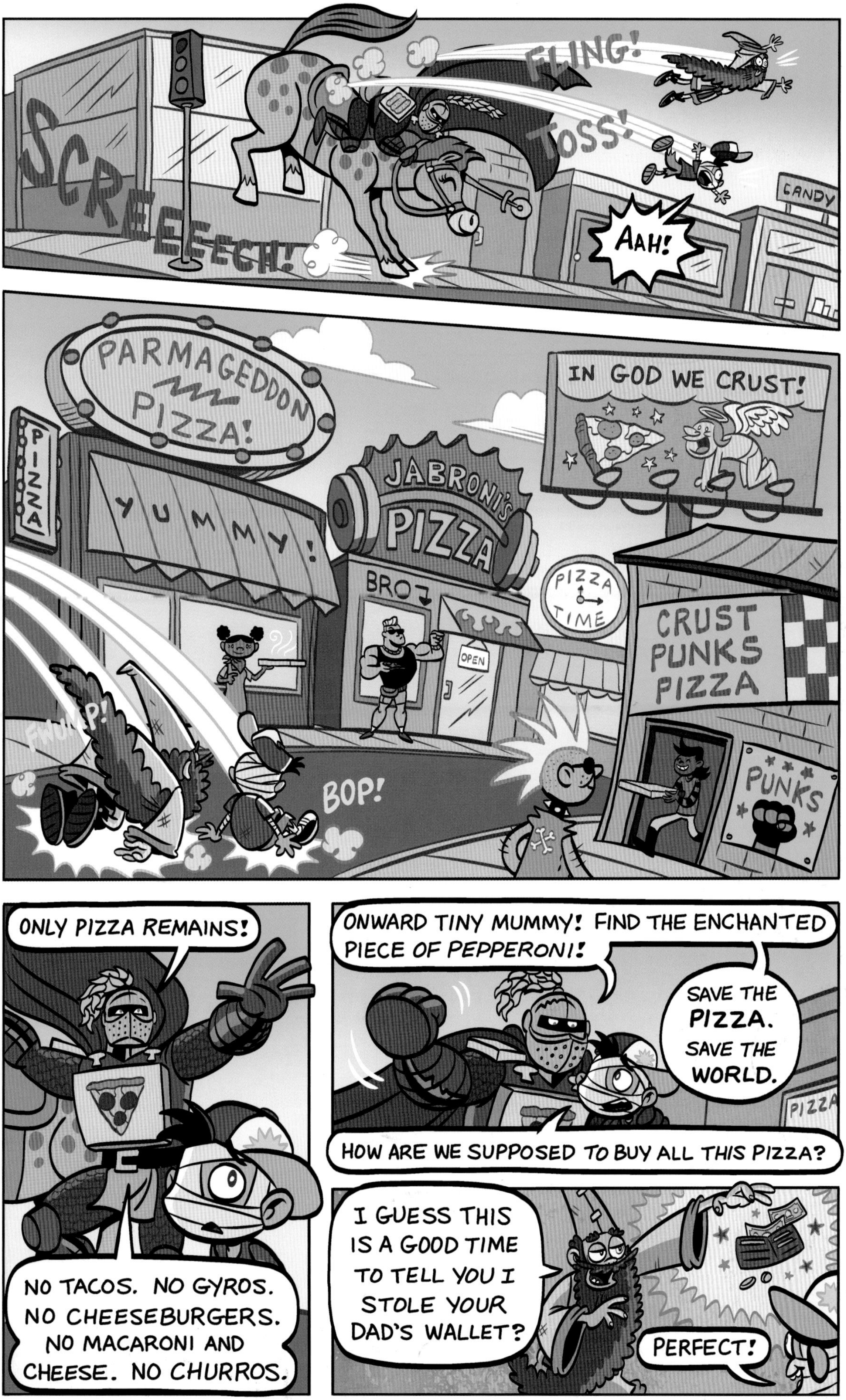
SCREEEEECH!
FLING!
TOSS!
AAH!
CANDY
PARMAGEDDON PIZZA!
PIZZA
YUMMY!
JABRONI'S PIZZA
BRO
OPEN
IN GOD WE CRUST!
PIZZA TIME
CRUST PUNKS PIZZA
PUNKS
FWUMP!
BOP!
ONLY PIZZA REMAINS!
NO TACOS. NO GYROS. NO CHEESEBURGERS. NO MACARONI AND CHEESE. NO CHURROS.
ONWARD TINY MUMMY! FIND THE ENCHANTED PIECE OF PEPPERONI!
SAVE THE PIZZA. SAVE THE WORLD.
PIZZA
HOW ARE WE SUPPOSED TO BUY ALL THIS PIZZA?
I GUESS THIS IS A GOOD TIME TO TELL YOU I STOLE YOUR DAD'S WALLET?
PERFECT!

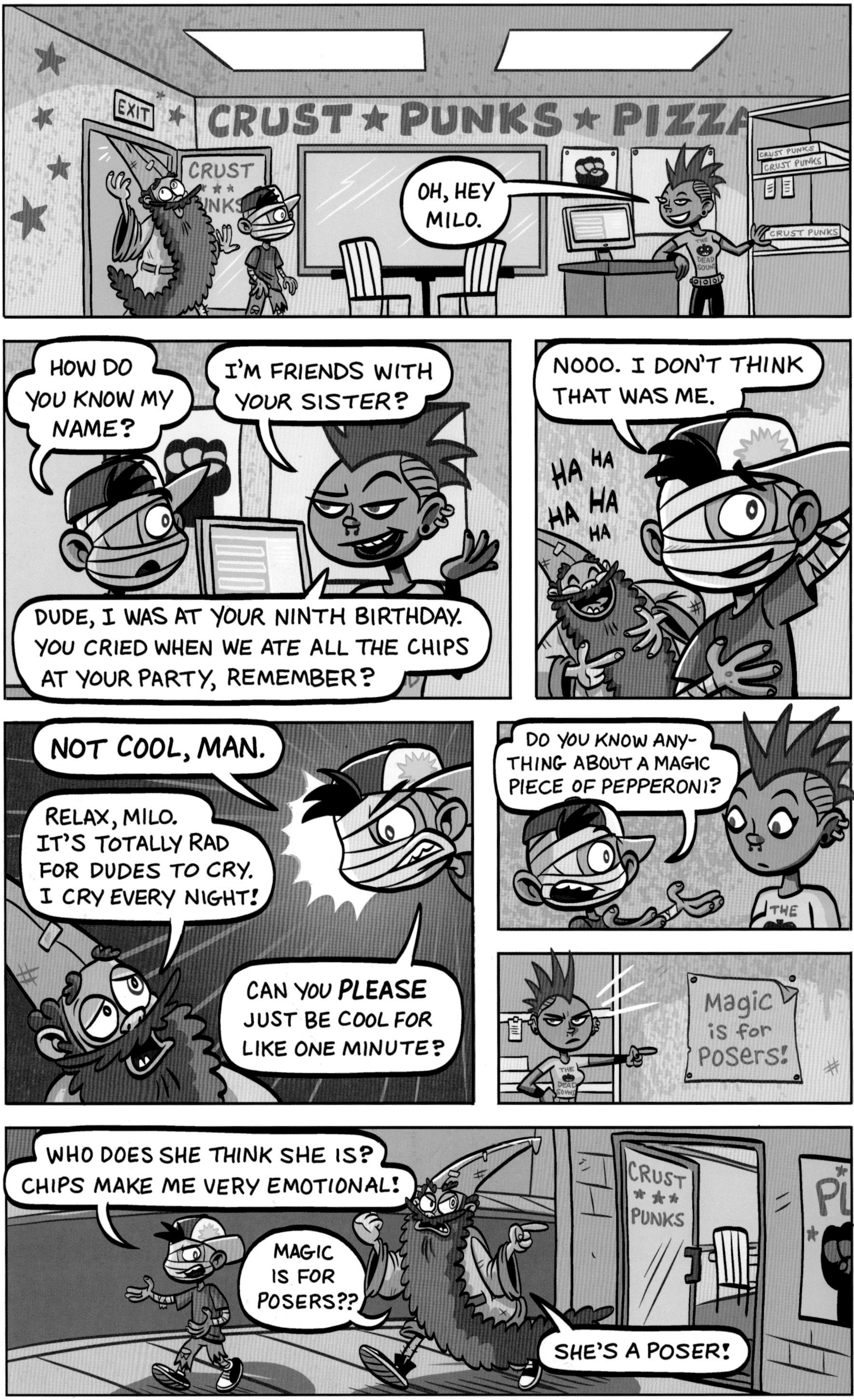
CRUST ★ PUNKS ★ PIZZA
EXIT
CRUST ★★★ PUNKS
OH, HEY MILO.
THE DEAD SOUND
CRUST PUNKS
CRUST PUNKS
CRUST PUNKS
HOW DO YOU KNOW MY NAME?
I'M FRIENDS WITH YOUR SISTER?
DUDE, I WAS AT YOUR NINTH BIRTHDAY. YOU CRIED WHEN WE ATE ALL THE CHIPS AT YOUR PARTY, REMEMBER?
NOOO. I DON'T THINK THAT WAS ME.
HA HA HA HA HA
NOT COOL, MAN.
RELAX, MILO. IT'S TOTALLY RAD FOR DUDES TO CRY. I CRY EVERY NIGHT!
CAN YOU PLEASE JUST BE COOL FOR LIKE ONE MINUTE?
DO YOU KNOW ANYTHING ABOUT A MAGIC PIECE OF PEPPERONI?
THE
Magic is for Posers!
THE DEAD SOUND
WHO DOES SHE THINK SHE IS? CHIPS MAKE ME VERY EMOTIONAL!
MAGIC IS FOR POSERS??
SHE'S A POSER!
CRUST ★★★ PUNKS

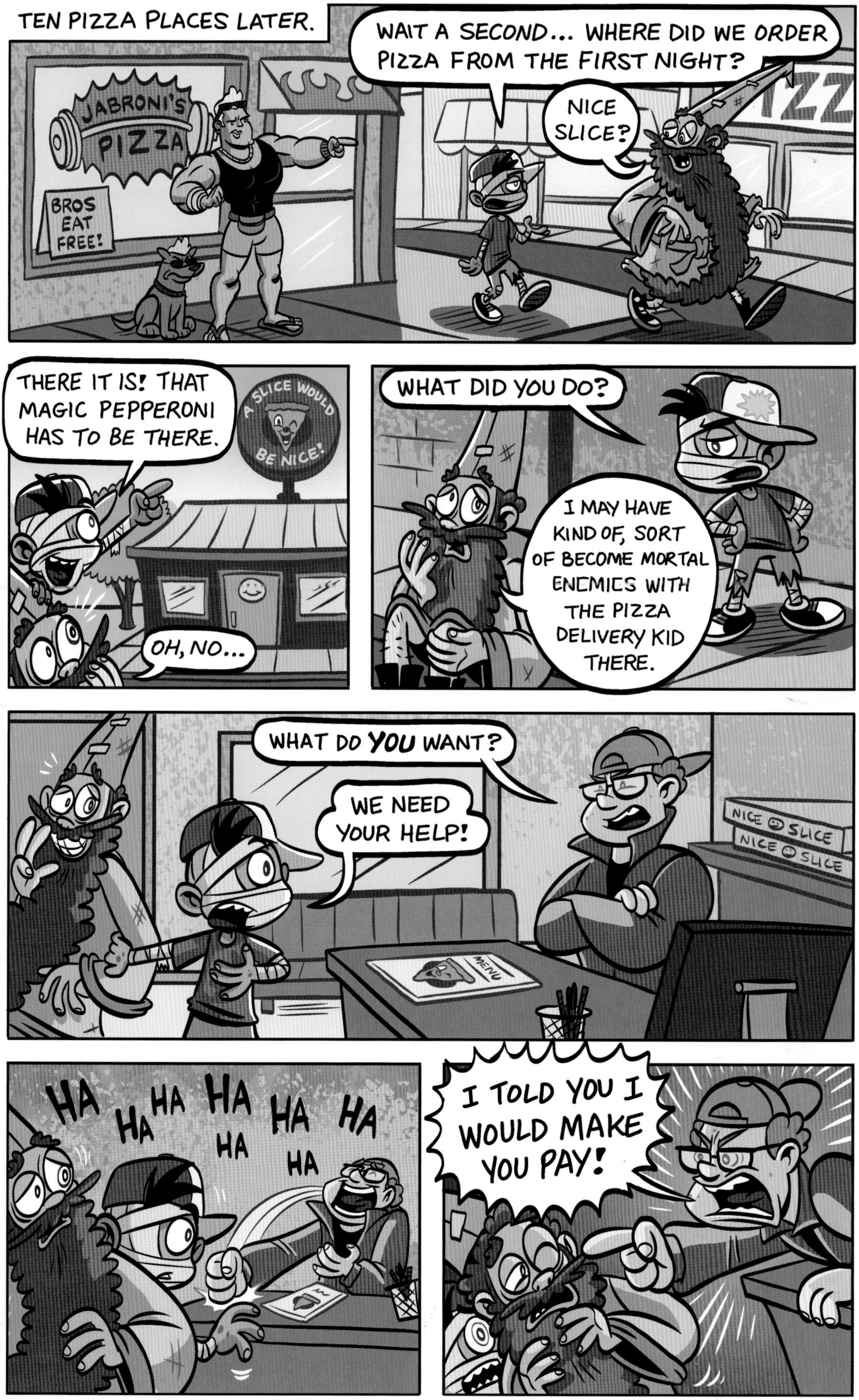
TEN PIZZA PLACES LATER.
WAIT A SECOND... WHERE DID WE ORDER PIZZA FROM THE FIRST NIGHT?
NICE SLICE?
JABRONI'S PIZZA
BROS EAT FREE!
THERE IT IS! THAT MAGIC PEPPERONI HAS TO BE THERE.
A SLICE WOULD BE NICE!
OH, NO...
WHAT DID YOU DO?
I MAY HAVE KIND OF, SORT OF BECOME MORTAL ENEMIES WITH THE PIZZA DELIVERY KID THERE.
WHAT DO YOU WANT?
WE NEED YOUR HELP!
NICE SLICE
NICE SLICE
MENU
HA HA HA HA HA HA HA HA HA
I TOLD YOU I WOULD MAKE YOU PAY!

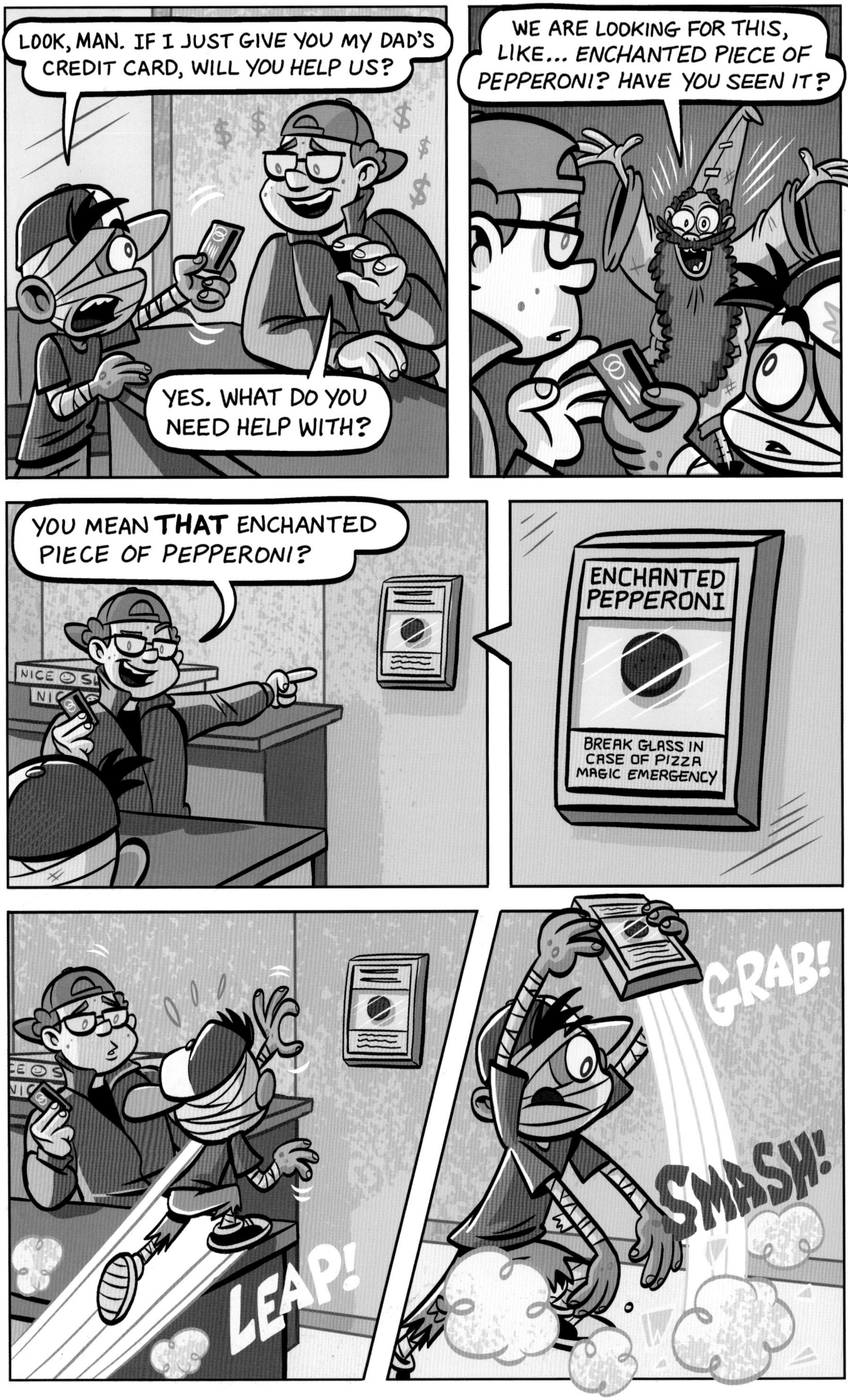
LOOK, MAN. IF I JUST GIVE YOU MY DAD'S CREDIT CARD, WILL YOU HELP US?
YES. WHAT DO YOU NEED HELP WITH?
WE ARE LOOKING FOR THIS, LIKE... ENCHANTED PIECE OF PEPPERONI? HAVE YOU SEEN IT?
YOU MEAN THAT ENCHANTED PIECE OF PEPPERONI?
ENCHANTED PEPPERONI
BREAK GLASS IN CASE OF PIZZA MAGIC EMERGENCY
LEAP!
GRAB!
SMASH!

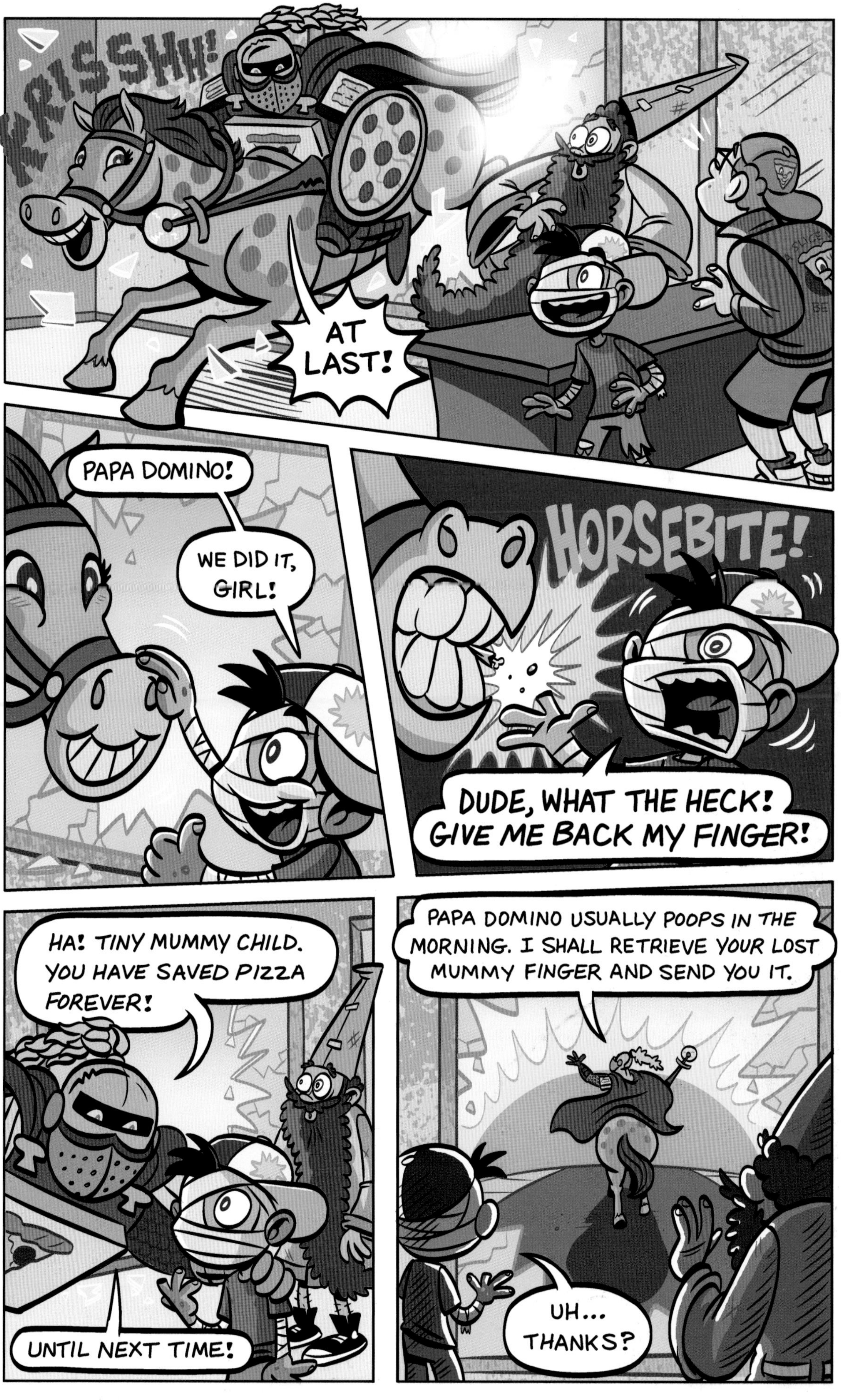
KRISSHH!
AT LAST!
PAPA DOMINO!
WE DID IT, GIRL!
HORSEBITE!
DUDE, WHAT THE HECK! GIVE ME BACK MY FINGER!
HA! TINY MUMMY CHILD. YOU HAVE SAVED PIZZA FOREVER!
UNTIL NEXT TIME!
PAPA DOMINO USUALLY POOPS IN THE MORNING. I SHALL RETRIEVE YOUR LOST MUMMY FINGER AND SEND YOU IT.
UH... THANKS?

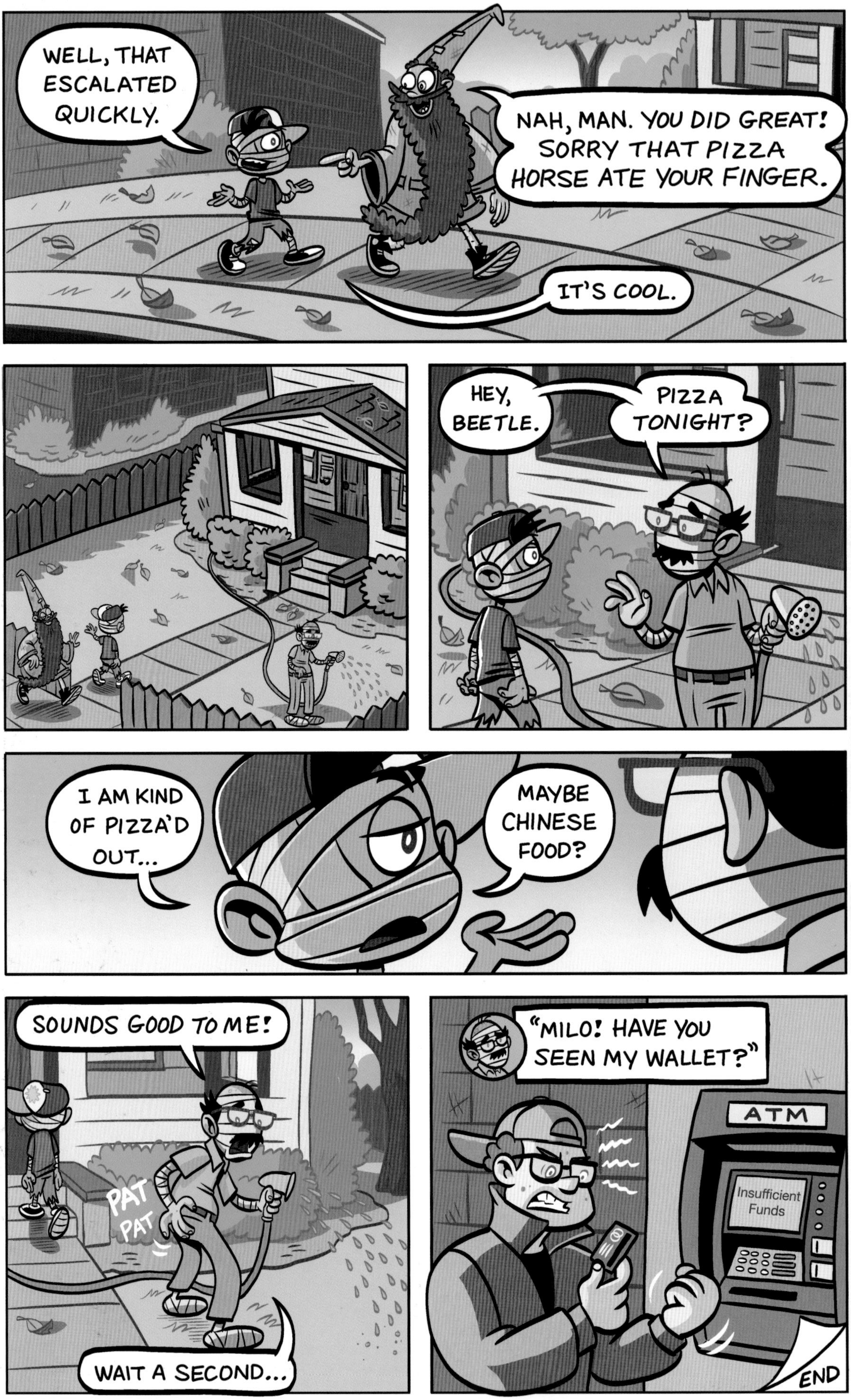
WELL, THAT ESCALATED QUICKLY.
NAH, MAN. YOU DID GREAT! SORRY THAT PIZZA HORSE ATE YOUR FINGER.
IT'S COOL.
HEY, BEETLE.
PIZZA TONIGHT?
I AM KIND OF PIZZA'D OUT...
MAYBE CHINESE FOOD?
SOUNDS GOOD TO ME!
PAT PAT
WAIT A SECOND...
"MILO! HAVE YOU SEEN MY WALLET?"
ATM
Insufficient Funds
END

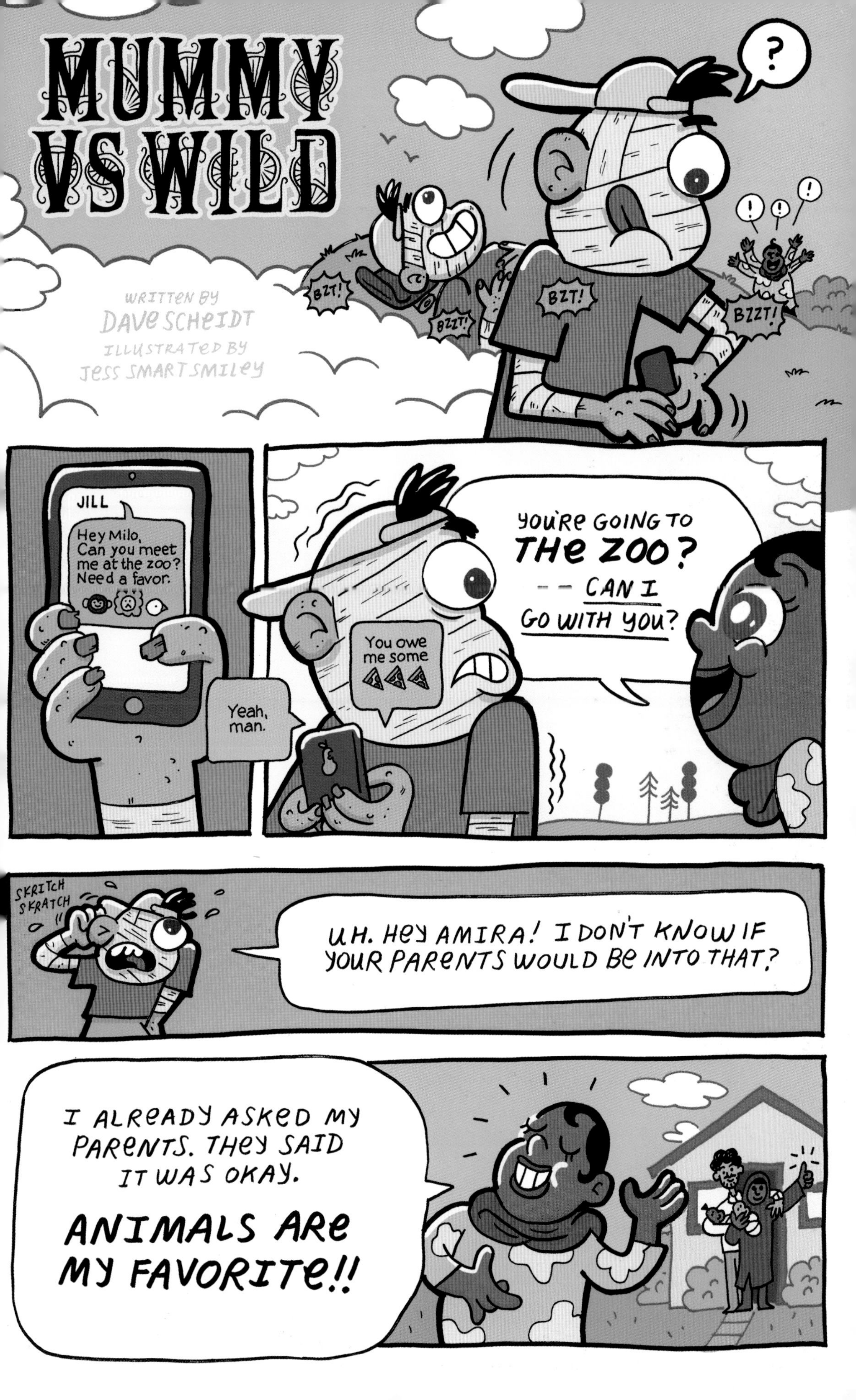
MUMMY VS WILD
WRITTEN BY DAVE SCHEIDT
ILLUSTRATED BY JESS SMART SMILEY
?
BZT!
BZZT!
BZT!
BZZT!
! ! !
JILL
Hey Milo, Can you meet me at the zoo? Need a favor.
Yeah, man.
You owe me some
YOU'RE GOING TO THE ZOO? -- CAN I GO WITH YOU?
SKRITCH SKRATCH
UH. HEY AMIRA! I DON'T KNOW IF YOUR PARENTS WOULD BE INTO THAT?
I ALREADY ASKED MY PARENTS. THEY SAID IT WAS OKAY.
ANIMALS ARE MY FAVORITE!!

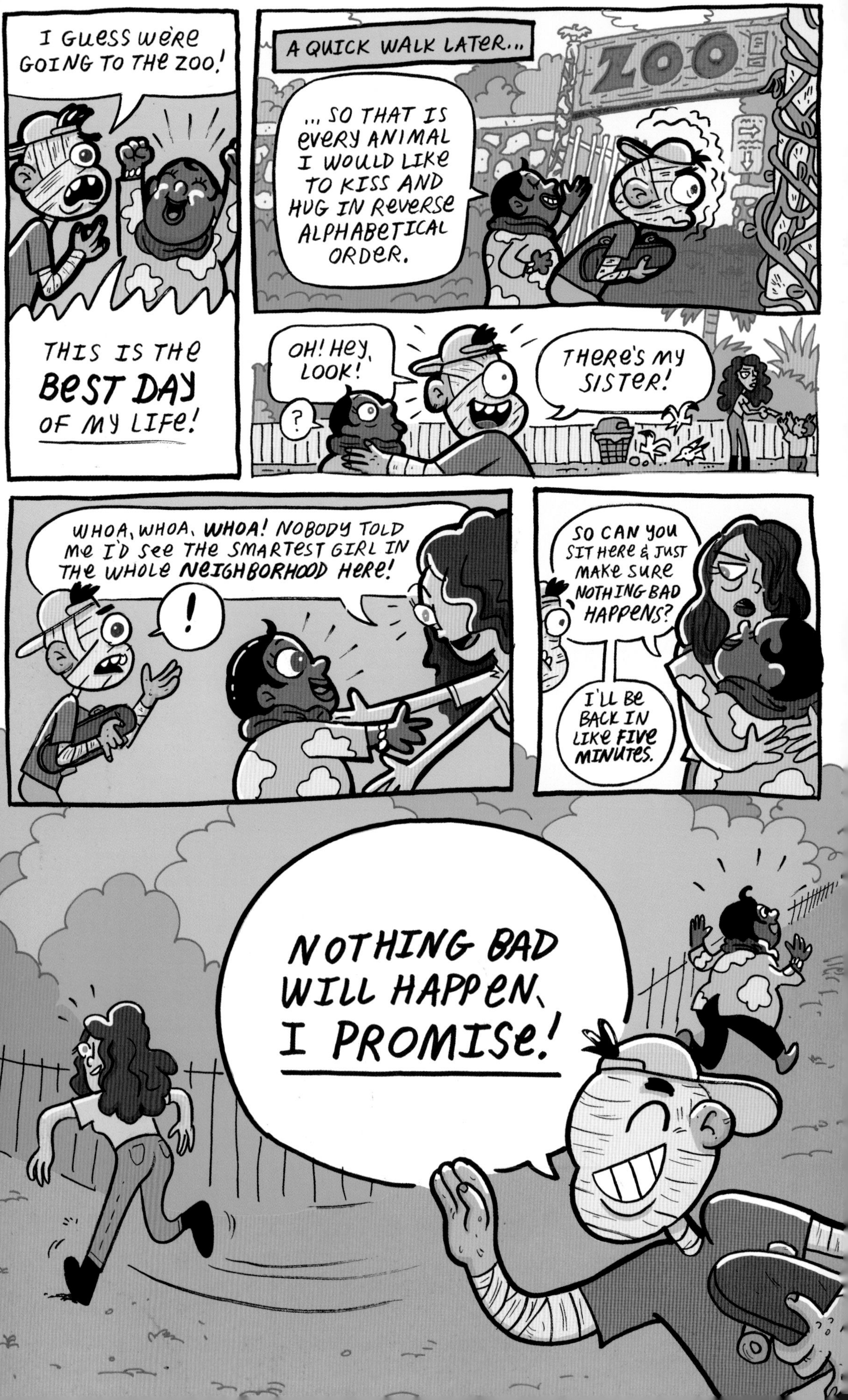
I GUESS WE'RE GOING TO THE ZOO!
THIS IS THE BEST DAY OF MY LIFE!
A QUICK WALK LATER...
ZOO
...SO THAT IS EVERY ANIMAL I WOULD LIKE TO KISS AND HUG IN REVERSE ALPHABETICAL ORDER.
OH! HEY, LOOK!
?
THERE'S MY SISTER!
WHOA, WHOA, WHOA! NOBODY TOLD ME I'D SEE THE SMARTEST GIRL IN THE WHOLE NEIGHBORHOOD HERE!
!
SO CAN YOU SIT HERE & JUST MAKE SURE NOTHING BAD HAPPENS?
I'LL BE BACK IN LIKE FIVE MINUTES.
NOTHING BAD WILL HAPPEN, I PROMISE!

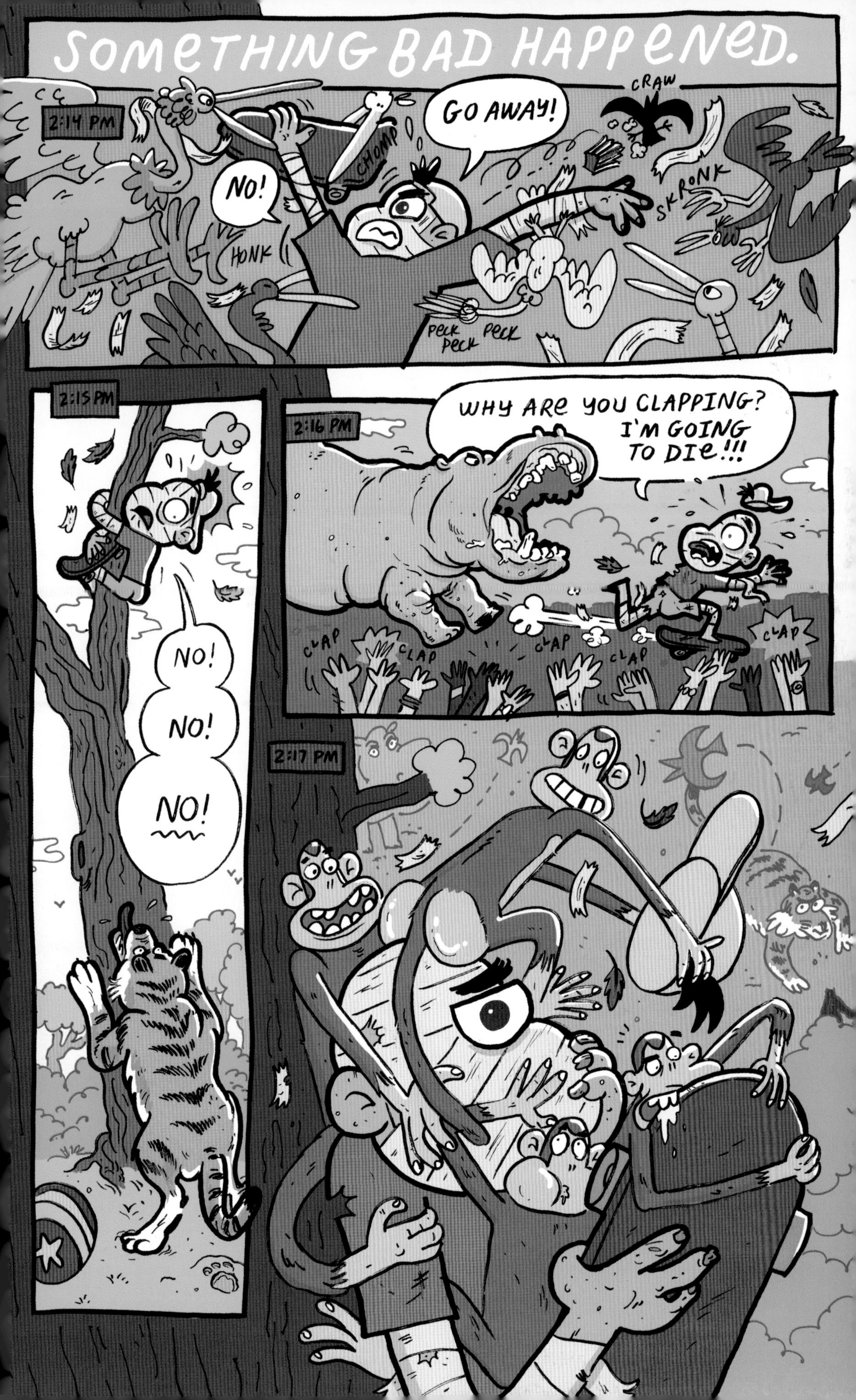
SOMETHING BAD HAPPENED.
2:14 PM
CRAW
GO AWAY!
CHOMP
NO!
SKRONK
HONK
PECK
PECK
PECK
2:15 PM
NO!
NO!
NO!
2:16 PM
WHY ARE YOU CLAPPING? I'M GOING TO DIE!!!
CLAP
CLAP
CLAP
CLAP
CLAP
2:17 PM

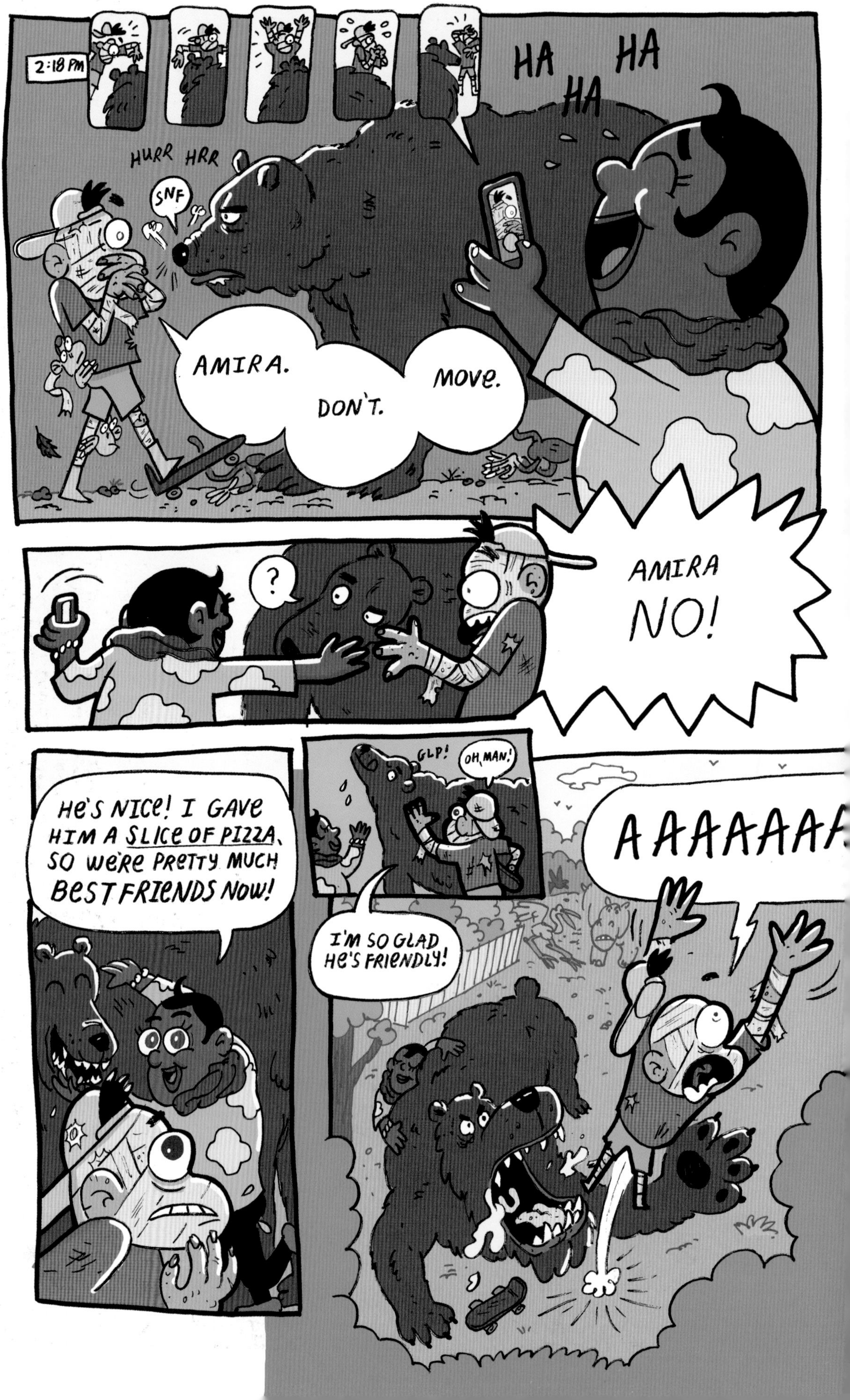
2:18 PM
HA HA HA
HURR HRR
SNF
AMIRA.
DON'T.
MOVE.
?
AMIRA NO!
HE'S NICE! I GAVE HIM A SLICE OF PIZZA, SO WE'RE PRETTY MUCH BEST FRIENDS NOW!
GLP!
OH, MAN!
I'M SO GLAD HE'S FRIENDLY!
AAAAAA

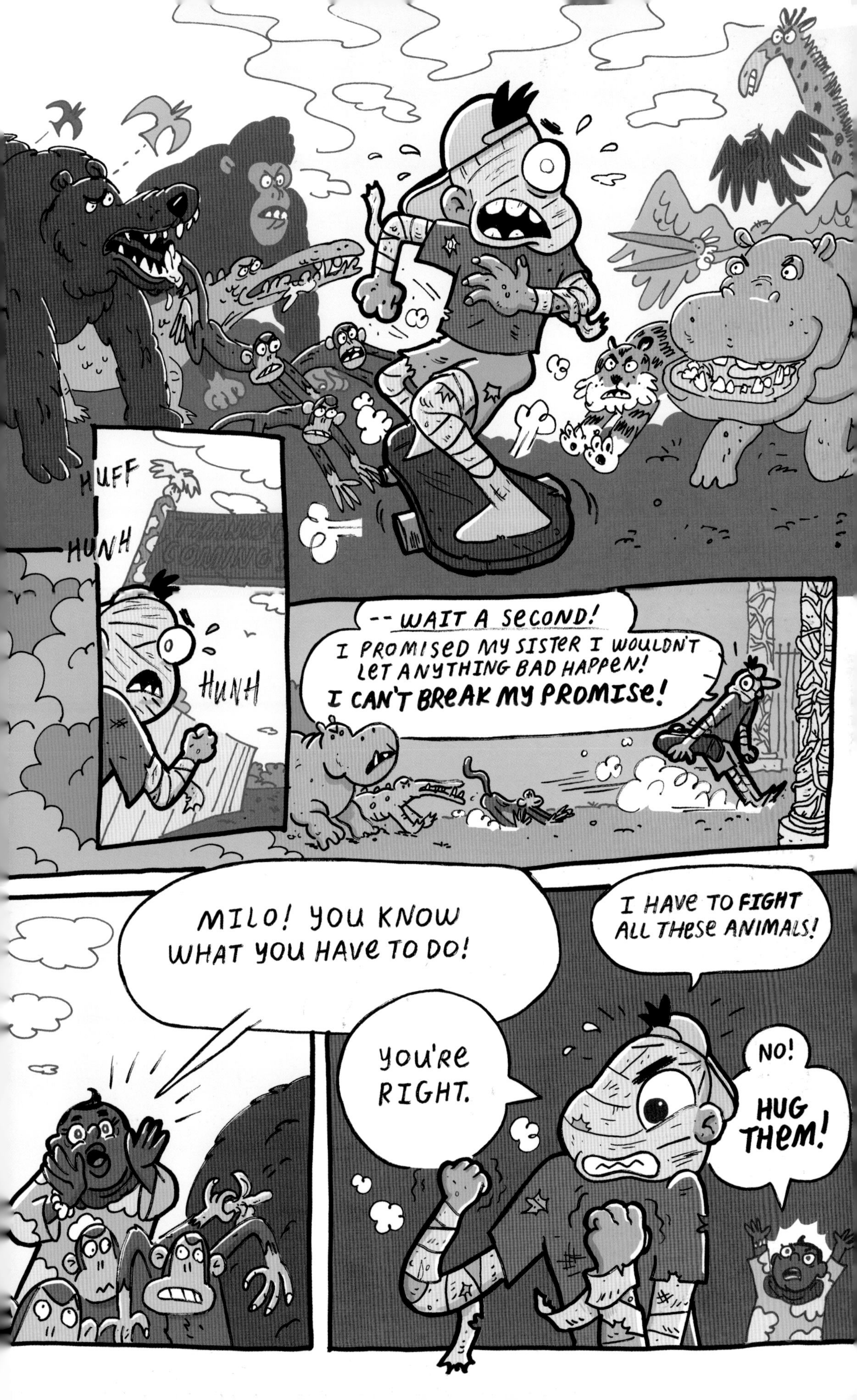
HUFF
HUNH
HUNH
-- WAIT A SECOND!
I PROMISED MY SISTER I WOULDN'T LET ANYTHING BAD HAPPEN!
I CAN'T BREAK MY PROMISE!
MILO! YOU KNOW WHAT YOU HAVE TO DO!
YOU'RE RIGHT.
I HAVE TO FIGHT ALL THESE ANIMALS!
NO!
HUG THEM!

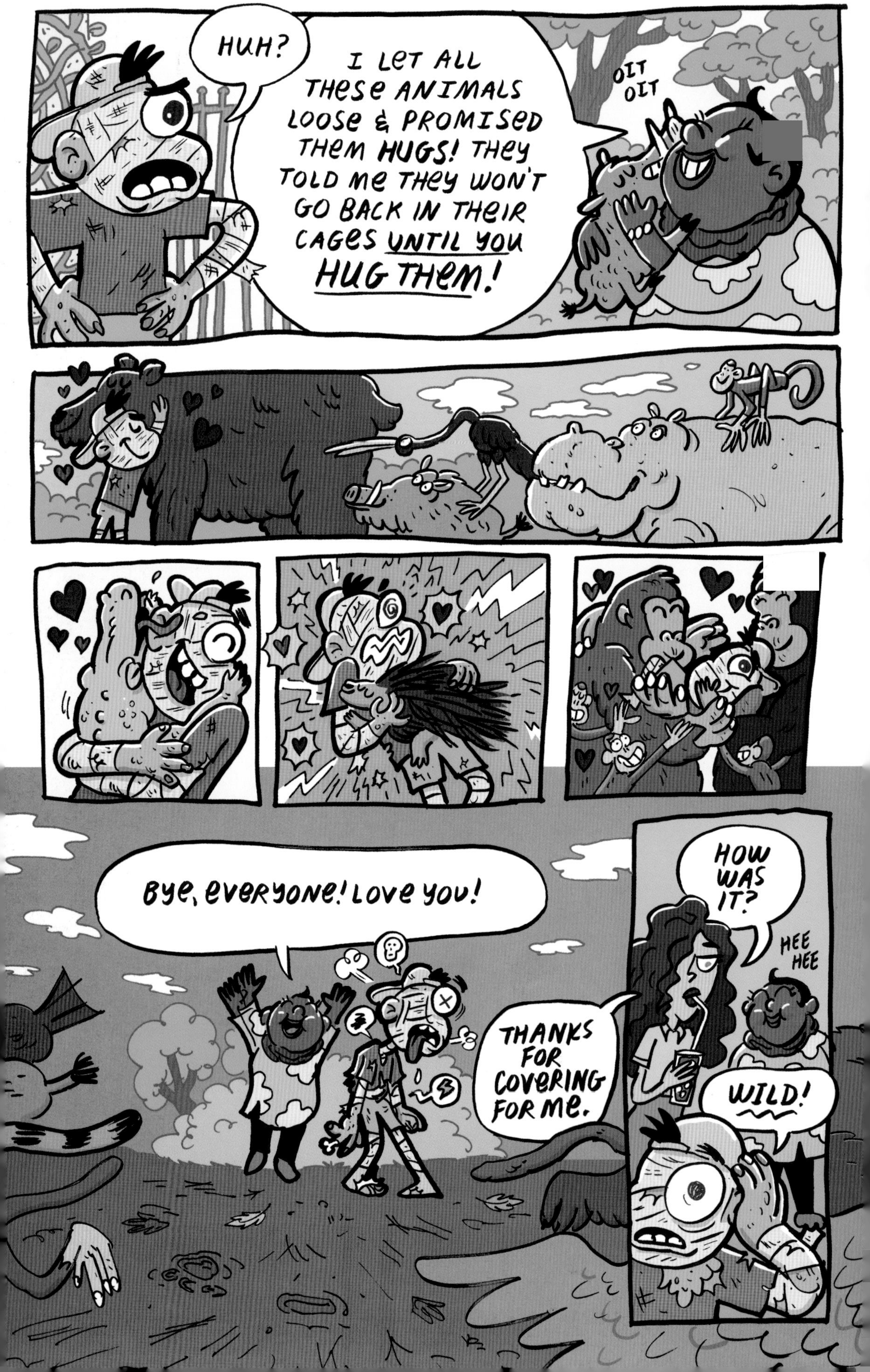
HUH?
I LET ALL THESE ANIMALS LOOSE & PROMISED THEM HUGS! THEY TOLD ME THEY WON'T GO BACK IN THEIR CAGES UNTIL YOU HUG THEM!
OIT OIT
BYE, EVERYONE! LOVE YOU!
HOW WAS IT?
HEE HEE
THANKS FOR COVERING FOR ME.
WILD!

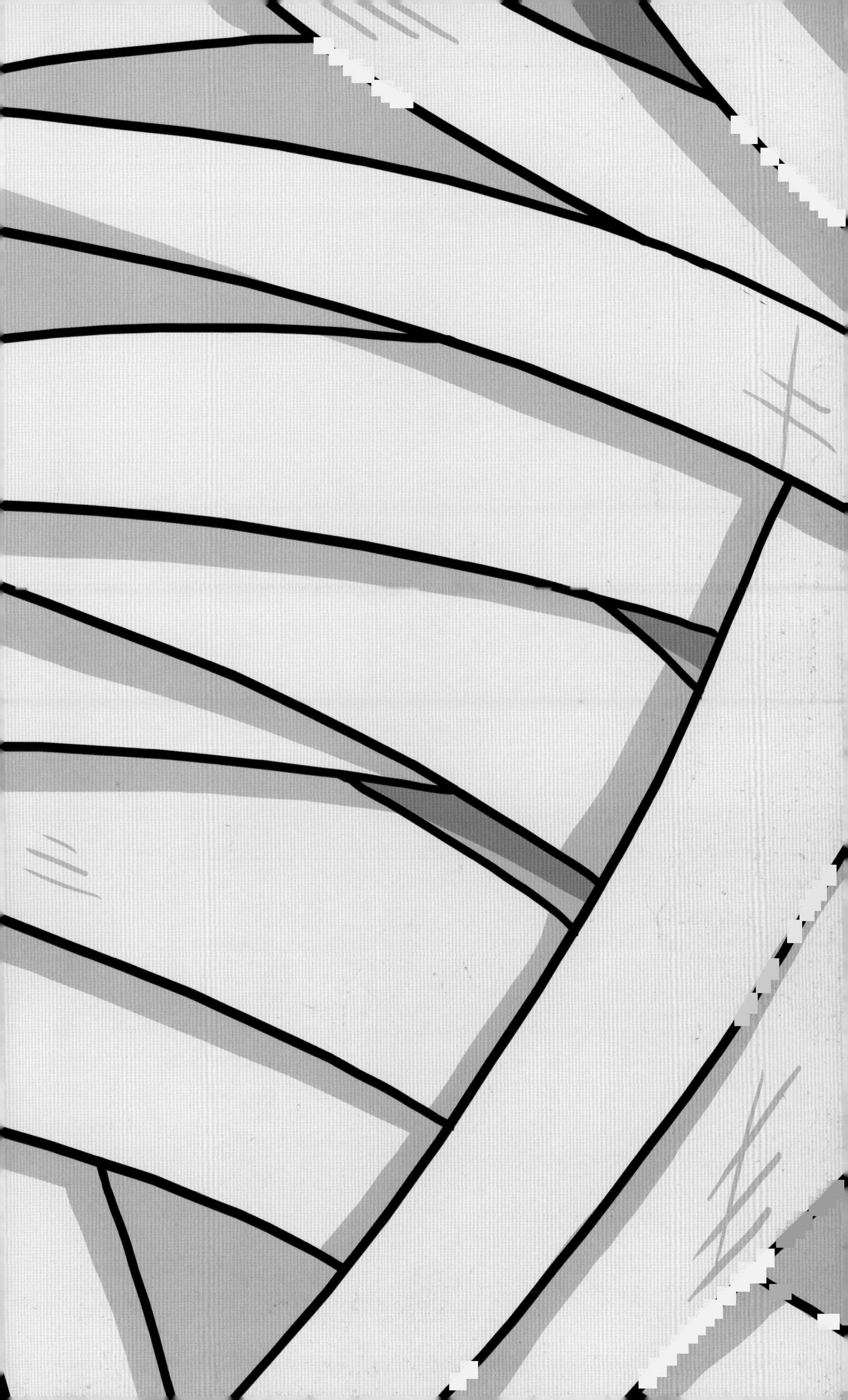

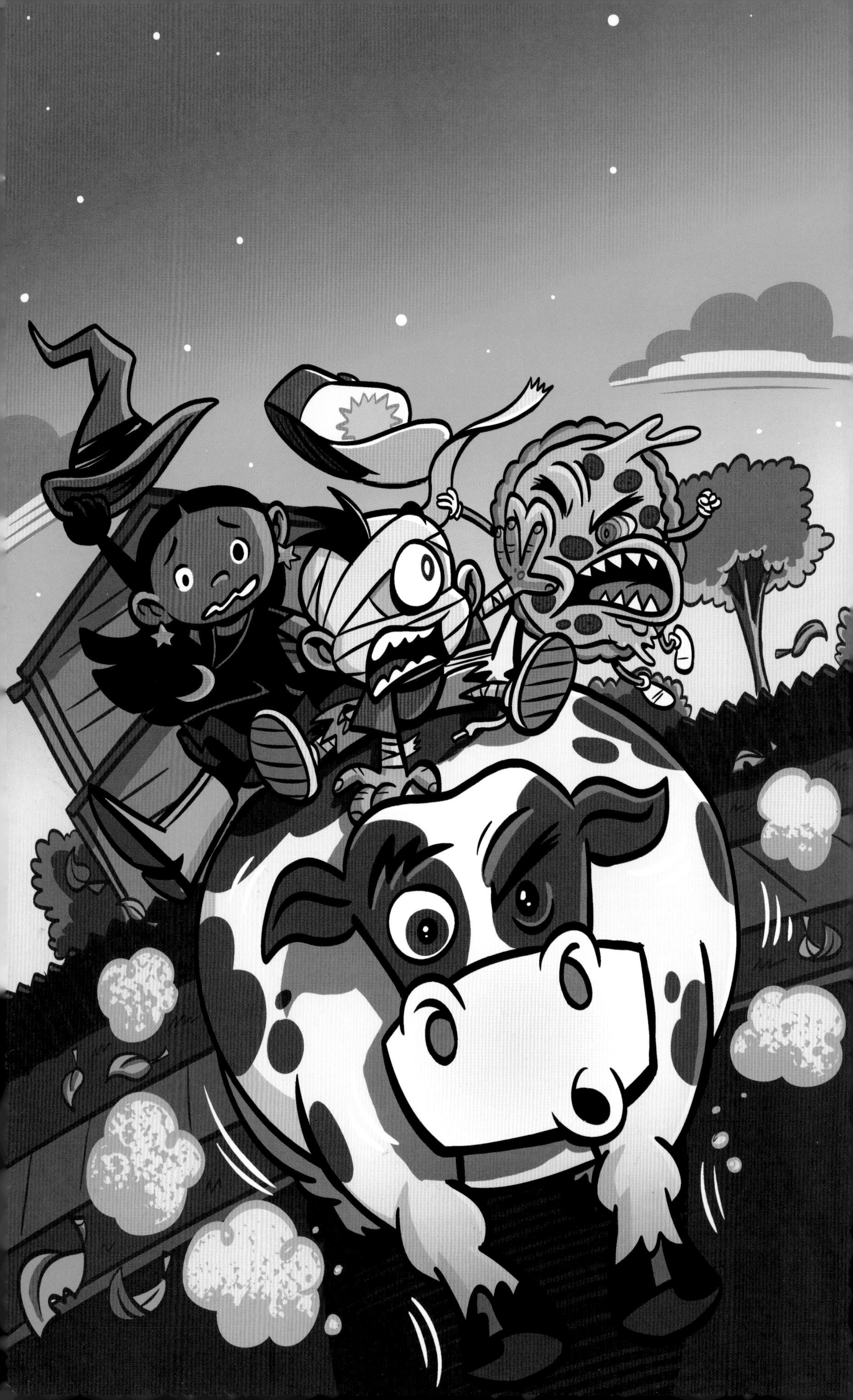

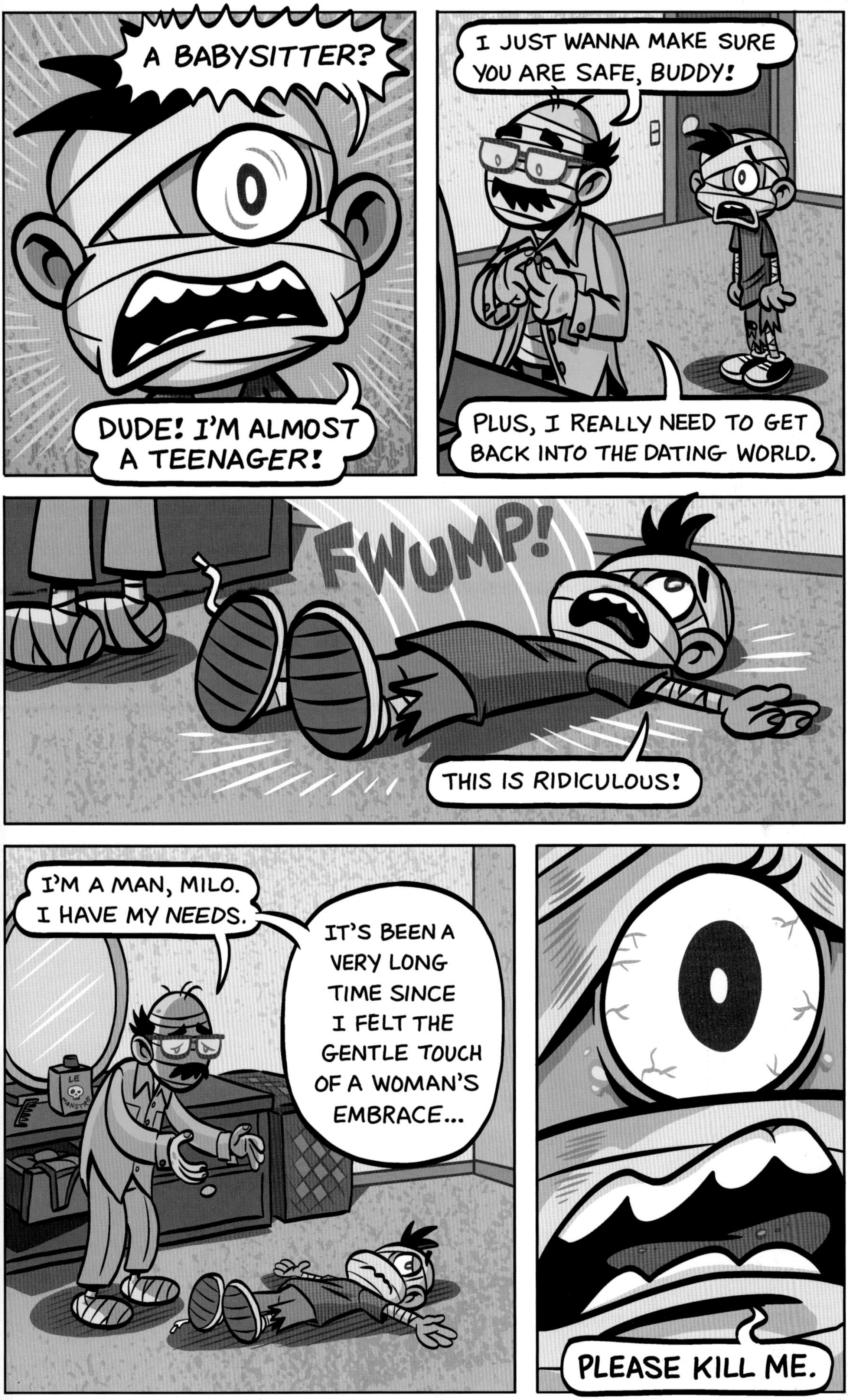
A BABYSITTER?
DUDE! I'M ALMOST A TEENAGER!
I JUST WANNA MAKE SURE YOU ARE SAFE, BUDDY!
PLUS, I REALLY NEED TO GET BACK INTO THE DATING WORLD.
FWUMP!
THIS IS RIDICULOUS!
I'M A MAN, MILO. I HAVE MY NEEDS.
IT'S BEEN A VERY LONG TIME SINCE I FELT THE GENTLE TOUCH OF A WOMAN'S EMBRACE...
LE MONSTRE
PLEASE KILL ME.

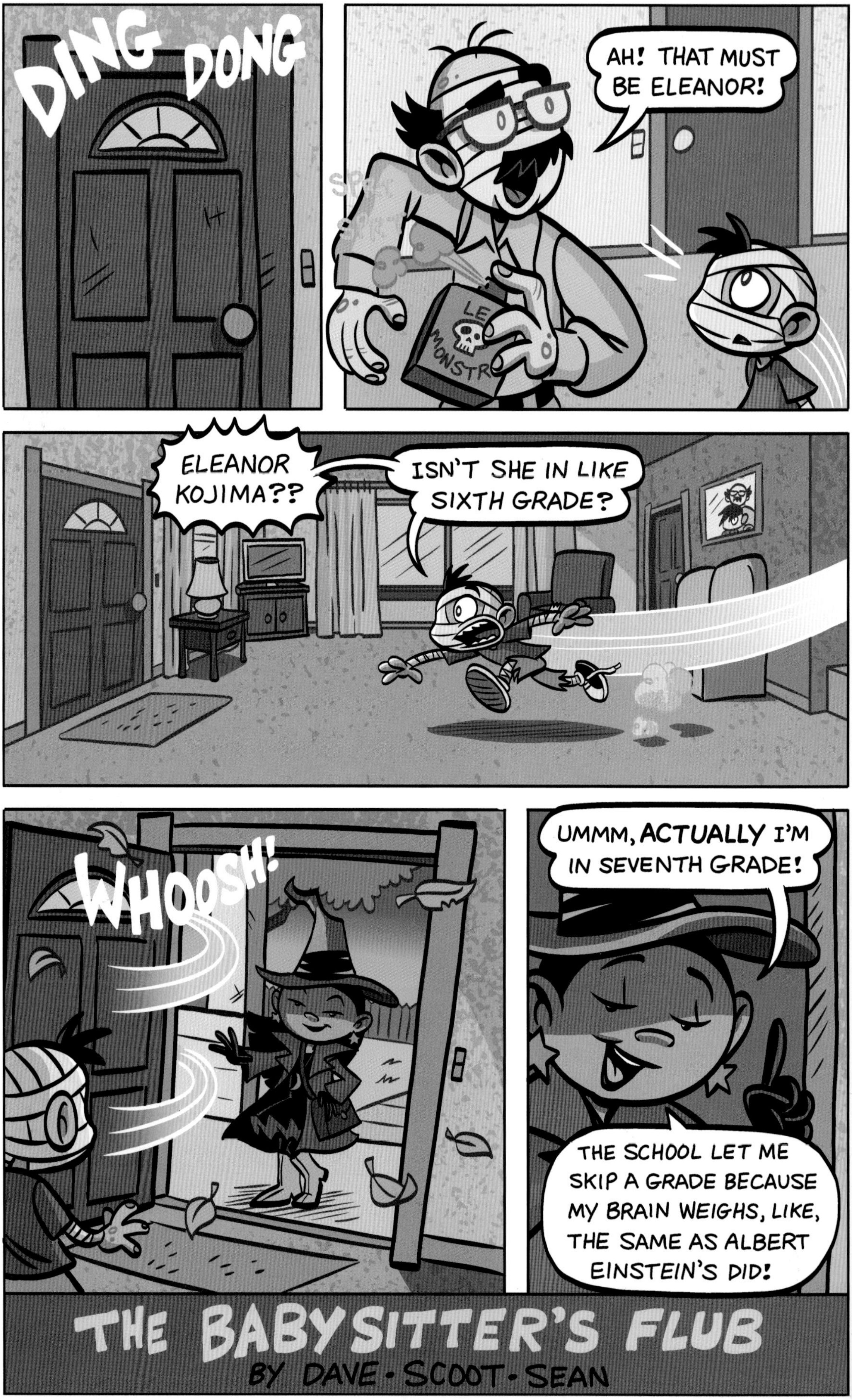
DING DONG
AH! THAT MUST BE ELEANOR!
LE MONSTR
ELEANOR KOJIMA??
ISN'T SHE IN LIKE SIXTH GRADE?
WHOOSH!
UMMM, ACTUALLY I'M IN SEVENTH GRADE!
THE SCHOOL LET ME SKIP A GRADE BECAUSE MY BRAIN WEIGHS, LIKE, THE SAME AS ALBERT EINSTEIN'S DID!
THE BABYSITTER'S FLUB
BY DAVE • SCOOT • SEAN

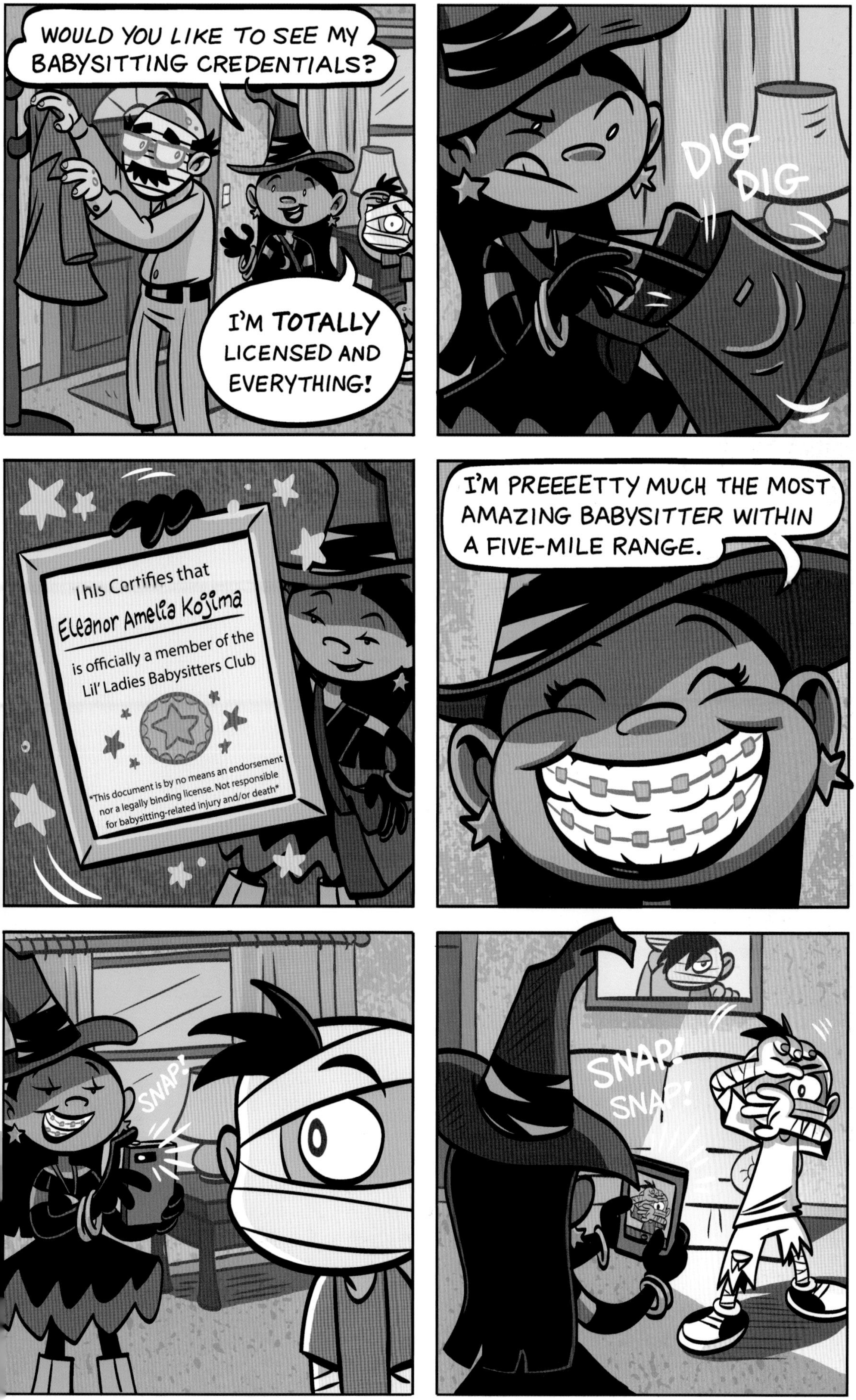

WOULD YOU LIKE TO SEE MY BABYSITTING CREDENTIALS?
I'M TOTALLY LICENSED AND EVERYTHING!
DIG
DIG
This Certifies that
Eleanor Amelia Kojima
is officially a member of the
Lil' Ladies Babysitters Club
This document is by no means an endorsement nor a legally binding license. Not responsible for babysitting-related injury and/or death
I'M PREEEETTY MUCH THE MOST AMAZING BABYSITTER WITHIN A FIVE-MILE RANGE.
SNAP!
SNAP!
SNAP!

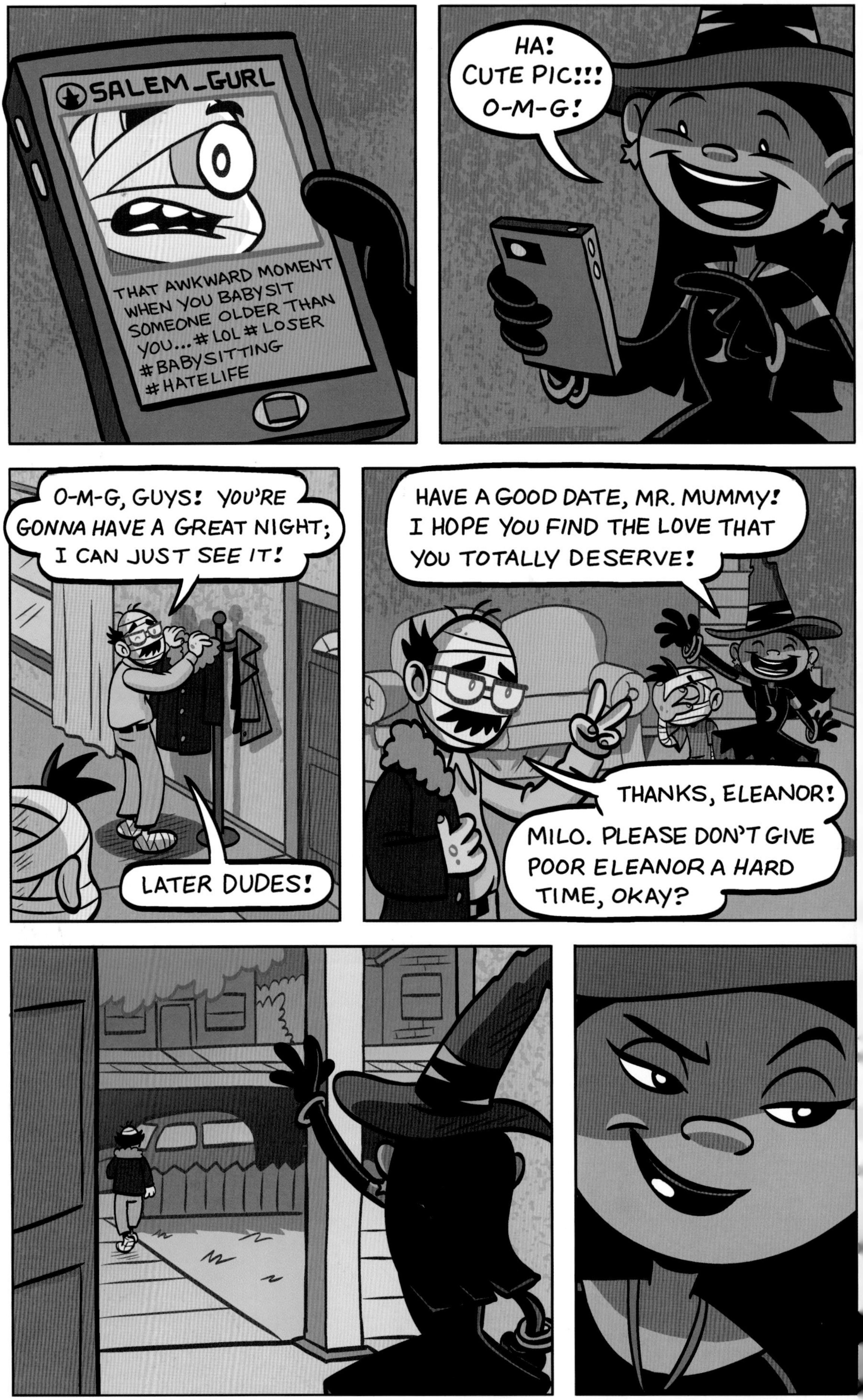
SALEM_GURL
THAT AWKWARD MOMENT WHEN YOU BABYSIT SOMEONE OLDER THAN YOU...# LOL # LOSER #BABYSITTING #HATELIFE
HA! CUTE PIC!!! O-M-G!
O-M-G, GUYS! YOU'RE GONNA HAVE A GREAT NIGHT; I CAN JUST SEE IT!
LATER DUDES!
HAVE A GOOD DATE, MR. MUMMY! I HOPE YOU FIND THE LOVE THAT YOU TOTALLY DESERVE!
THANKS, ELEANOR!
MILO. PLEASE DON'T GIVE POOR ELEANOR A HARD TIME, OKAY?

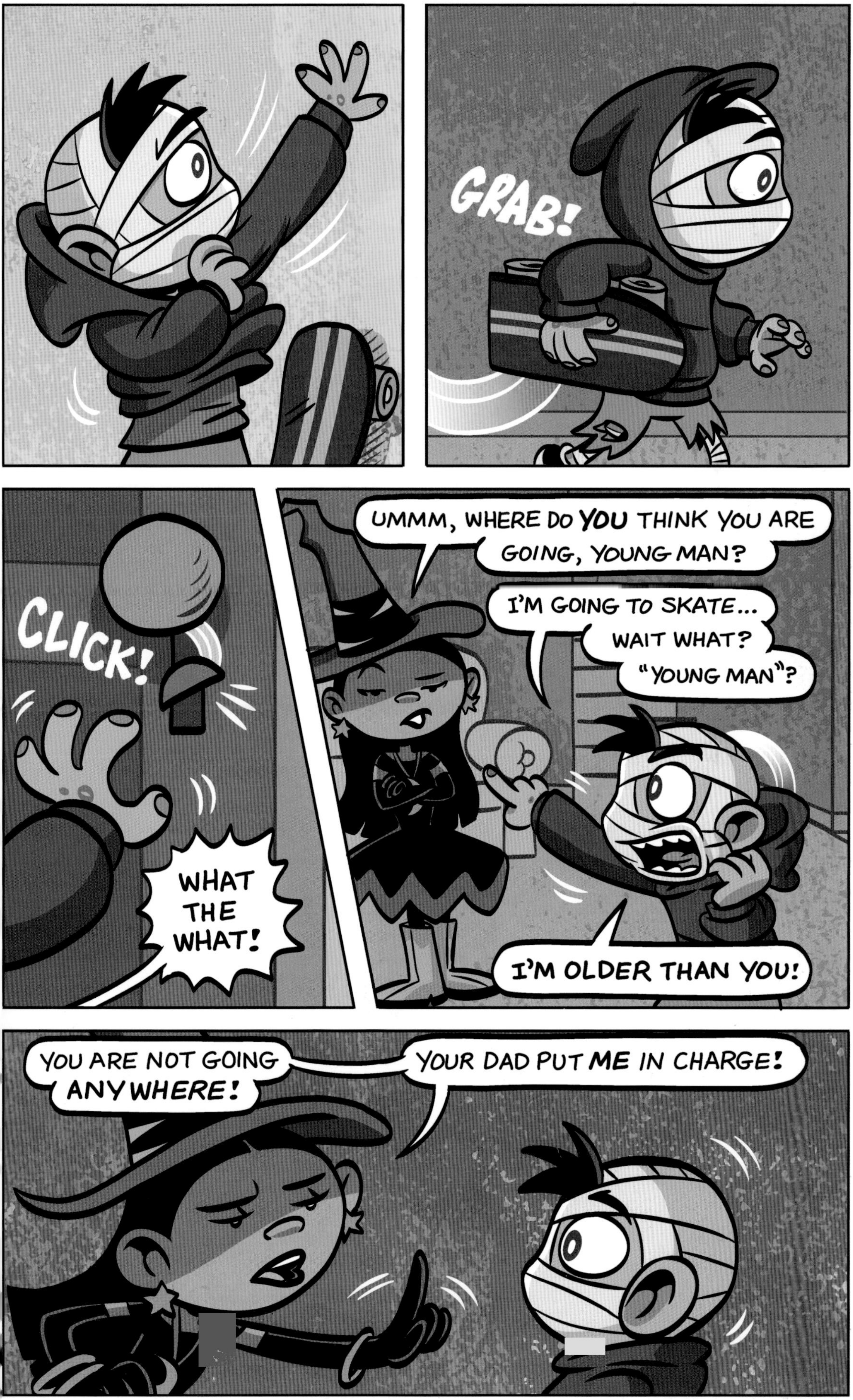
GRAB!
CLICK!
UMMM, WHERE DO YOU THINK YOU ARE GOING, YOUNG MAN?
I'M GOING TO SKATE...
WAIT WHAT?
"YOUNG MAN"?
WHAT THE WHAT!
I'M OLDER THAN YOU!
YOU ARE NOT GOING ANYWHERE!
YOUR DAD PUT ME IN CHARGE!

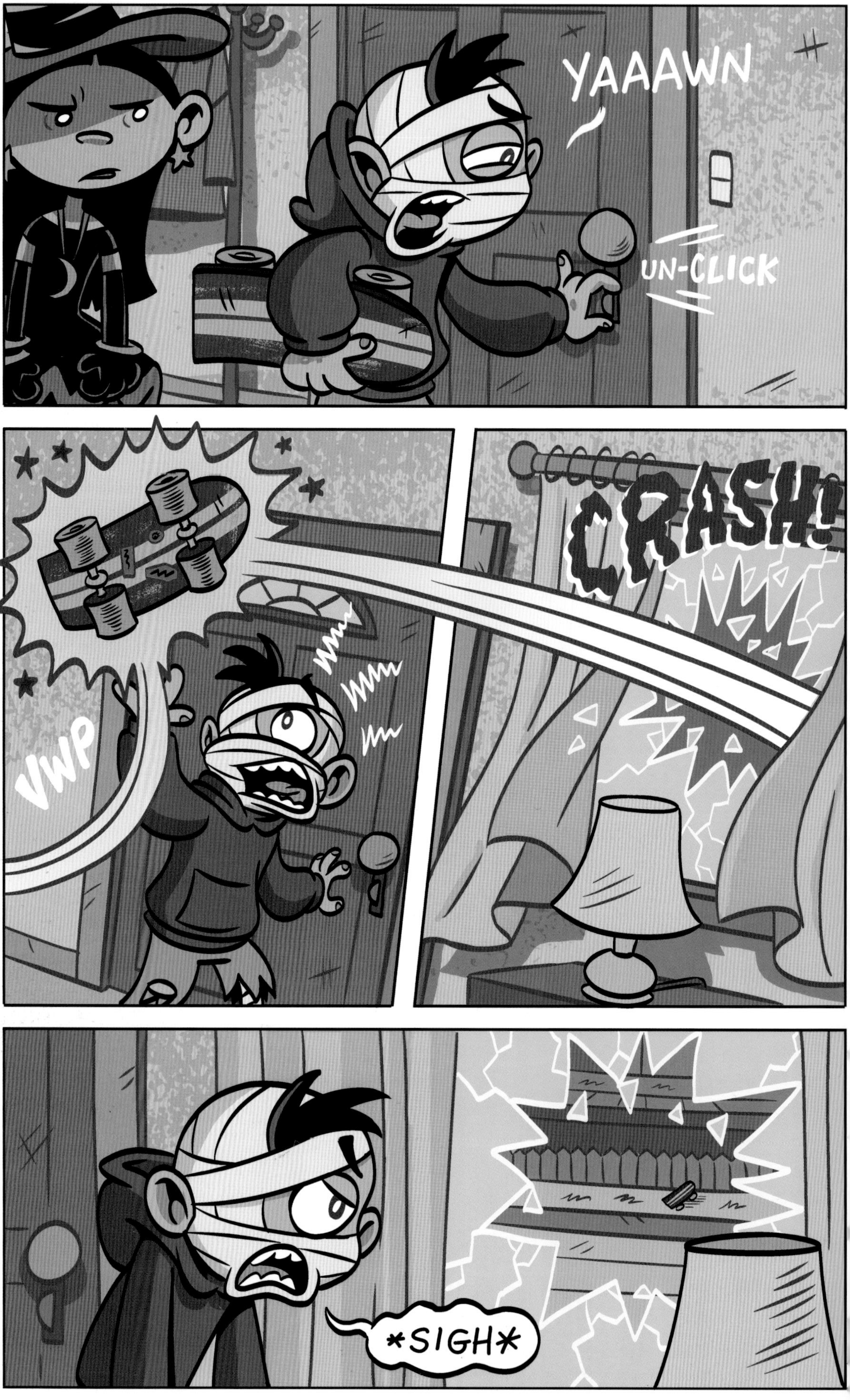
YAAAWN
UN-CLICK
VWP
CRASH!
SIGH

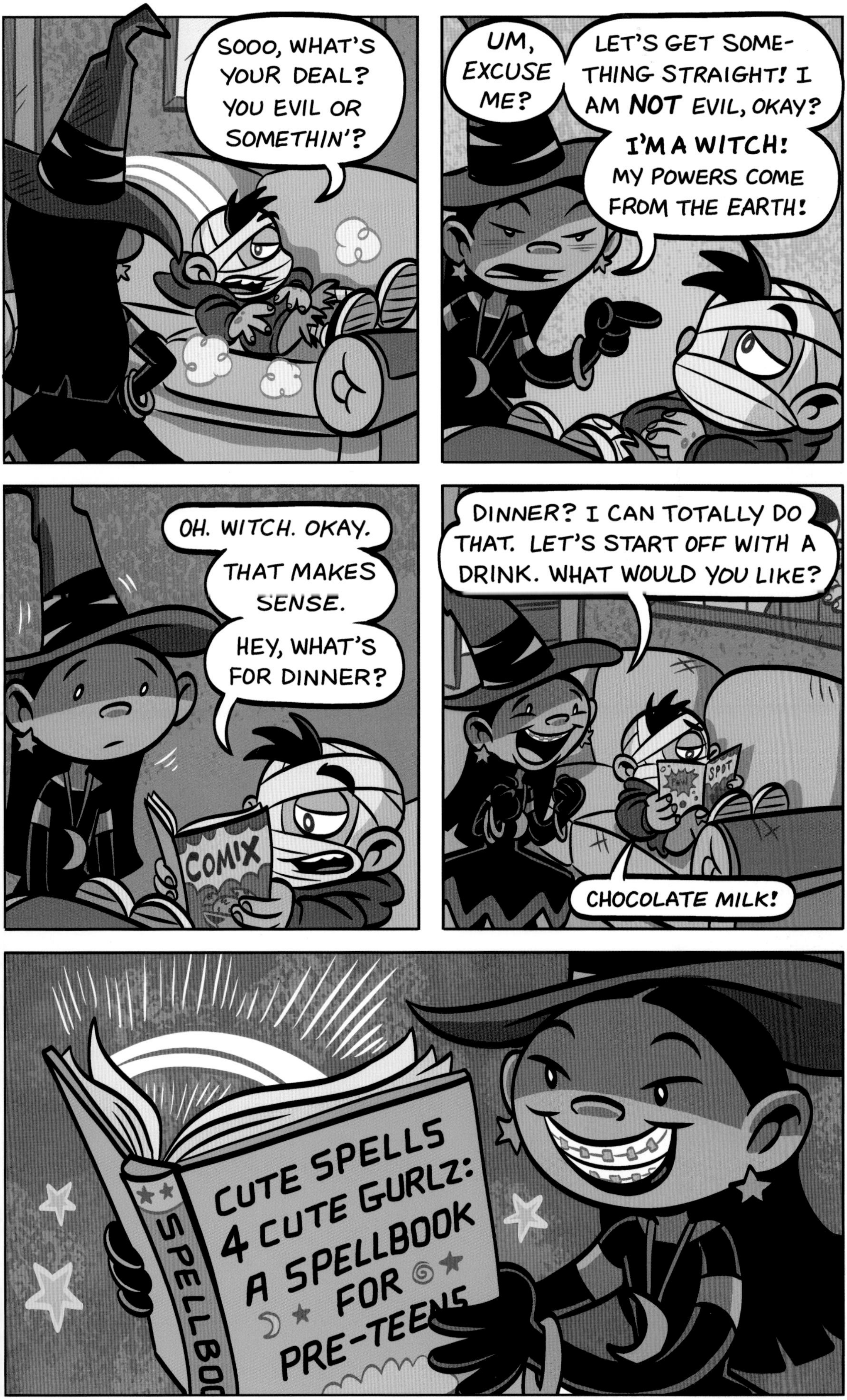
SOOO, WHAT'S YOUR DEAL? YOU EVIL OR SOMETHIN'?
UM, EXCUSE ME?
LET'S GET SOMETHING STRAIGHT! I AM **NOT** EVIL, OKAY?
I'M A WITCH! MY POWERS COME FROM THE EARTH!
OH. WITCH. OKAY.
THAT MAKES SENSE.
HEY, WHAT'S FOR DINNER?
COMIX
DINNER? I CAN TOTALLY DO THAT. LET'S START OFF WITH A DRINK. WHAT WOULD YOU LIKE?
CHOCOLATE MILK!
CUTE SPELLS 4 CUTE GURLZ: A SPELLBOOK FOR PRE-TEENS
SPELLBOO

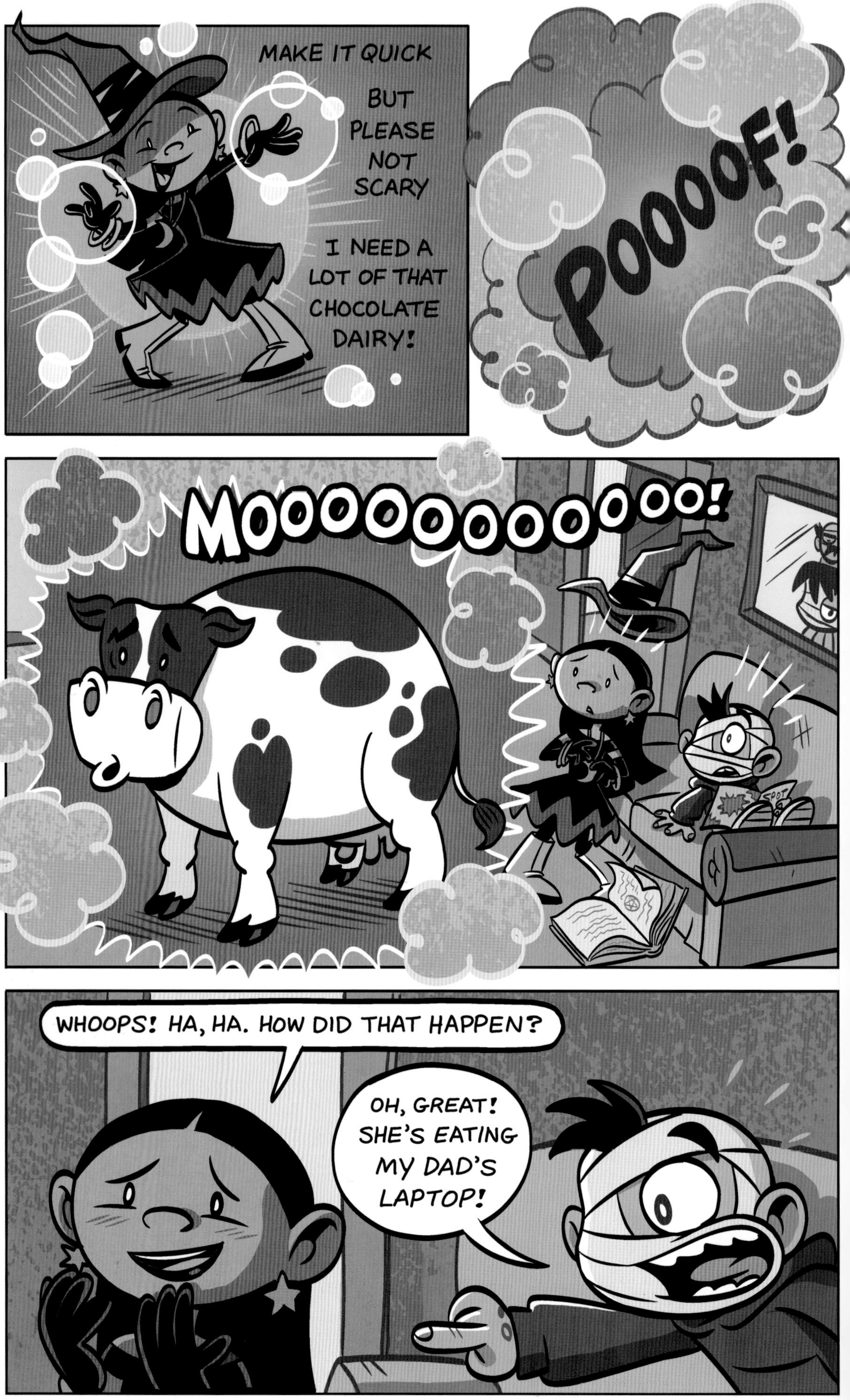
MAKE IT QUICK
BUT PLEASE NOT SCARY
I NEED A LOT OF THAT CHOCOLATE DAIRY!
POOOOOF!
MOOOOOOOOOOOO!
SPOT
WHOOPS! HA, HA. HOW DID THAT HAPPEN?
OH, GREAT! SHE'S EATING MY DAD'S LAPTOP!

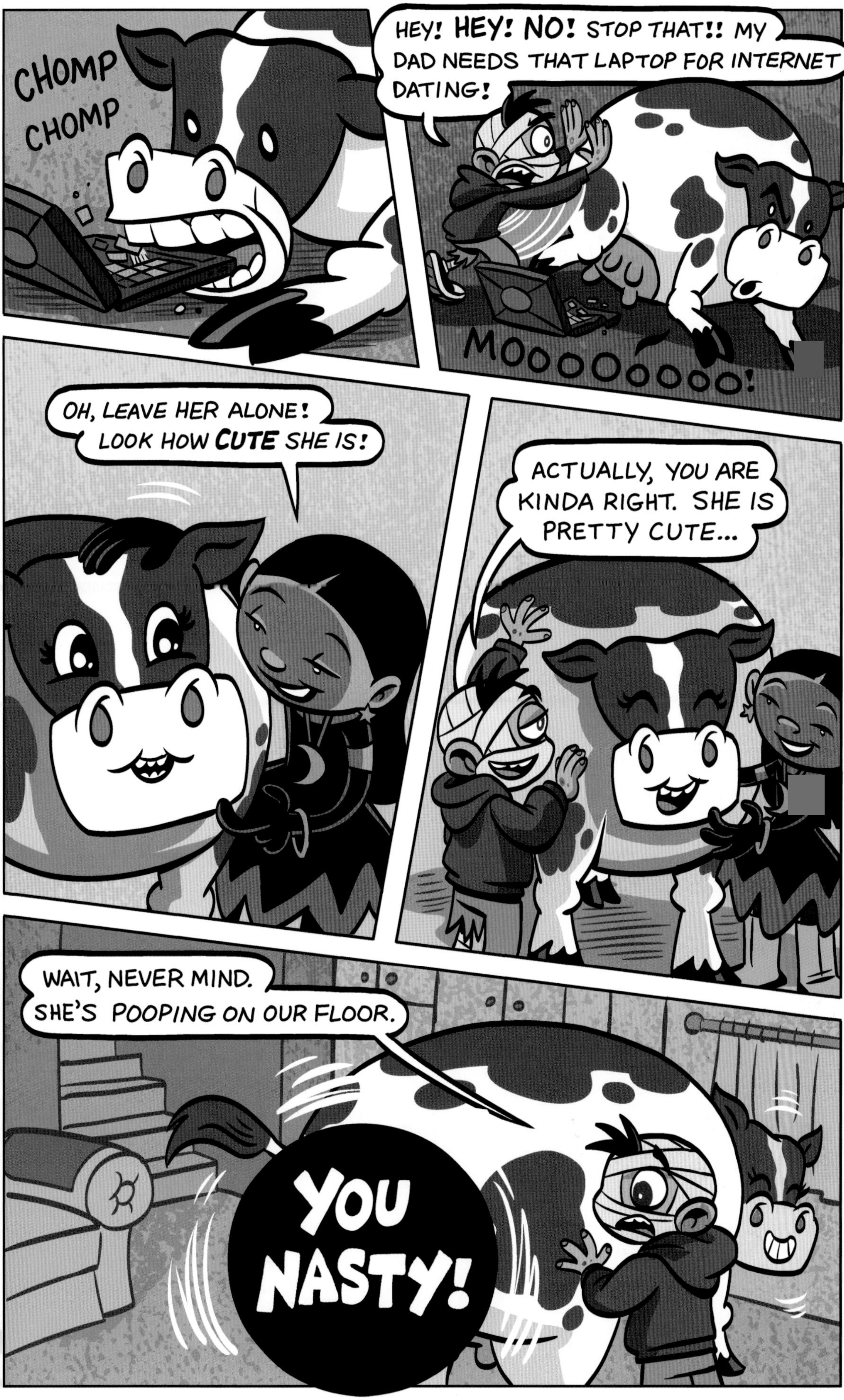
CHOMP
CHOMP
HEY! HEY! NO! STOP THAT!! MY DAD NEEDS THAT LAPTOP FOR INTERNET DATING!
MOOOOOOOOO!
OH, LEAVE HER ALONE! LOOK HOW CUTE SHE IS!
ACTUALLY, YOU ARE KINDA RIGHT. SHE IS PRETTY CUTE...
WAIT, NEVER MIND. SHE'S POOPING ON OUR FLOOR.
YOU NASTY!

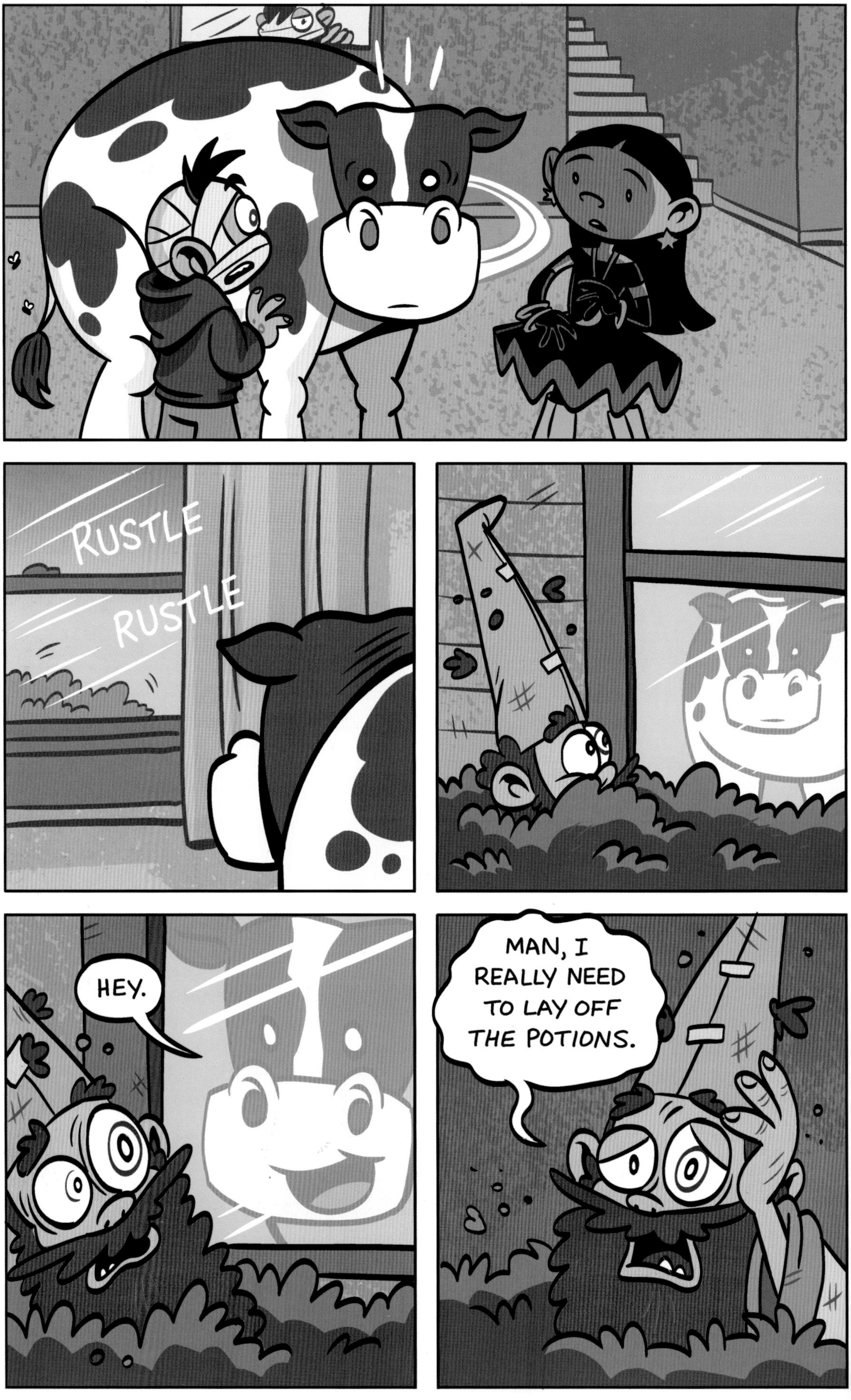
RUSTLE
RUSTLE
HEY.
MAN, I REALLY NEED TO LAY OFF THE POTIONS.

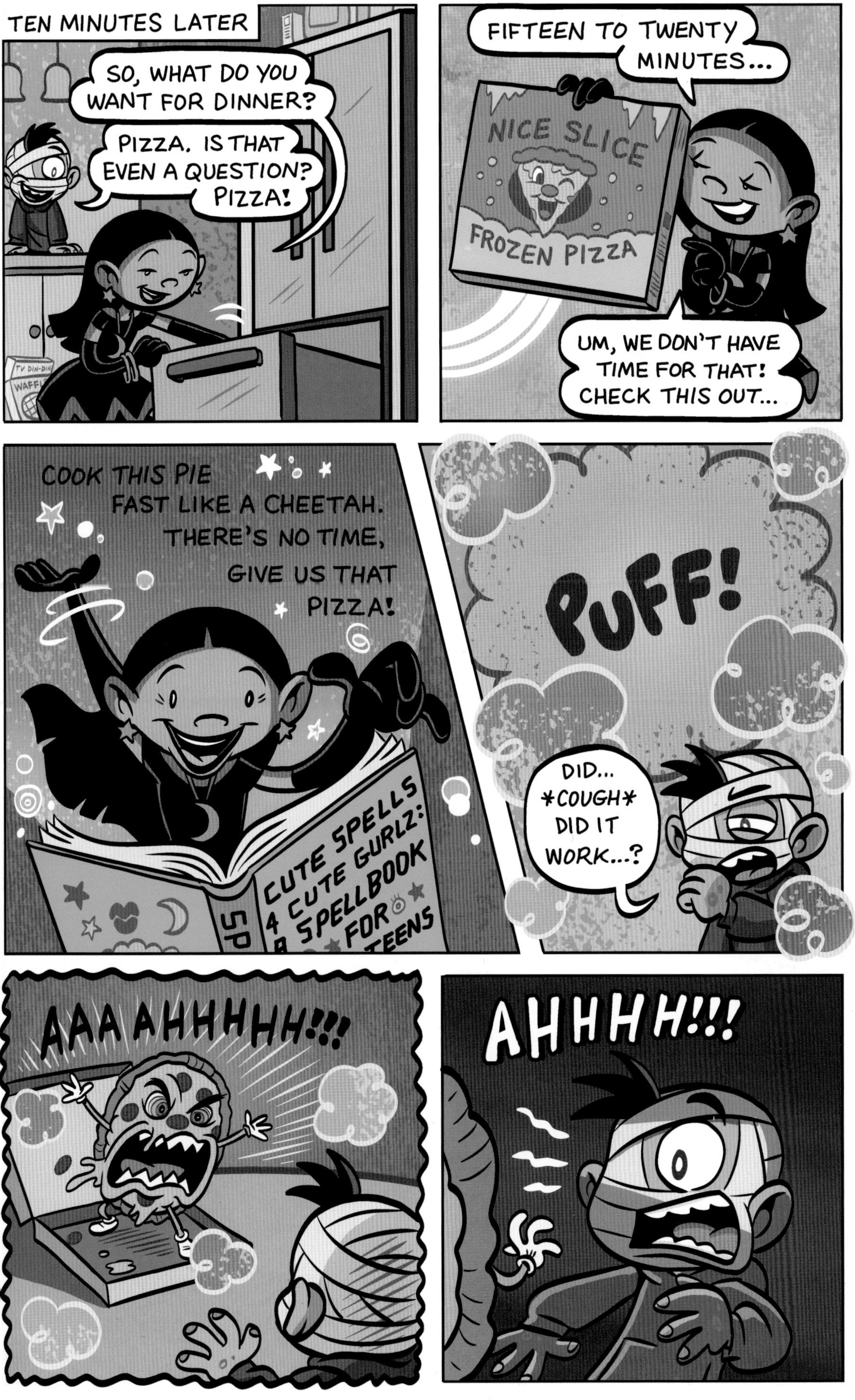
TEN MINUTES LATER
SO, WHAT DO YOU WANT FOR DINNER?
PIZZA. IS THAT EVEN A QUESTION? PIZZA!
TV DIN-DIN
WAFFL
FIFTEEN TO TWENTY MINUTES...
NICE SLICE
FROZEN PIZZA
UM, WE DON'T HAVE TIME FOR THAT! CHECK THIS OUT...
COOK THIS PIE
FAST LIKE A CHEETAH.
THERE'S NO TIME,
GIVE US THAT
PIZZA!
CUTE SPELLS 4 CUTE GURLZ: A SPELLBOOK FOR TEENS
PUFF!
DID... *COUGH* DID IT WORK...?
AAA AHHHHHH!!!
AHHHH!!!

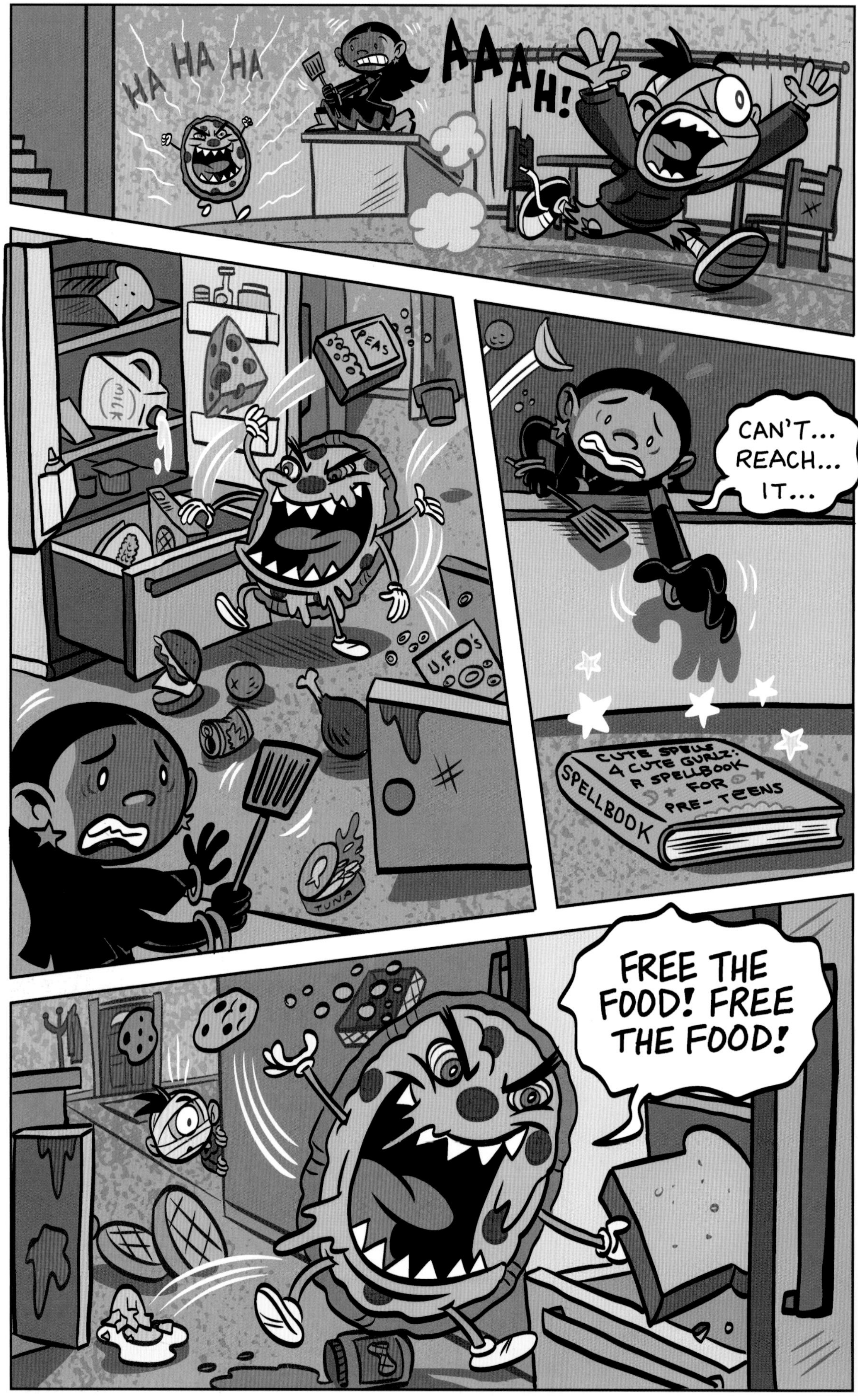
HA HA HA
AAAAH!
PEAS
MILK
U.F.O's
TUNA
CAN'T... REACH... IT...
CUTE SPELLS 4 CUTE GURLZ: A SPELLBOOK FOR PRE-TEENS
SPELLBOOK
FREE THE FOOD! FREE THE FOOD!

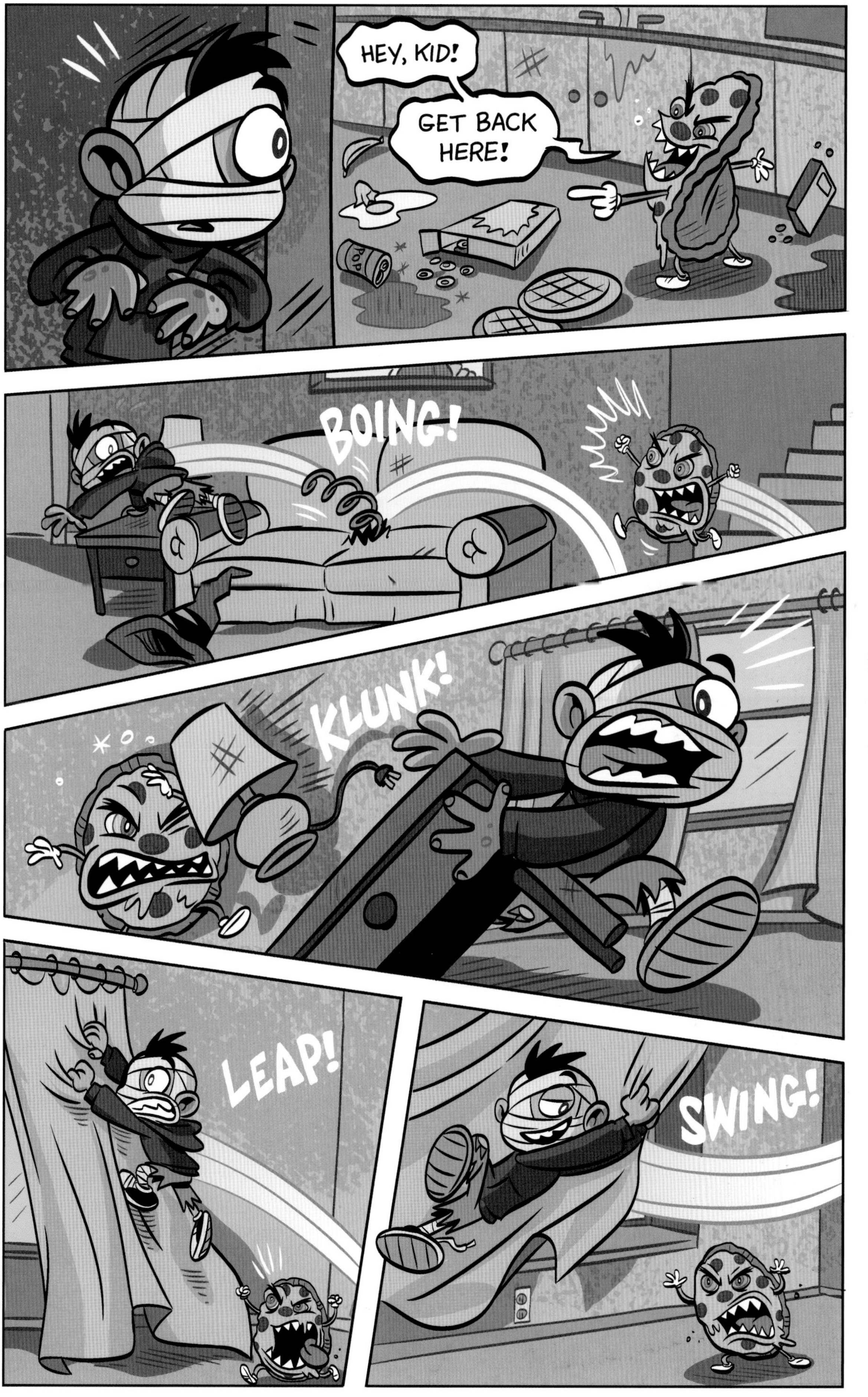
HEY, KID!
GET BACK HERE!
POP
BOING!
KLUNK!
LEAP!
SWING!

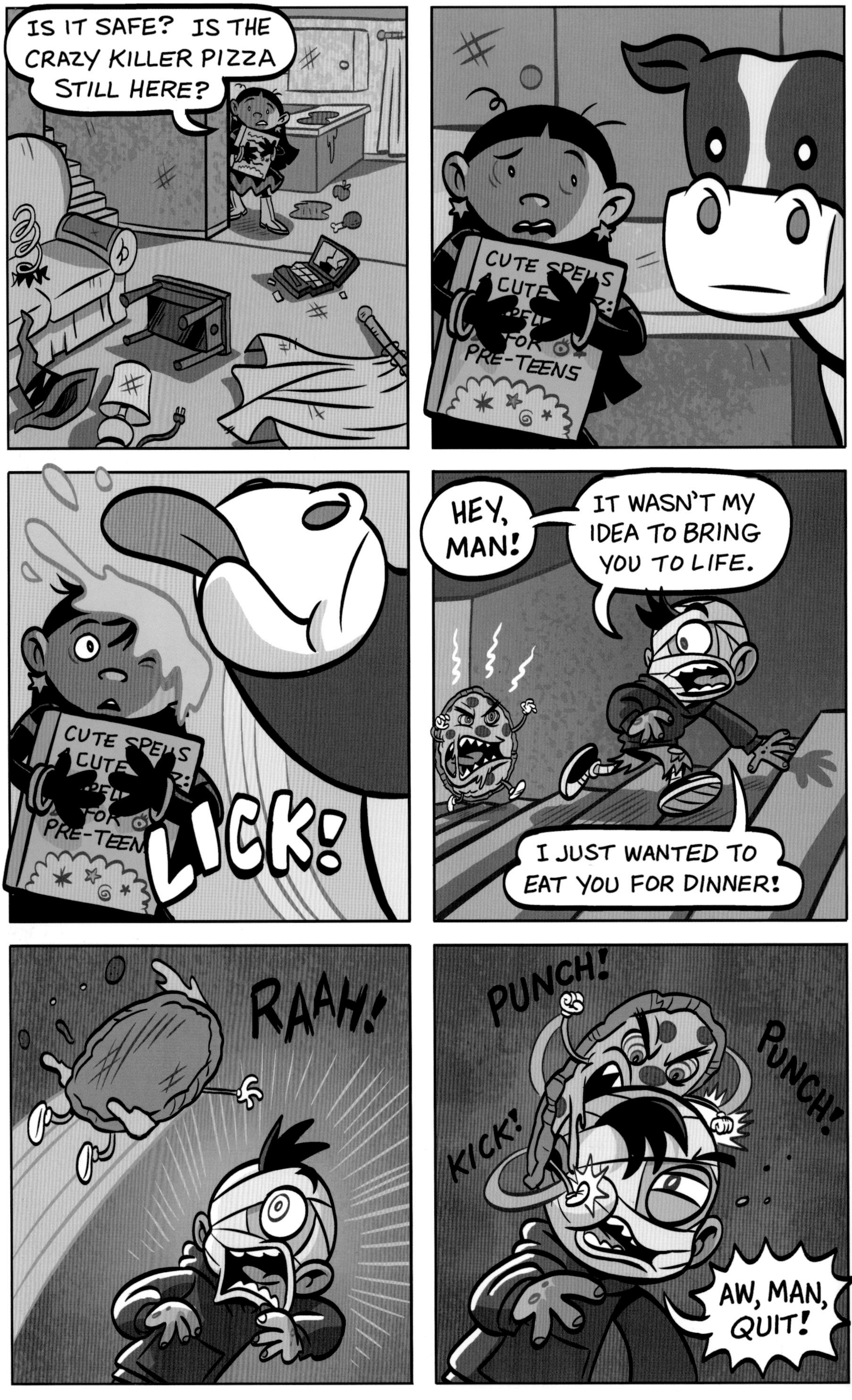
IS IT SAFE? IS THE CRAZY KILLER PIZZA STILL HERE?
FOR PRE-TEENS
LICK!
HEY, MAN!
IT WASN'T MY IDEA TO BRING YOU TO LIFE.
I JUST WANTED TO EAT YOU FOR DINNER!
RAAH!
PUNCH!
KICK!
PUNCH!
AW, MAN, QUIT!

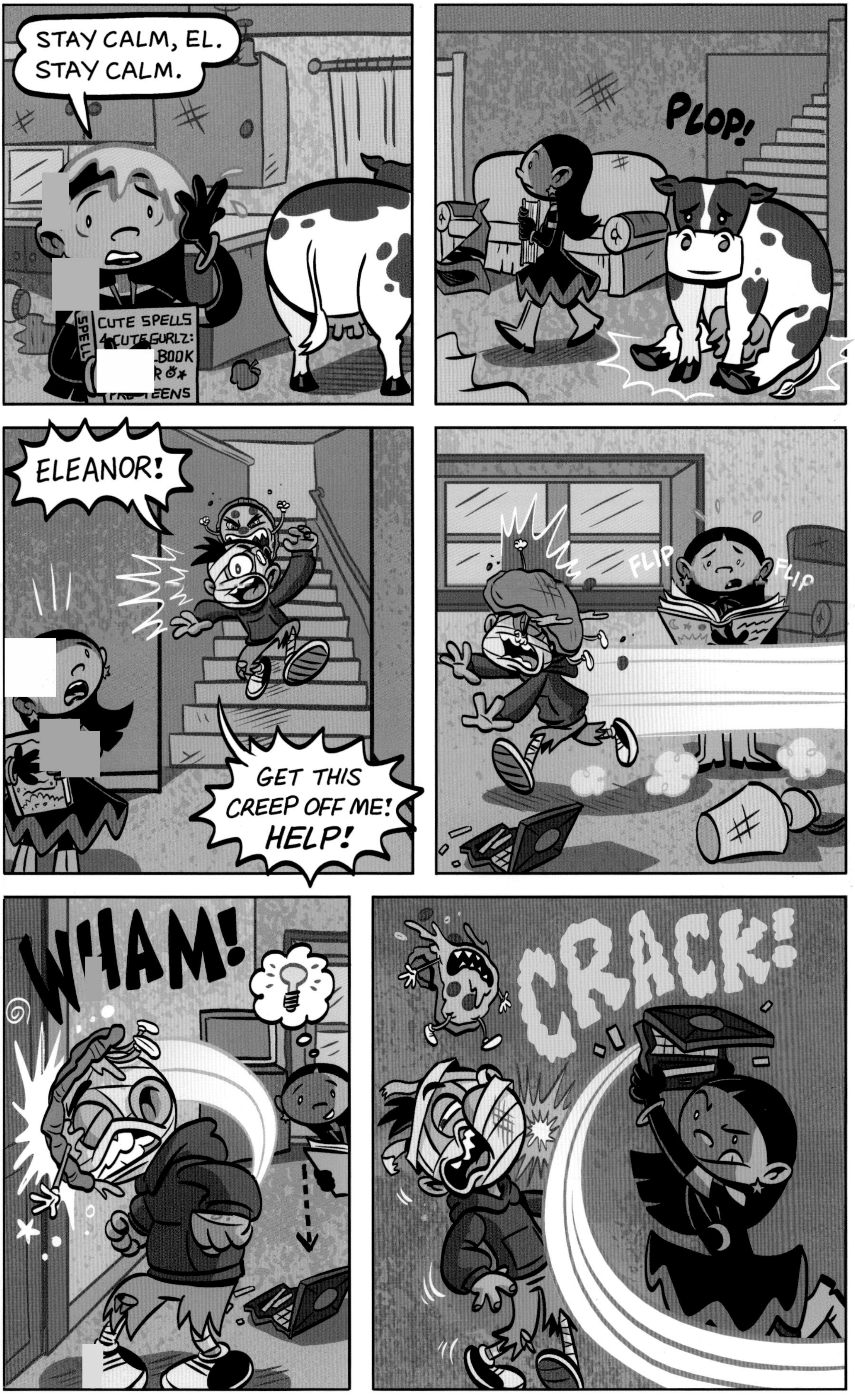

STAY CALM, EL.
STAY CALM.
SPELL
CUTE SPELLS
4 CUTE GURLZ:
BOOK
PLOP!
ELEANOR!
GET THIS CREEP OFF ME! HELP!
FLIP
FLIP
WHAM!
CRACK!

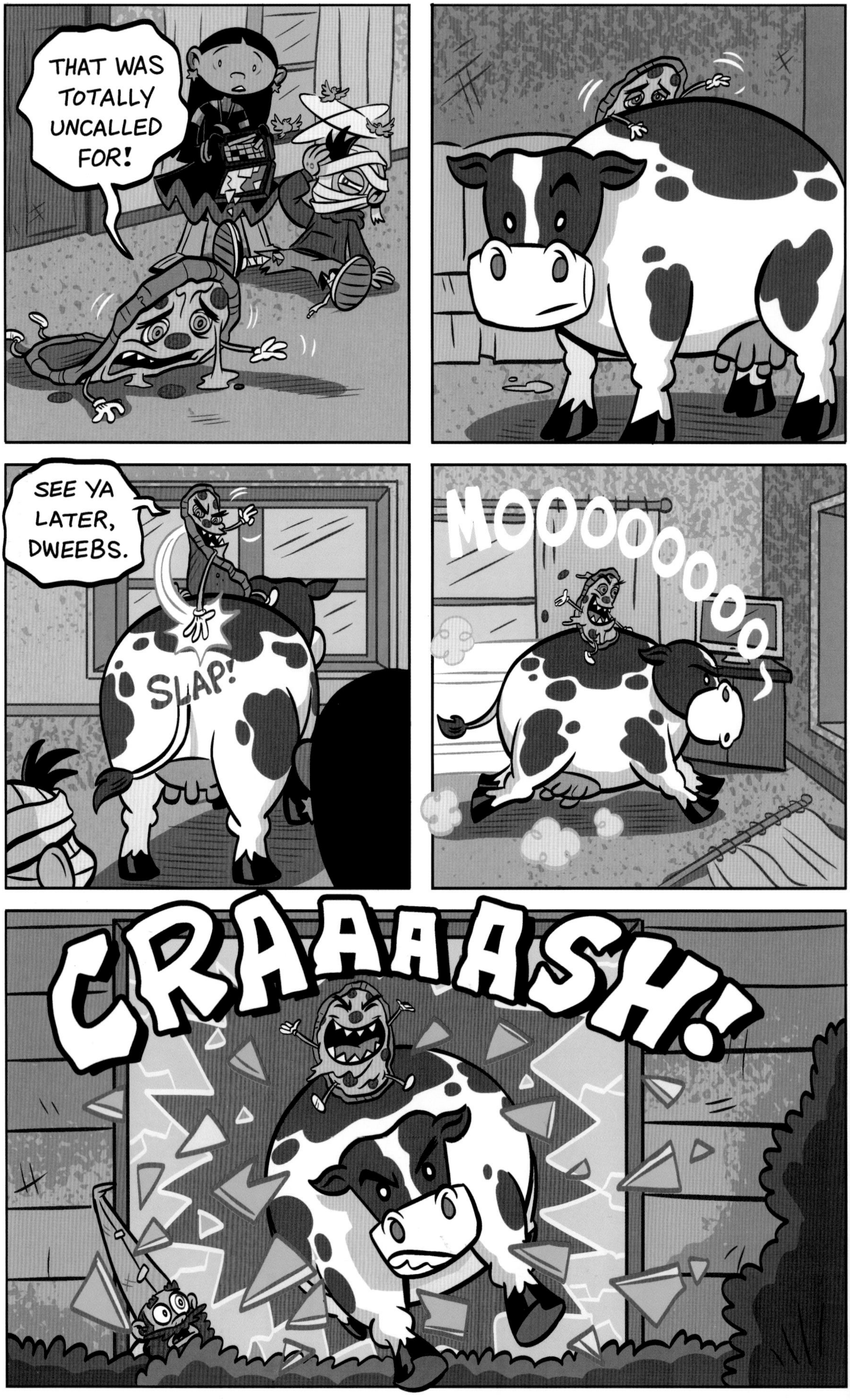
THAT WAS TOTALLY UNCALLED FOR!
SEE YA LATER, DWEEBS.
SLAP!
MOOOOOOOOO
CRAAAASH!

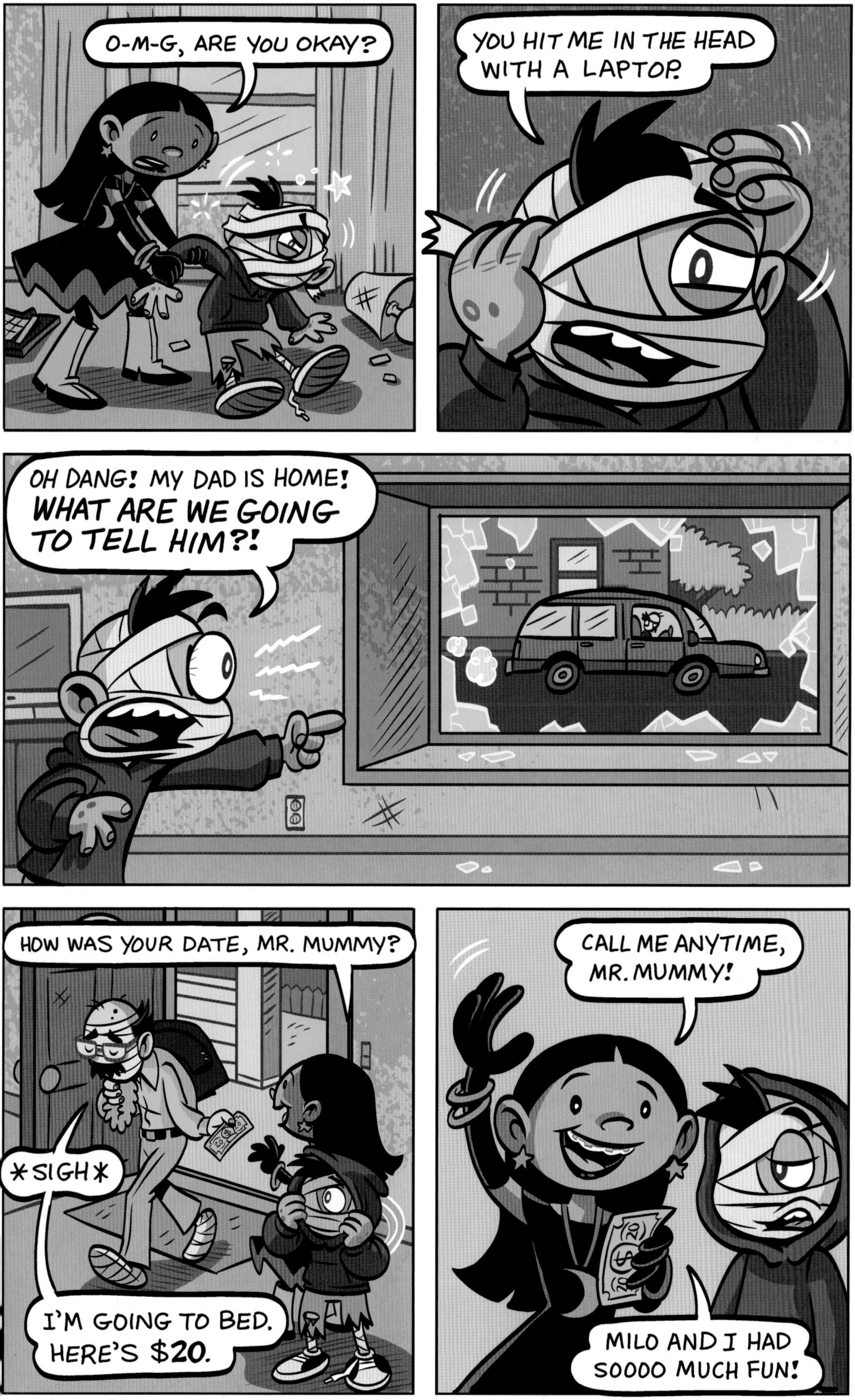
O-M-G, ARE YOU OKAY?
YOU HIT ME IN THE HEAD WITH A LAPTOP.
OH DANG! MY DAD IS HOME! WHAT ARE WE GOING TO TELL HIM?!
HOW WAS YOUR DATE, MR. MUMMY?
SIGH
I'M GOING TO BED. HERE'S $20.
CALL ME ANYTIME, MR. MUMMY!
MILO AND I HAD SOOOO MUCH FUN!

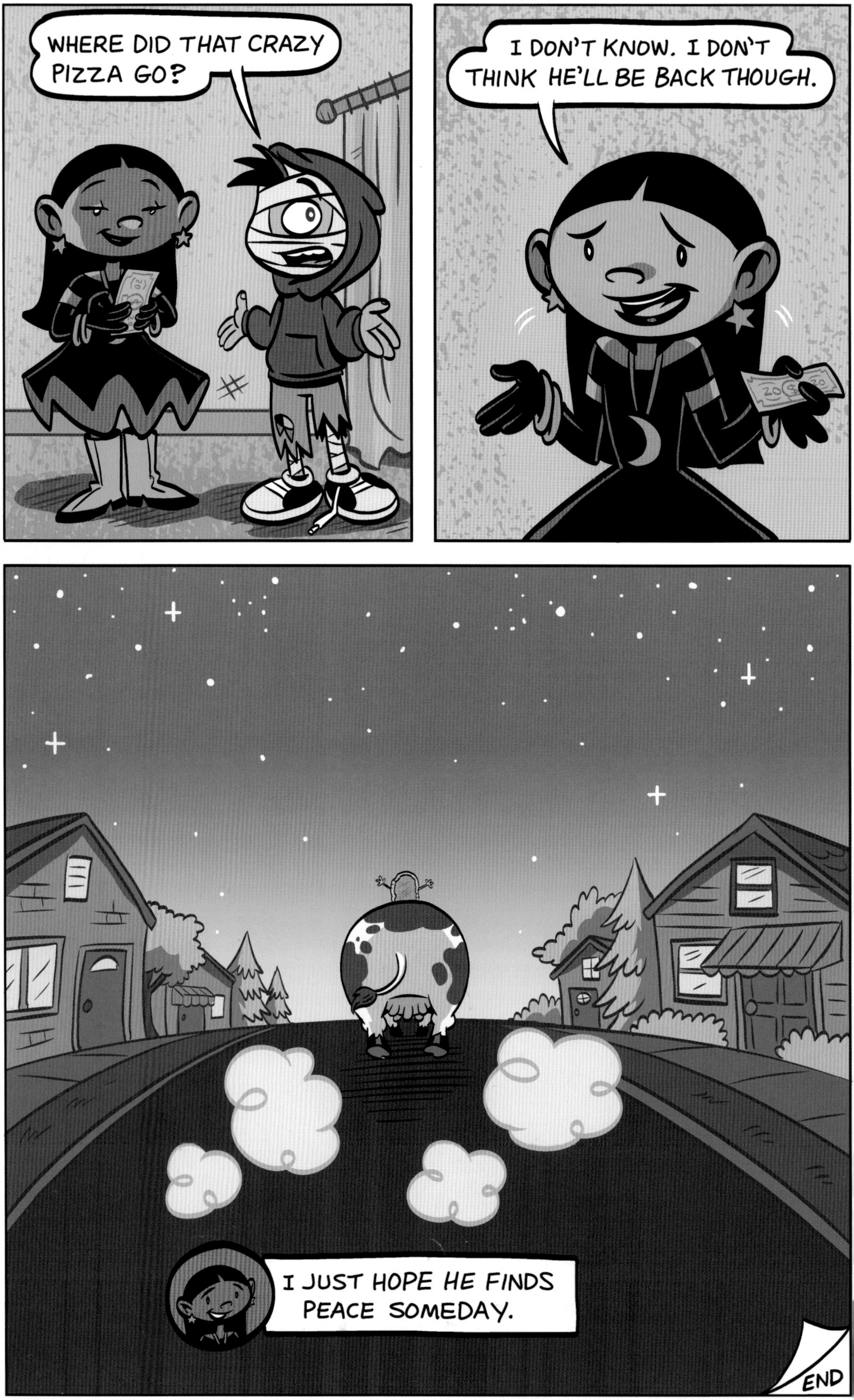
WHERE DID THAT CRAZY PIZZA GO?
I DON'T KNOW. I DON'T THINK HE'LL BE BACK THOUGH.
I JUST HOPE HE FINDS PEACE SOMEDAY.
END

THE Ewww-y Decimal System

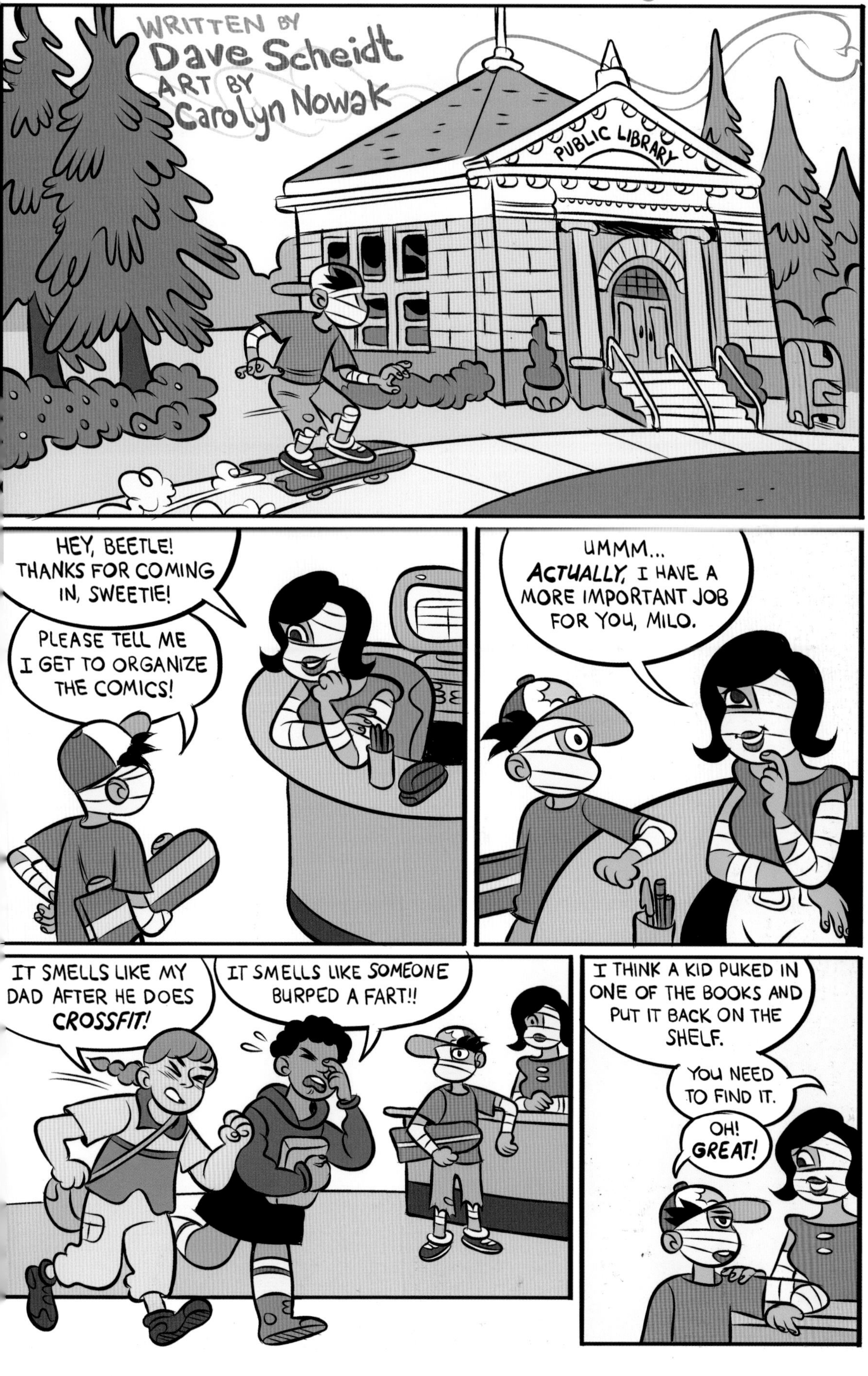

WRITTEN BY Dave Scheidt
ART BY Carolyn Nowak
PUBLIC LIBRARY
HEY, BEETLE! THANKS FOR COMING IN, SWEETIE!
PLEASE TELL ME I GET TO ORGANIZE THE COMICS!
UMMM... ACTUALLY, I HAVE A MORE IMPORTANT JOB FOR YOU, MILO.
IT SMELLS LIKE MY DAD AFTER HE DOES CROSSFIT!
IT SMELLS LIKE SOMEONE BURPED A FART!!
I THINK A KID PUKED IN ONE OF THE BOOKS AND PUT IT BACK ON THE SHELF.
YOU NEED TO FIND IT.
OH! GREAT!

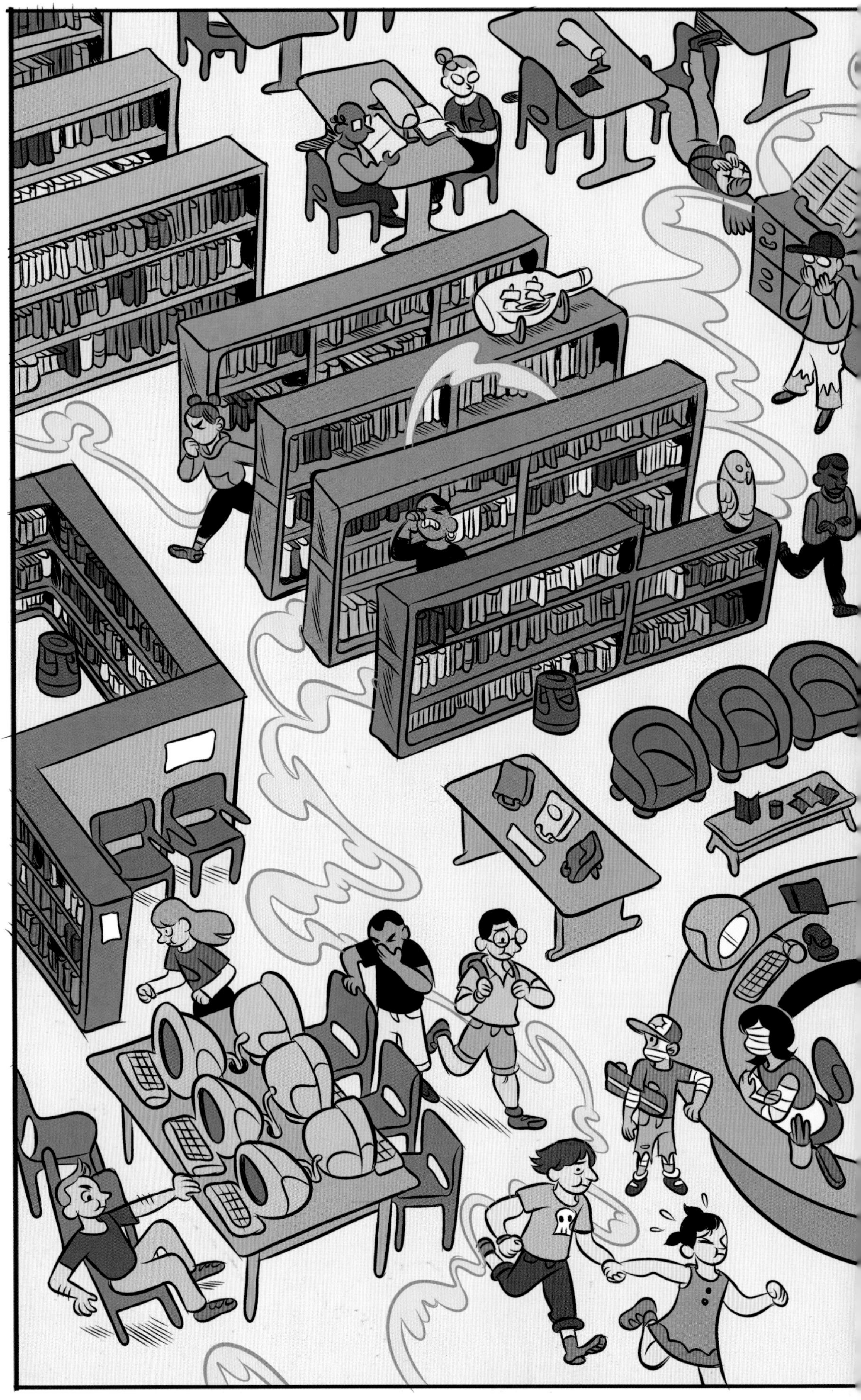

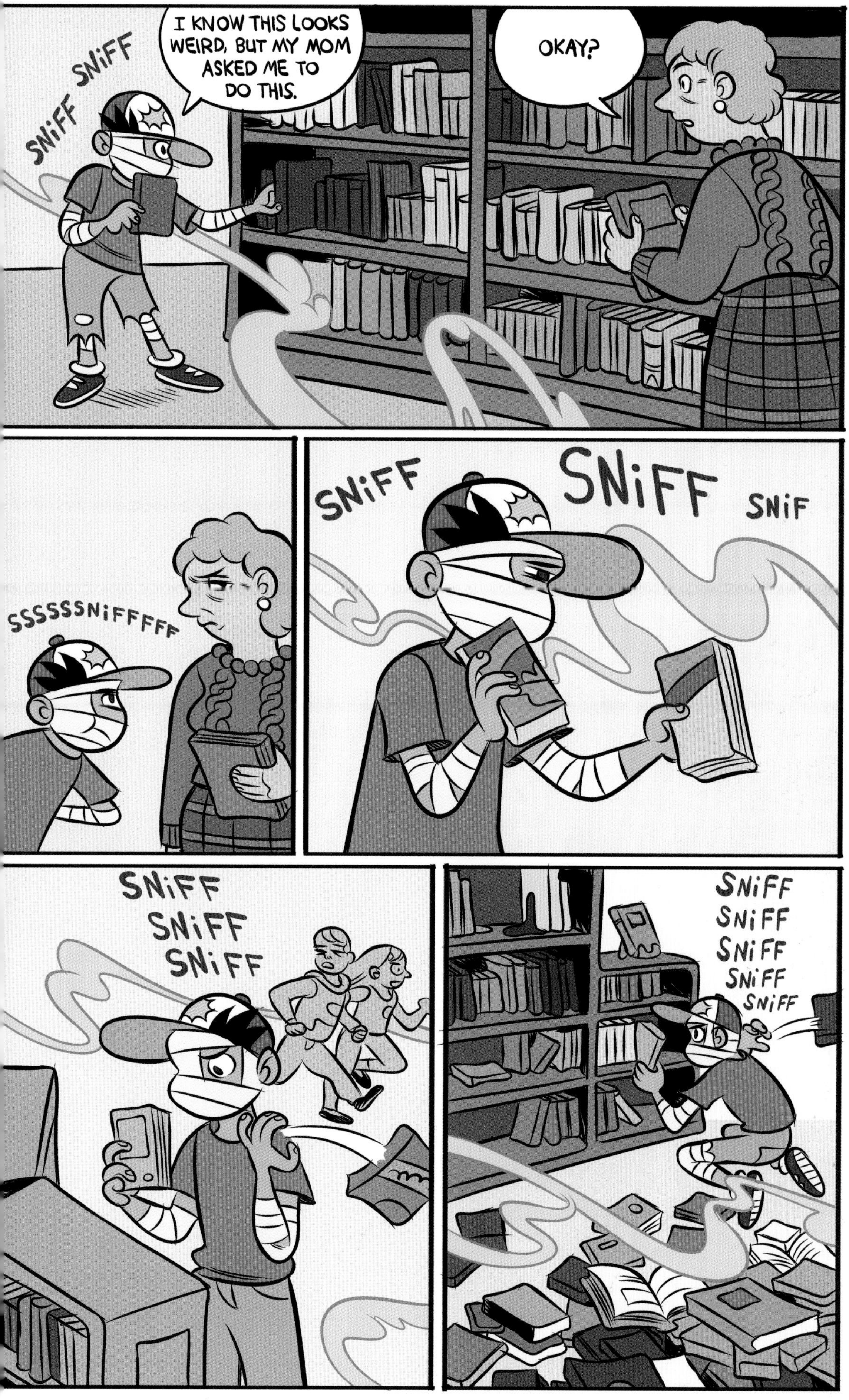
SNIFF SNIFF
I KNOW THIS LOOKS WEIRD, BUT MY MOM ASKED ME TO DO THIS.
OKAY?
SSSSSSNIFFFFF
SNIFF
SNIFF
SNIF
SNIFF
SNIFF
SNIFF
SNIFF
SNIFF
SNIFF
SNIFF
SNIFF

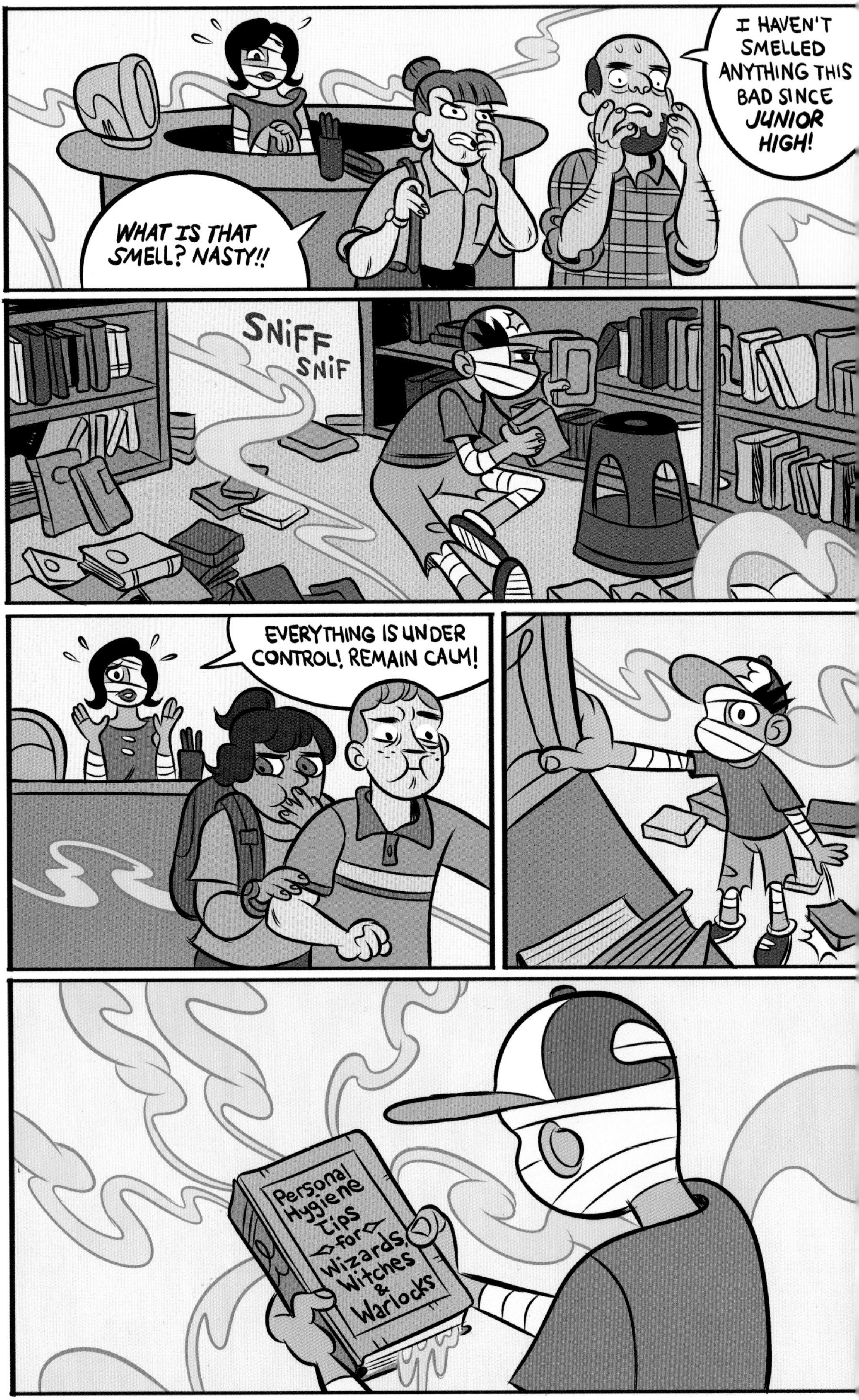
I HAVEN'T SMELLED ANYTHING THIS BAD SINCE JUNIOR HIGH!
WHAT IS THAT SMELL? NASTY!!
SNIFF SNIF
EVERYTHING IS UNDER CONTROL! REMAIN CALM!
Personal Hygiene Tips for Wizards, Witches & Warlocks

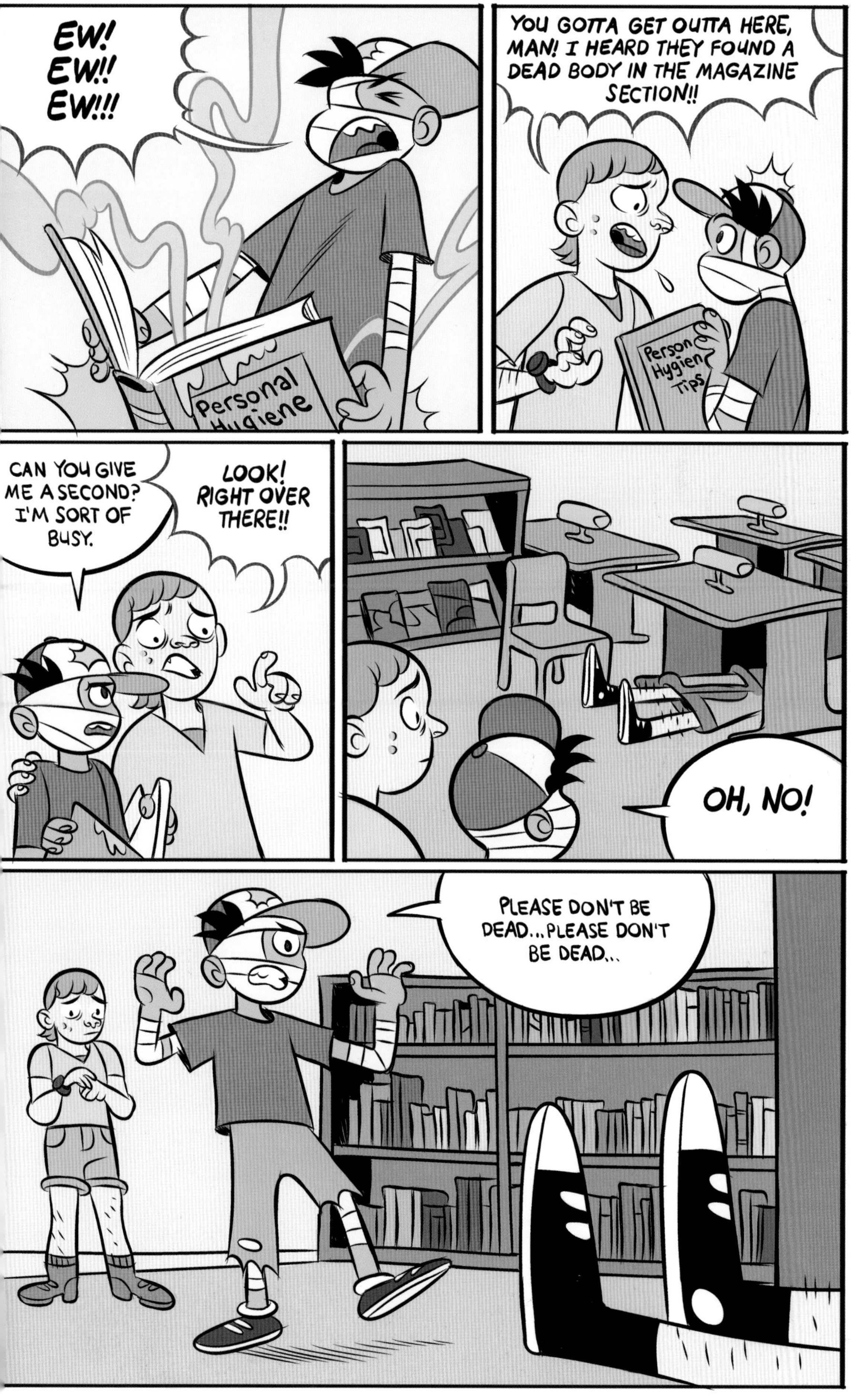
EW!
EW!!
EW!!!
Personal Hygiene
YOU GOTTA GET OUTTA HERE, MAN! I HEARD THEY FOUND A DEAD BODY IN THE MAGAZINE SECTION!!
Person Hygien Tips
CAN YOU GIVE ME A SECOND? I'M SORT OF BUSY.
LOOK! RIGHT OVER THERE!!
OH, NO!
PLEASE DON'T BE DEAD... PLEASE DON'T BE DEAD...

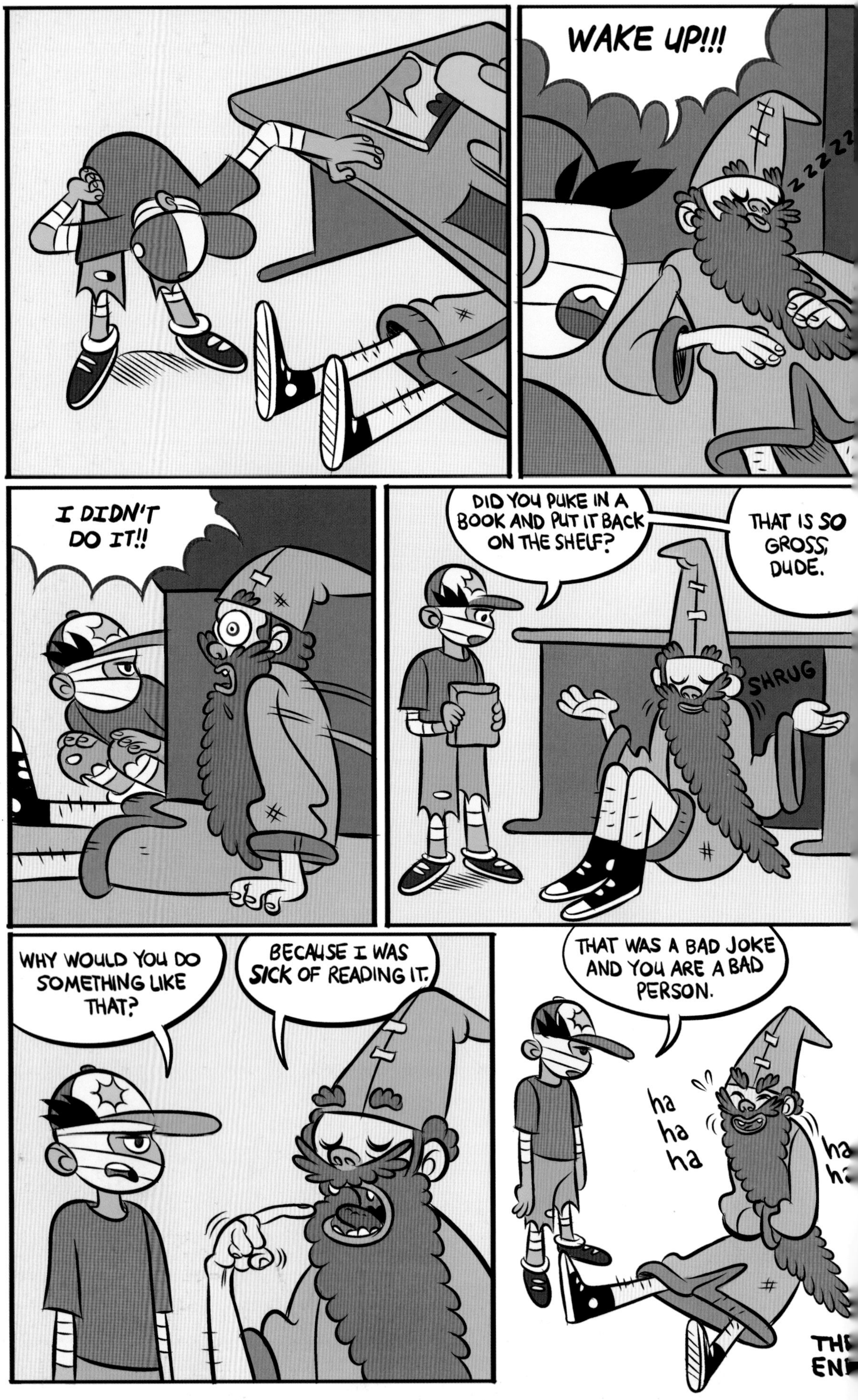
WAKE UP!!!
zzzzz
I DIDN'T DO IT!!
DID YOU PUKE IN A BOOK AND PUT IT BACK ON THE SHELF?
THAT IS SO GROSS, DUDE.
SHRUG
WHY WOULD YOU DO SOMETHING LIKE THAT?
BECAUSE I WAS SICK OF READING IT.
THAT WAS A BAD JOKE AND YOU ARE A BAD PERSON.
ha ha ha

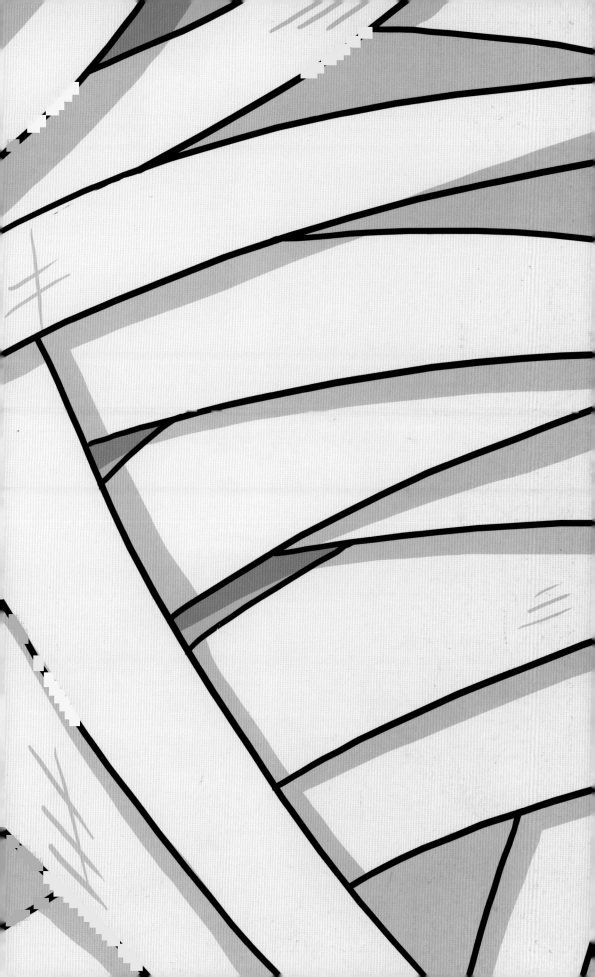

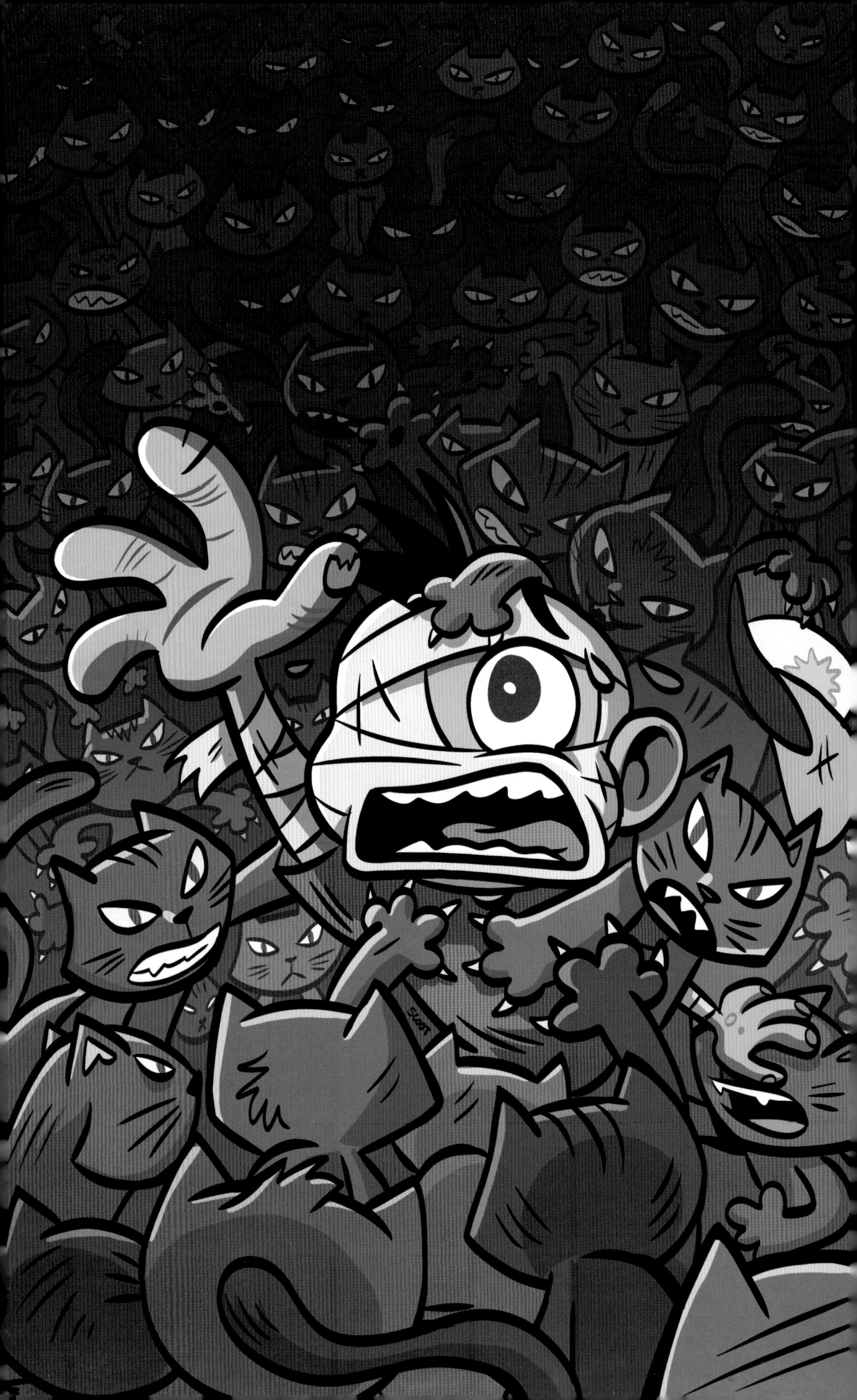

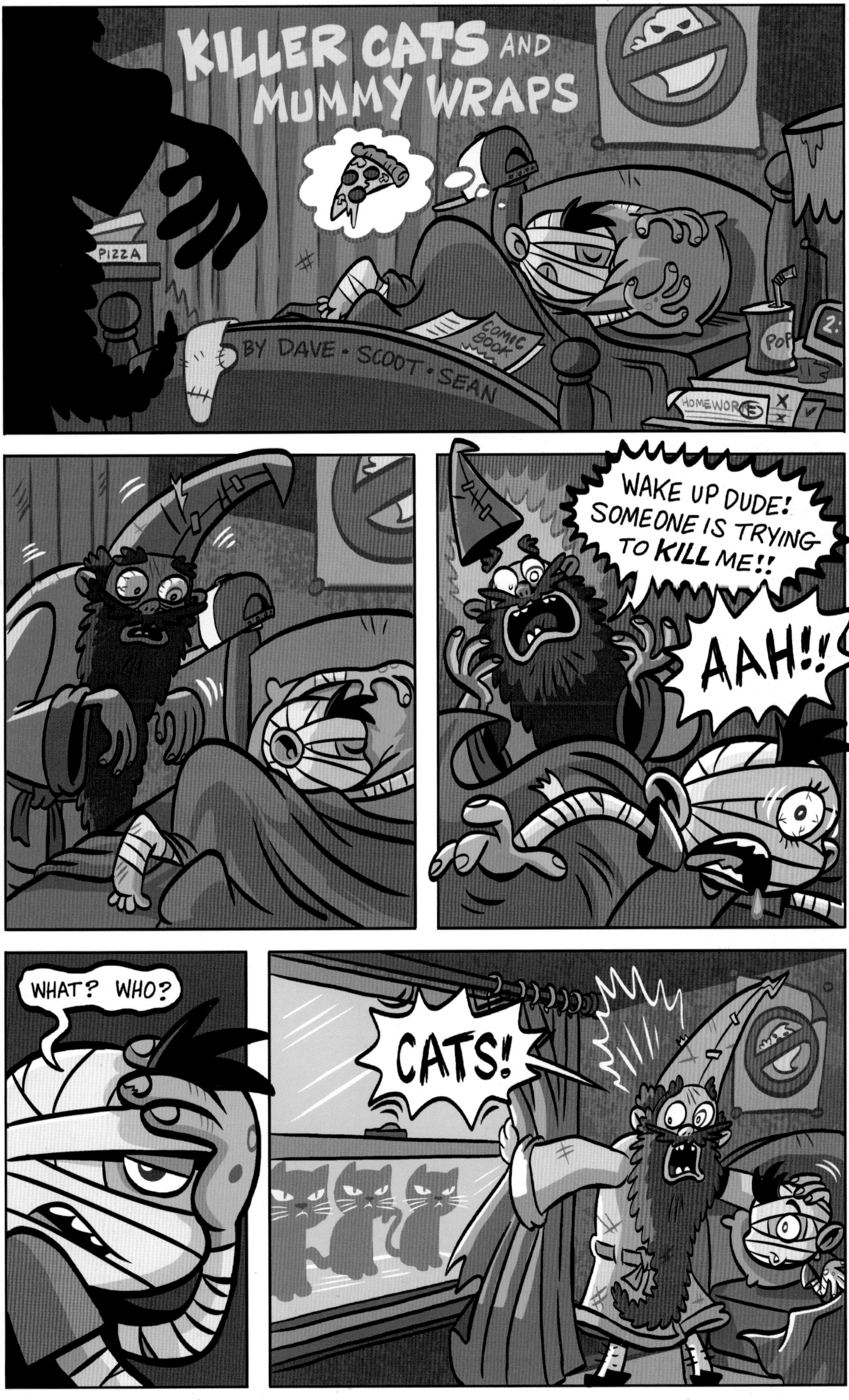
KILLER CATS AND MUMMY WRAPS
PIZZA
BY DAVE • SCOOT • SEAN
COMIC BOOK
POP
HOMEWORK
WAKE UP DUDE! SOMEONE IS TRYING TO KILL ME!!
AAH!!
WHAT? WHO?
CATS!

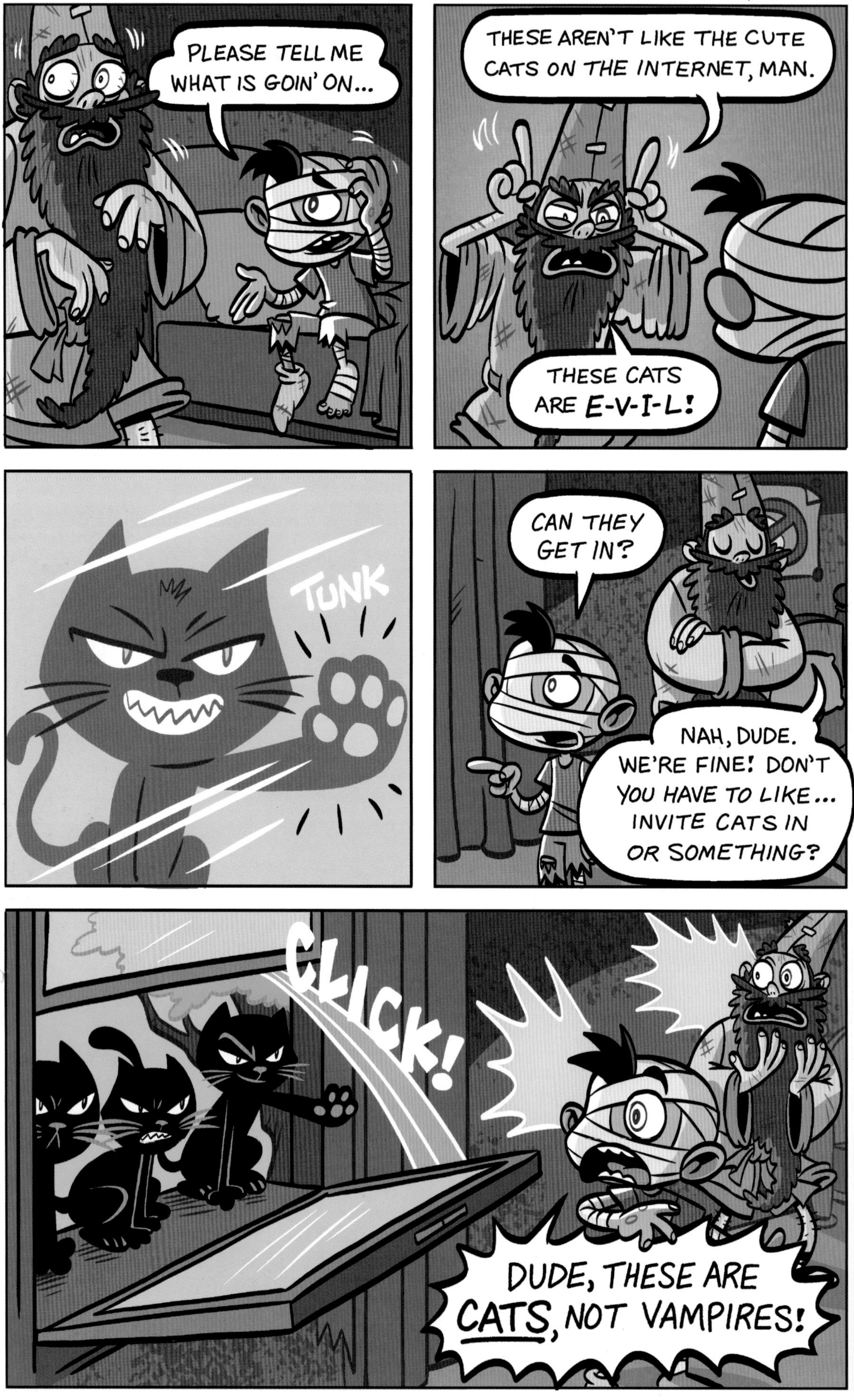
PLEASE TELL ME WHAT IS GOIN' ON...
THESE AREN'T LIKE THE CUTE CATS ON THE INTERNET, MAN.
THESE CATS ARE E-V-I-L!
TUNK
CAN THEY GET IN?
NAH, DUDE. WE'RE FINE! DON'T YOU HAVE TO LIKE... INVITE CATS IN OR SOMETHING?
CLICK!
DUDE, THESE ARE CATS, NOT VAMPIRES!

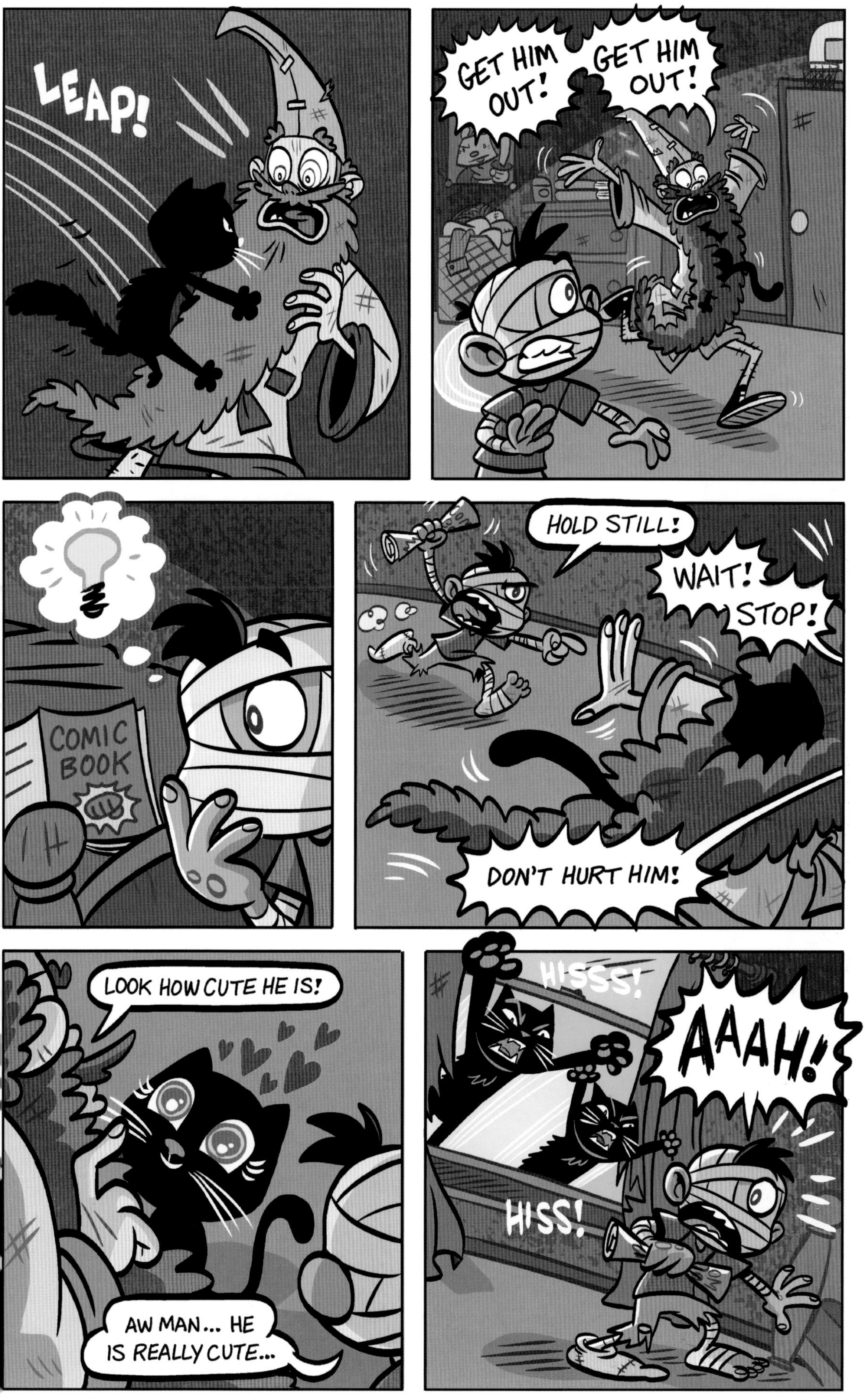
LEAP!
GET HIM OUT!
GET HIM OUT!
COMIC BOOK
HOLD STILL!
WAIT!
STOP!
DON'T HURT HIM!
LOOK HOW CUTE HE IS!
AW MAN... HE IS REALLY CUTE...
HISSS!
AAAH!
HISS!

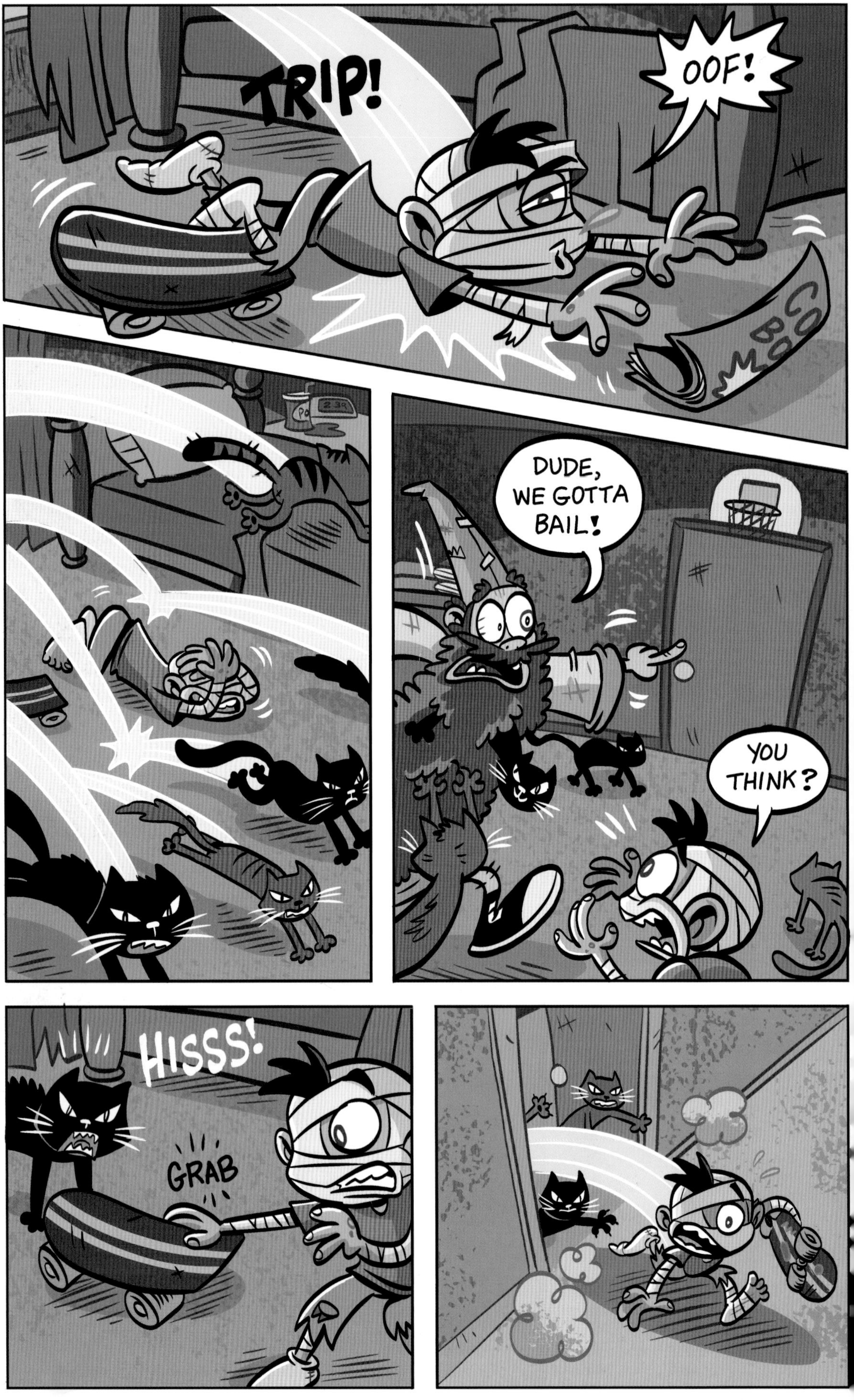
TRIP!
OOF!
DUDE, WE GOTTA BAIL!
YOU THINK?
HISSS!
GRAB

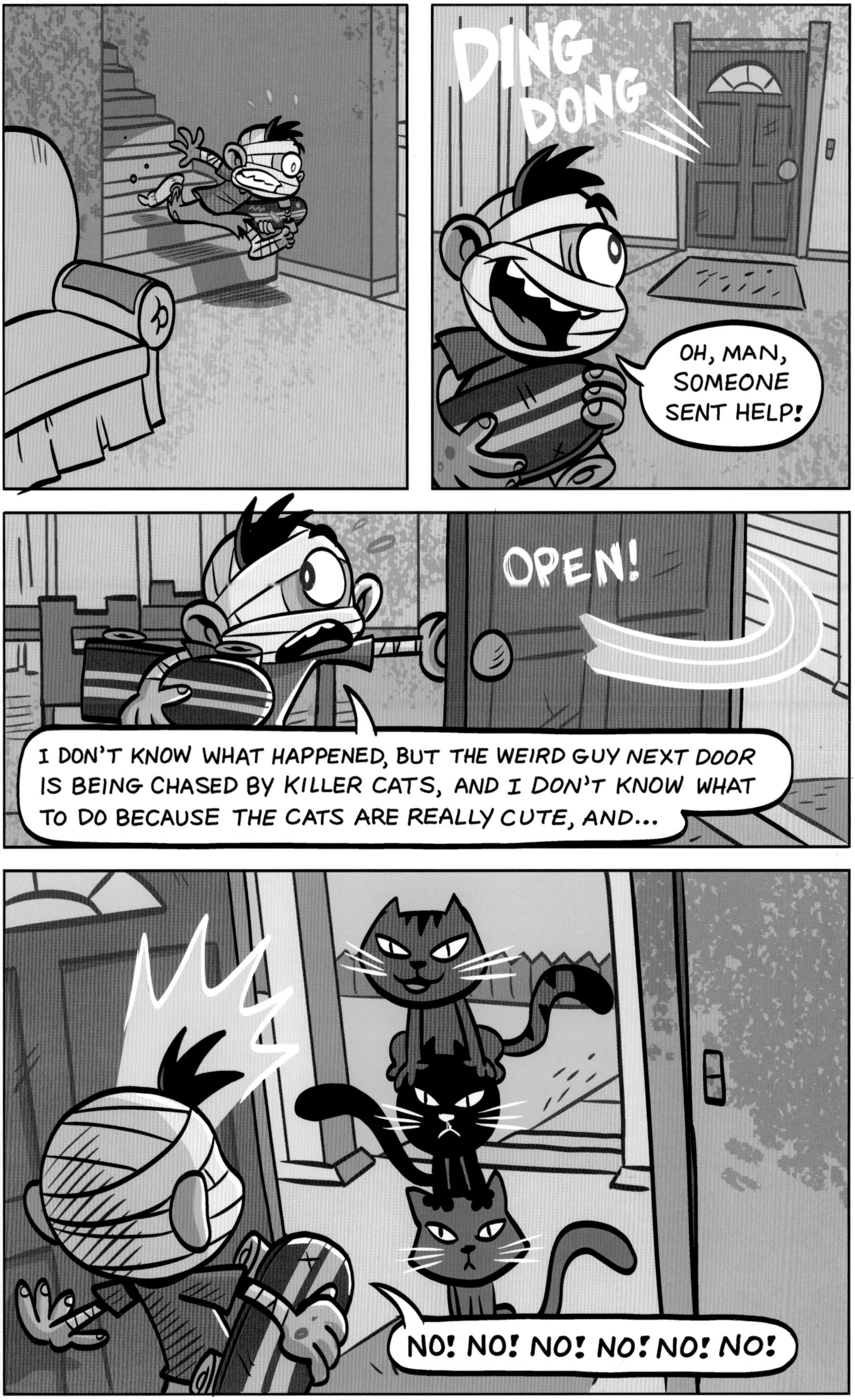
DING DONG
OH, MAN, SOMEONE SENT HELP!
OPEN!
I DON'T KNOW WHAT HAPPENED, BUT THE WEIRD GUY NEXT DOOR IS BEING CHASED BY KILLER CATS, AND I DON'T KNOW WHAT TO DO BECAUSE THE CATS ARE REALLY CUTE, AND...
NO! NO! NO! NO! NO! NO!

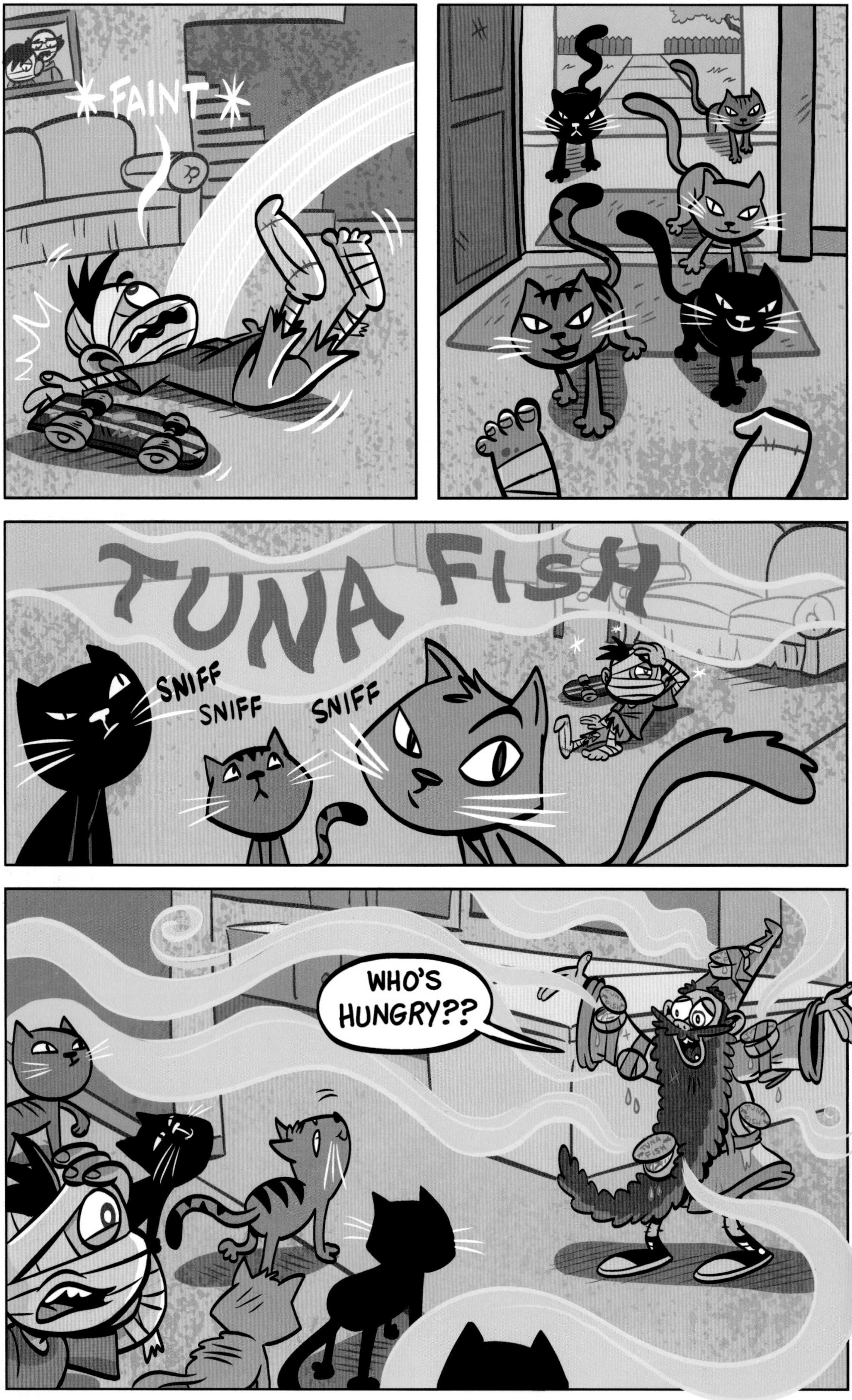
FAINT
TUNA FISH
SNIFF
SNIFF
SNIFF
WHO'S HUNGRY??
TUNA FISH

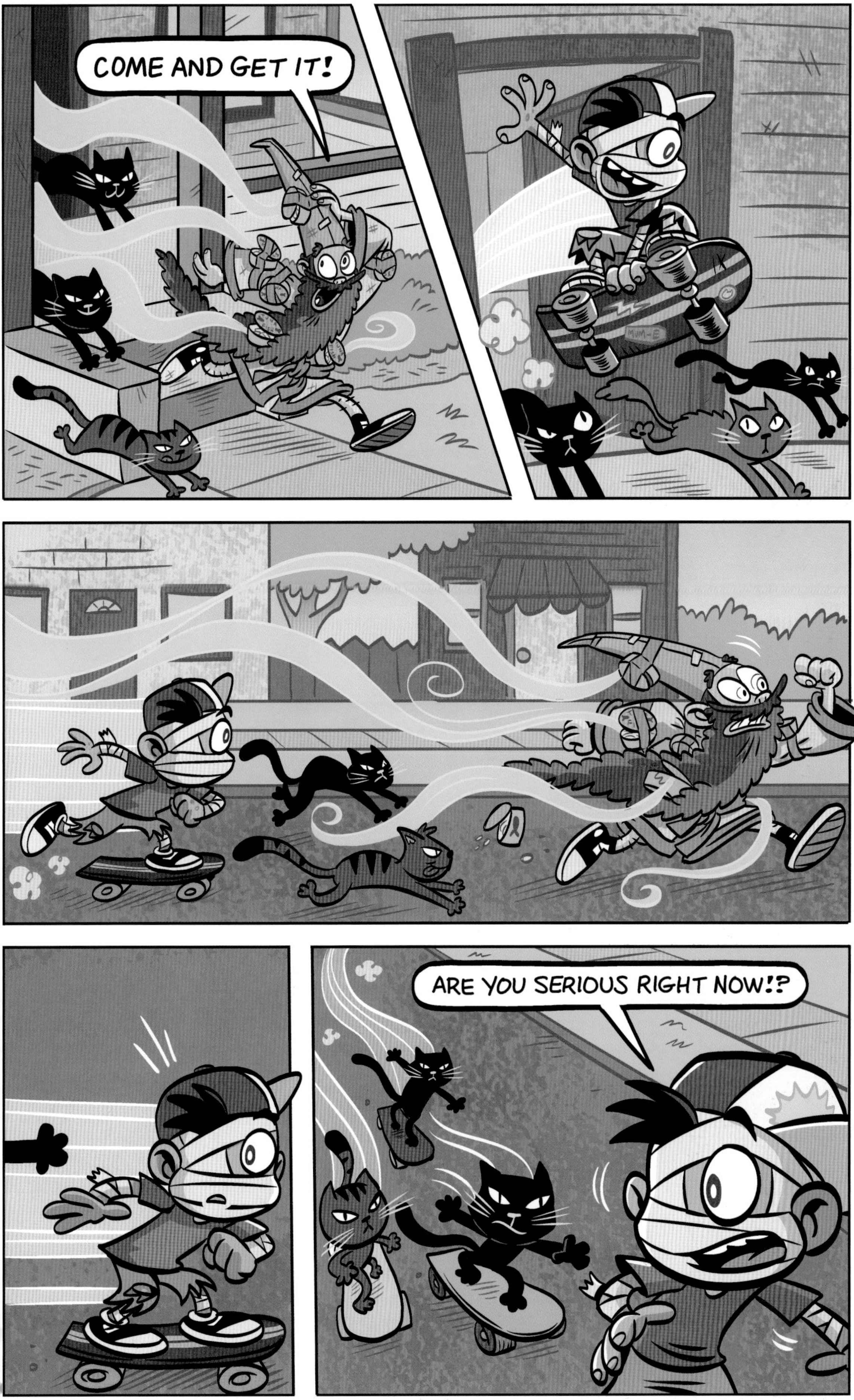
COME AND GET IT!
MUM-E
ARE YOU SERIOUS RIGHT NOW!?

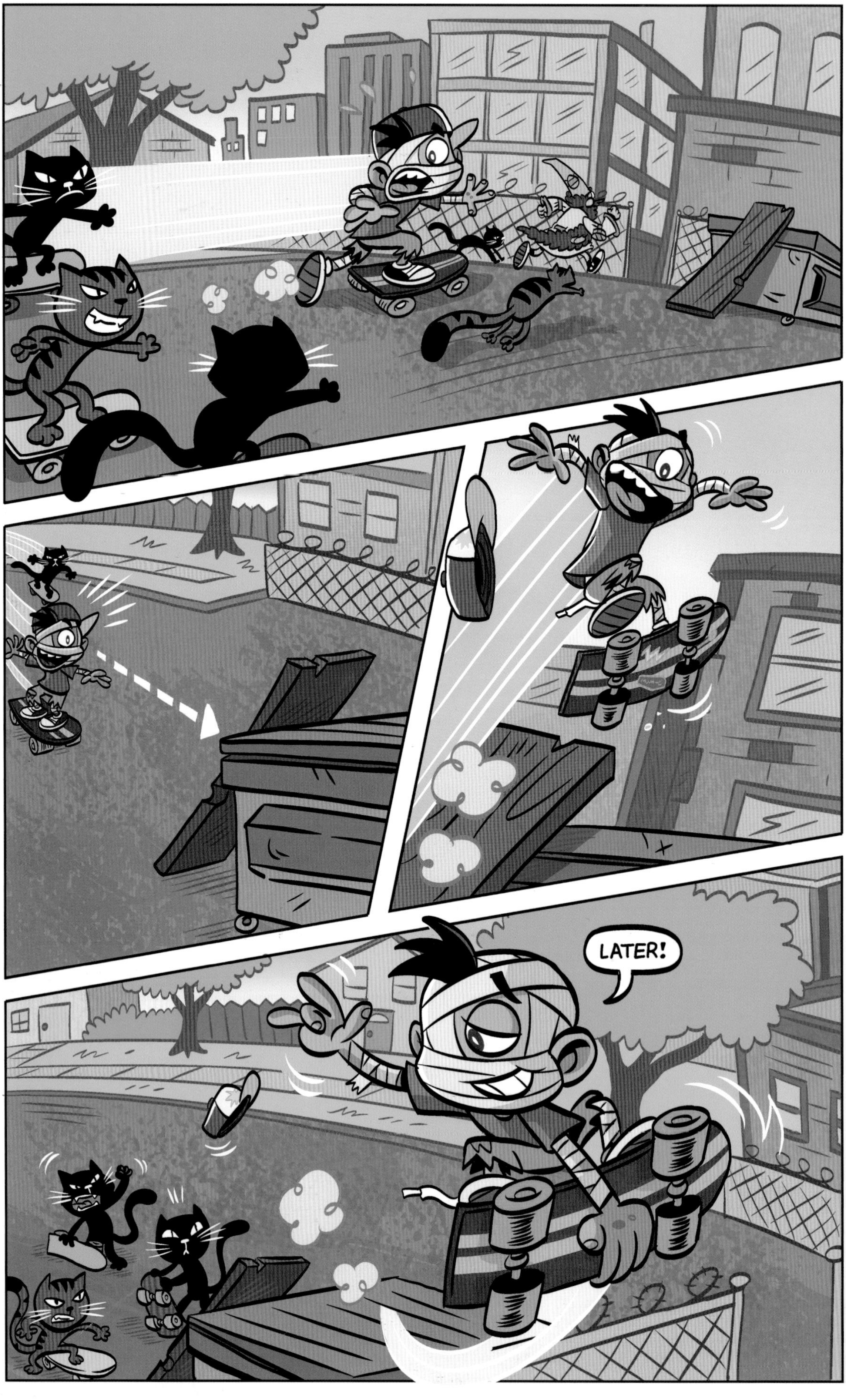
LATER!

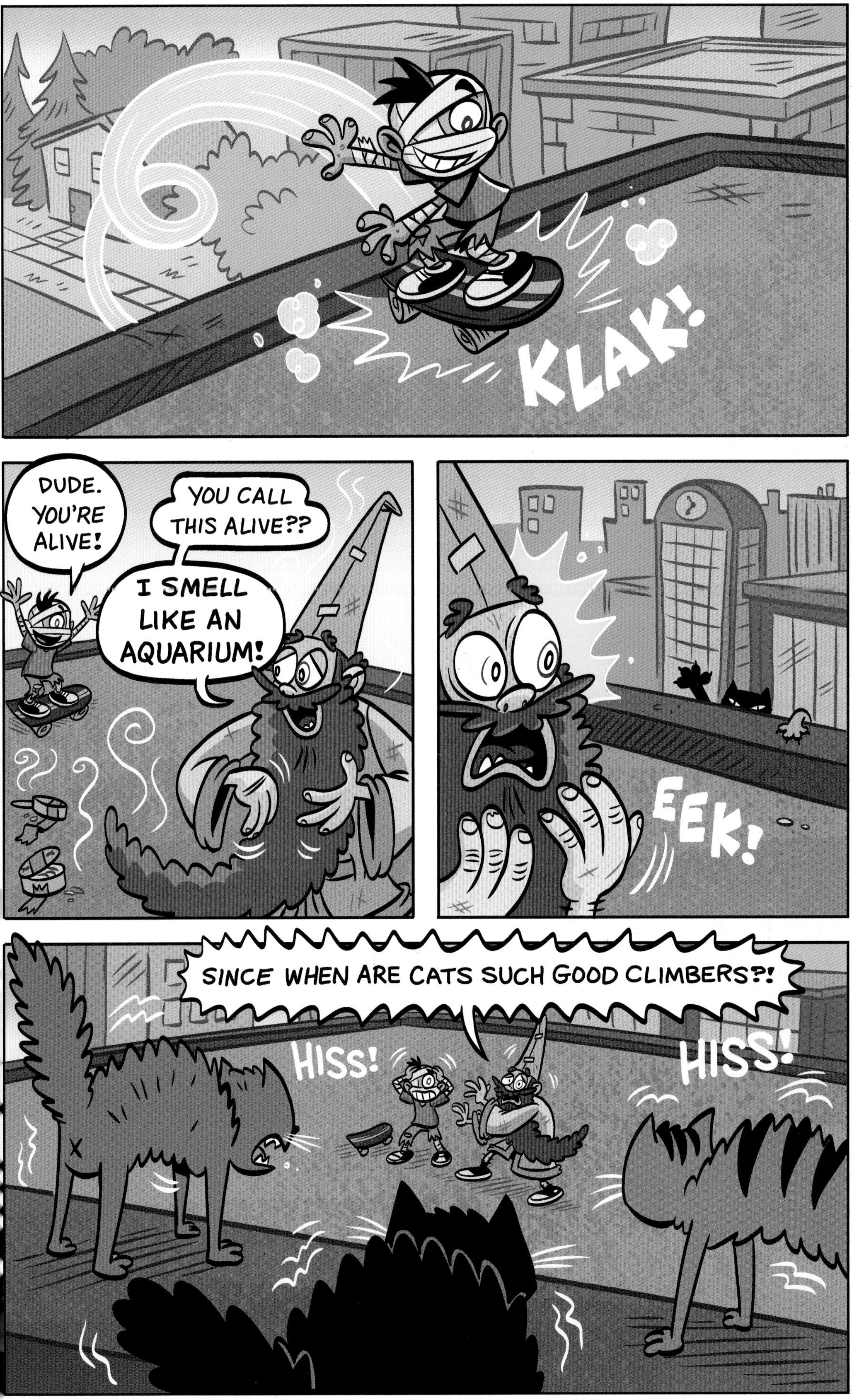
KLAK!
DUDE. YOU'RE ALIVE!
YOU CALL THIS ALIVE??
I SMELL LIKE AN AQUARIUM!
EEK!
SINCE WHEN ARE CATS SUCH GOOD CLIMBERS?!
HISS!
HISS!

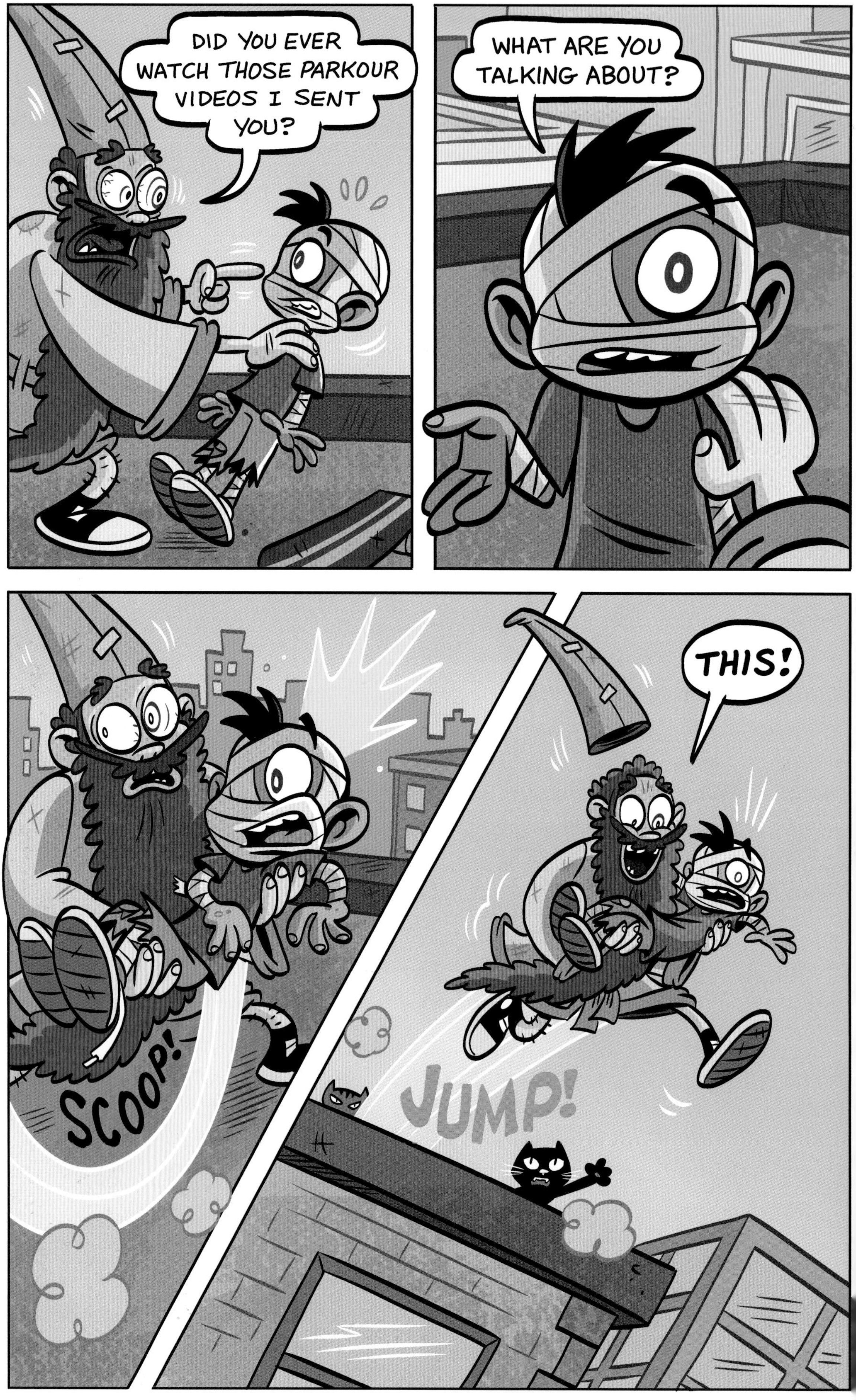
DID YOU EVER WATCH THOSE PARKOUR VIDEOS I SENT YOU?
WHAT ARE YOU TALKING ABOUT?
SCOOP!
THIS!
JUMP!

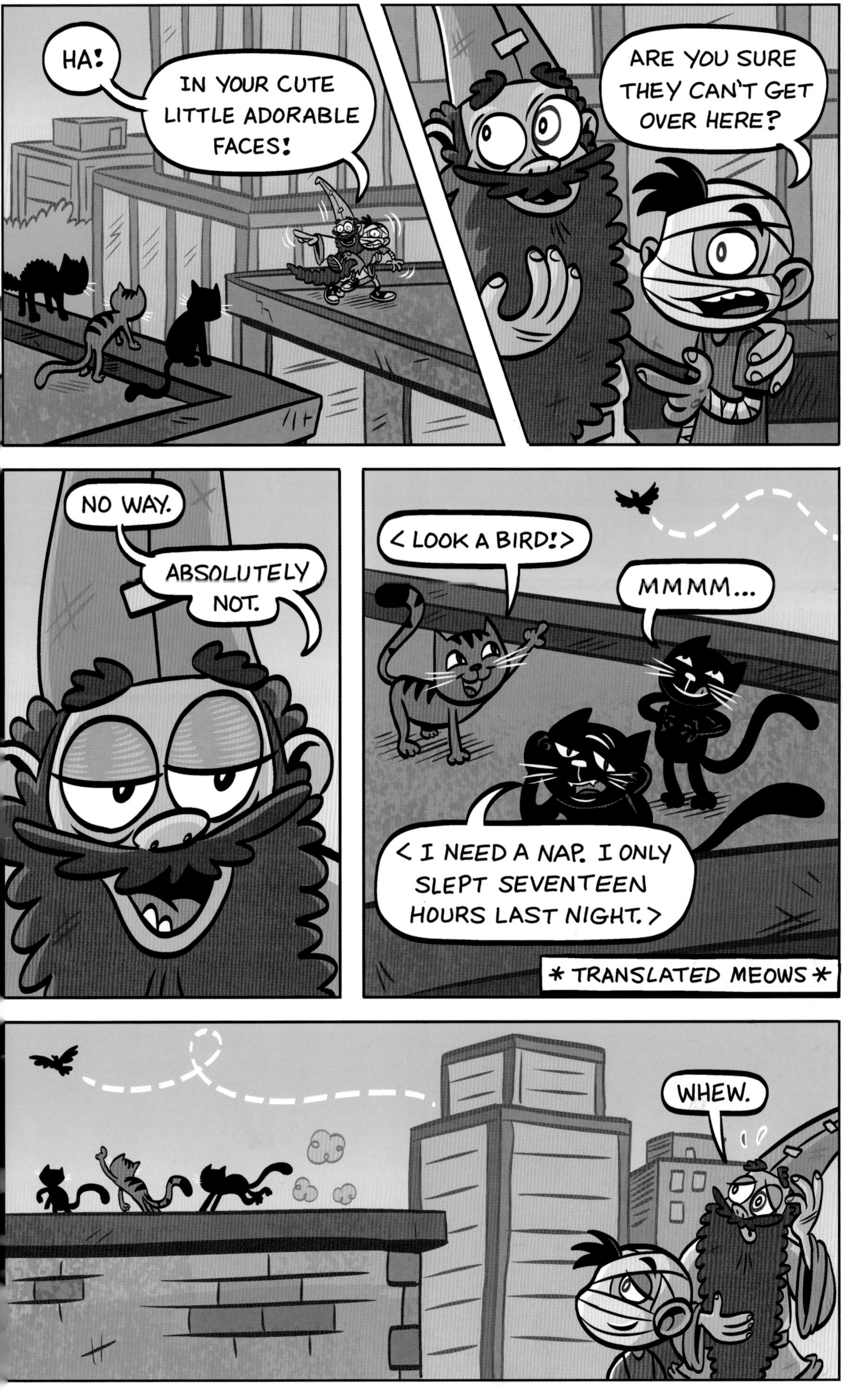
HA!
IN YOUR CUTE LITTLE ADORABLE FACES!
ARE YOU SURE THEY CAN'T GET OVER HERE?
NO WAY.
ABSOLUTELY NOT.
< LOOK A BIRD! >
MMMM...
< I NEED A NAP. I ONLY SLEPT SEVENTEEN HOURS LAST NIGHT. >
* TRANSLATED MEOWS *
WHEW.

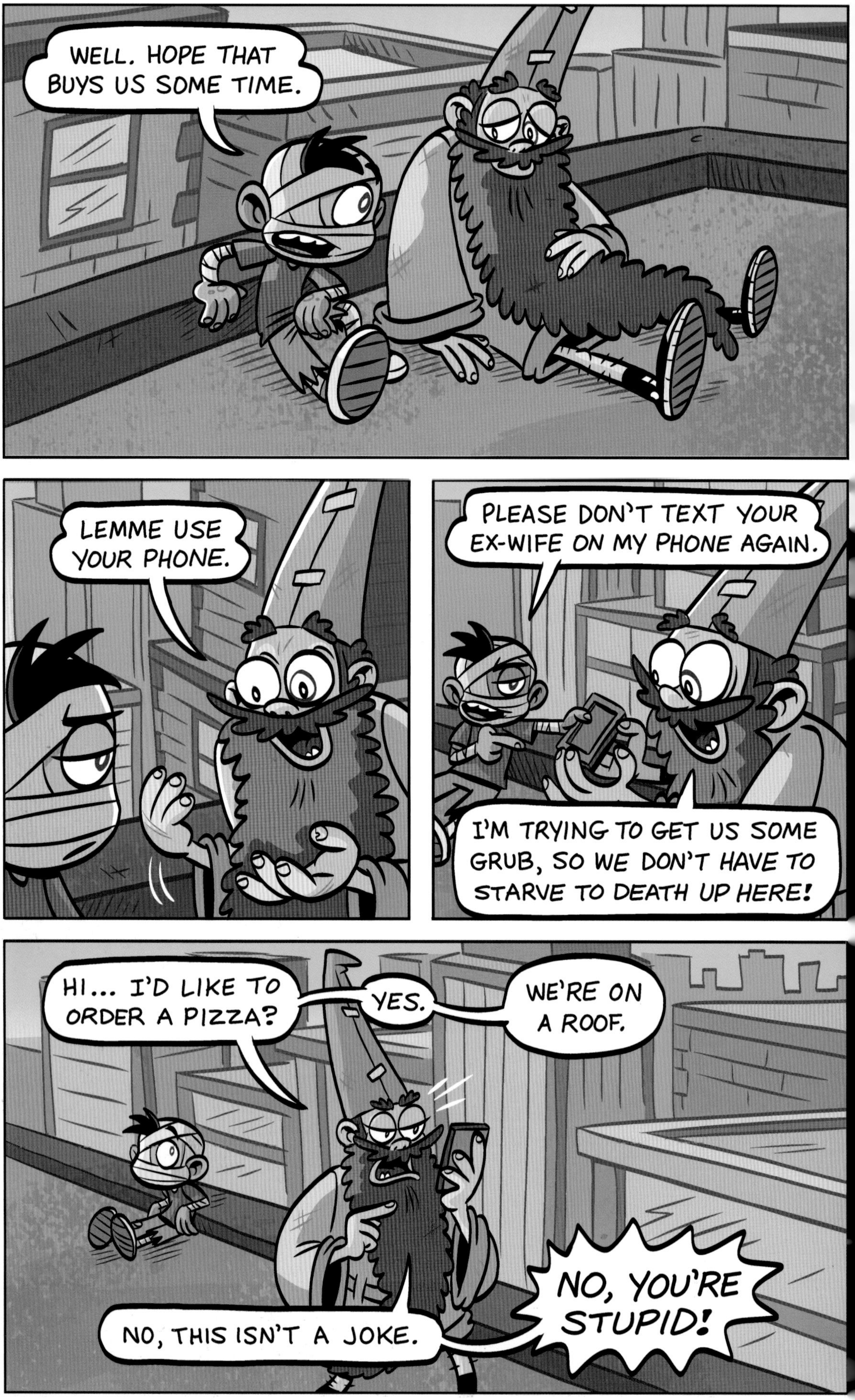
WELL. HOPE THAT BUYS US SOME TIME.
LEMME USE YOUR PHONE.
PLEASE DON'T TEXT YOUR EX-WIFE ON MY PHONE AGAIN.
I'M TRYING TO GET US SOME GRUB, SO WE DON'T HAVE TO STARVE TO DEATH UP HERE!
HI... I'D LIKE TO ORDER A PIZZA?
YES.
WE'RE ON A ROOF.
NO, THIS ISN'T A JOKE.
NO, YOU'RE STUPID!

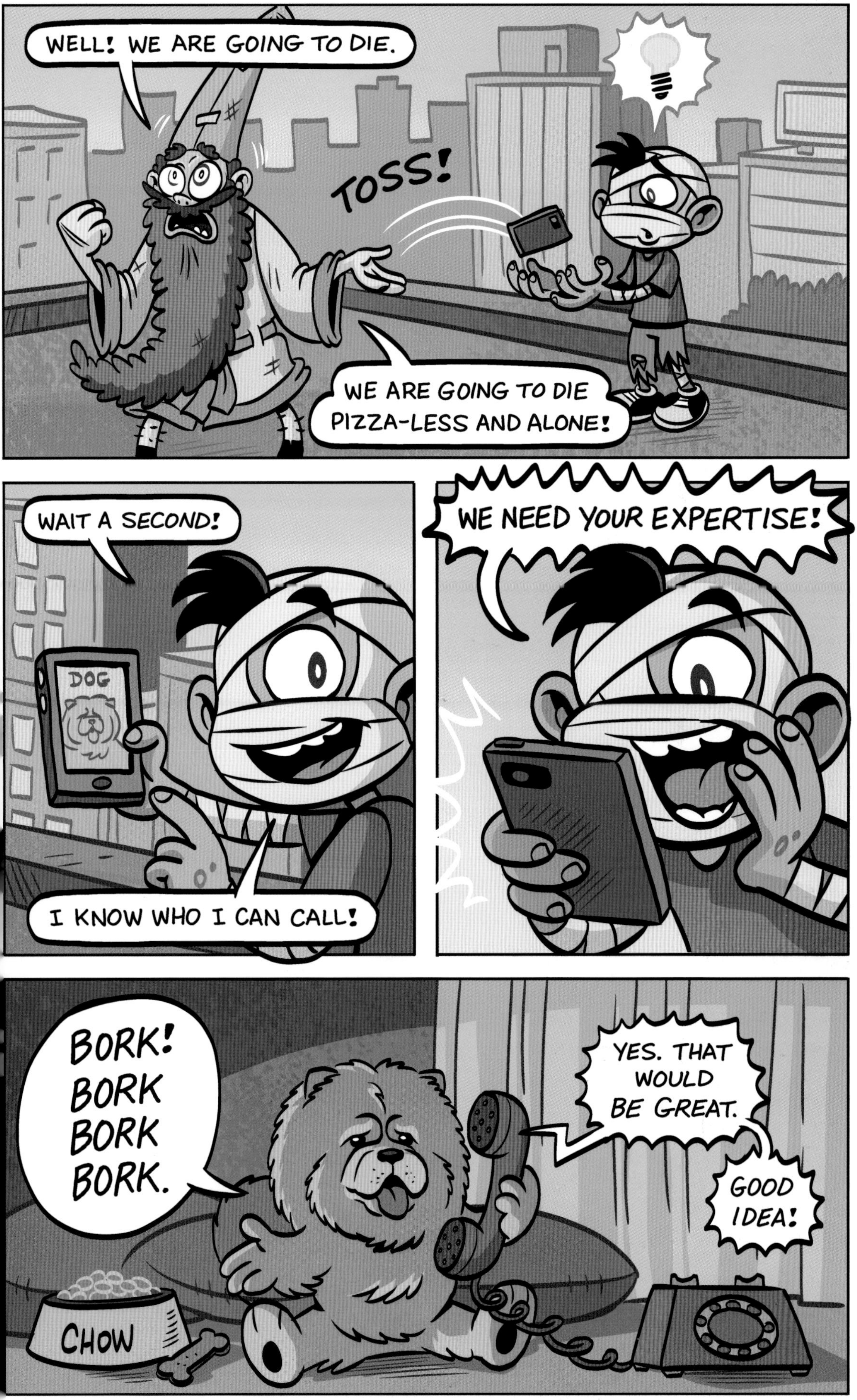
WELL! WE ARE GOING TO DIE.
TOSS!
WE ARE GOING TO DIE PIZZA-LESS AND ALONE!
WAIT A SECOND!
DOG
I KNOW WHO I CAN CALL!
WE NEED YOUR EXPERTISE!
BORK! BORK BORK BORK.
YES. THAT WOULD BE GREAT.
GOOD IDEA!
CHOW

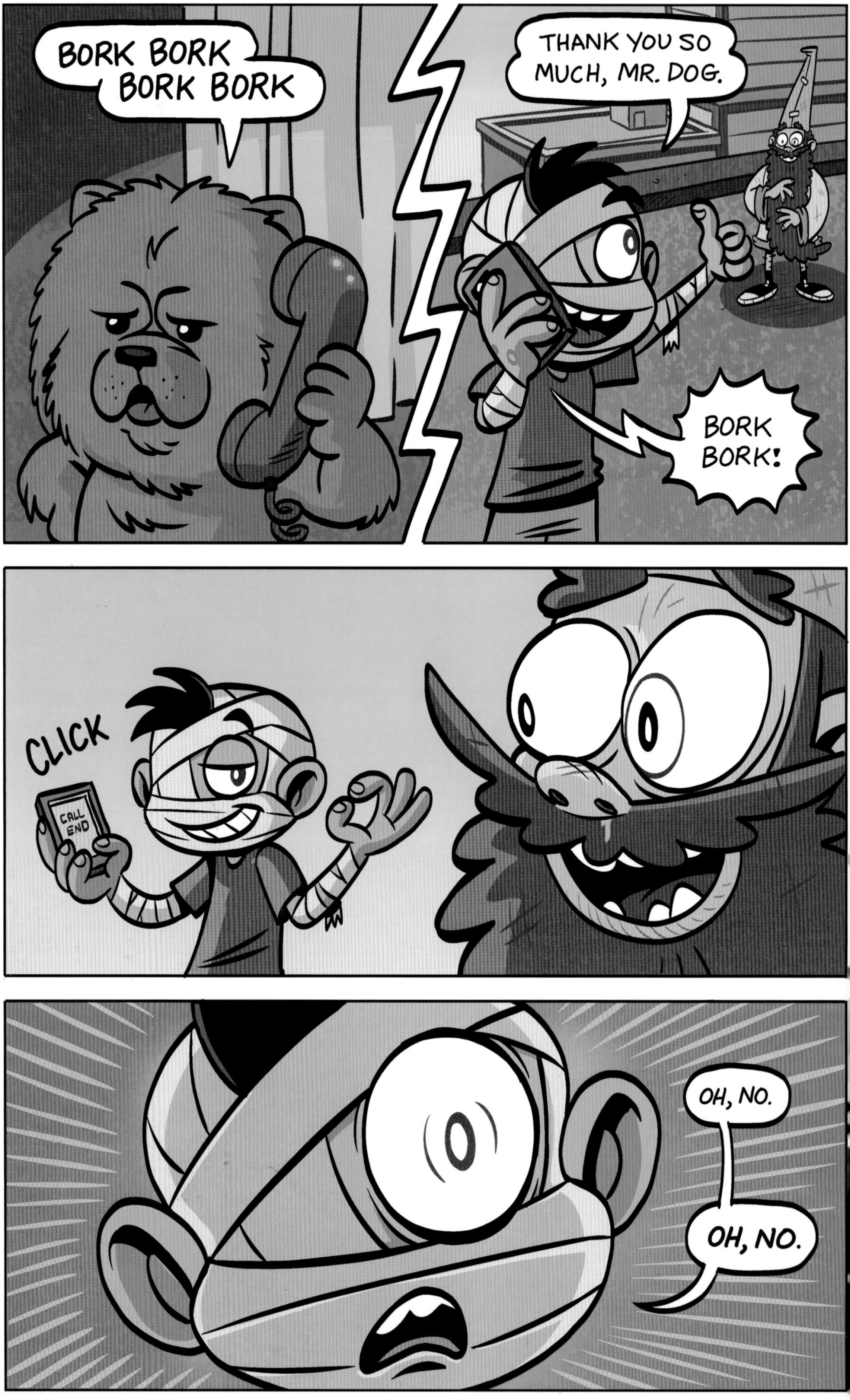
BORK BORK
BORK BORK
THANK YOU SO
MUCH, MR. DOG.
BORK
BORK!
CLICK
CALL
END
OH, NO.
OH, NO.

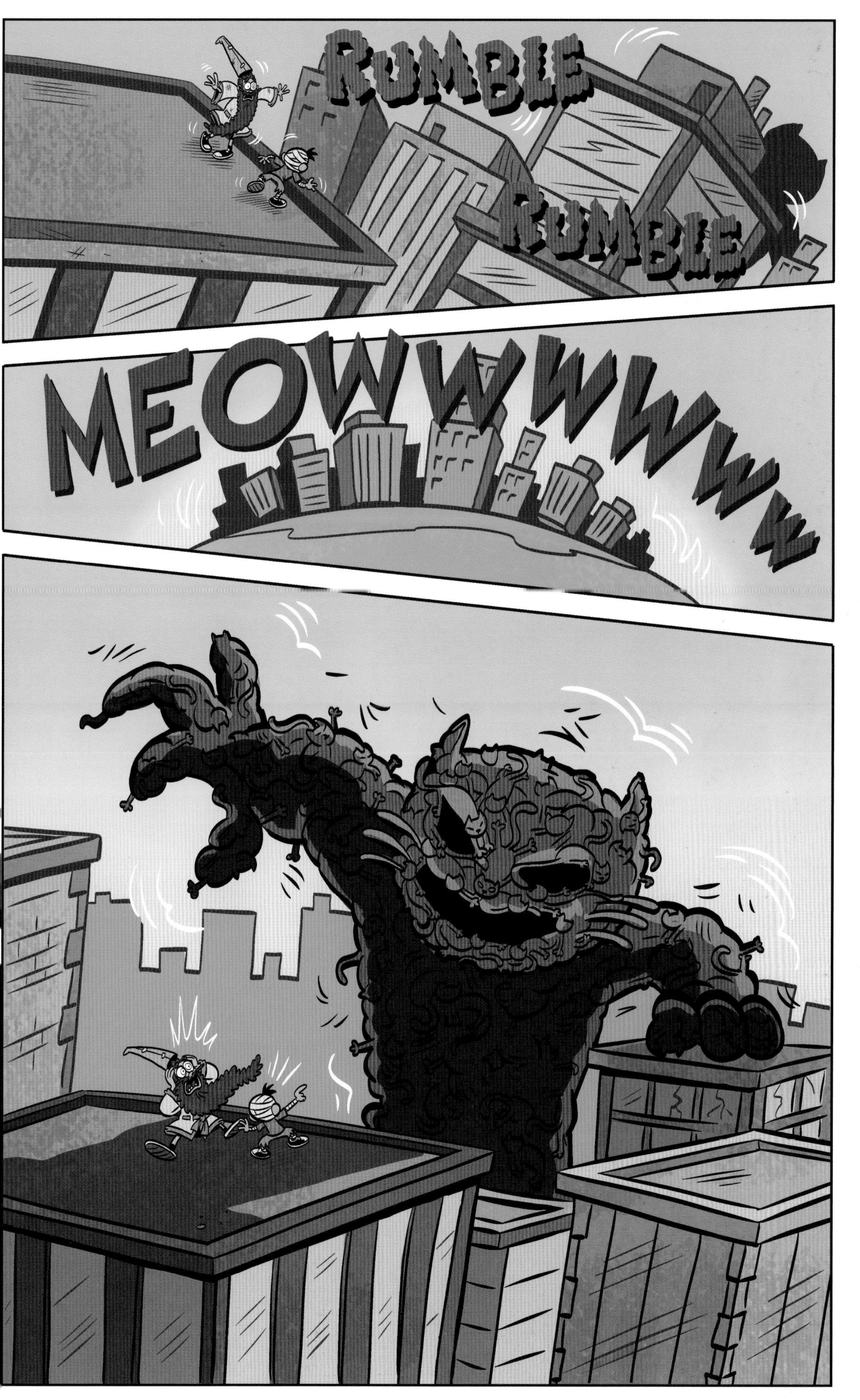
RUMBLE
RUMBLE
MEOWWWWWWW

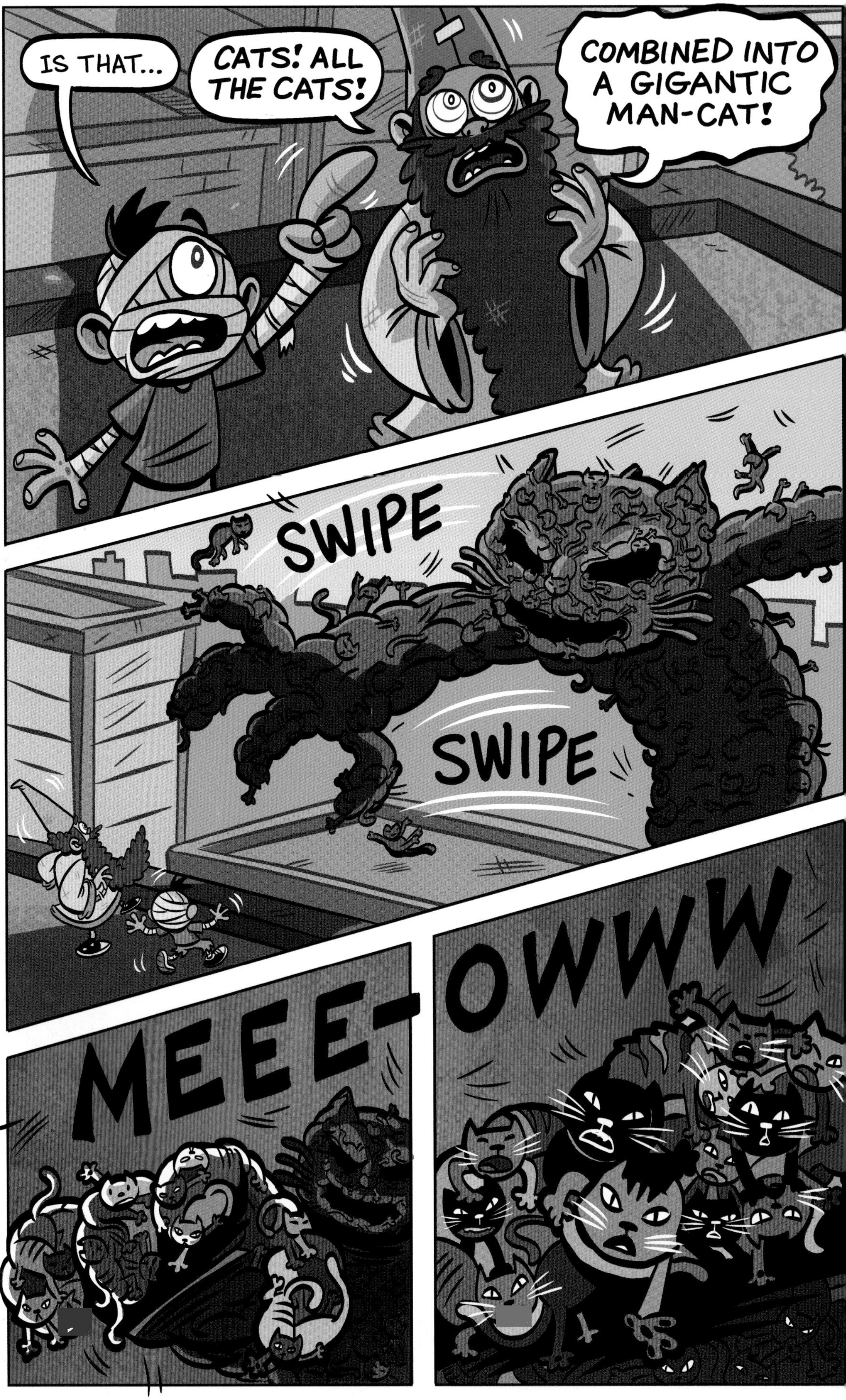
IS THAT...
CATS! ALL THE CATS!
COMBINED INTO A GIGANTIC MAN-CAT!
SWIPE
SWIPE
MEEE-OWWW

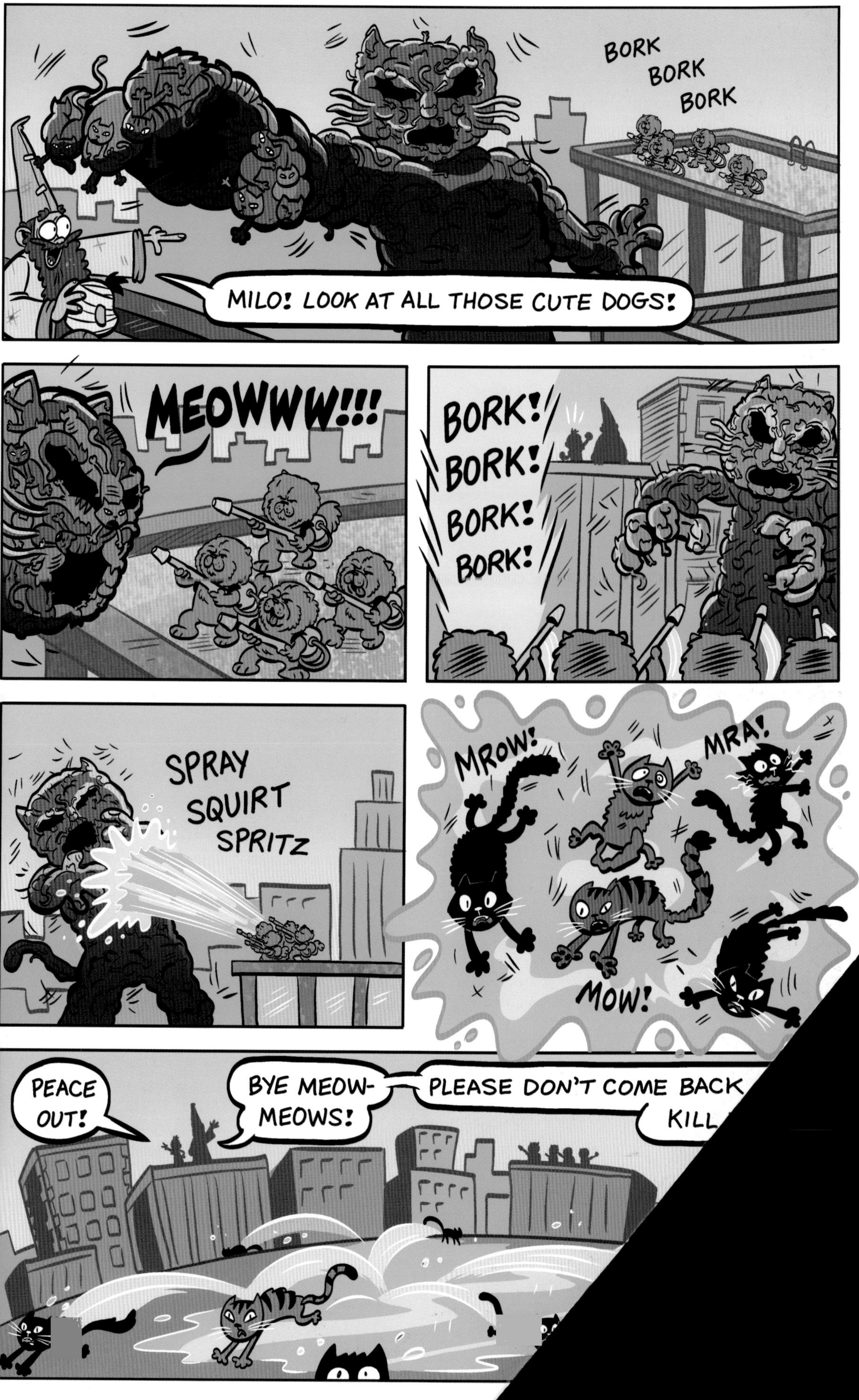
BORK
BORK
BORK
MILO! LOOK AT ALL THOSE CUTE DOGS!
MEOWWW!!!
BORK!
BORK!
BORK!
BORK!
SPRAY
SQUIRT
SPRITZ
MROW!
MRA!
MOW!
PEACE OUT!
BYE MEOW-MEOWS!
PLEASE DON'T COME BACK [redacted] KILL[redacted]

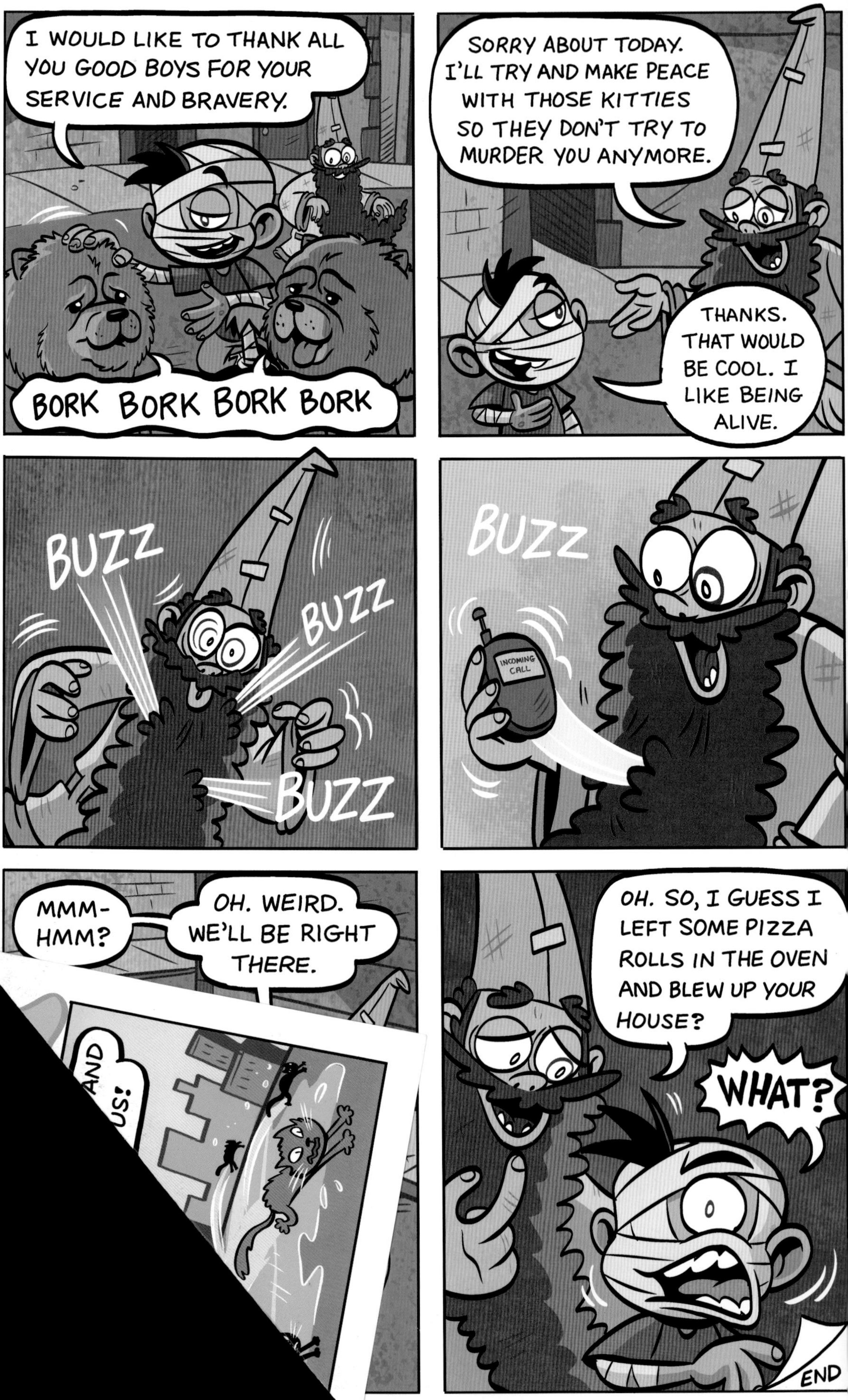
I WOULD LIKE TO THANK ALL YOU GOOD BOYS FOR YOUR SERVICE AND BRAVERY.
BORK BORK BORK BORK
SORRY ABOUT TODAY. I'LL TRY AND MAKE PEACE WITH THOSE KITTIES SO THEY DON'T TRY TO MURDER YOU ANYMORE.
THANKS. THAT WOULD BE COOL. I LIKE BEING ALIVE.
BUZZ
BUZZ
BUZZ
BUZZ
INCOMING CALL
MMM-HMM?
OH. WEIRD. WE'LL BE RIGHT THERE.
OH. SO, I GUESS I LEFT SOME PIZZA ROLLS IN THE OVEN AND BLEW UP YOUR HOUSE?
WHAT?
END

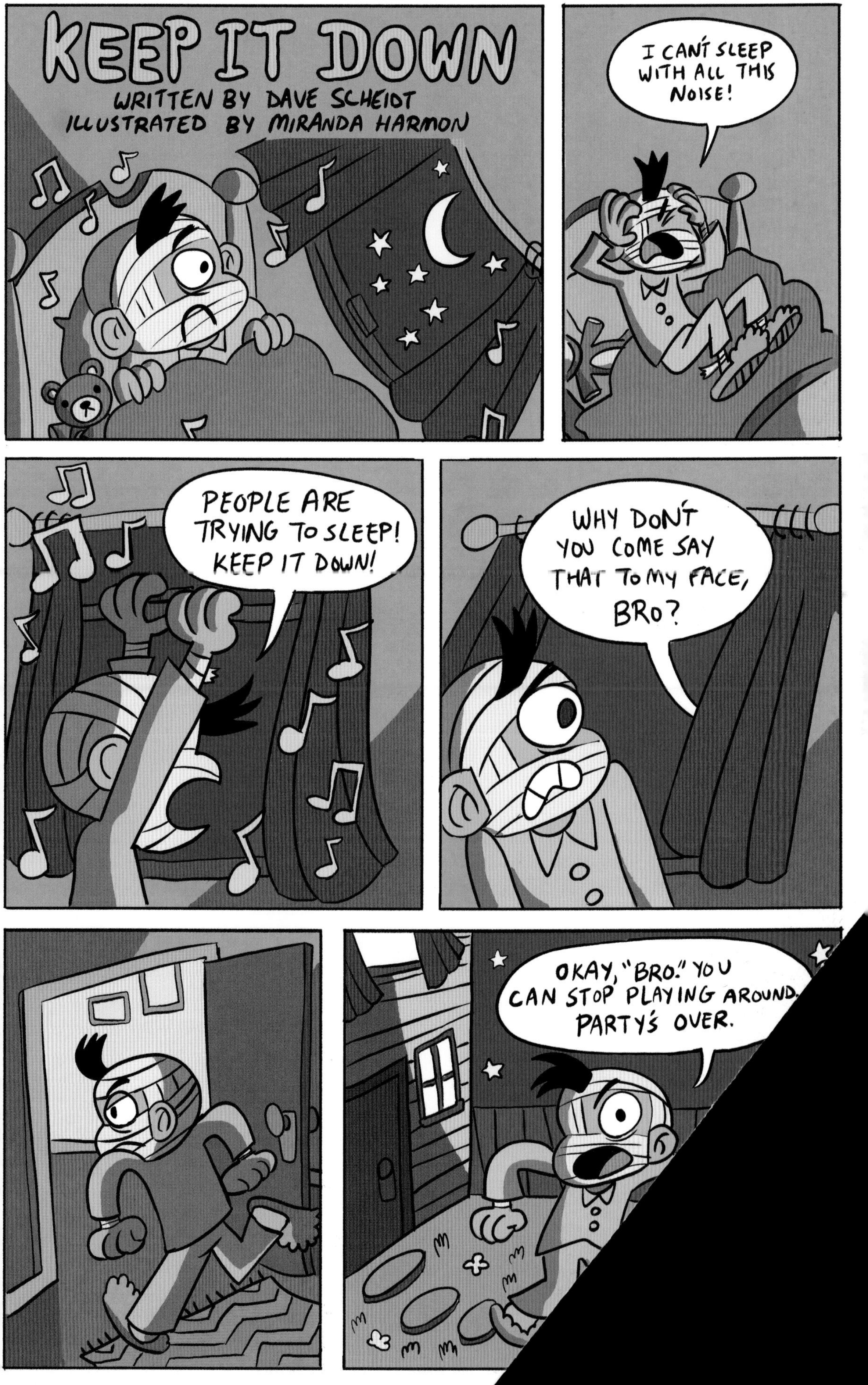
KEEP IT DOWN
WRITTEN BY DAVE SCHEIDT
ILLUSTRATED BY MIRANDA HARMON
I CAN'T SLEEP WITH ALL THIS NOISE!
PEOPLE ARE TRYING TO SLEEP! KEEP IT DOWN!
WHY DON'T YOU COME SAY THAT TO MY FACE, BRO?
OKAY, "BRO." YOU CAN STOP PLAYING AROUND. PARTY'S OVER.

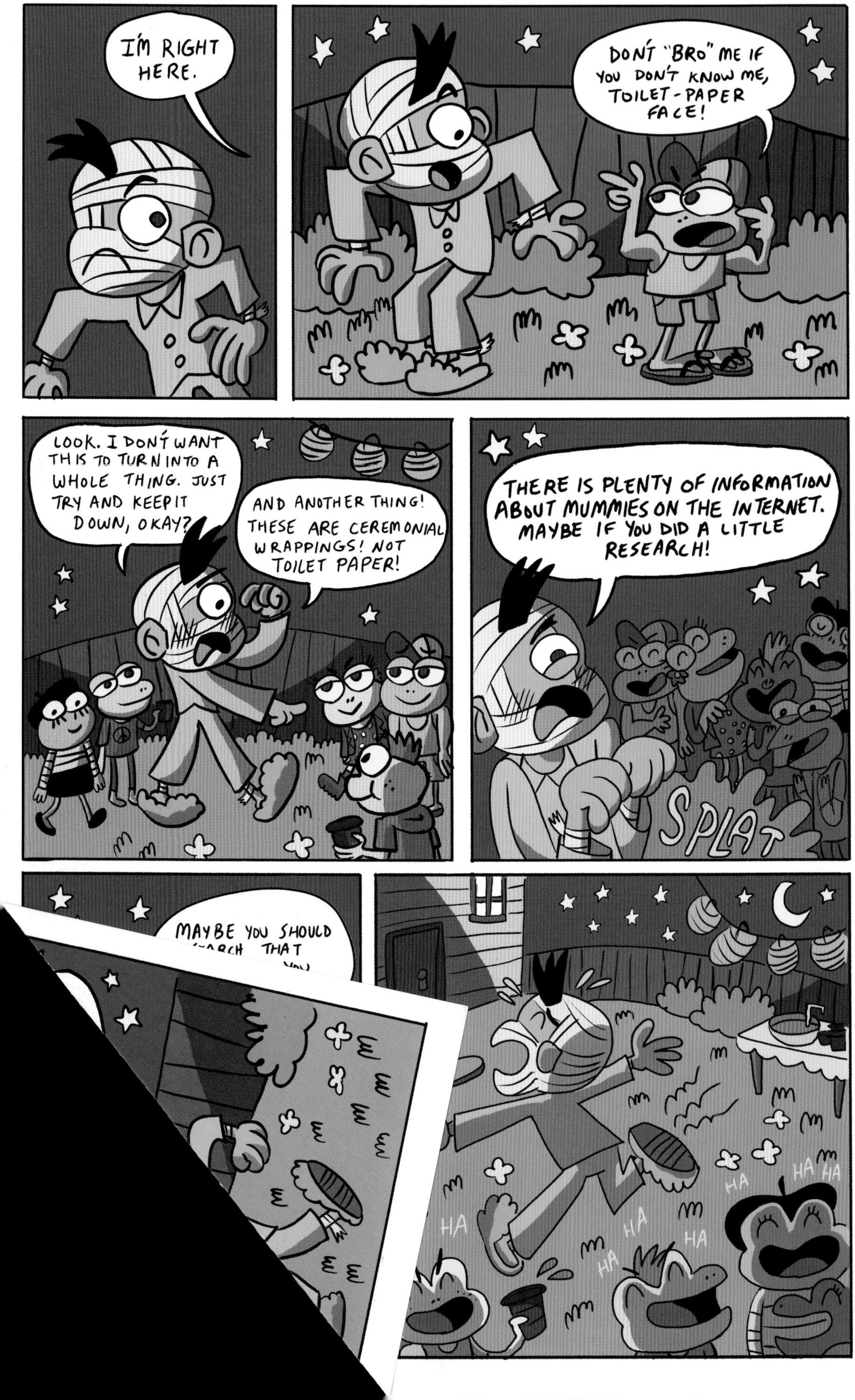
I'M RIGHT HERE.
DON'T "BRO" ME IF YOU DON'T KNOW ME, TOILET-PAPER FACE!
LOOK. I DON'T WANT THIS TO TURN INTO A WHOLE THING. JUST TRY AND KEEP IT DOWN, OKAY?
AND ANOTHER THING! THESE ARE CEREMONIAL WRAPPINGS! NOT TOILET PAPER!
THERE IS PLENTY OF INFORMATION ABOUT MUMMIES ON THE INTERNET. MAYBE IF YOU DID A LITTLE RESEARCH!
SPLAT
MAYBE YOU SHOULD
THAT
HA HA HA
HA HA HA HA HA

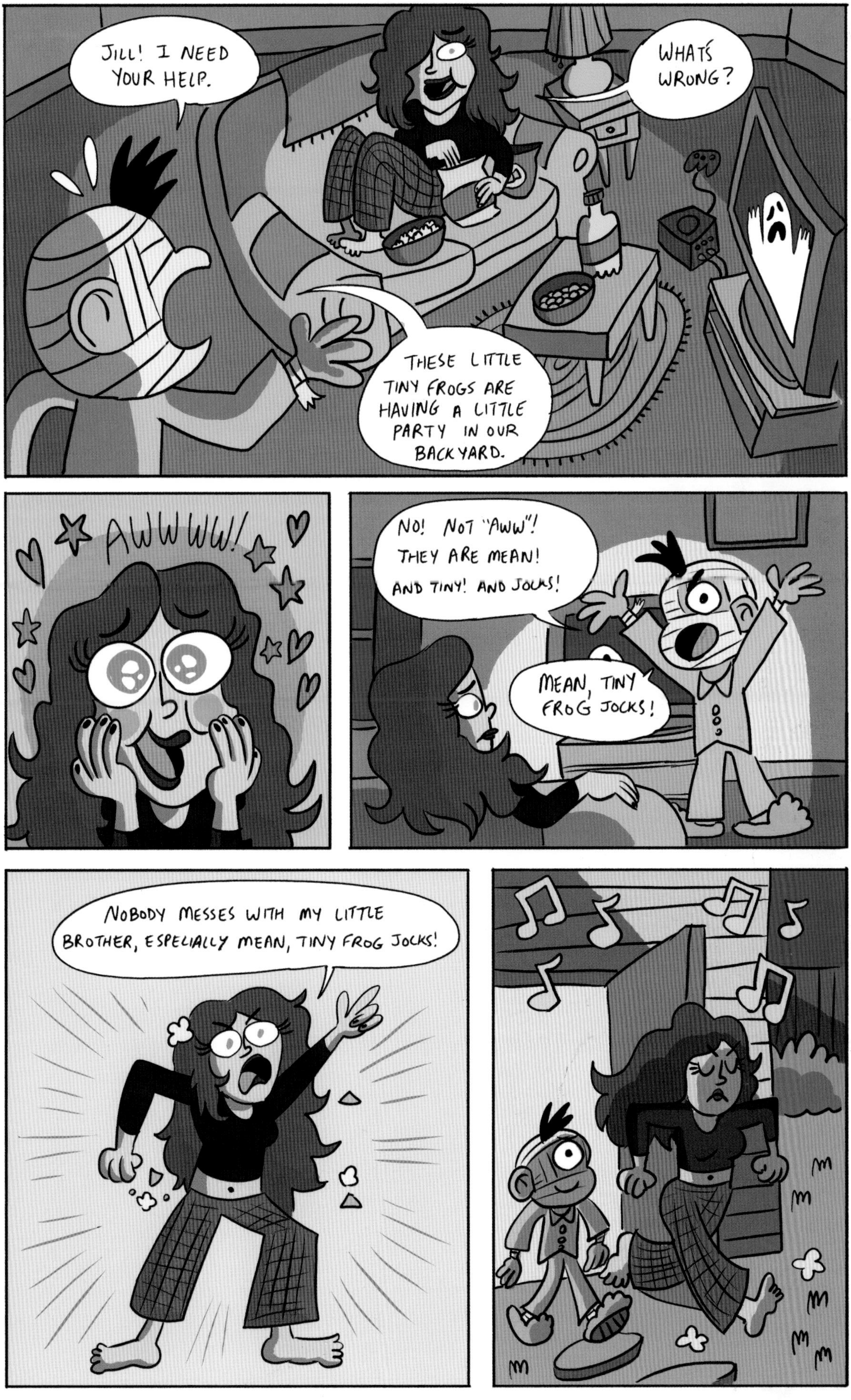
JILL! I NEED YOUR HELP.
WHAT'S WRONG?
THESE LITTLE TINY FROGS ARE HAVING A LITTLE PARTY IN OUR BACKYARD.
AWWWW!
NO! NOT "AWW"! THEY ARE MEAN! AND TINY! AND JOCKS!
MEAN, TINY FROG JOCKS!
NOBODY MESSES WITH MY LITTLE BROTHER, ESPECIALLY MEAN, TINY FROG JOCKS!

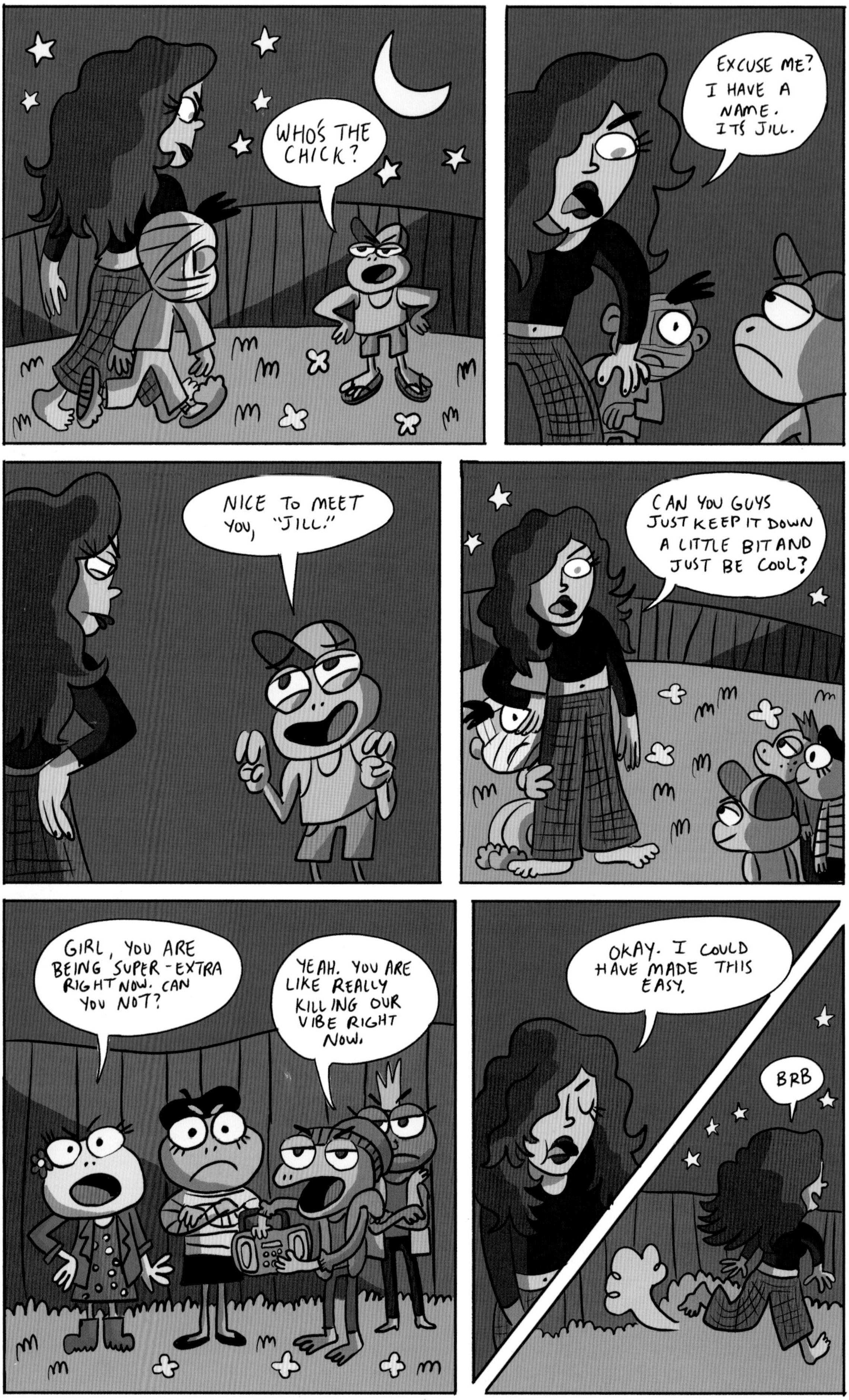
WHO'S THE CHICK?
EXCUSE ME? I HAVE A NAME. IT'S JILL.
NICE TO MEET YOU, "JILL."
CAN YOU GUYS JUST KEEP IT DOWN A LITTLE BIT AND JUST BE COOL?
GIRL, YOU ARE BEING SUPER-EXTRA RIGHT NOW. CAN YOU NOT?
YEAH. YOU ARE LIKE REALLY KILLING OUR VIBE RIGHT NOW.
OKAY. I COULD HAVE MADE THIS EASY.
BRB

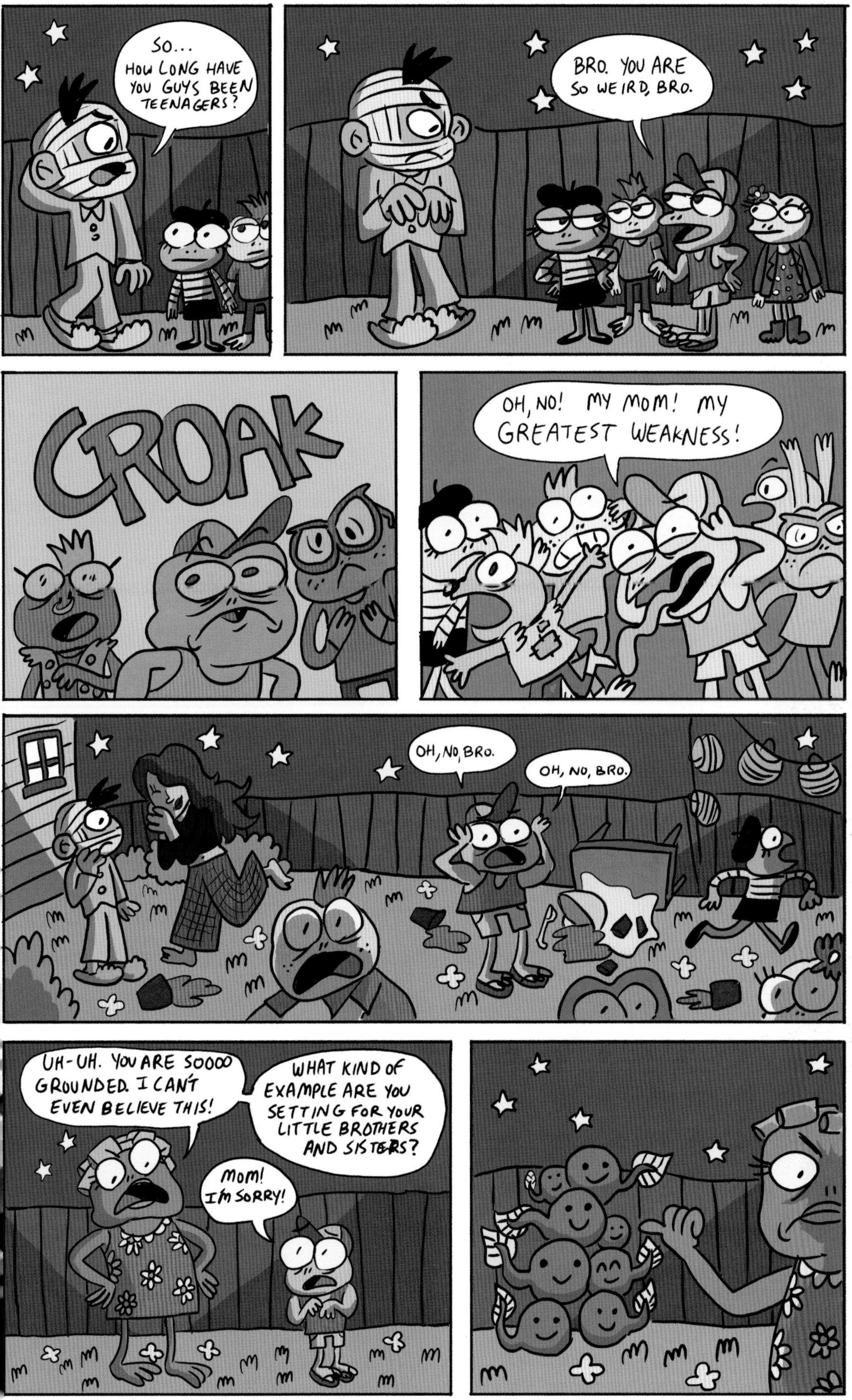
SO... HOW LONG HAVE YOU GUYS BEEN TEENAGERS?
BRO. YOU ARE SO WEIRD, BRO.
CROAK
OH, NO! MY MOM! MY GREATEST WEAKNESS!
OH, NO, BRO.
OH, NO, BRO.
UH-UH. YOU ARE SOOOO GROUNDED. I CAN'T EVEN BELIEVE THIS!
WHAT KIND OF EXAMPLE ARE YOU SETTING FOR YOUR LITTLE BROTHERS AND SISTERS?
MOM! I'M SORRY!

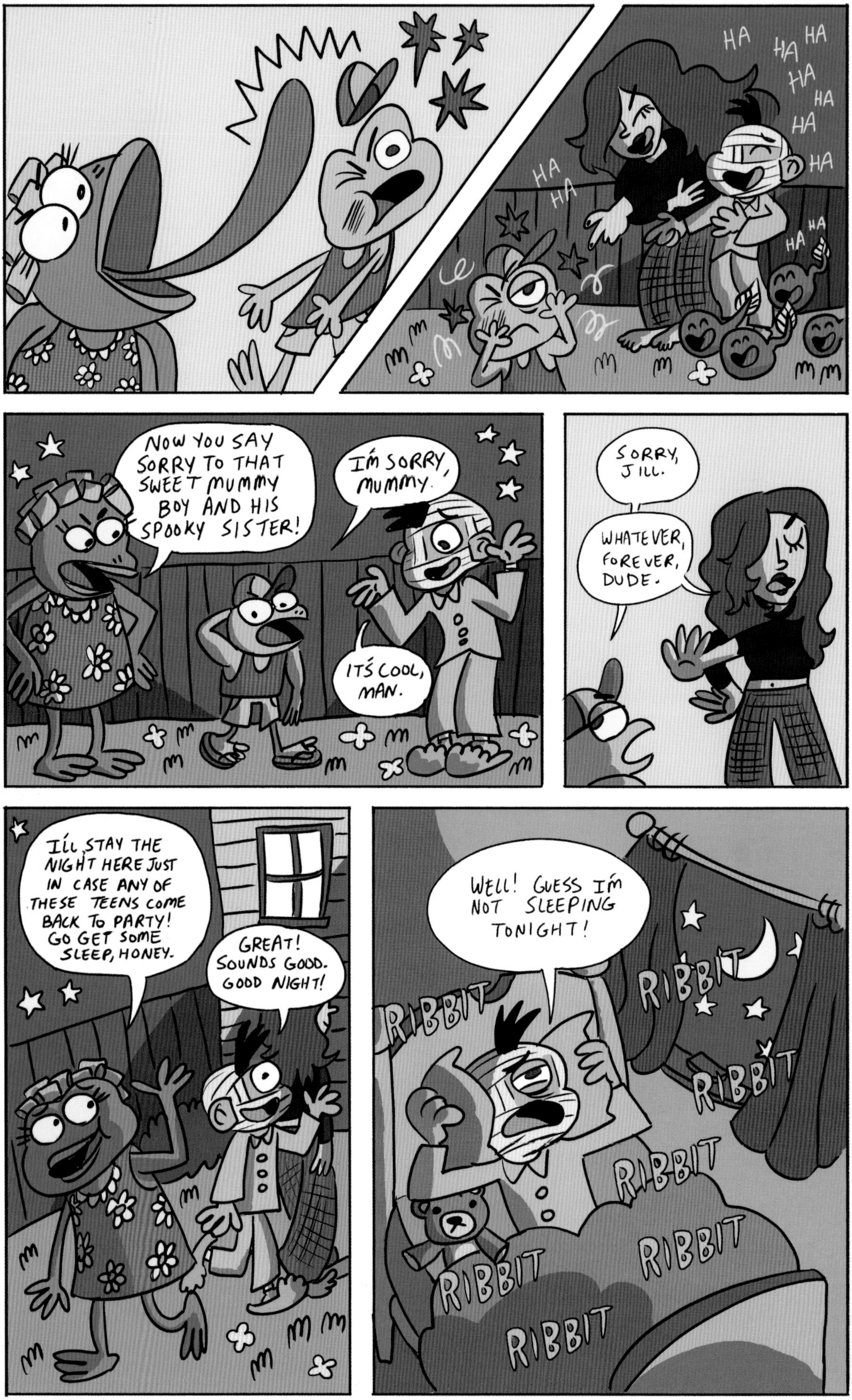
HA HA HA HA HA HA HA
HA HA
HA HA
NOW YOU SAY SORRY TO THAT SWEET MUMMY BOY AND HIS SPOOKY SISTER!
I'M SORRY, MUMMY.
IT'S COOL, MAN.
SORRY, JILL.
WHATEVER, FOREVER, DUDE.
I'LL STAY THE NIGHT HERE JUST IN CASE ANY OF THESE TEENS COME BACK TO PARTY! GO GET SOME SLEEP, HONEY.
GREAT! SOUNDS GOOD. GOOD NIGHT!
WELL! GUESS I'M NOT SLEEPING TONIGHT!
RIBBIT RIBBIT RIBBIT RIBBIT RIBBIT RIBBIT RIBBIT

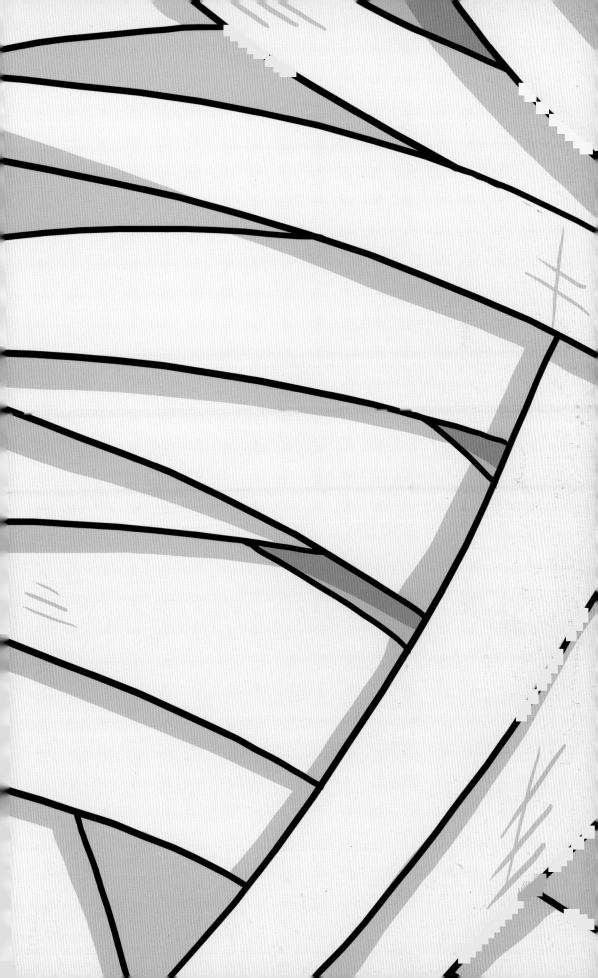

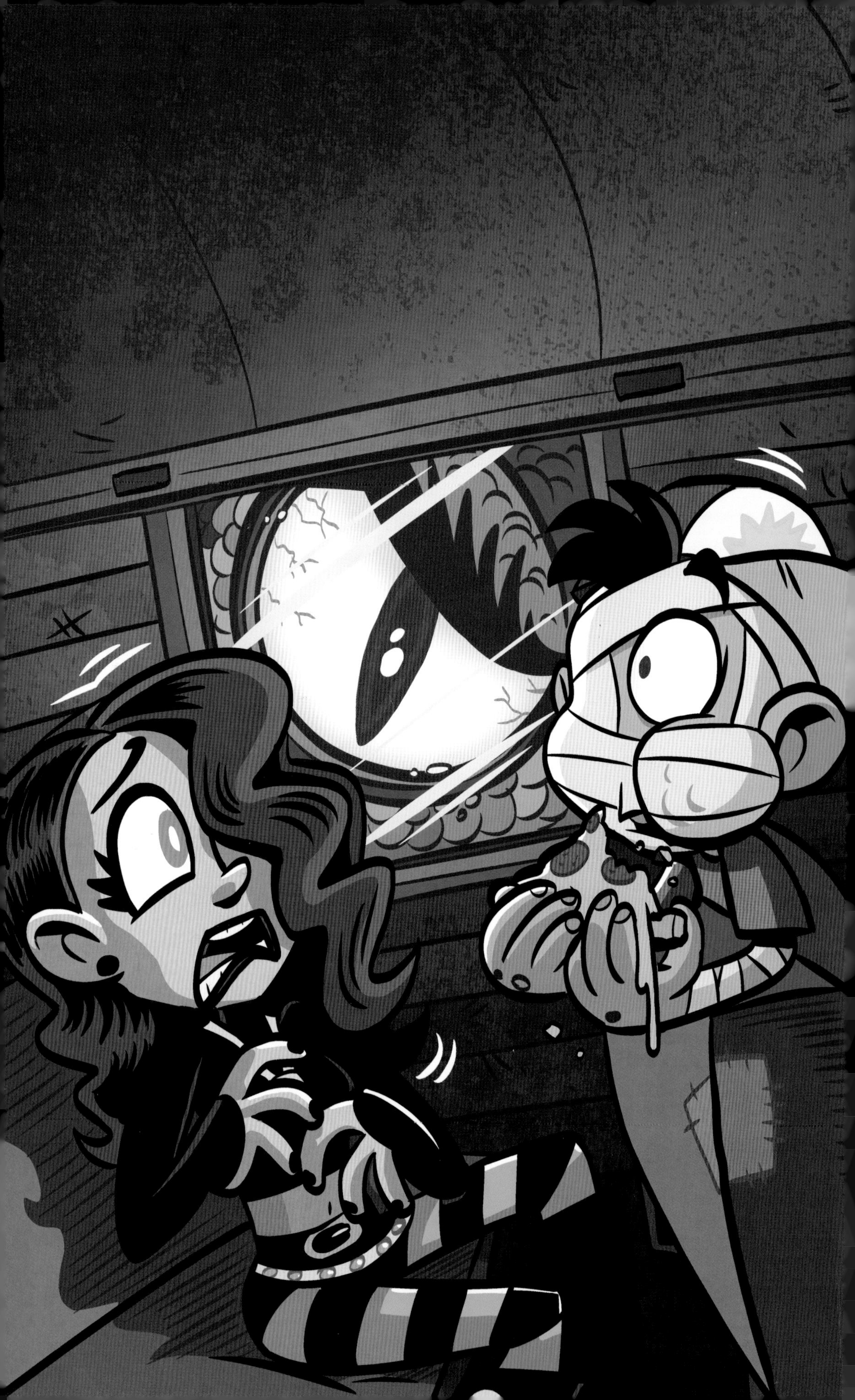

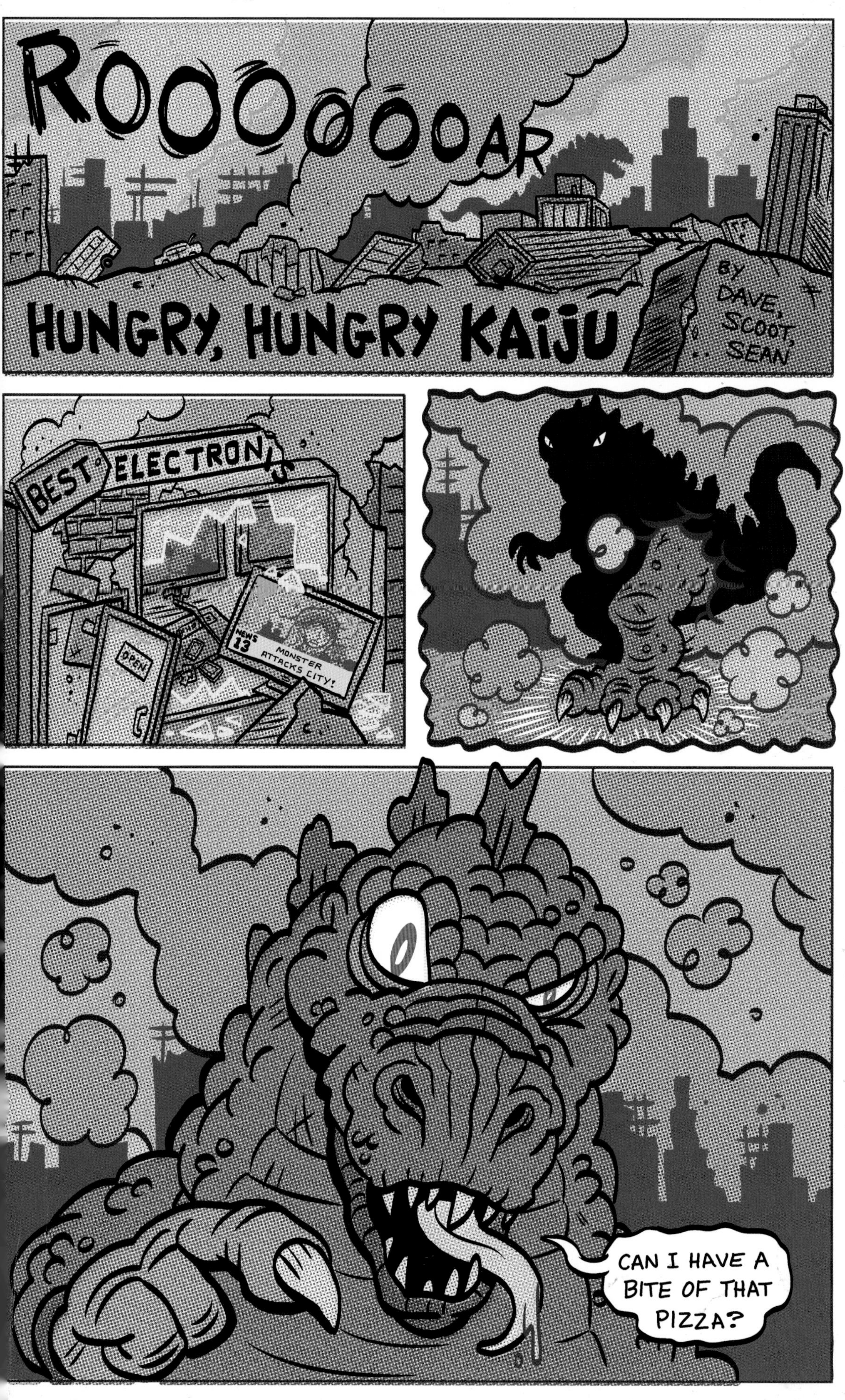
ROOOOOOAR
HUNGRY, HUNGRY KAIJU
BY DAVE, SCOOT, SEAN
BEST ELECTRON
NEWS 13
MONSTER ATTACKS CITY!
OPEN
CAN I HAVE A BITE OF THAT PIZZA?

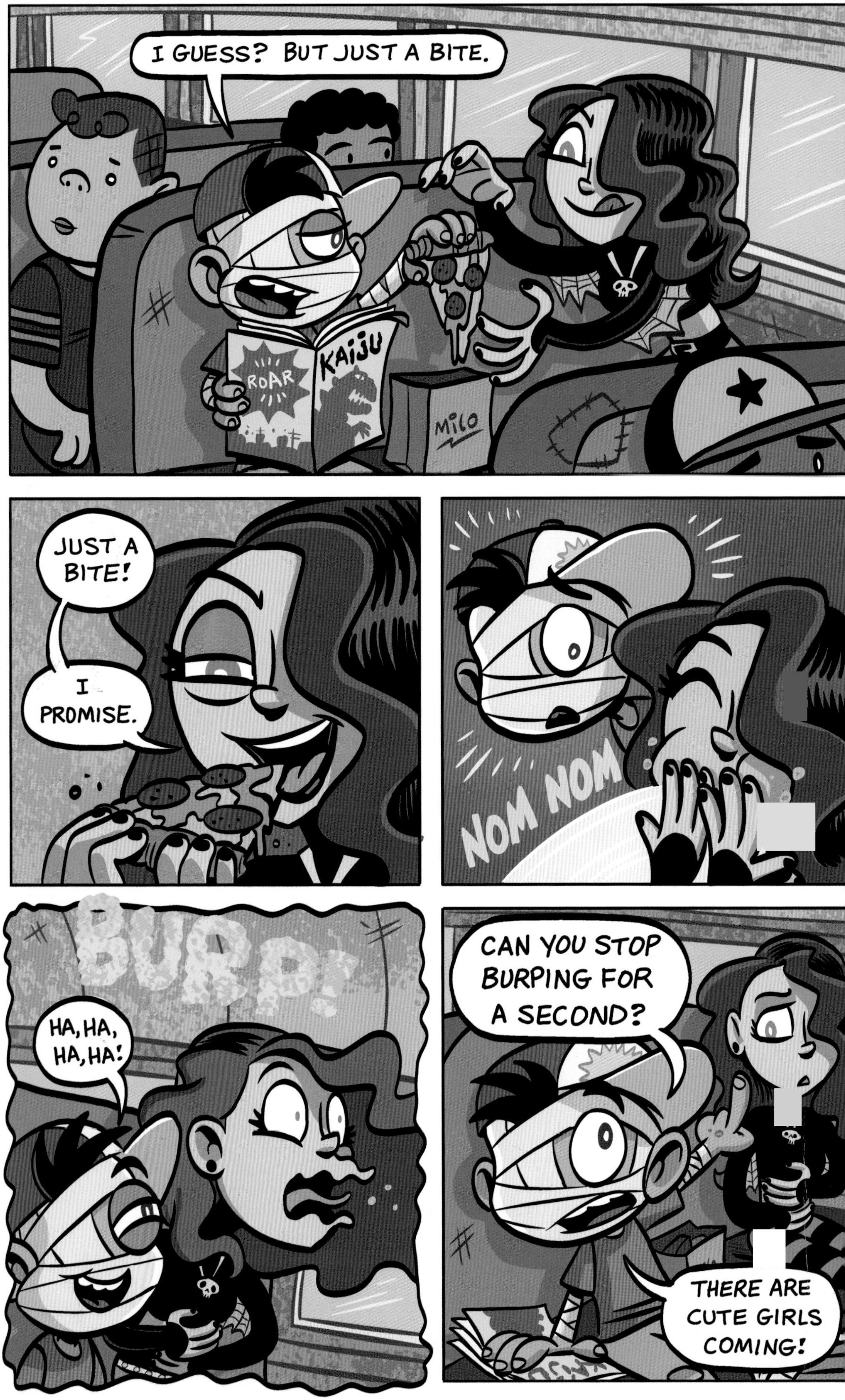
I GUESS? BUT JUST A BITE.
ROAR
KAIJU
MILO
JUST A BITE!
I PROMISE.
NOM NOM
BURP!
HA, HA, HA, HA!
CAN YOU STOP BURPING FOR A SECOND?
THERE ARE CUTE GIRLS COMING!

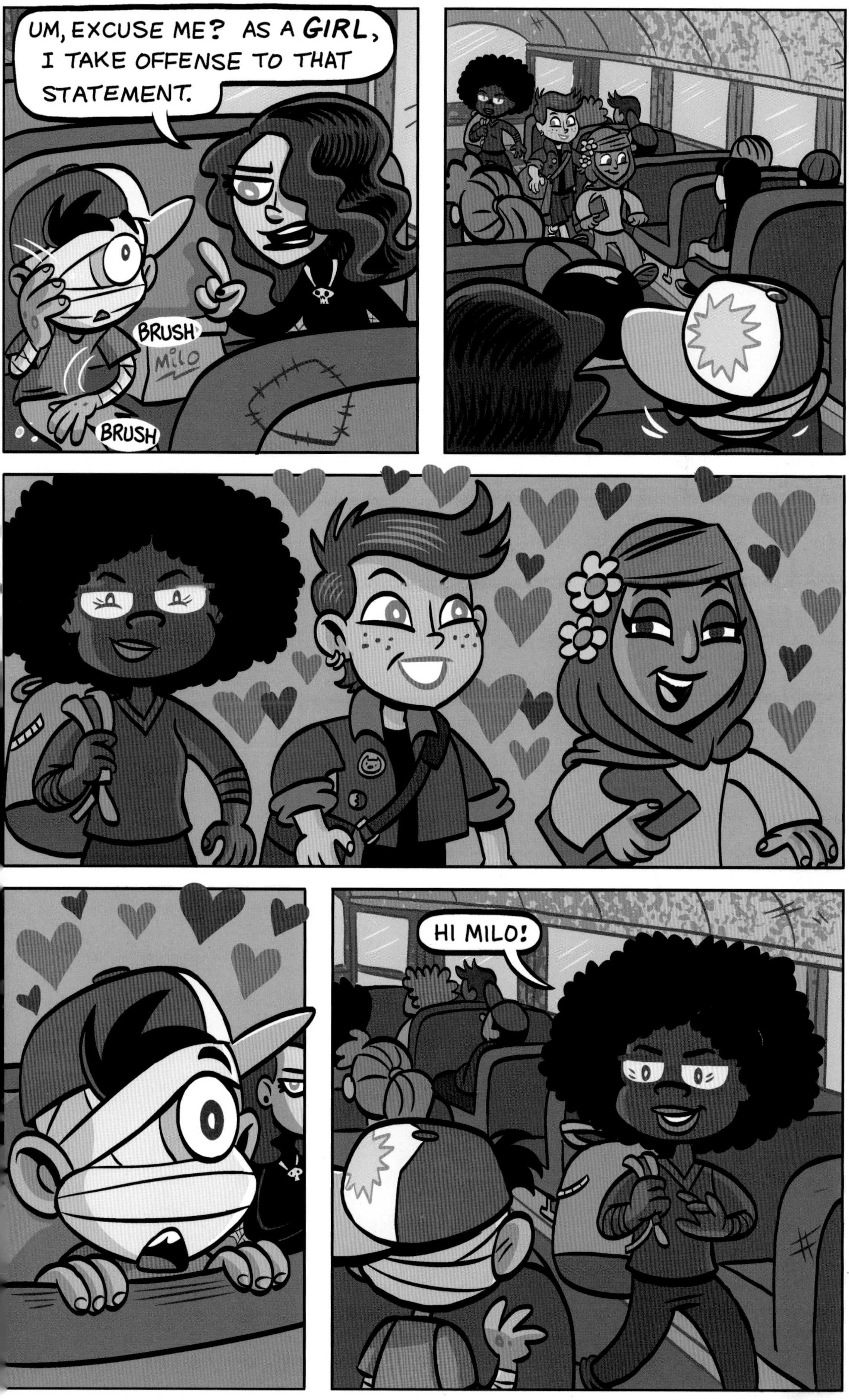
UM, EXCUSE ME? AS A GIRL, I TAKE OFFENSE TO THAT STATEMENT.
BRUSH
MILO
BRUSH
HI MILO!

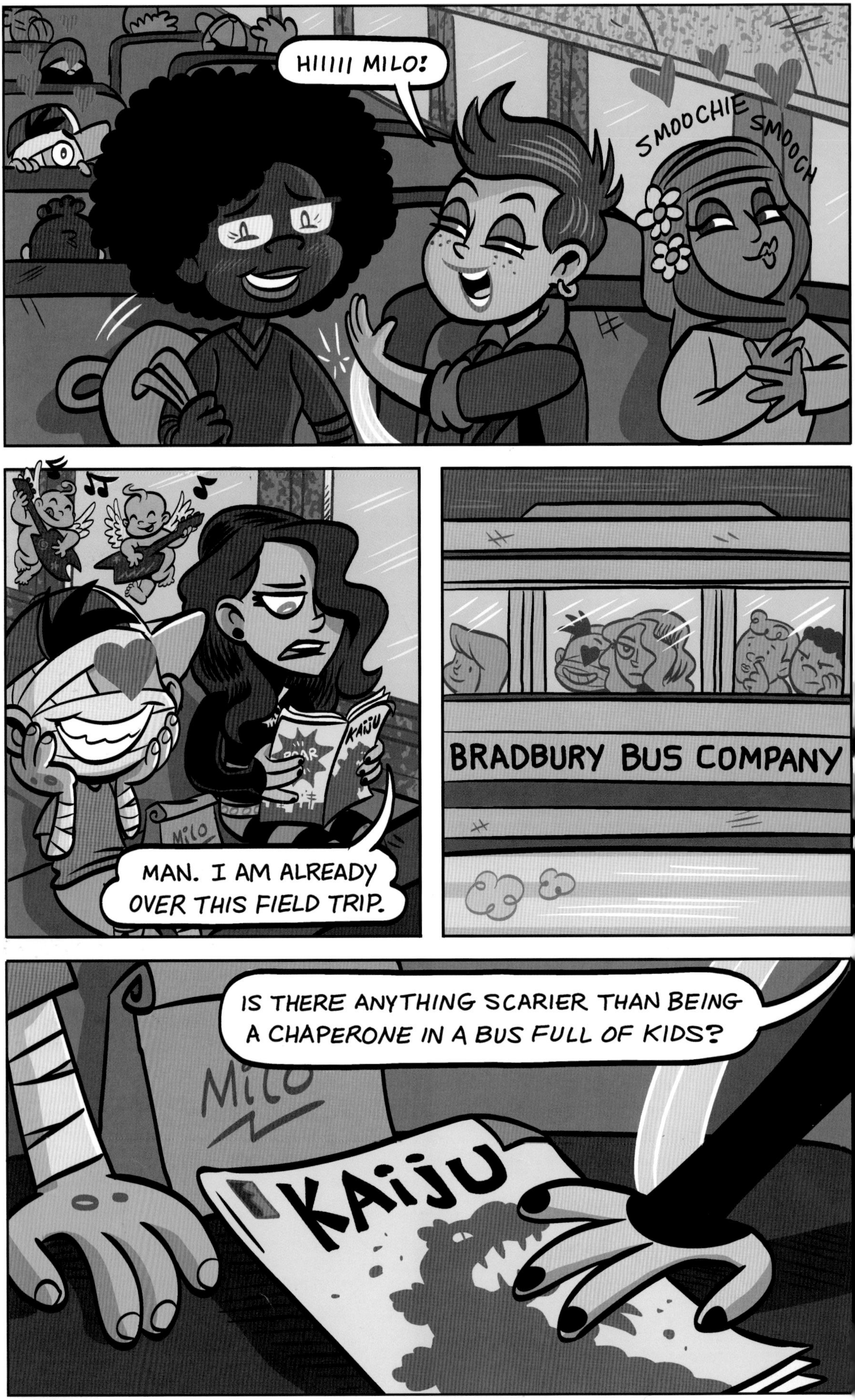
HIIIII MILO!
SMOOCHIE SMOOCH
MAN. I AM ALREADY OVER THIS FIELD TRIP.
BRADBURY BUS COMPANY
IS THERE ANYTHING SCARIER THAN BEING A CHAPERONE IN A BUS FULL OF KIDS?
MILO
KAIJU

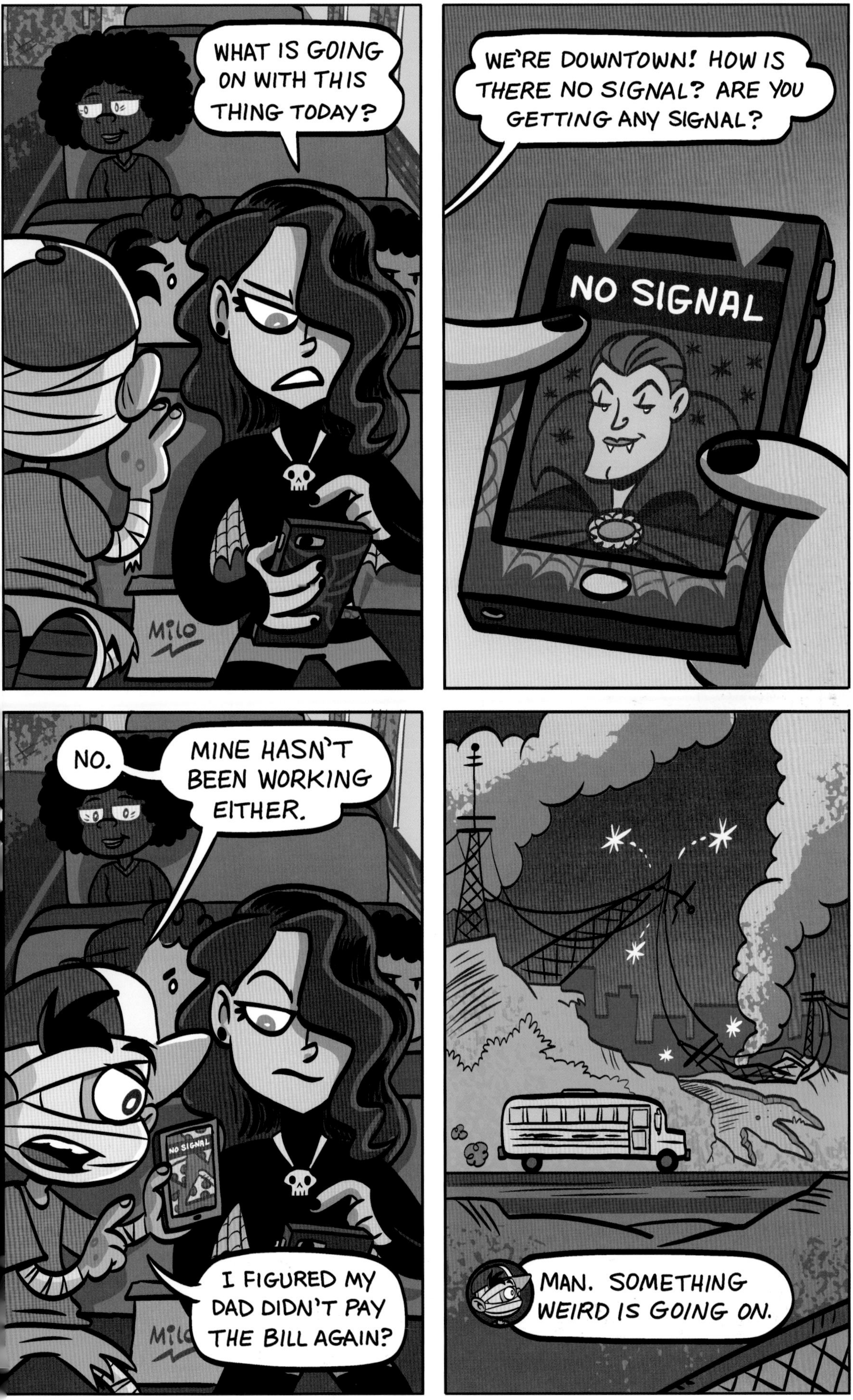
WHAT IS GOING ON WITH THIS THING TODAY?
WE'RE DOWNTOWN! HOW IS THERE NO SIGNAL? ARE YOU GETTING ANY SIGNAL?
NO SIGNAL
MILO
NO.
MINE HASN'T BEEN WORKING EITHER.
NO SIGNAL
I FIGURED MY DAD DIDN'T PAY THE BILL AGAIN?
MAN. SOMETHING WEIRD IS GOING ON.

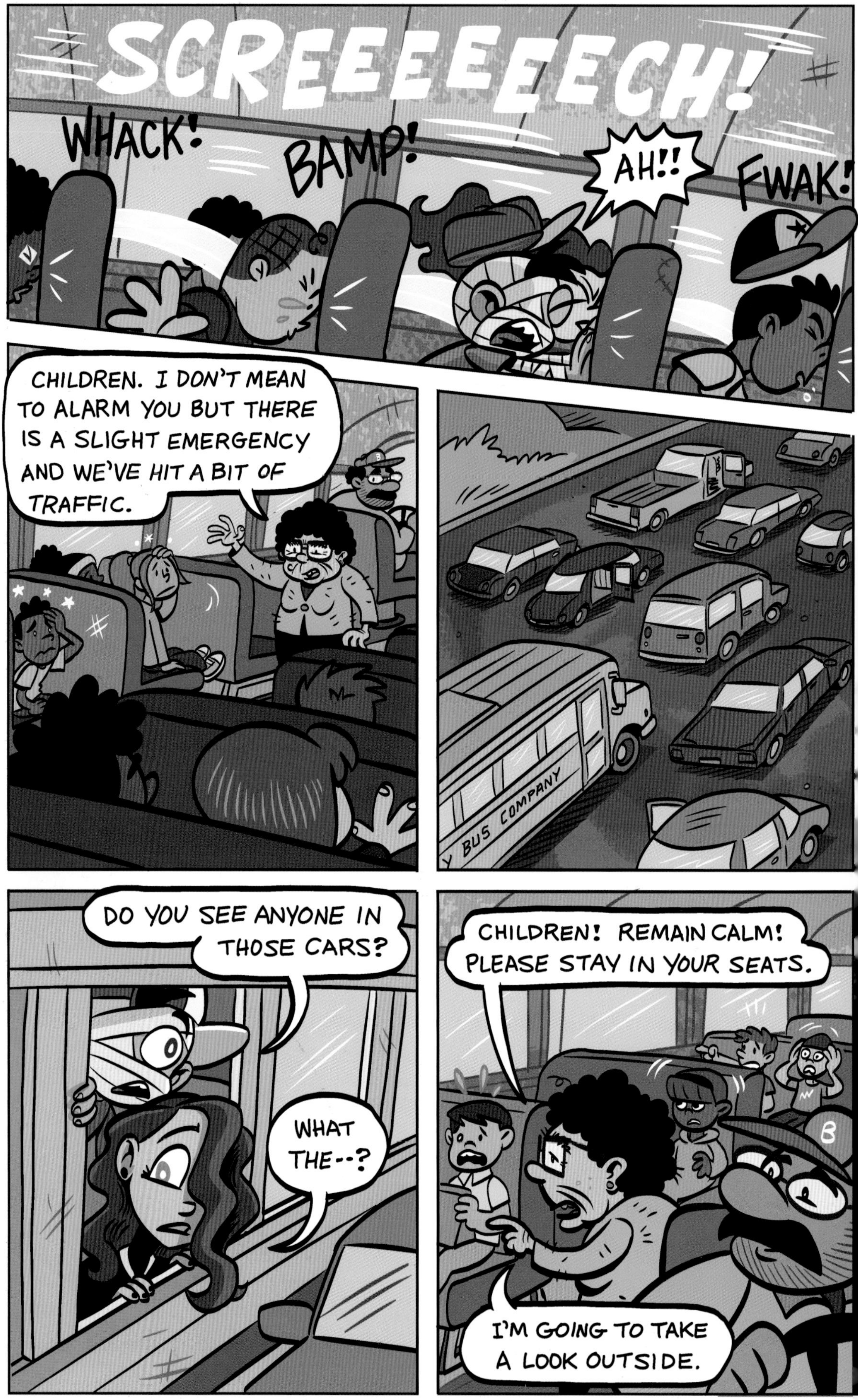
SCREEEEEECH!
WHACK!
BAMP!
AH!!
FWAK!
CHILDREN. I DON'T MEAN TO ALARM YOU BUT THERE IS A SLIGHT EMERGENCY AND WE'VE HIT A BIT OF TRAFFIC.
BUS COMPANY
DO YOU SEE ANYONE IN THOSE CARS?
WHAT THE--?
CHILDREN! REMAIN CALM! PLEASE STAY IN YOUR SEATS.
I'M GOING TO TAKE A LOOK OUTSIDE.

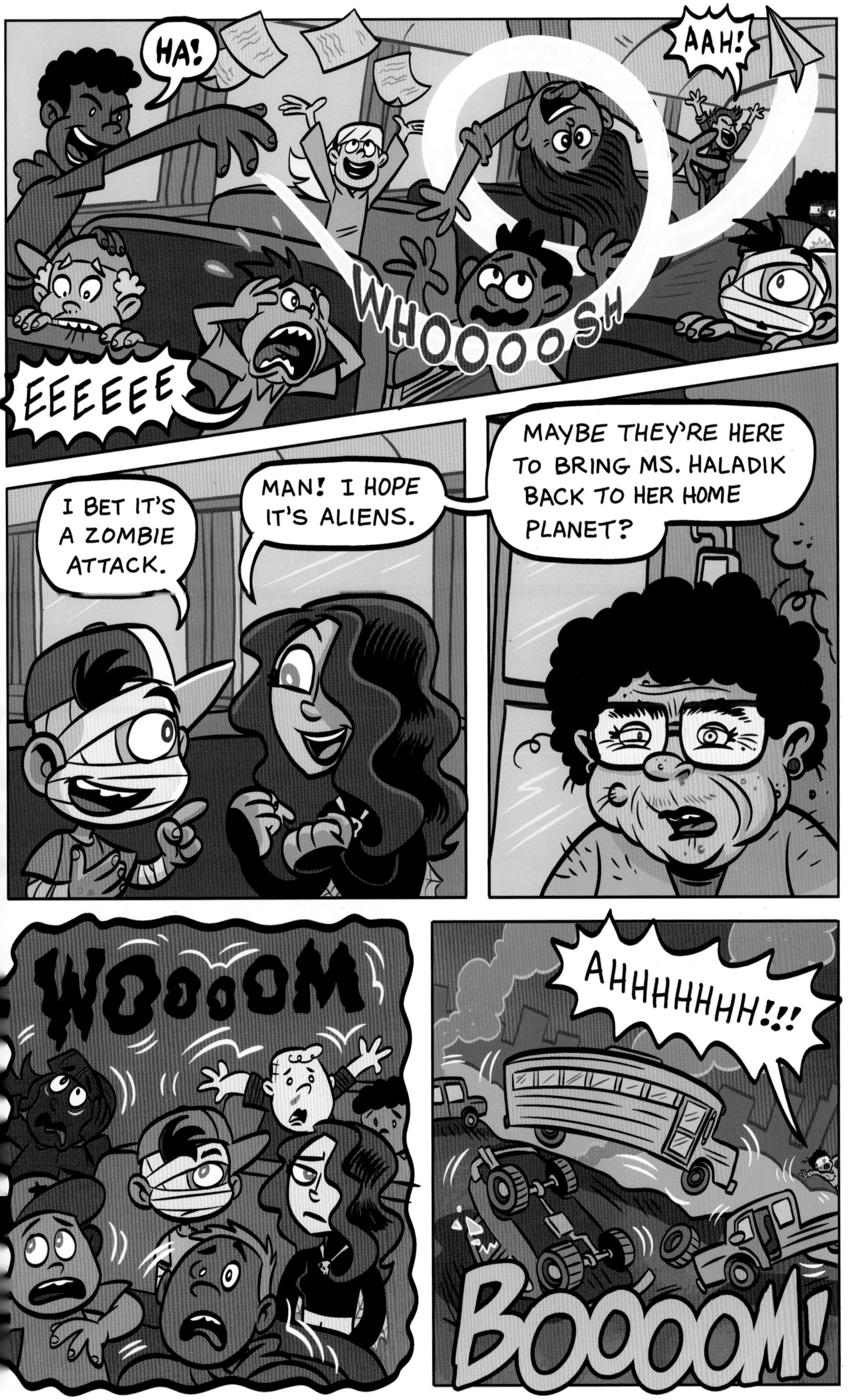
HA!
AAH!
WHOOOOOSH
EEEEEE
I BET IT'S A ZOMBIE ATTACK.
MAN! I HOPE IT'S ALIENS.
MAYBE THEY'RE HERE TO BRING MS. HALADIK BACK TO HER HOME PLANET?
WOOOOM
AHHHHHHHH!!!
BOOOOM!

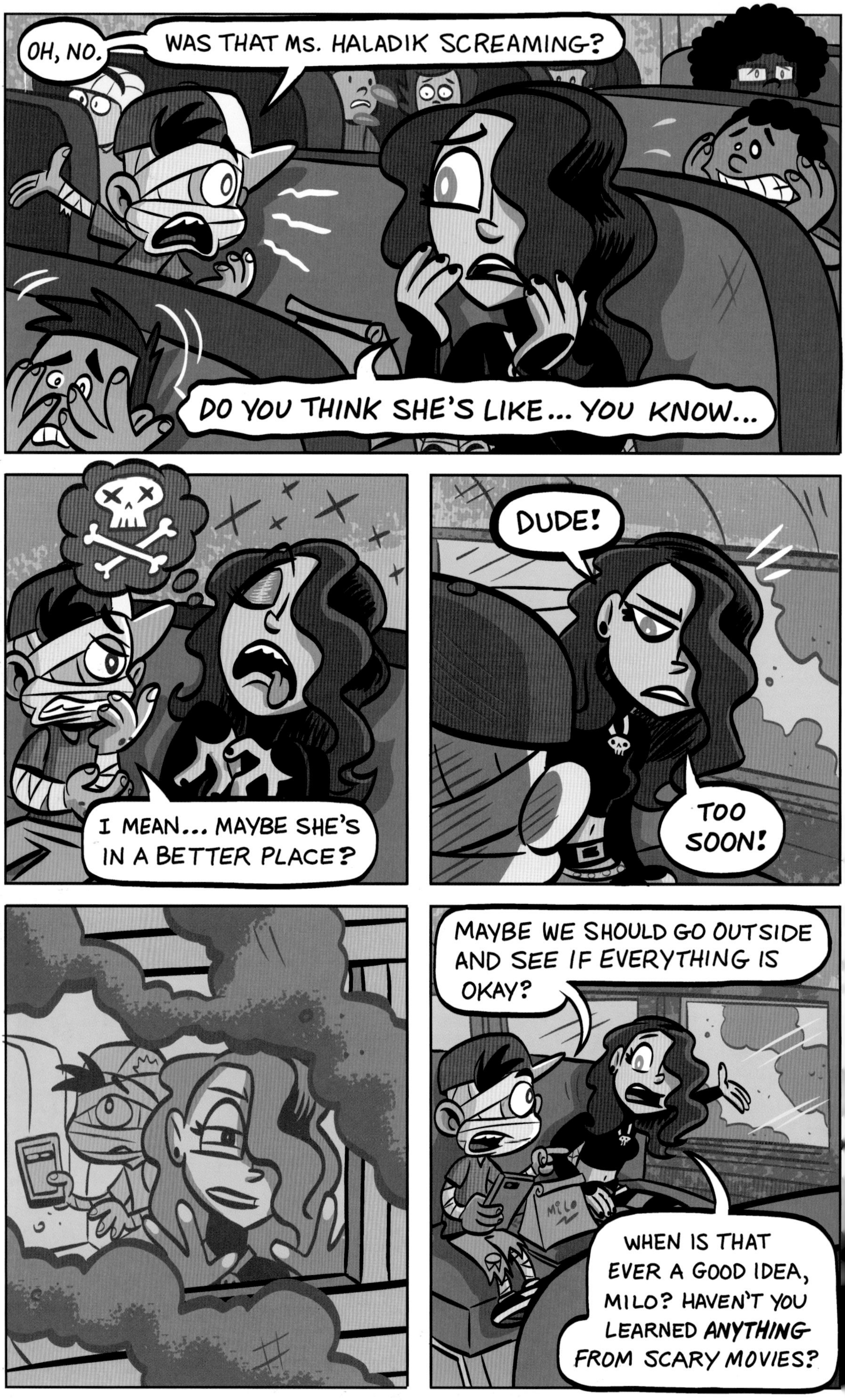
OH, NO.
WAS THAT Ms. HALADIK SCREAMING?
DO YOU THINK SHE'S LIKE... YOU KNOW...
I MEAN... MAYBE SHE'S IN A BETTER PLACE?
DUDE!
TOO SOON!
MAYBE WE SHOULD GO OUTSIDE AND SEE IF EVERYTHING IS OKAY?
MILO
WHEN IS THAT EVER A GOOD IDEA, MILO? HAVEN'T YOU LEARNED ***ANYTHING*** FROM SCARY MOVIES?

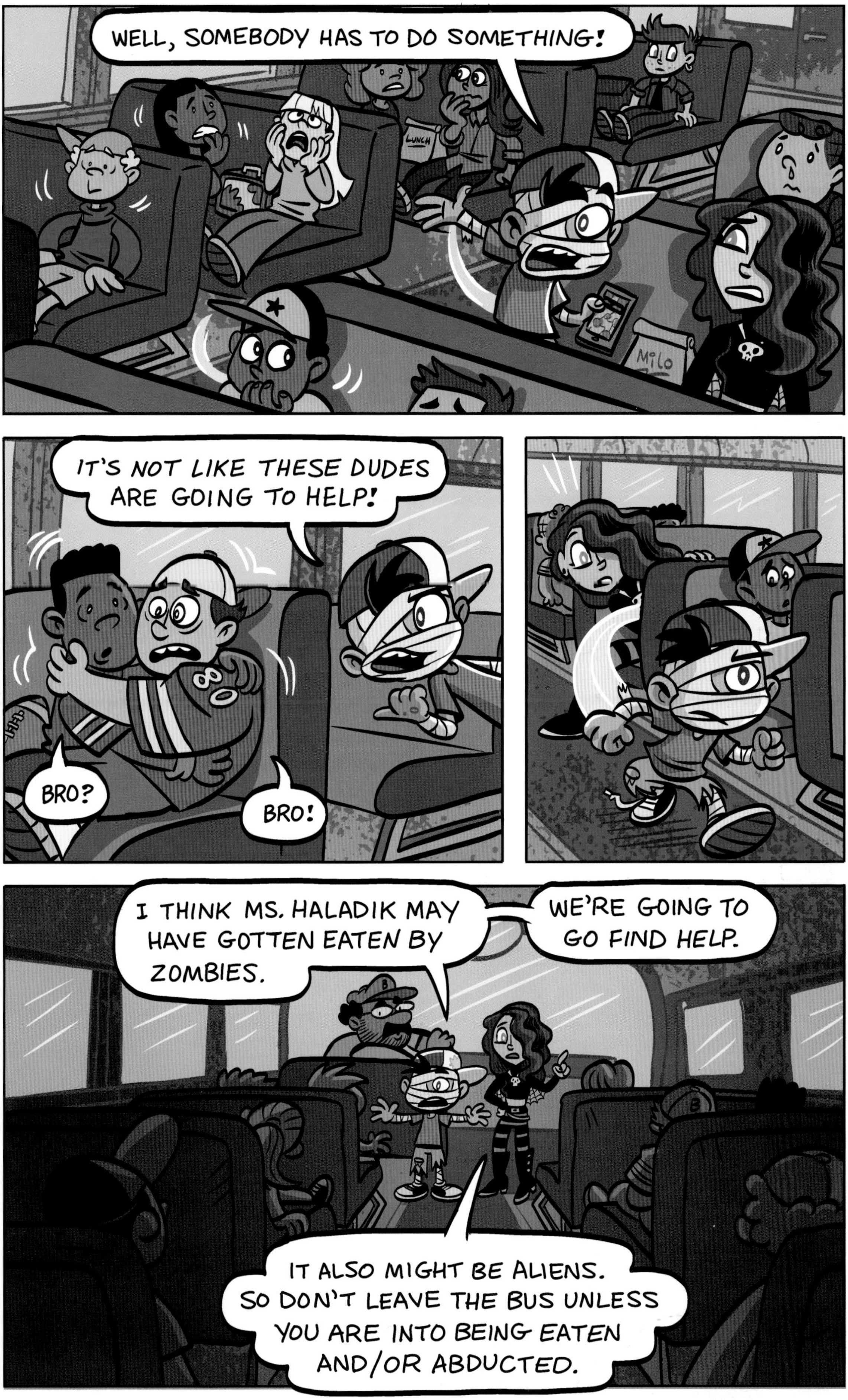
WELL, SOMEBODY HAS TO DO SOMETHING!
LUNCH
MILO
IT'S NOT LIKE THESE DUDES ARE GOING TO HELP!
BRO?
BRO!
I THINK MS. HALADIK MAY HAVE GOTTEN EATEN BY ZOMBIES.
WE'RE GOING TO GO FIND HELP.
IT ALSO MIGHT BE ALIENS. SO DON'T LEAVE THE BUS UNLESS YOU ARE INTO BEING EATEN AND/OR ABDUCTED.

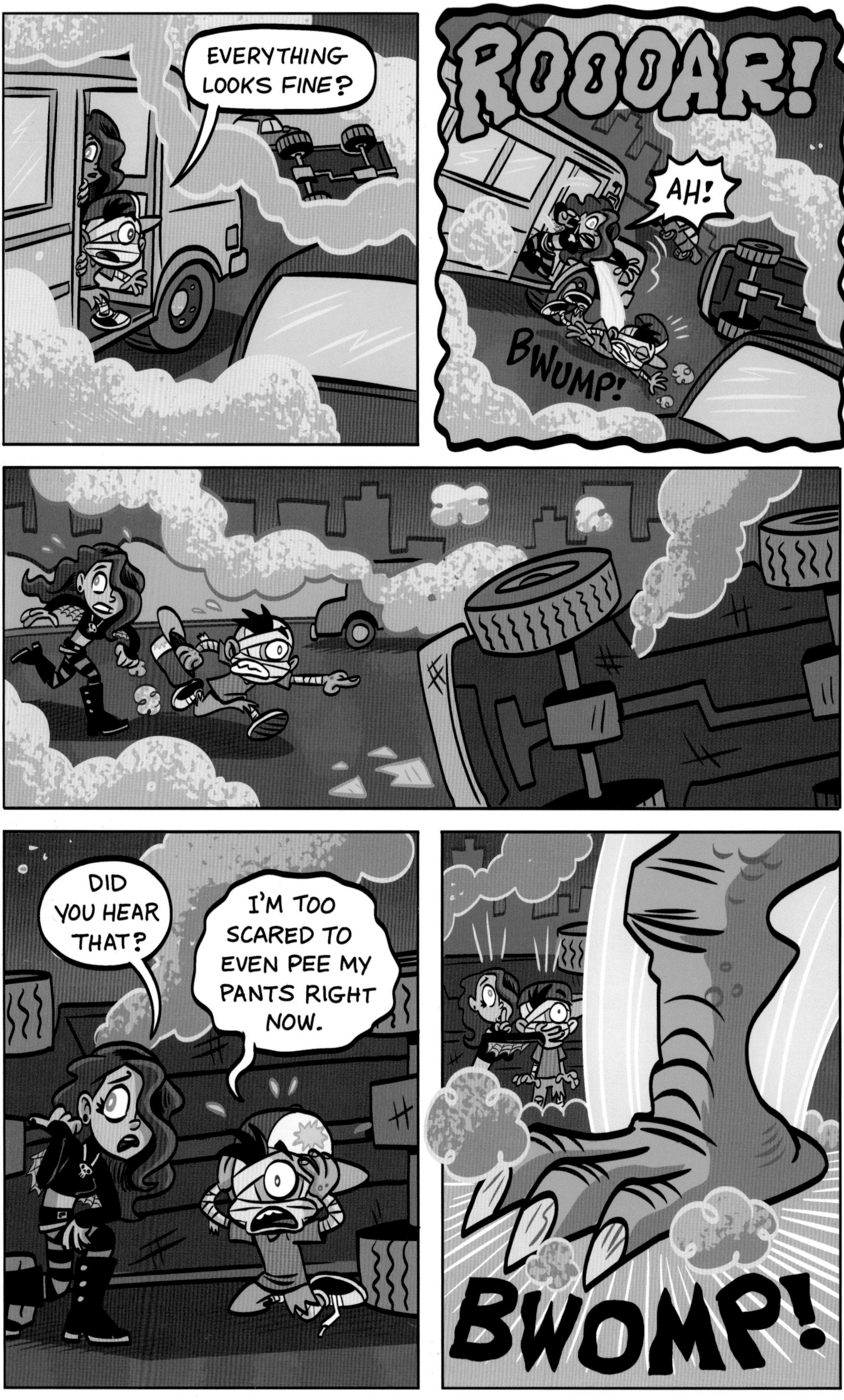
EVERYTHING LOOKS FINE?
ROOOAR!
AH!
BWUMP!
DID YOU HEAR THAT?
I'M TOO SCARED TO EVEN PEE MY PANTS RIGHT NOW.
BWOMP!

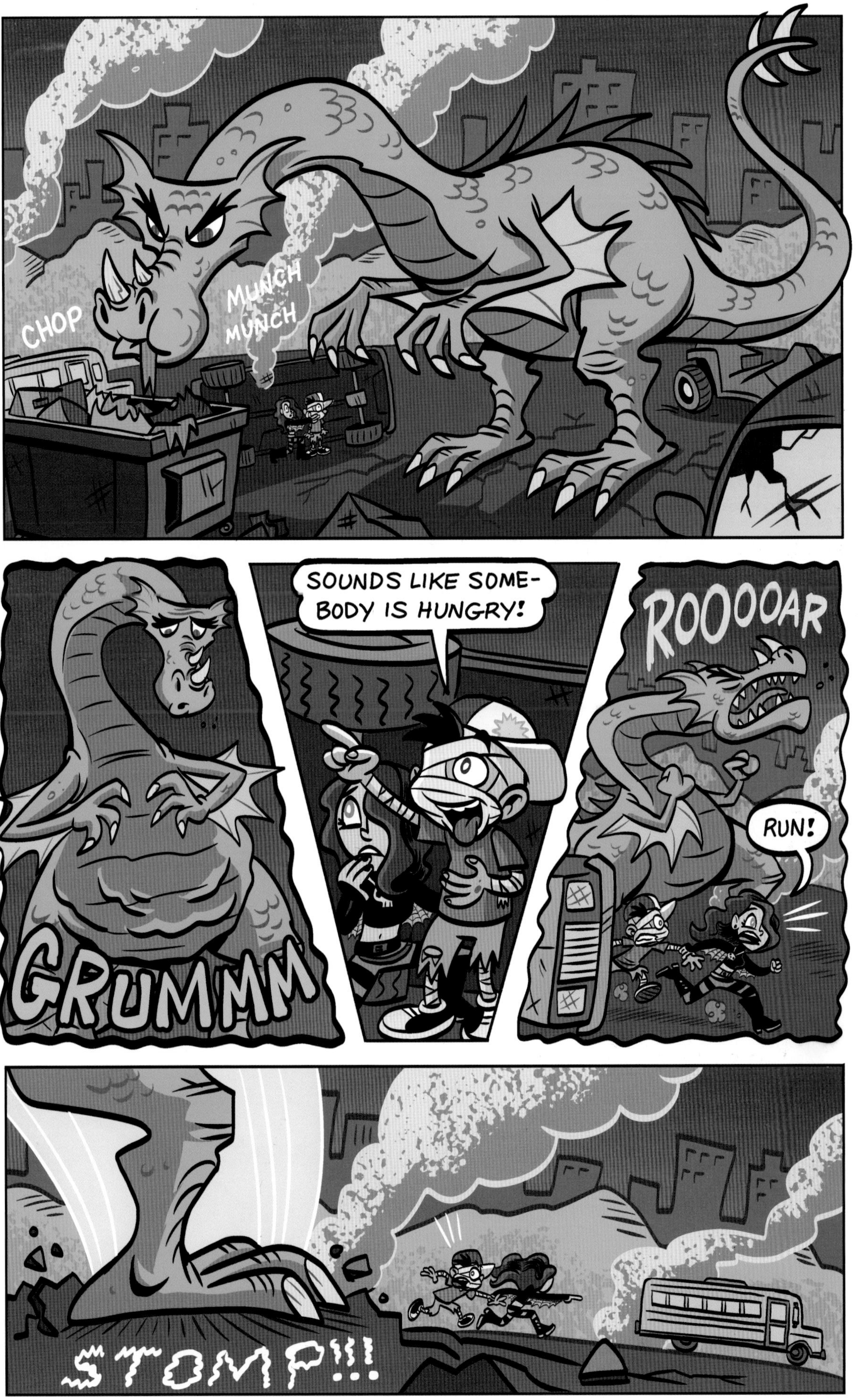
CHOP
MUNCH
MUNCH
GRUMMM
SOUNDS LIKE SOME-BODY IS HUNGRY!
ROOOOAR
RUN!
STOMP!!!

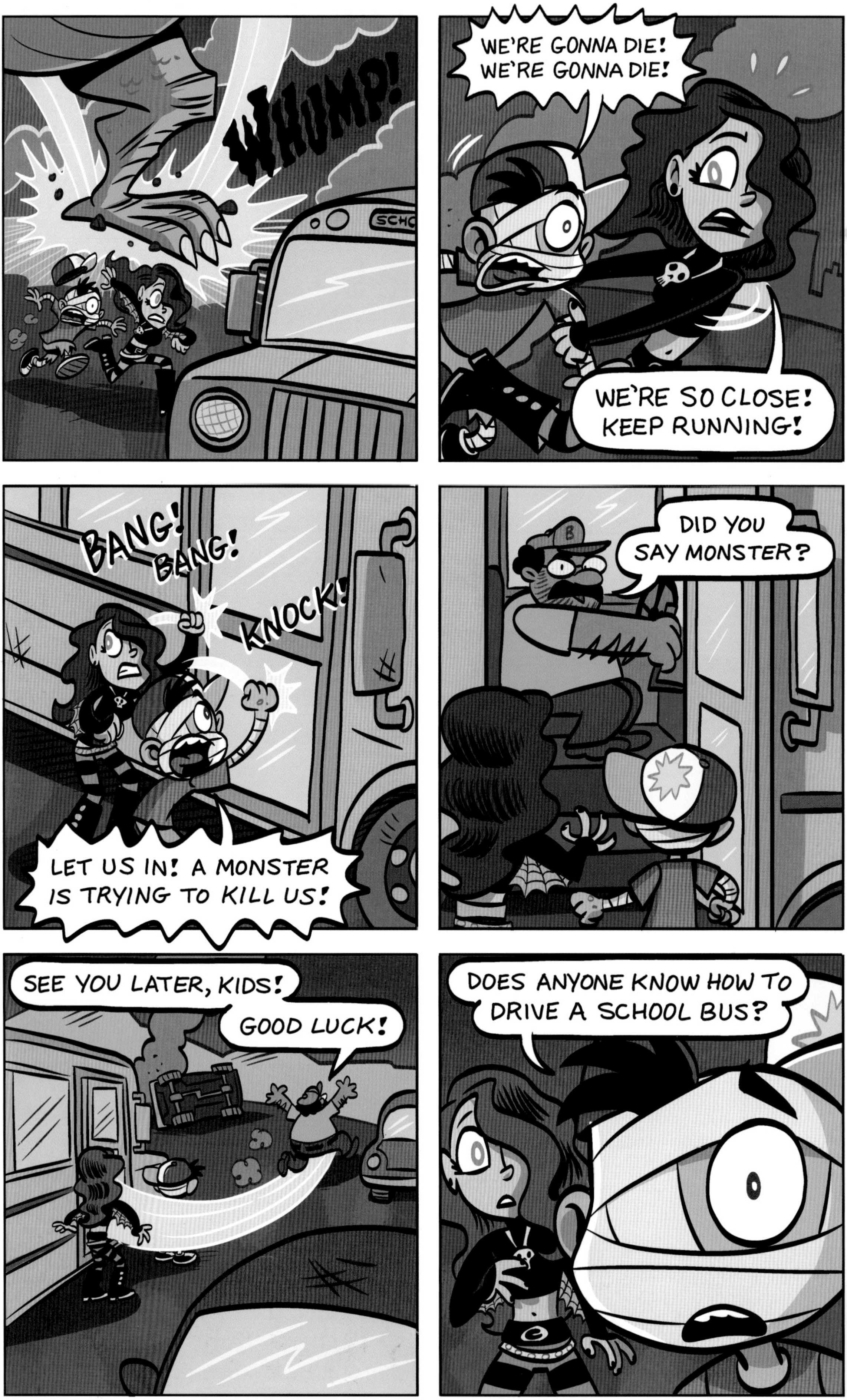
WHUMP!
WE'RE GONNA DIE! WE'RE GONNA DIE!
WE'RE SO CLOSE! KEEP RUNNING!
BANG! BANG!
KNOCK!
LET US IN! A MONSTER IS TRYING TO KILL US!
DID YOU SAY MONSTER?
SEE YOU LATER, KIDS!
GOOD LUCK!
DOES ANYONE KNOW HOW TO DRIVE A SCHOOL BUS?

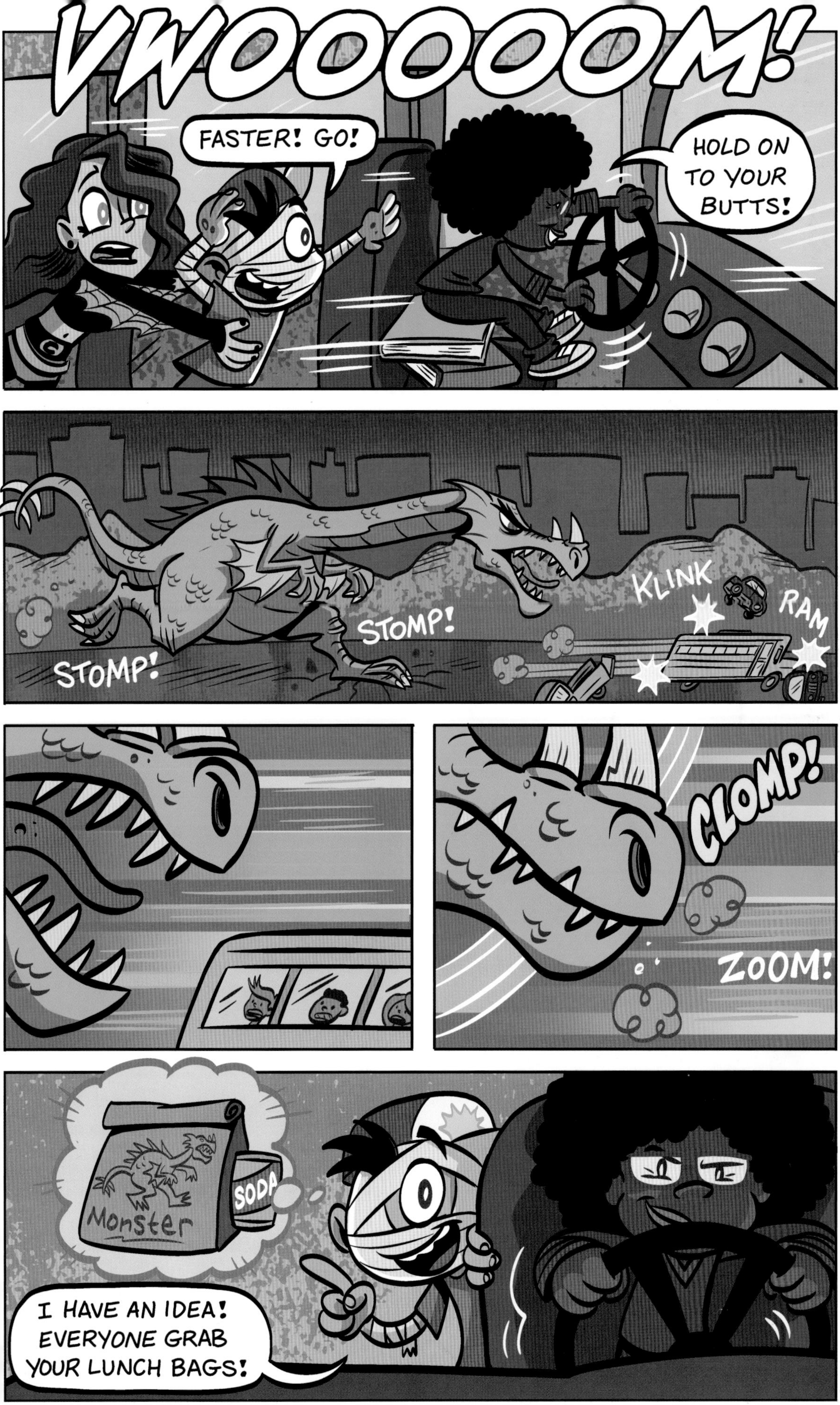
VWOOOOOM!
FASTER! GO!
HOLD ON TO YOUR BUTTS!
STOMP!
STOMP!
KLINK
RAM
CLOMP!
ZOOM!
Monster
SODA
I HAVE AN IDEA! EVERYONE GRAB YOUR LUNCH BAGS!

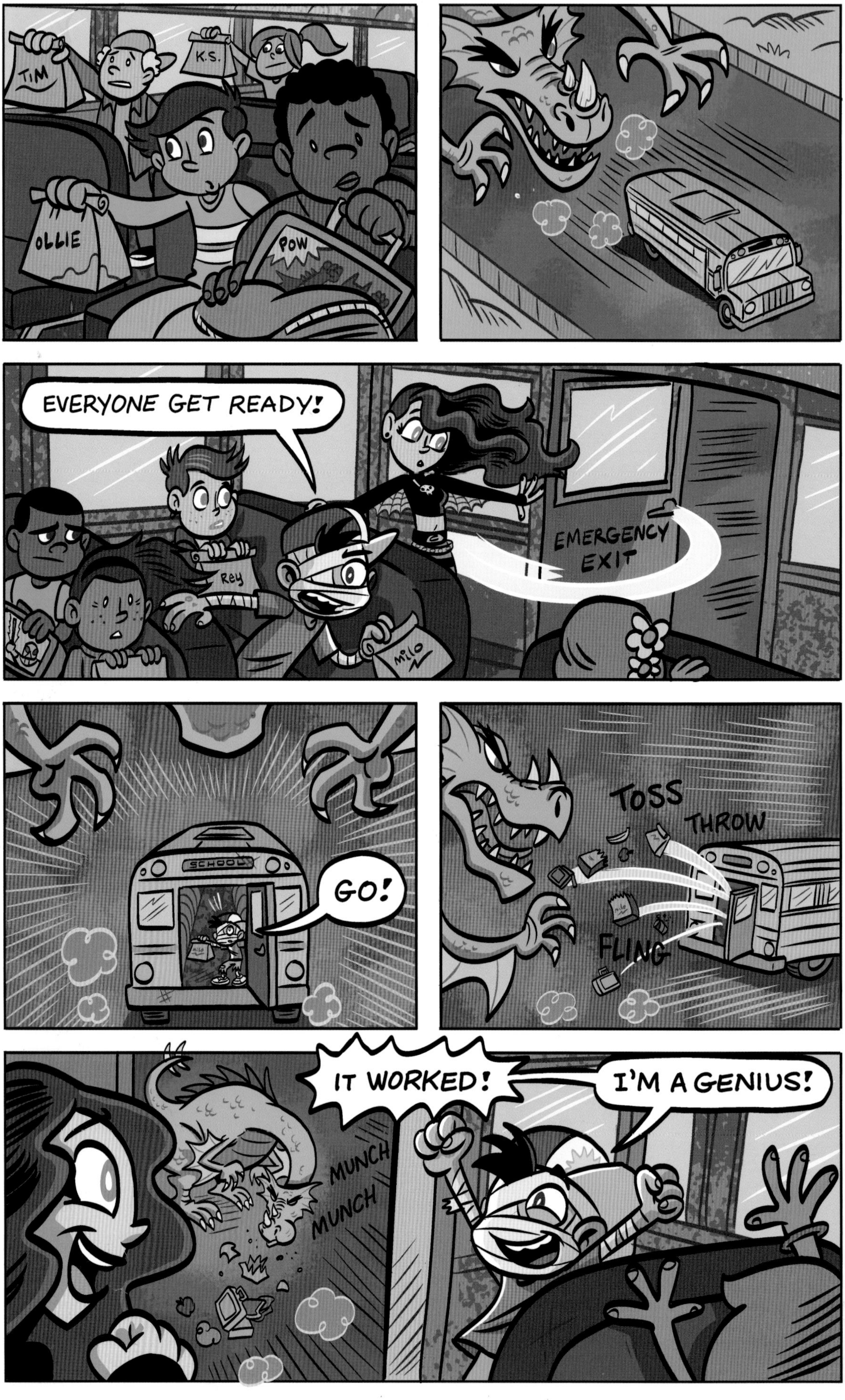
TIM
K.S.
OLLIE
POW
EVERYONE GET READY!
Rey
EMERGENCY EXIT
MILO
SCHOOL
GO!
TOSS
THROW
FLING
IT WORKED!
I'M A GENIUS!
MUNCH
MUNCH

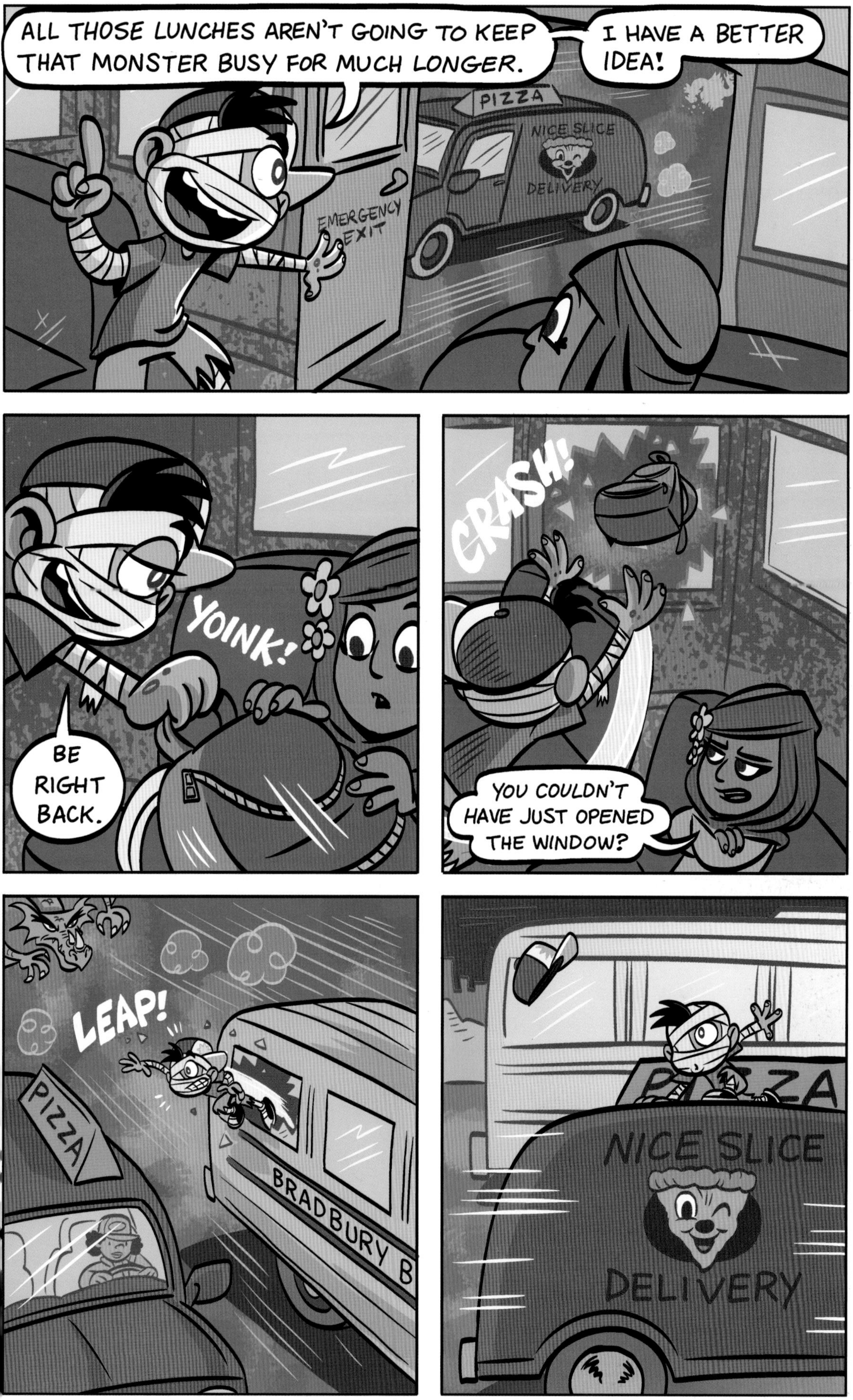
ALL THOSE LUNCHES AREN'T GOING TO KEEP THAT MONSTER BUSY FOR MUCH LONGER.
I HAVE A BETTER IDEA!
PIZZA
NICE SLICE
DELIVERY
EMERGENCY EXIT
YOINK!
BE RIGHT BACK.
CRASH!
YOU COULDN'T HAVE JUST OPENED THE WINDOW?
LEAP!
PIZZA
BRADBURY B
PIZZA
NICE SLICE
DELIVERY

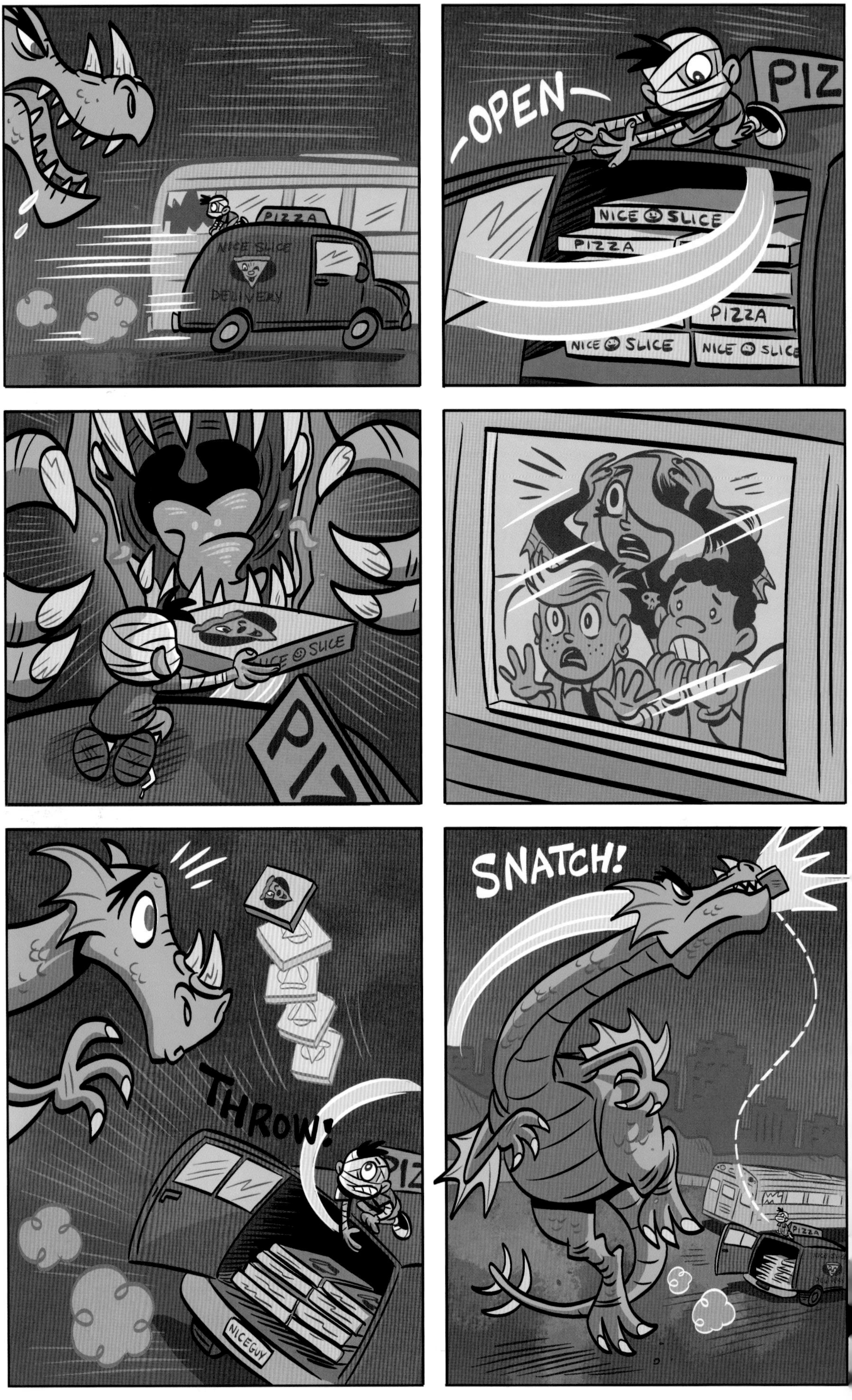
PIZZA
NICE SLICE
DELIVERY
OPEN
PIZ
NICE SLICE
PIZZA
PIZZA
NICE SLICE
NICE SLICE
NICE SLICE
PIZ
THROW!
PIZ
NICEGUY
SNATCH!
PIZZA

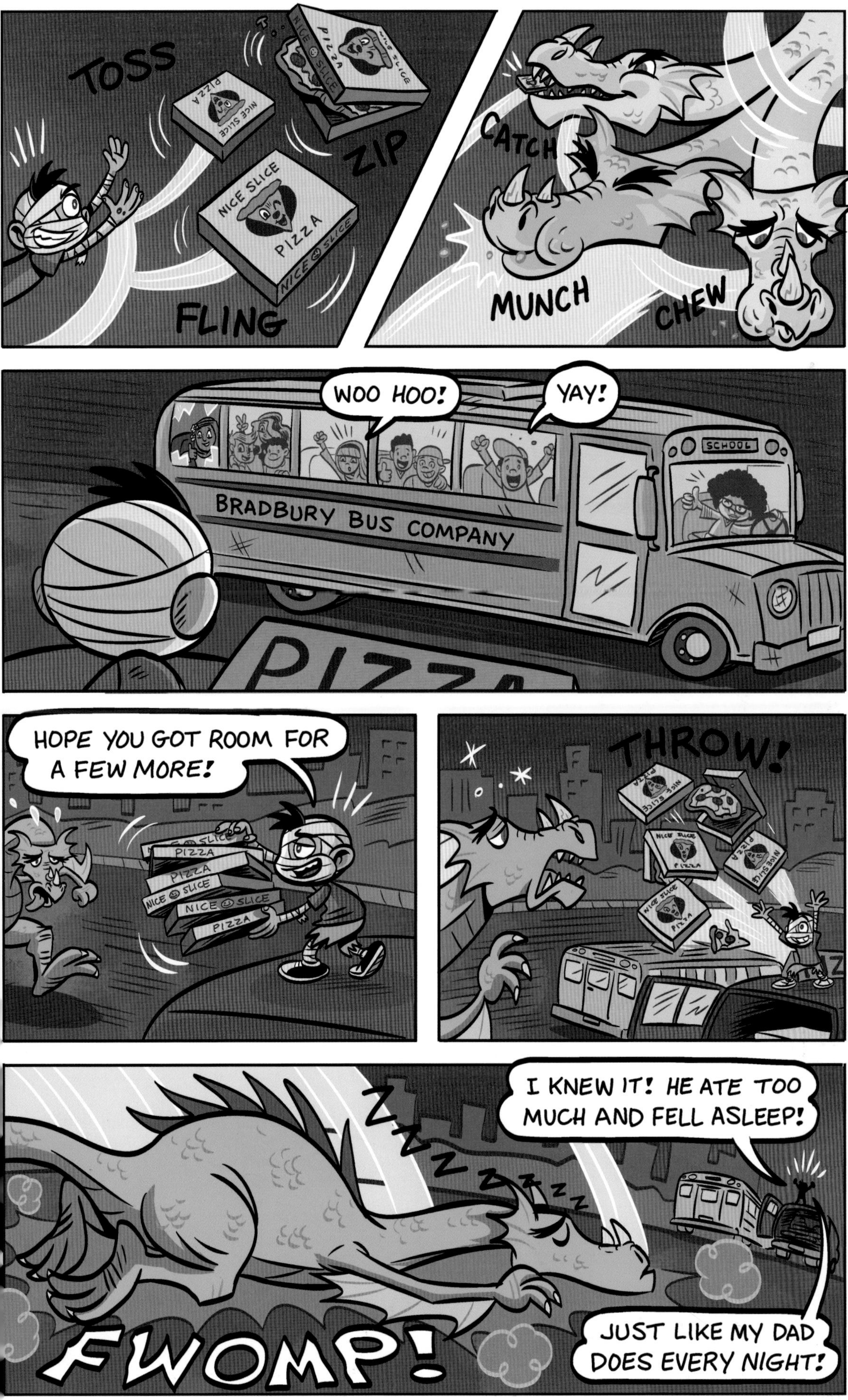
TOSS
ZIP
NICE SLICE PIZZA
FLING
CATCH
MUNCH
CHEW
WOO HOO!
YAY!
SCHOOL
BRADBURY BUS COMPANY
PIZZA
HOPE YOU GOT ROOM FOR A FEW MORE!
THROW!
ZZZZZZ
I KNEW IT! HE ATE TOO MUCH AND FELL ASLEEP!
JUST LIKE MY DAD DOES EVERY NIGHT!
FWOMP!

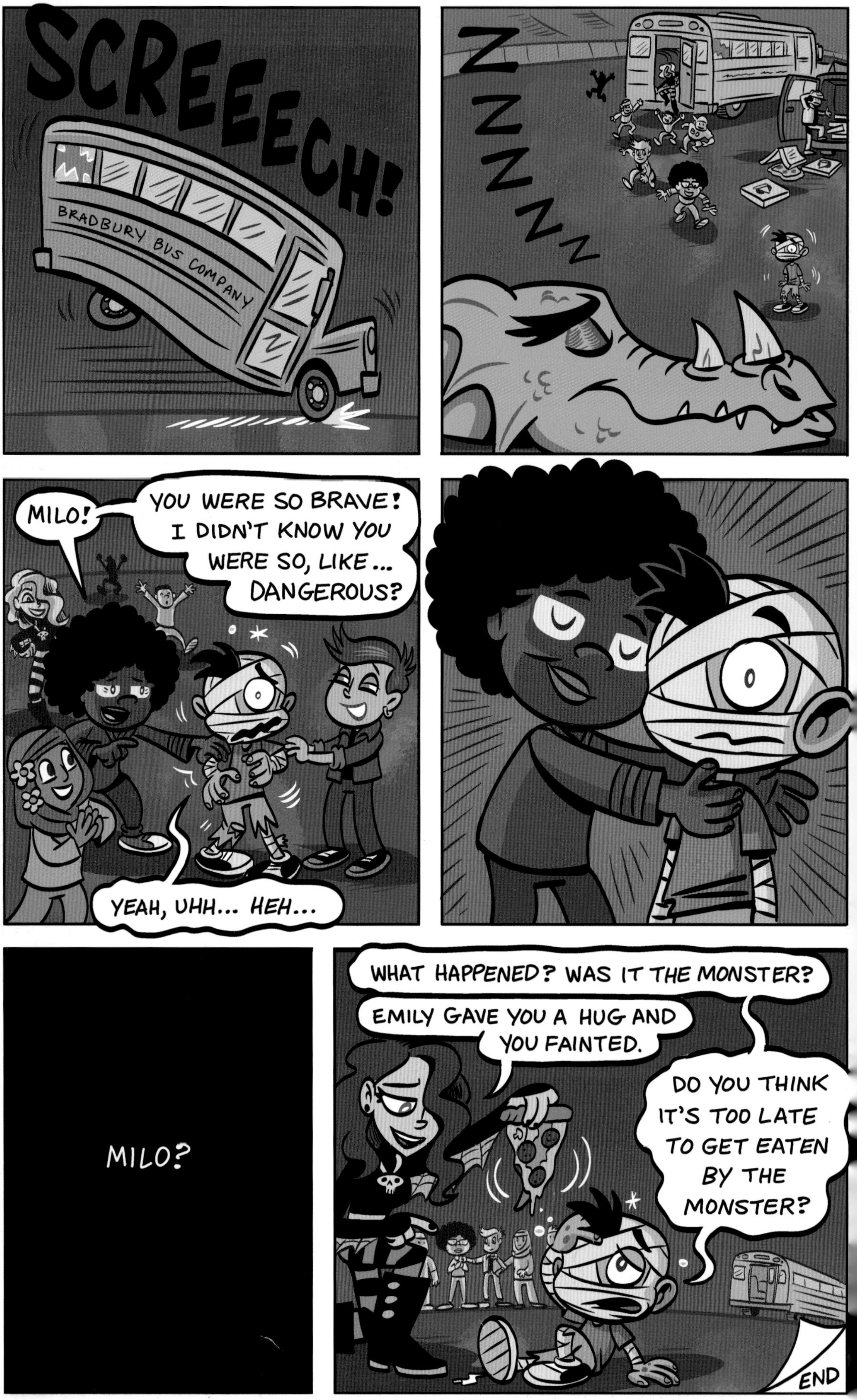
SCREEECH!
BRADBURY BUS COMPANY
ZZZZZ
MILO!
YOU WERE SO BRAVE! I DIDN'T KNOW YOU WERE SO, LIKE... DANGEROUS?
YEAH, UHH... HEH...
MILO?
WHAT HAPPENED? WAS IT THE MONSTER?
EMILY GAVE YOU A HUG AND YOU FAINTED.
DO YOU THINK IT'S TOO LATE TO GET EATEN BY THE MONSTER?
END

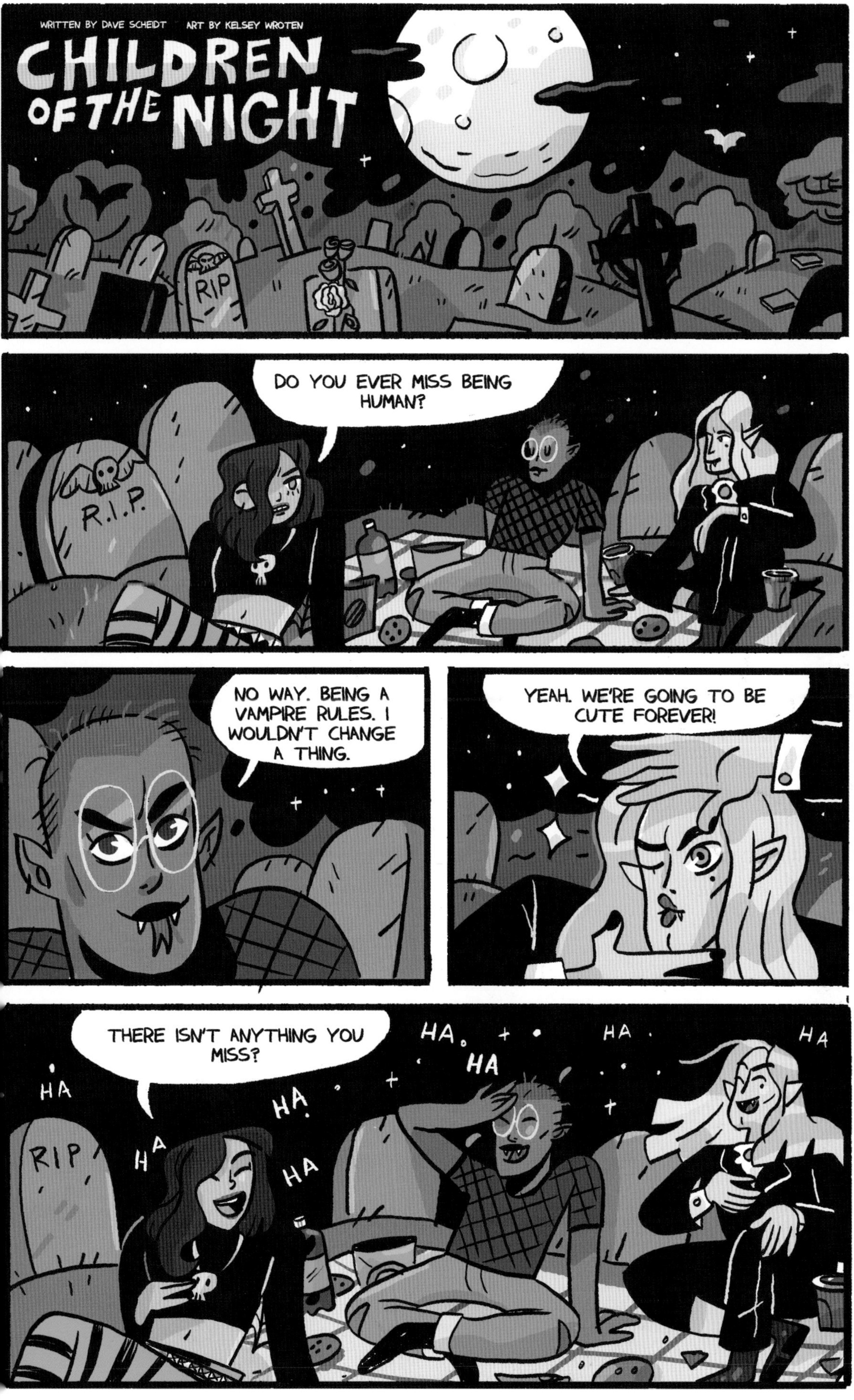
WRITTEN BY DAVE SCHEIDT
ART BY KELSEY WROTEN
CHILDREN OF THE NIGHT
RIP
R.I.P.
DO YOU EVER MISS BEING HUMAN?
NO WAY. BEING A VAMPIRE RULES. I WOULDN'T CHANGE A THING.
YEAH. WE'RE GOING TO BE CUTE FOREVER!
THERE ISN'T ANYTHING YOU MISS?
HA HA HA HA HA HA HA HA HA
RIP

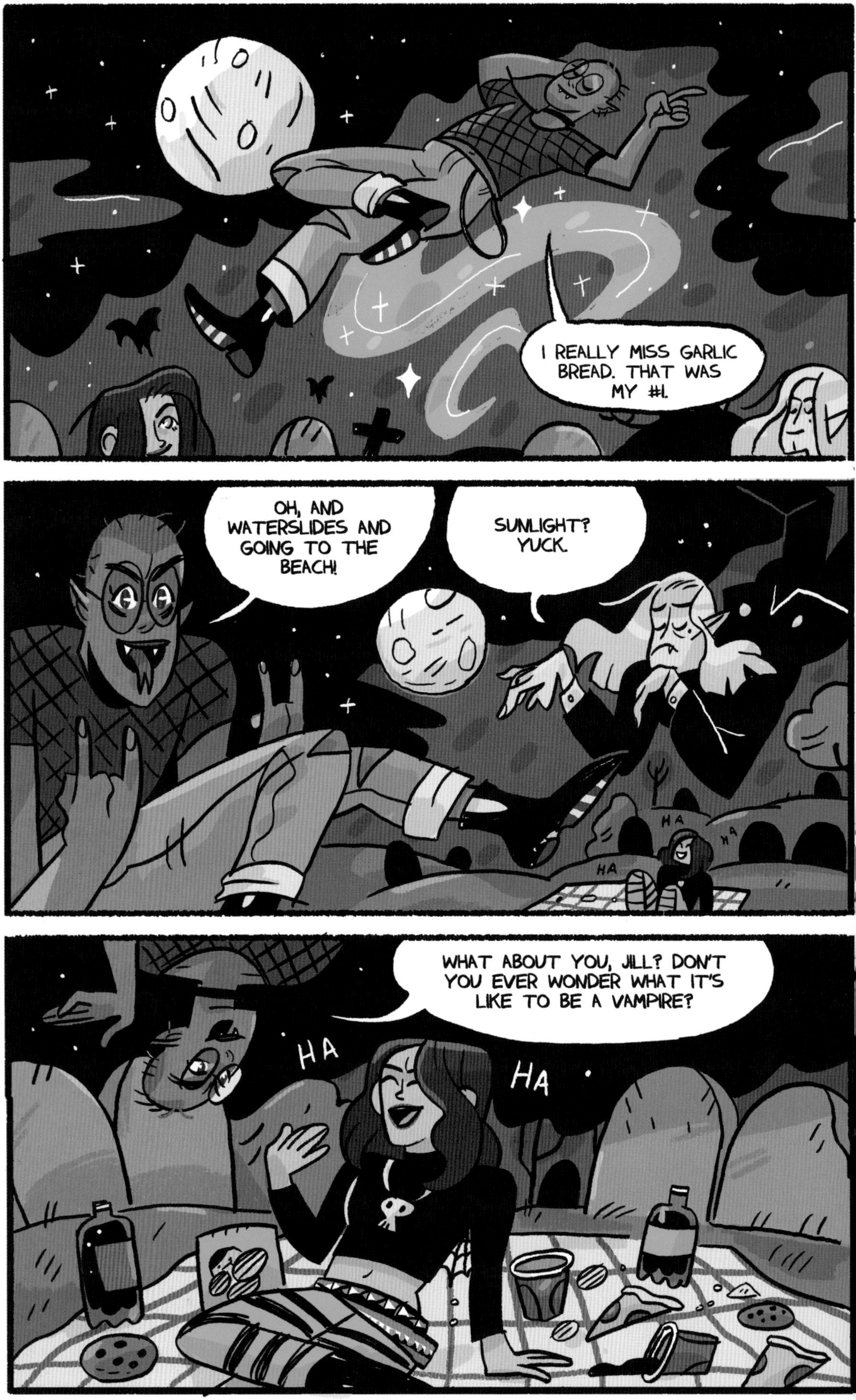
I REALLY MISS GARLIC BREAD. THAT WAS MY #1.
OH, AND WATERSLIDES AND GOING TO THE BEACH!
SUNLIGHT? YUCK.
HA
HA
HA
WHAT ABOUT YOU, JILL? DON'T YOU EVER WONDER WHAT IT'S LIKE TO BE A VAMPIRE?
HA
HA

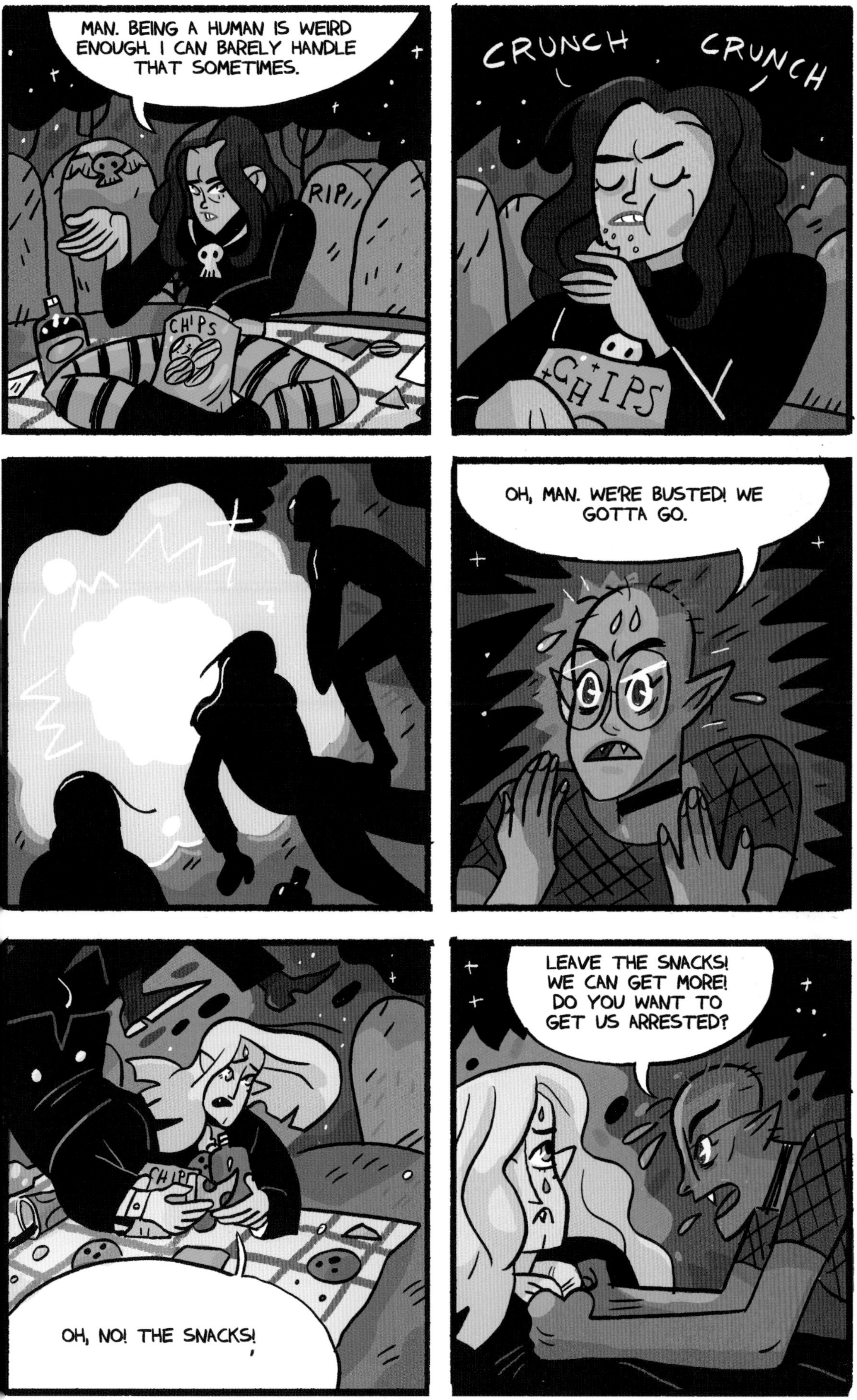
MAN. BEING A HUMAN IS WEIRD ENOUGH. I CAN BARELY HANDLE THAT SOMETIMES.
RIP
CHIPS
CRUNCH CRUNCH
CHIPS
OH, MAN. WE'RE BUSTED! WE GOTTA GO.
OH, NO! THE SNACKS!
LEAVE THE SNACKS! WE CAN GET MORE! DO YOU WANT TO GET US ARRESTED?

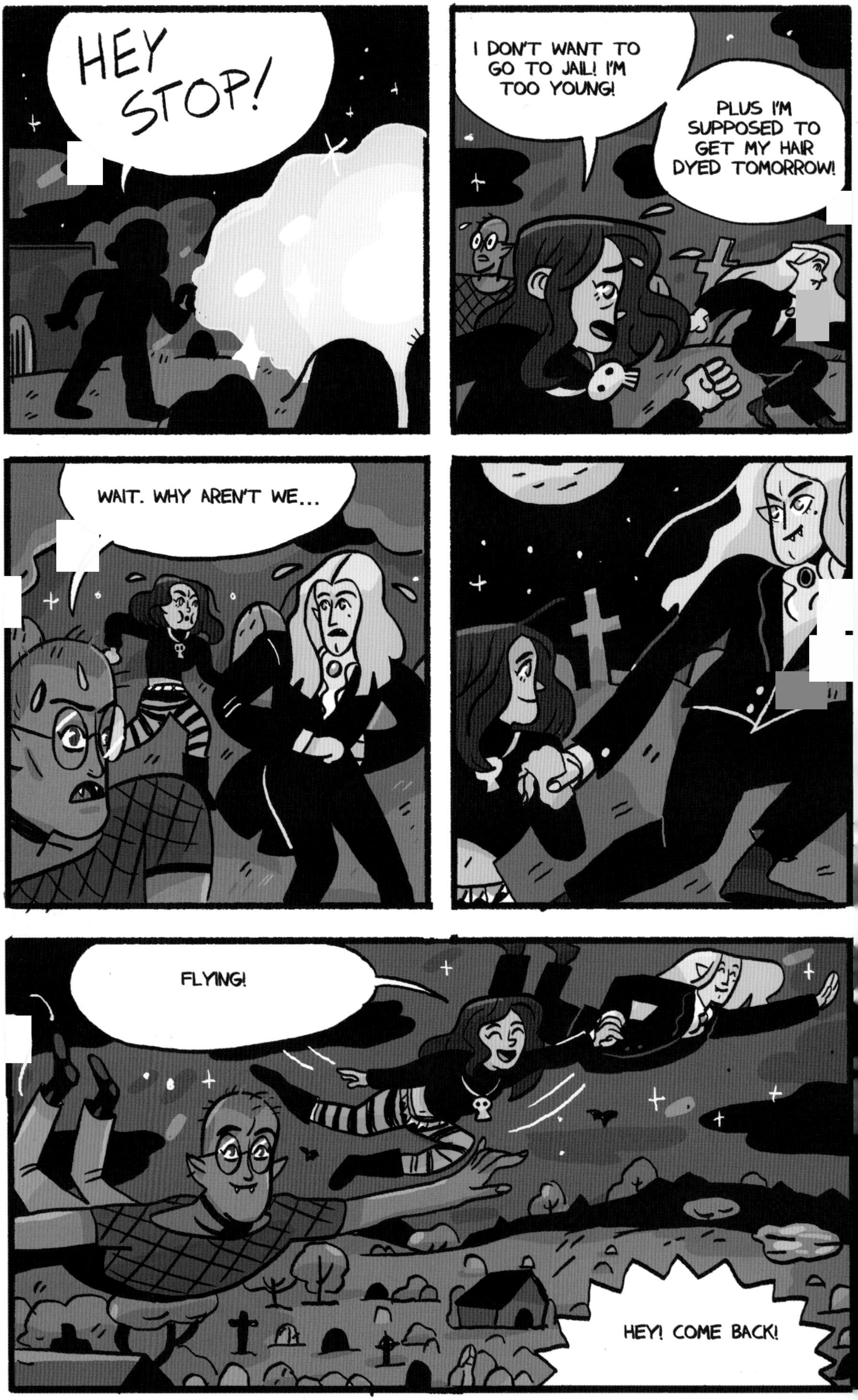
HEY STOP!
I DON'T WANT TO GO TO JAIL! I'M TOO YOUNG!
PLUS I'M SUPPOSED TO GET MY HAIR DYED TOMORROW!
WAIT. WHY AREN'T WE...
FLYING!
HEY! COME BACK!

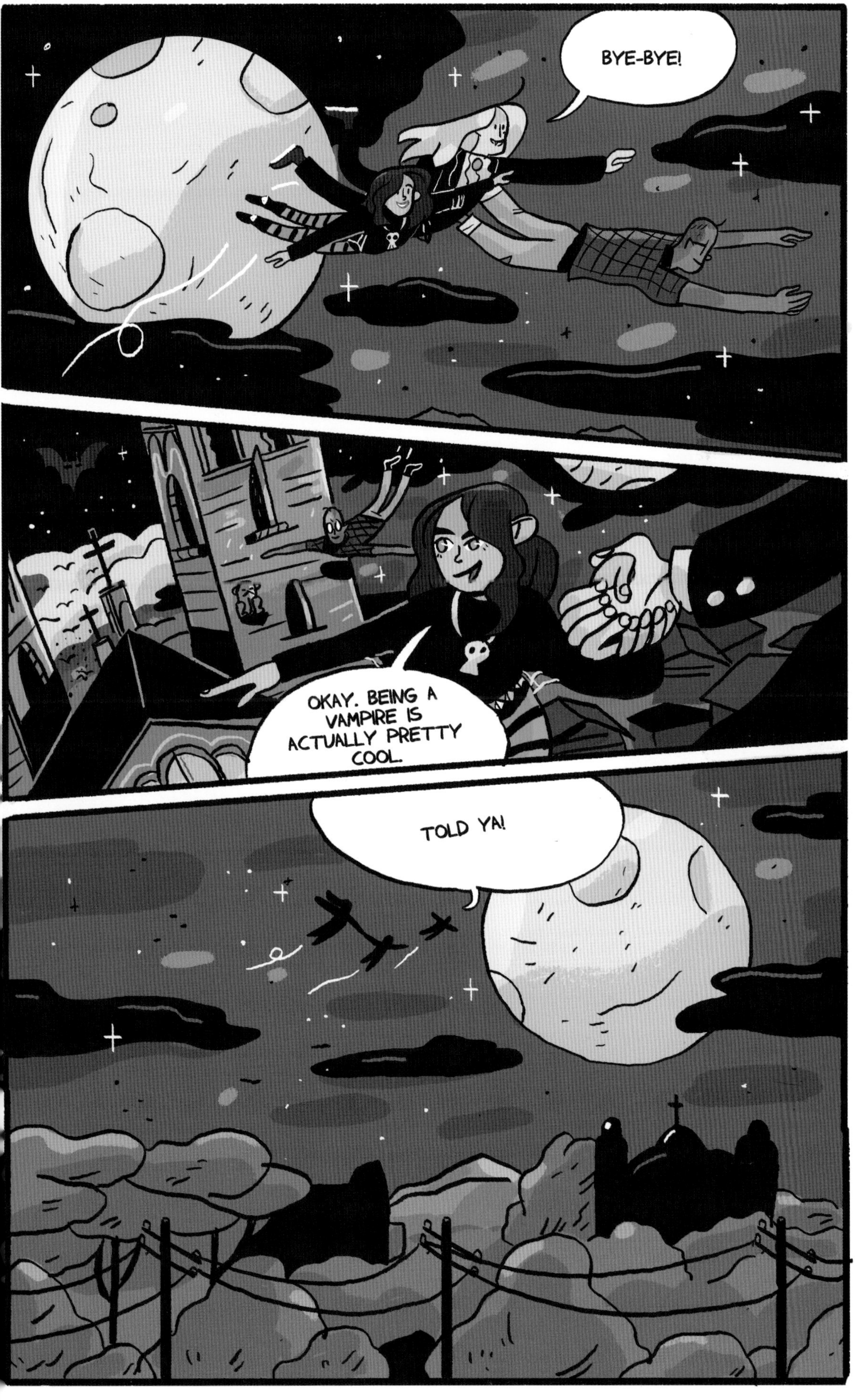
BYE-BYE!
OKAY. BEING A VAMPIRE IS ACTUALLY PRETTY COOL.
TOLD YA!

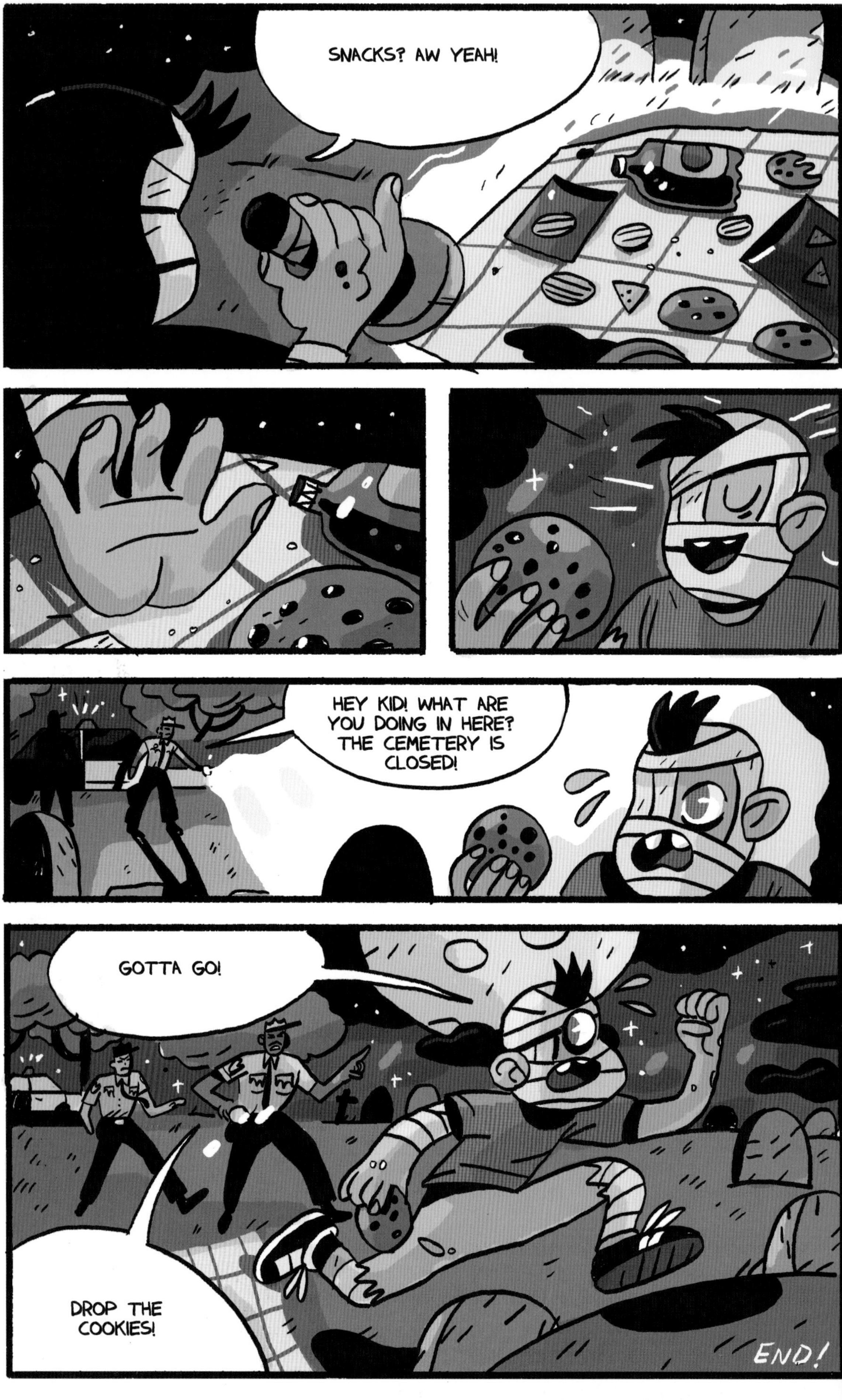
SNACKS? AW YEAH!
HEY KID! WHAT ARE YOU DOING IN HERE? THE CEMETERY IS CLOSED!
GOTTA GO!
DROP THE COOKIES!
END!

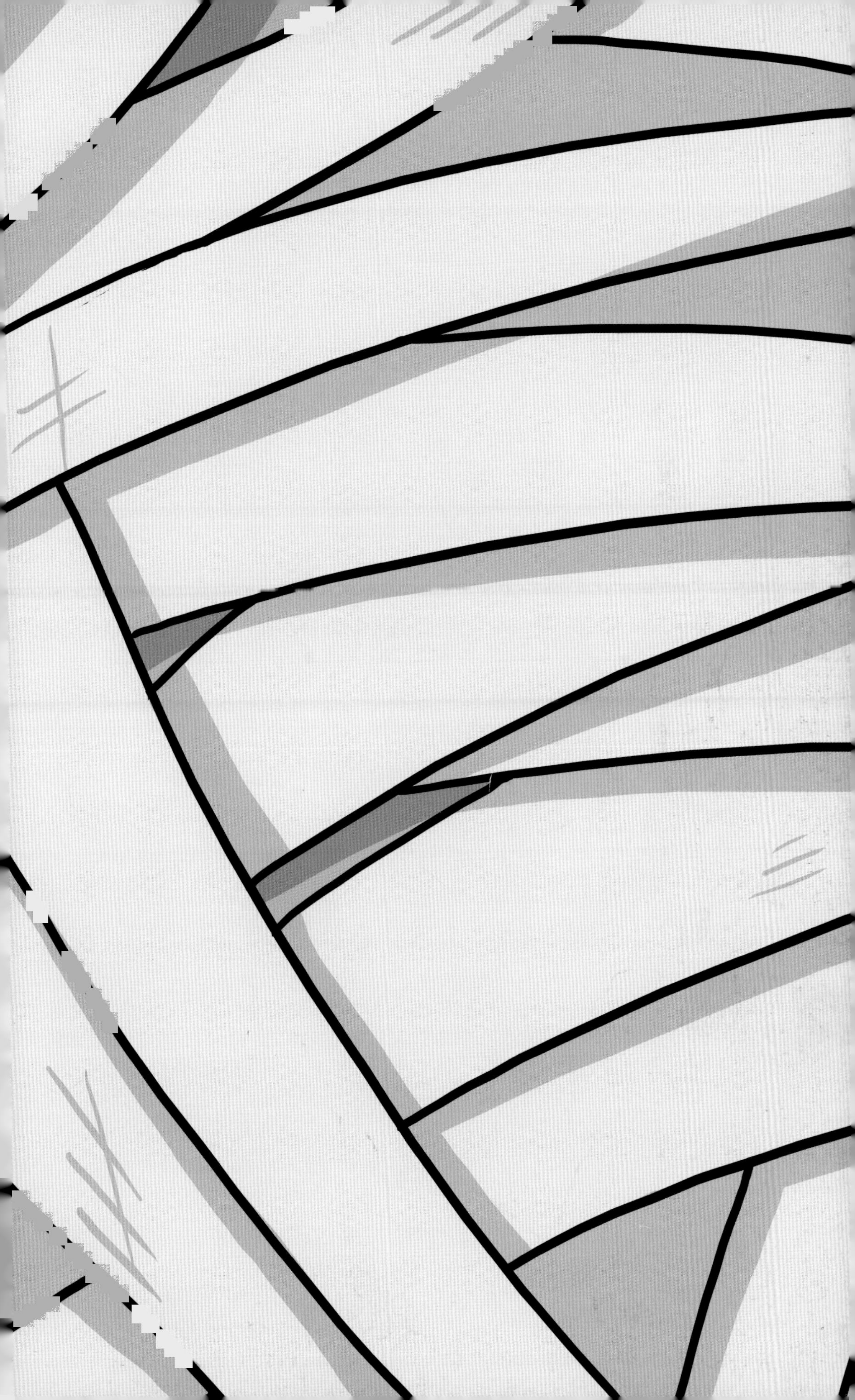

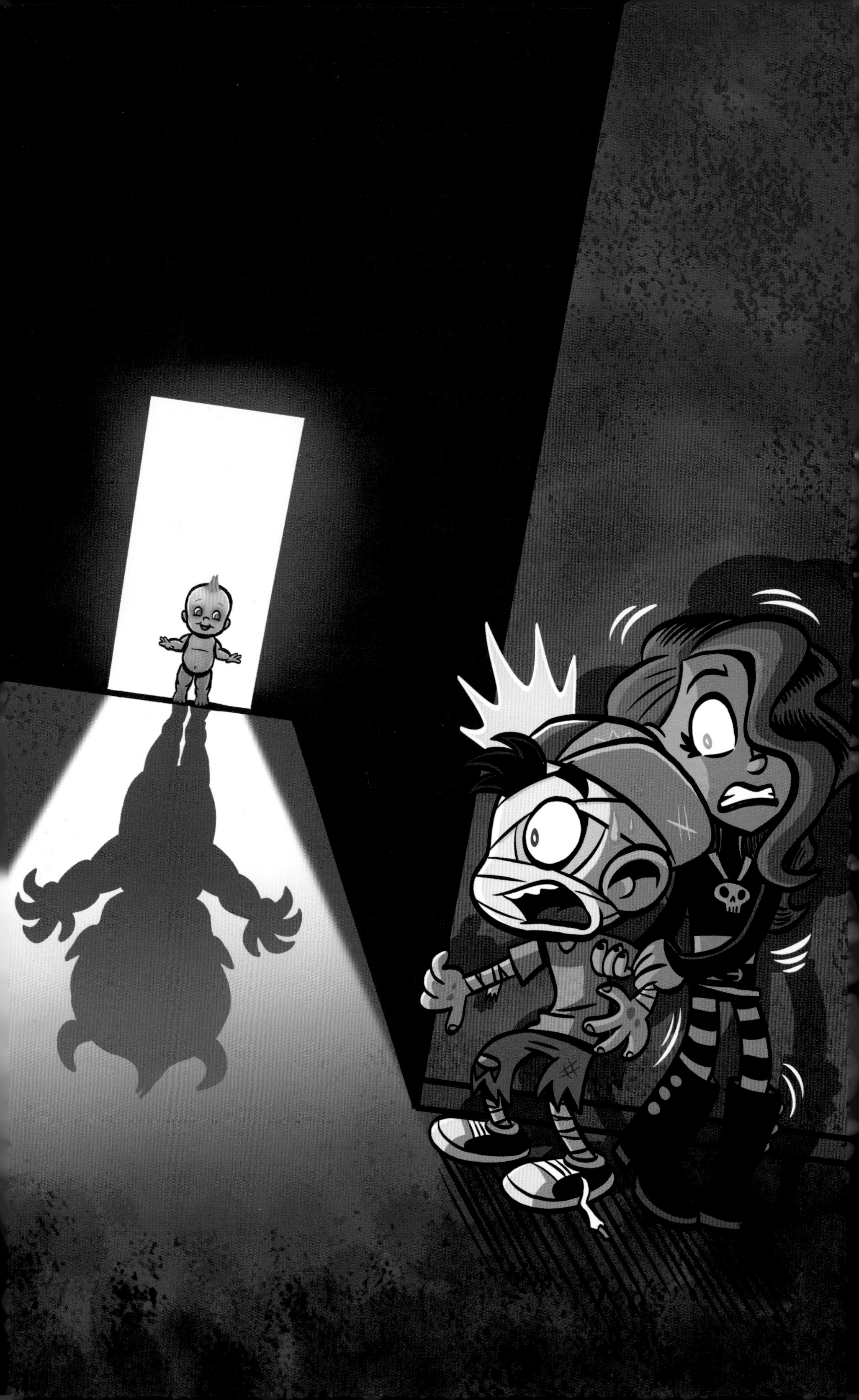

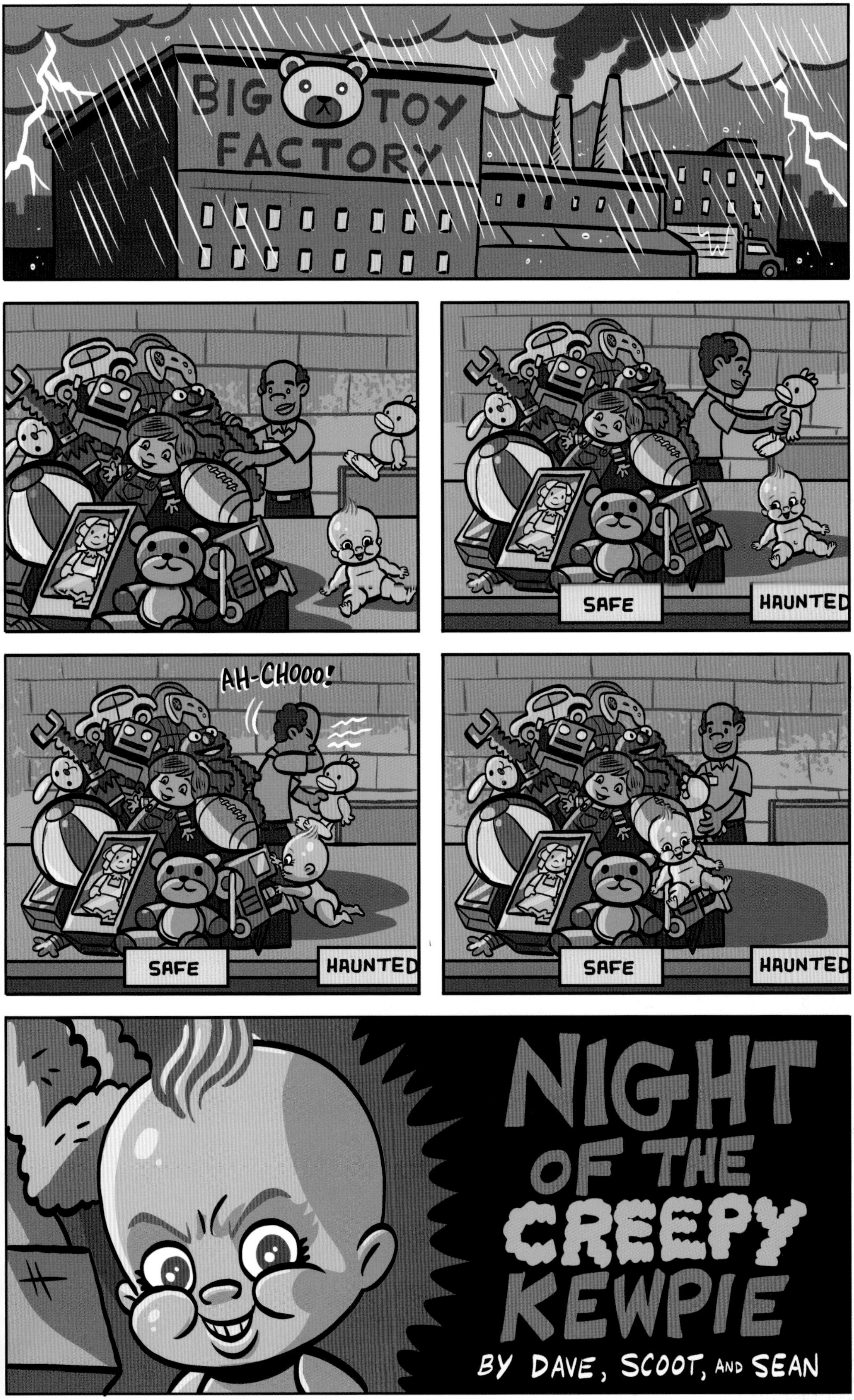
BIG TOY FACTORY
SAFE
HAUNTED
AH-CHOOO!
SAFE
HAUNTED
SAFE
HAUNTED
NIGHT OF THE CREEPY KEWPIE
BY DAVE, SCOOT, AND SEAN

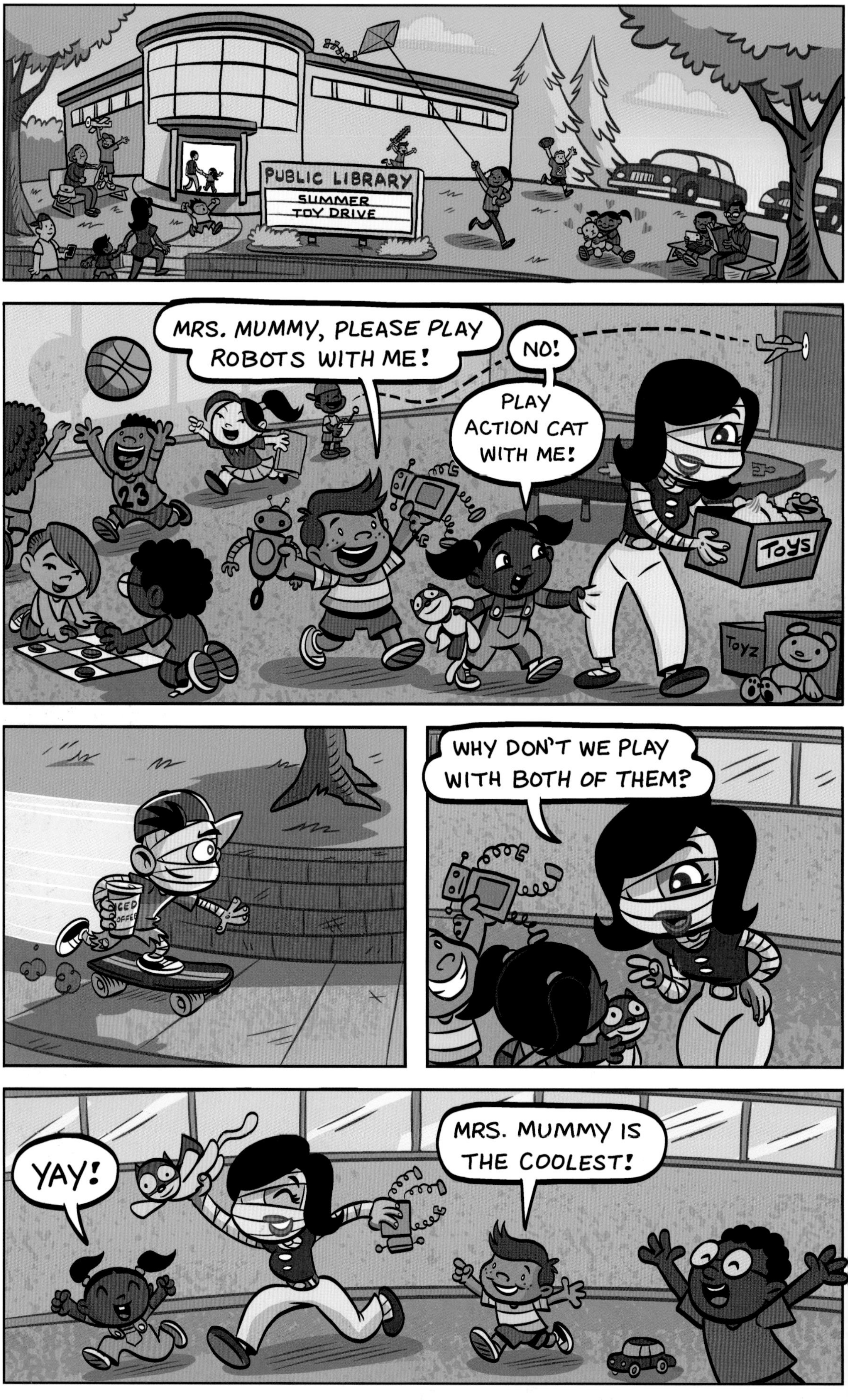
PUBLIC LIBRARY
SUMMER
TOY DRIVE
MRS. MUMMY, PLEASE PLAY ROBOTS WITH ME!
NO!
PLAY ACTION CAT WITH ME!
TOYS
TOYZ
ICED COFFEE
WHY DON'T WE PLAY WITH BOTH OF THEM?
YAY!
MRS. MUMMY IS THE COOLEST!

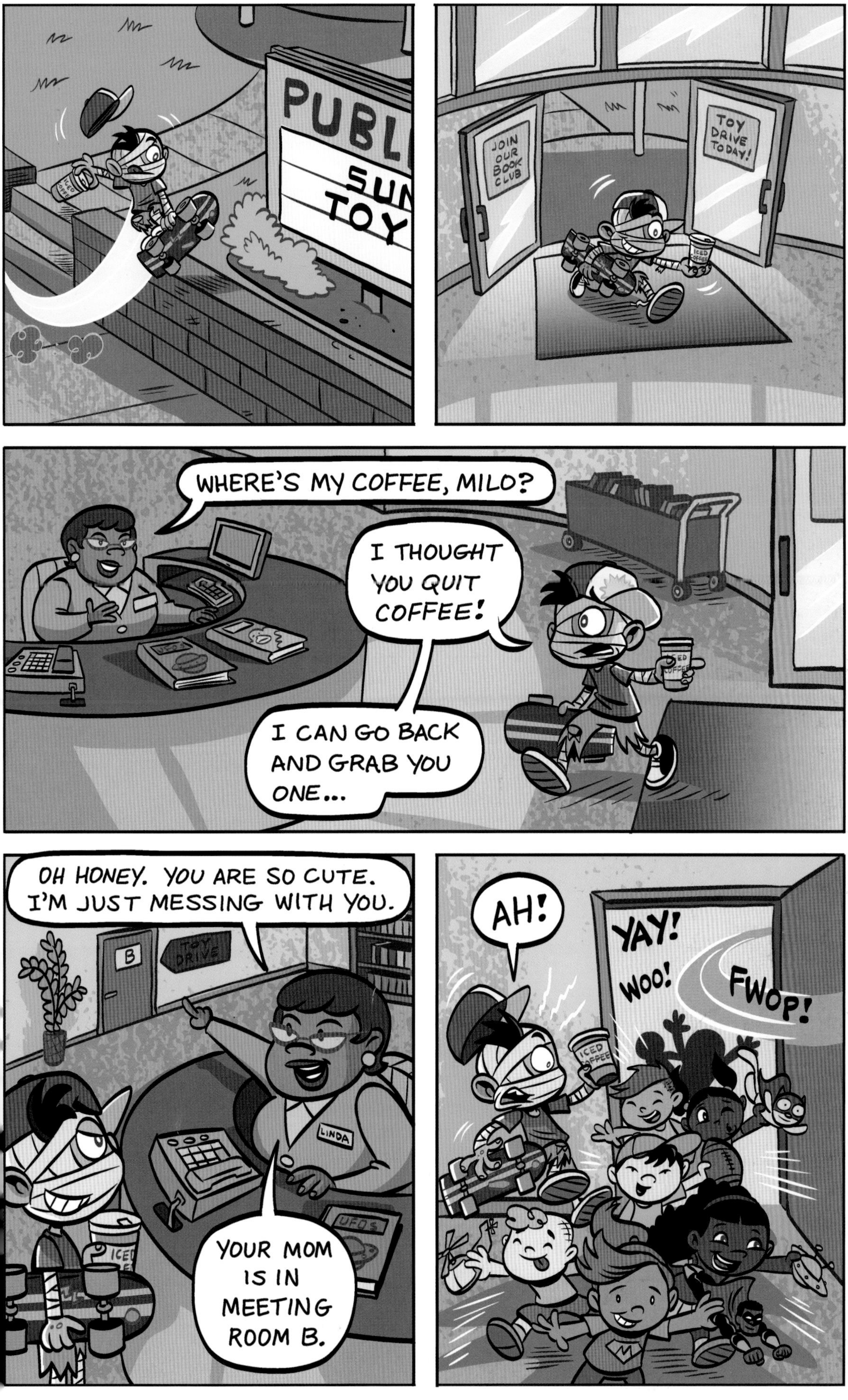
PUBL
SUN
TOY
ICED COFFEE
JOIN OUR BOOK CLUB
TOY DRIVE TODAY!
ICED COFFEE
WHERE'S MY COFFEE, MILO?
I THOUGHT YOU QUIT COFFEE!
I CAN GO BACK AND GRAB YOU ONE...
UFOS
ICED COFFEE
OH HONEY. YOU ARE SO CUTE. I'M JUST MESSING WITH YOU.
B
TOY DRIVE
LINDA
UFOs
YOUR MOM IS IN MEETING ROOM B.
AH!
ICED COFFEE
YAY!
WOO!
FWOP!

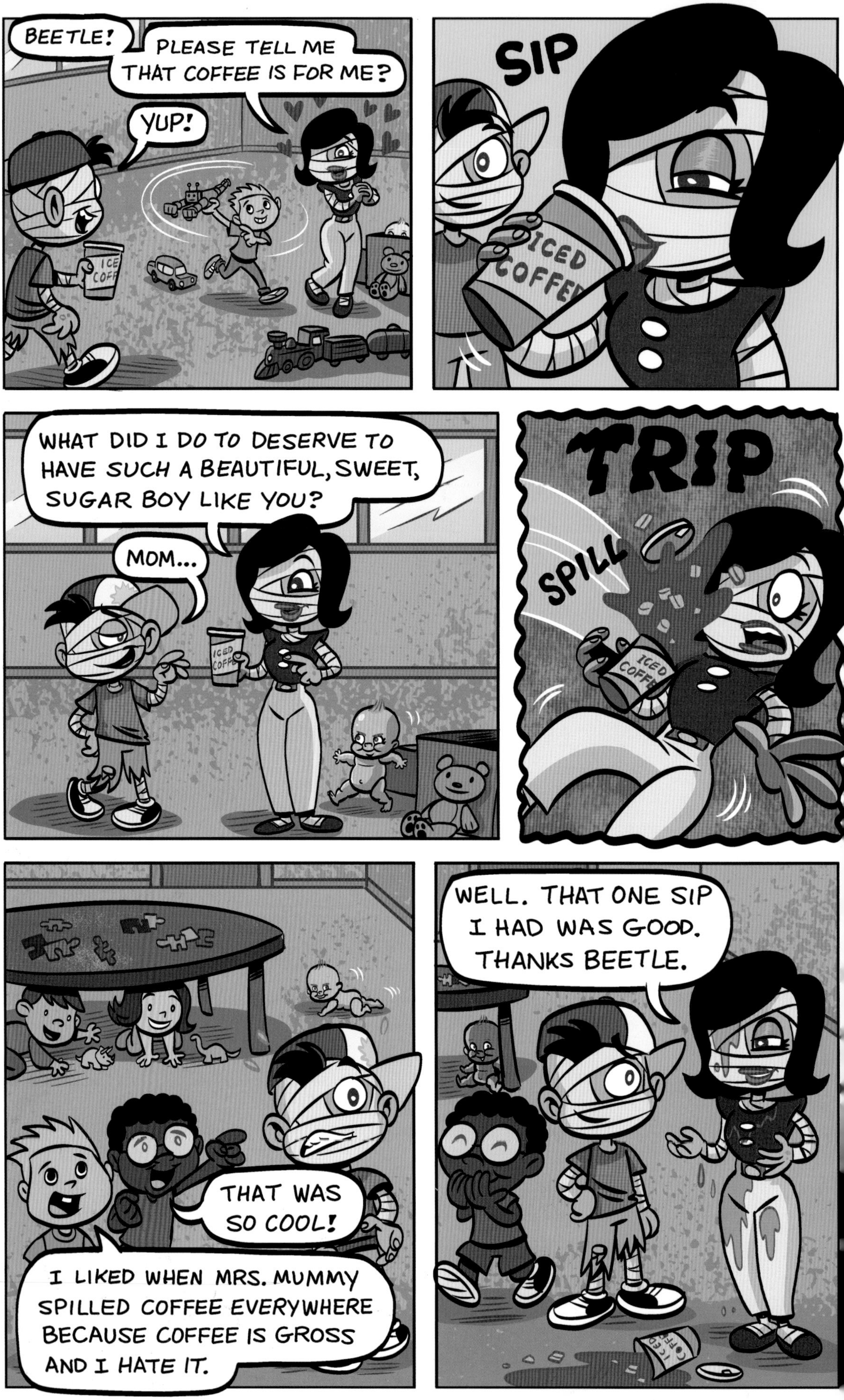
BEETLE!
PLEASE TELL ME THAT COFFEE IS FOR ME?
YUP!
ICED COFF
SIP
ICED COFFE
WHAT DID I DO TO DESERVE TO HAVE SUCH A BEAUTIFUL, SWEET, SUGAR BOY LIKE YOU?
MOM...
ICED COFF
TRIP
SPILL
ICED COFFE
THAT WAS SO COOL!
I LIKED WHEN MRS. MUMMY SPILLED COFFEE EVERYWHERE BECAUSE COFFEE IS GROSS AND I HATE IT.
WELL. THAT ONE SIP I HAD WAS GOOD. THANKS BEETLE.

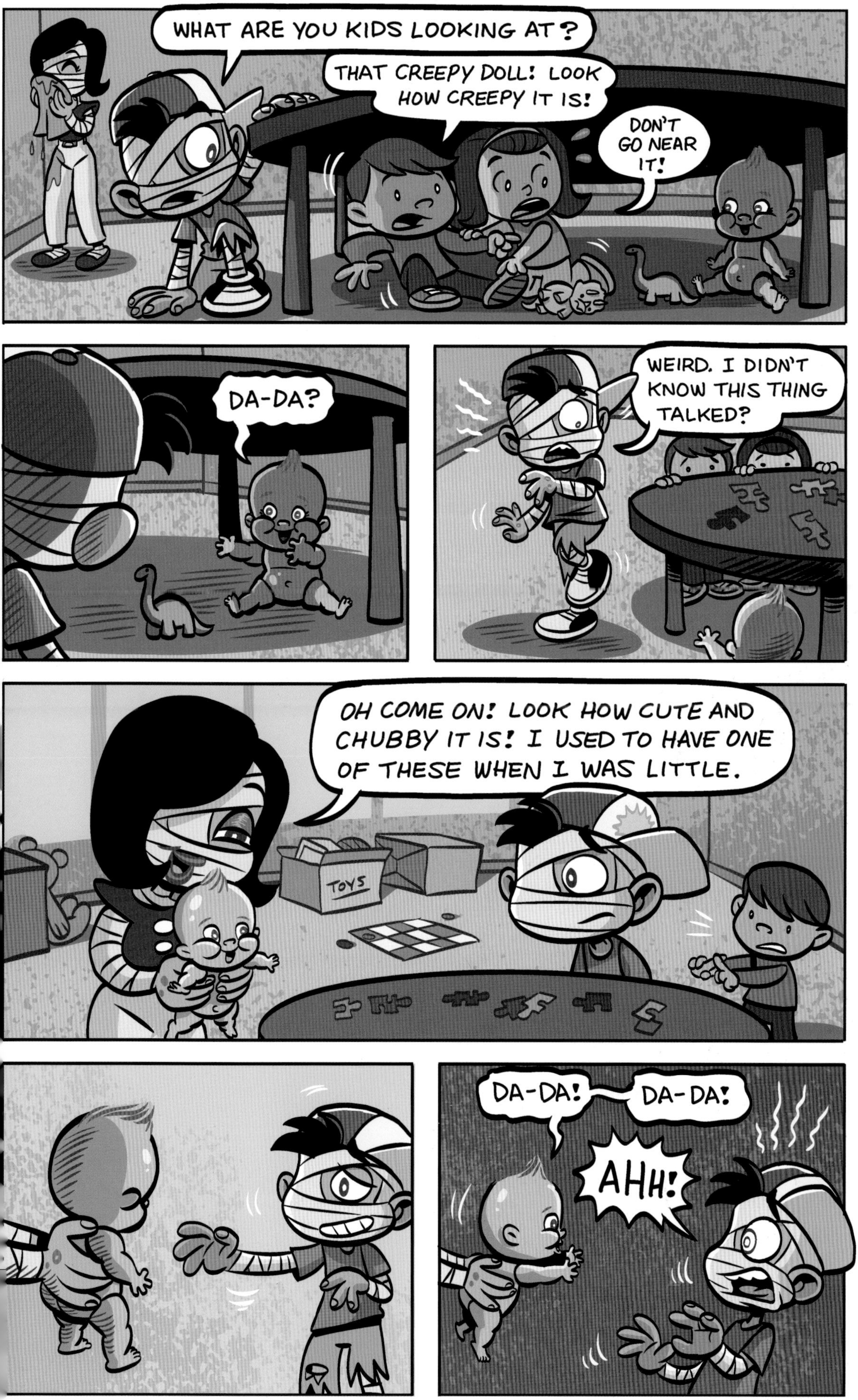
WHAT ARE YOU KIDS LOOKING AT?
THAT CREEPY DOLL! LOOK HOW CREEPY IT IS!
DON'T GO NEAR IT!
DA-DA?
WEIRD. I DIDN'T KNOW THIS THING TALKED?
OH COME ON! LOOK HOW CUTE AND CHUBBY IT IS! I USED TO HAVE ONE OF THESE WHEN I WAS LITTLE.
TOYS
DA-DA!
DA-DA!
AHH!

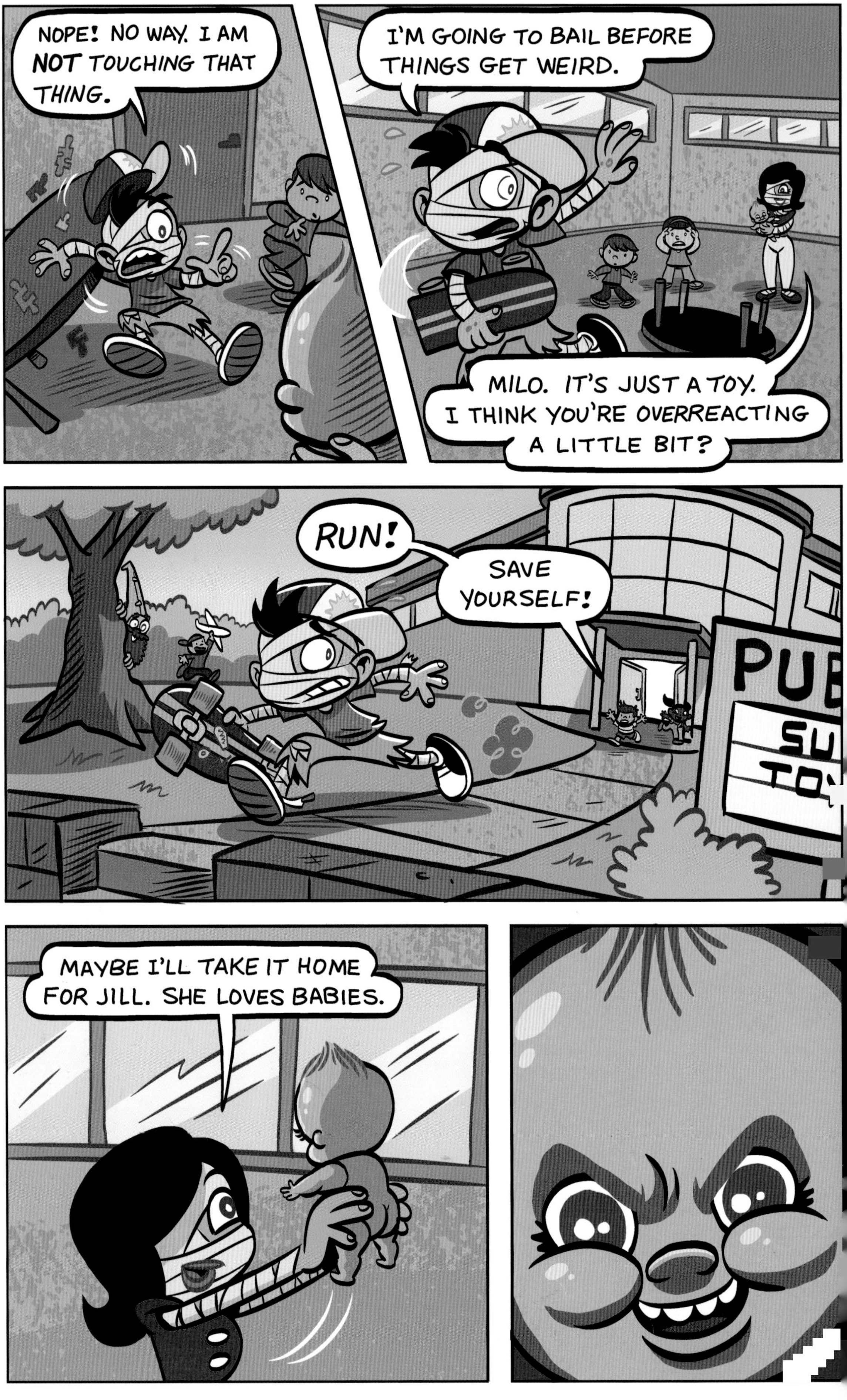
NOPE! NO WAY. I AM **NOT** TOUCHING THAT THING.
I'M GOING TO BAIL BEFORE THINGS GET WEIRD.
MILO. IT'S JUST A TOY. I THINK YOU'RE OVERREACTING A LITTLE BIT?
RUN!
SAVE YOURSELF!
PUB
SU
TO
MAYBE I'LL TAKE IT HOME FOR JILL. SHE LOVES BABIES.

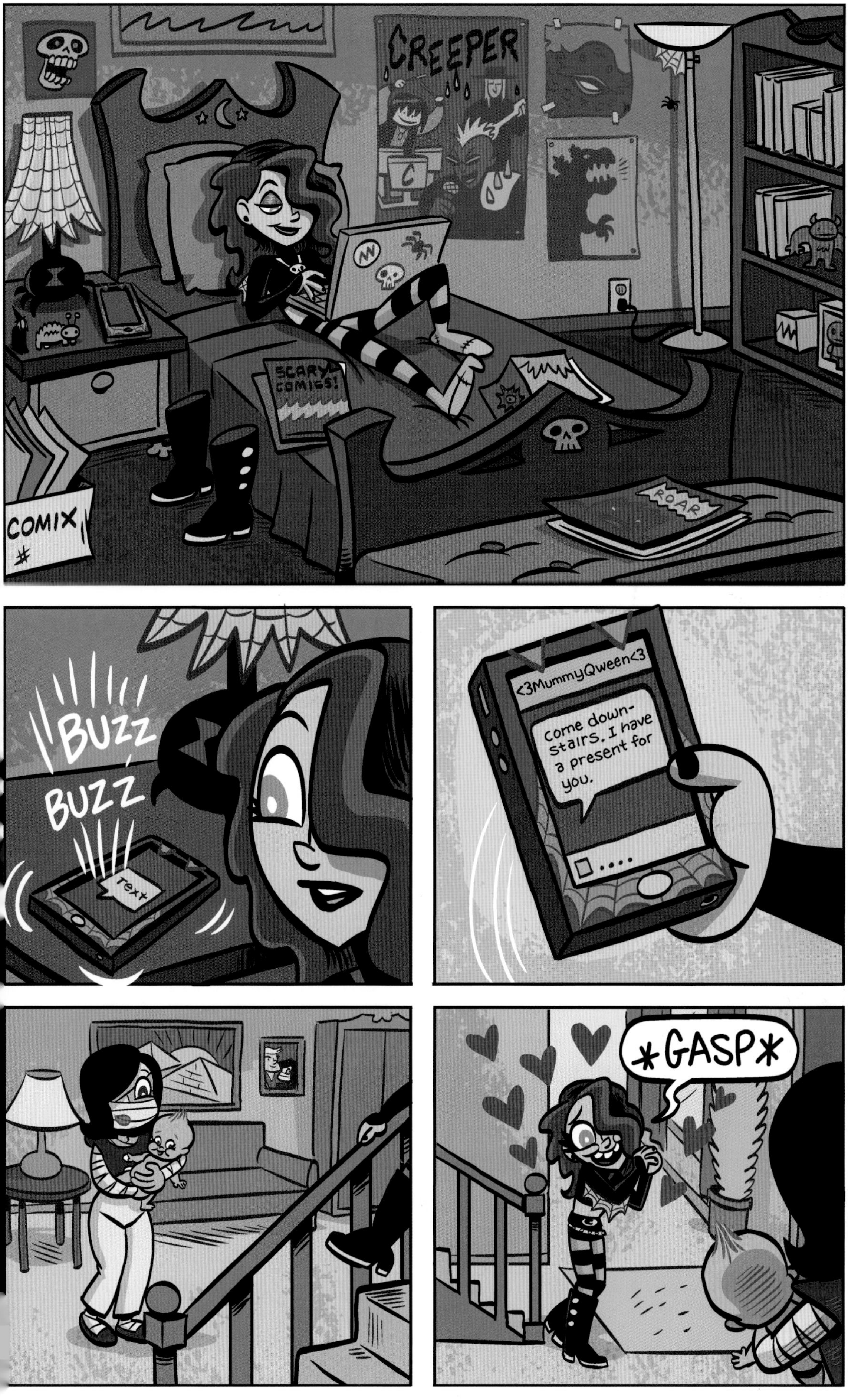
CREEPER
SCARY COMICS!
ROAR
COMIX
BUZZ
BUZZ
Text
<3MummyQween<3
come down-stairs. I have a present for you.
GASP

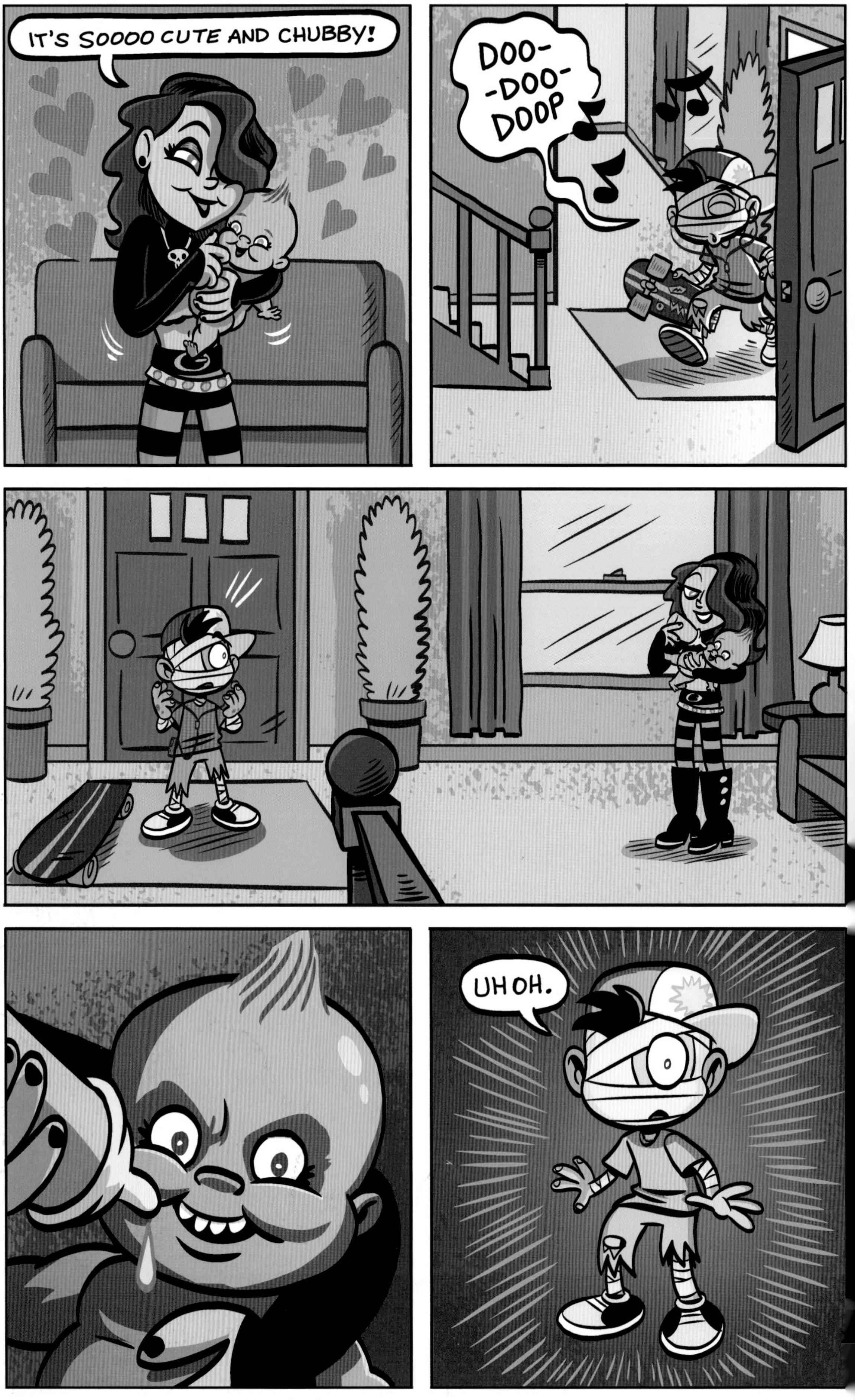
IT'S SOOOO CUTE AND CHUBBY!
DOO-
-DOO-
DOOP
UH OH.

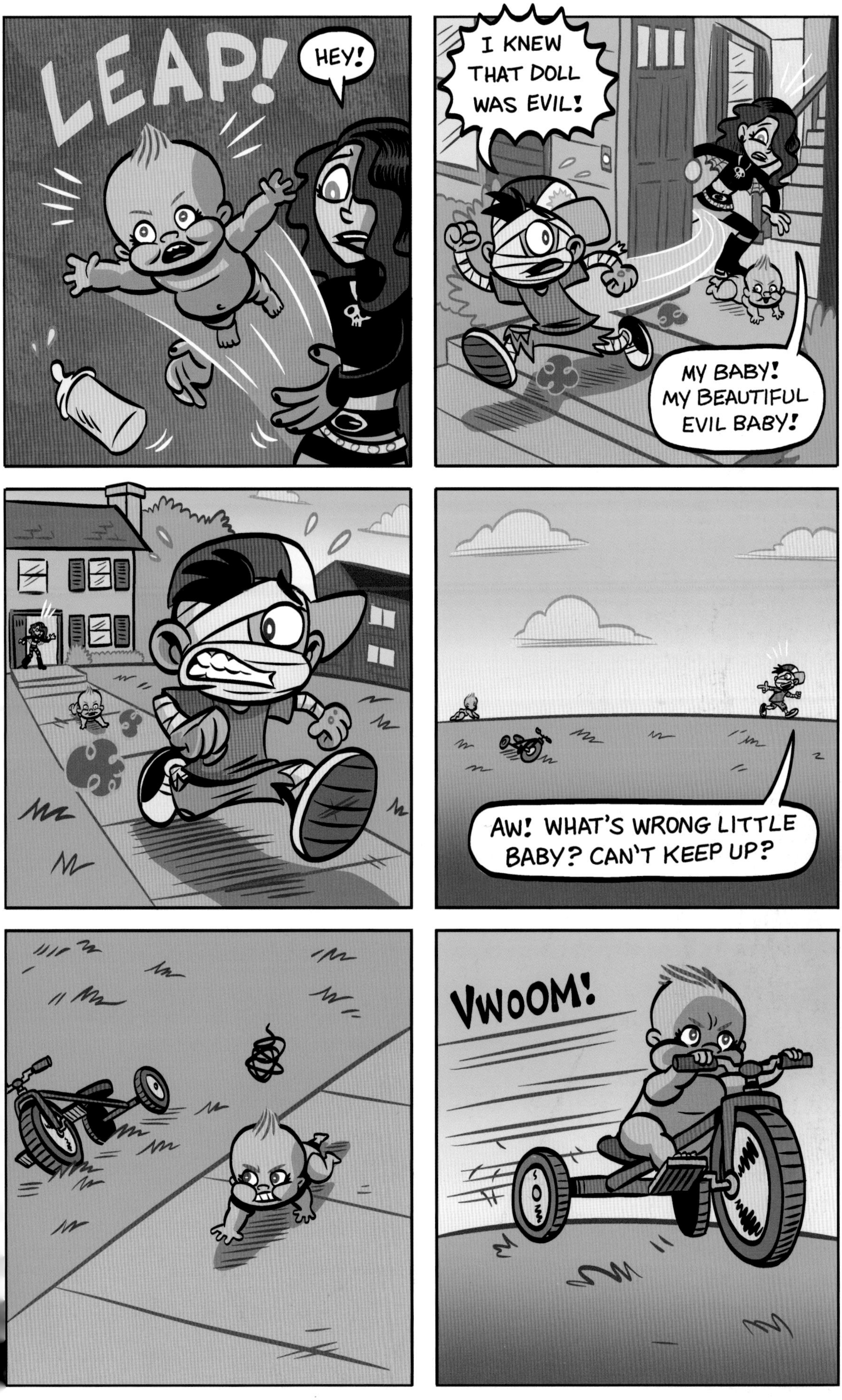
LEAP!
HEY!
I KNEW THAT DOLL WAS EVIL!
MY BABY! MY BEAUTIFUL EVIL BABY!
AW! WHAT'S WRONG LITTLE BABY? CAN'T KEEP UP?
VWOOM!

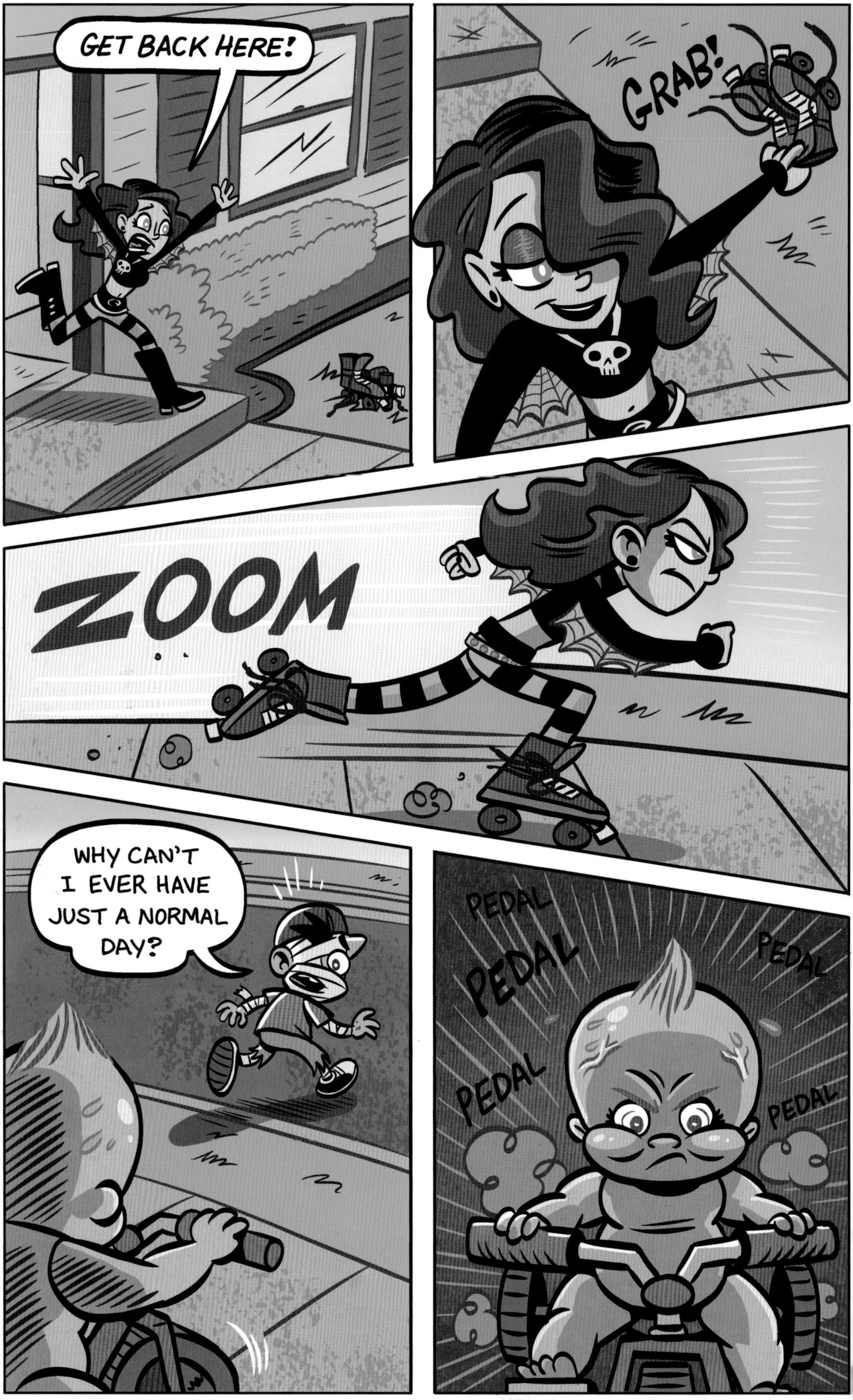
GET BACK HERE!
GRAB!
ZOOM
WHY CAN'T I EVER HAVE JUST A NORMAL DAY?
PEDAL
PEDAL
PEDAL
PEDAL
PEDAL

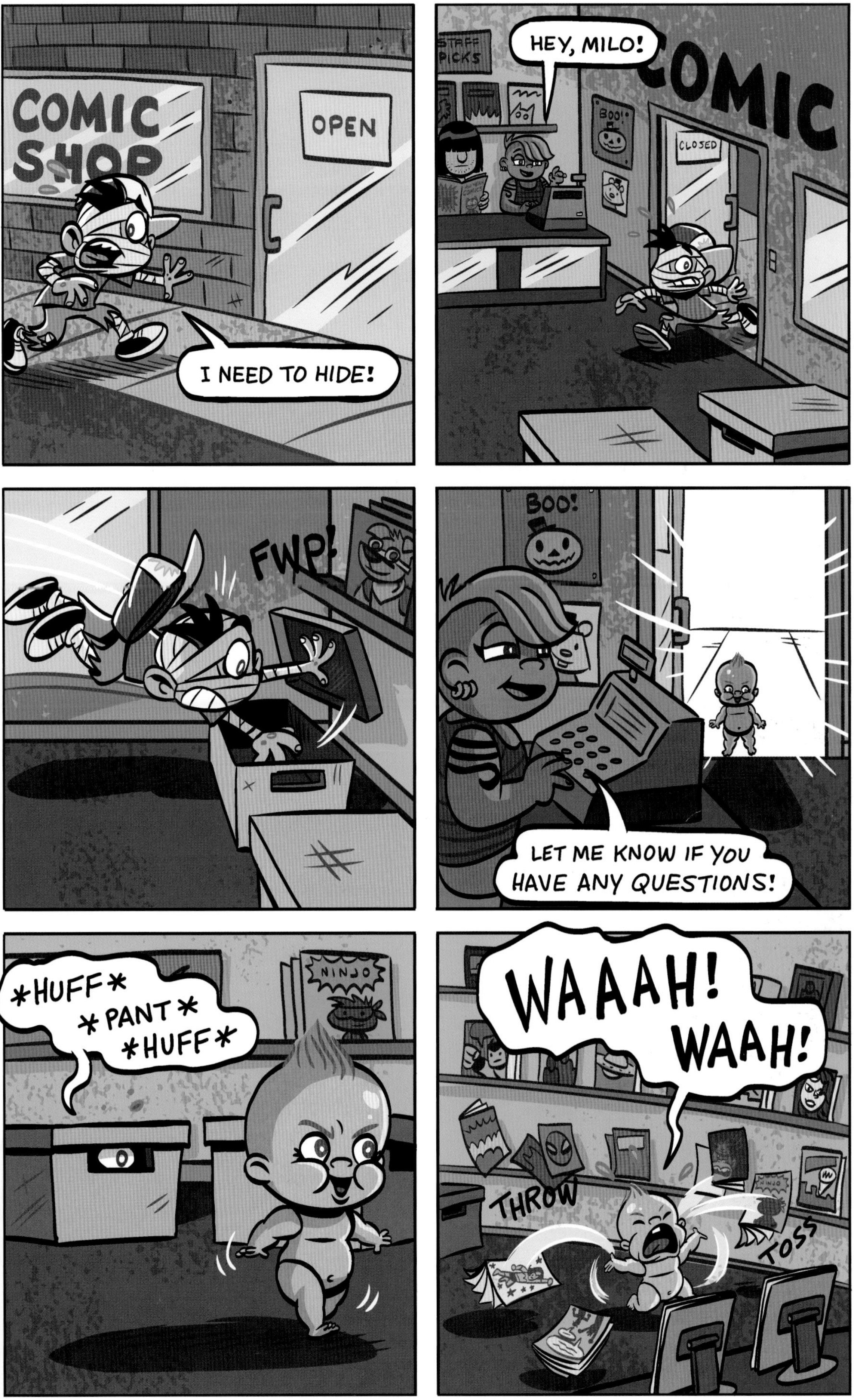
COMIC SHOP
OPEN
I NEED TO HIDE!
STAFF PICKS
HEY, MILO!
COMIC
BOO!
CLOSED
FWP!
BOO!
LET ME KNOW IF YOU HAVE ANY QUESTIONS!
HUFF *PANT* *HUFF*
NINJO
WAAAH! WAAH!
THROW
TOSS

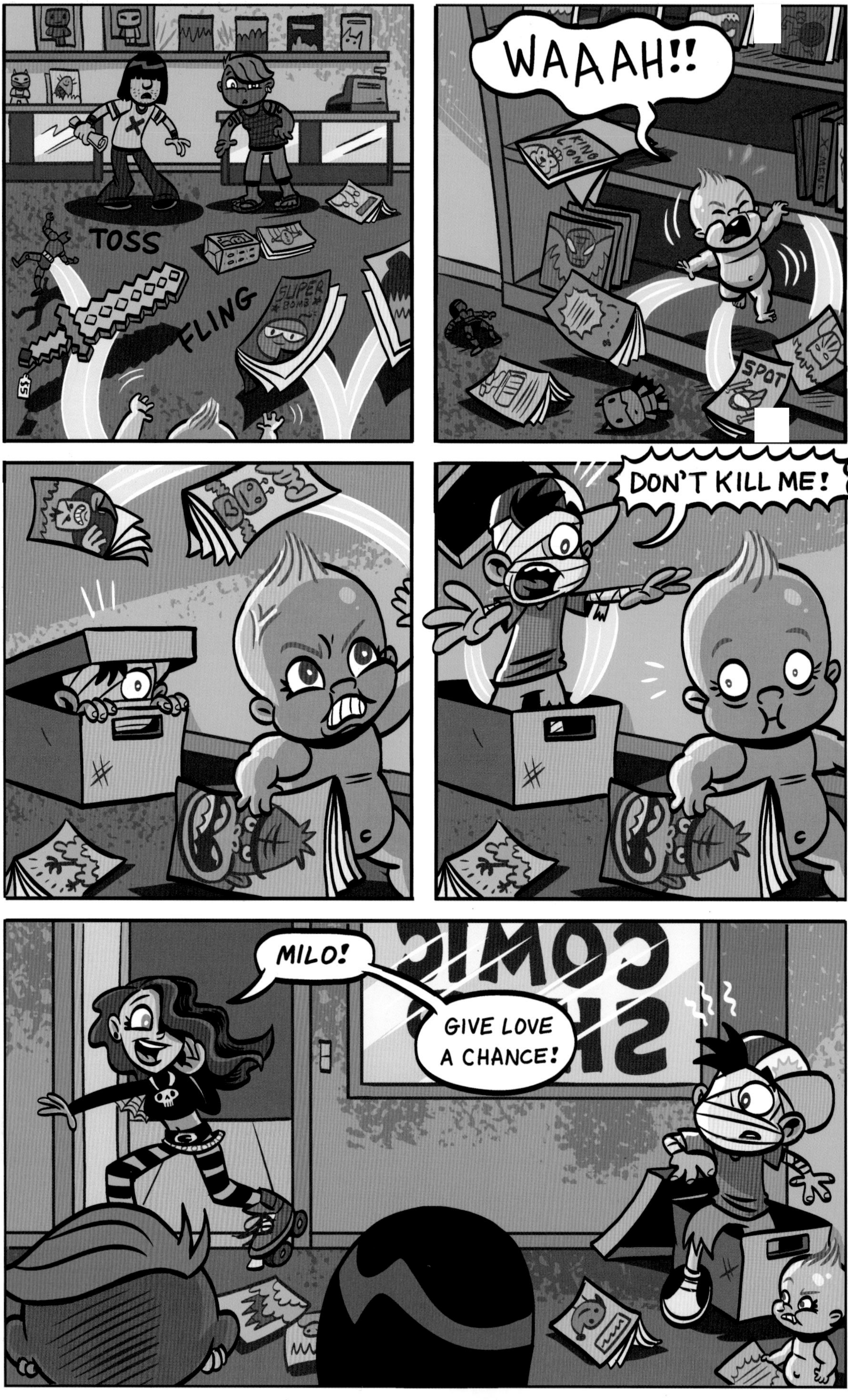
TOSS
FLING
SUPER BOMB
WAAAH!!
KING LION
SPOT
DON'T KILL ME!
MILO!
GIVE LOVE A CHANCE!

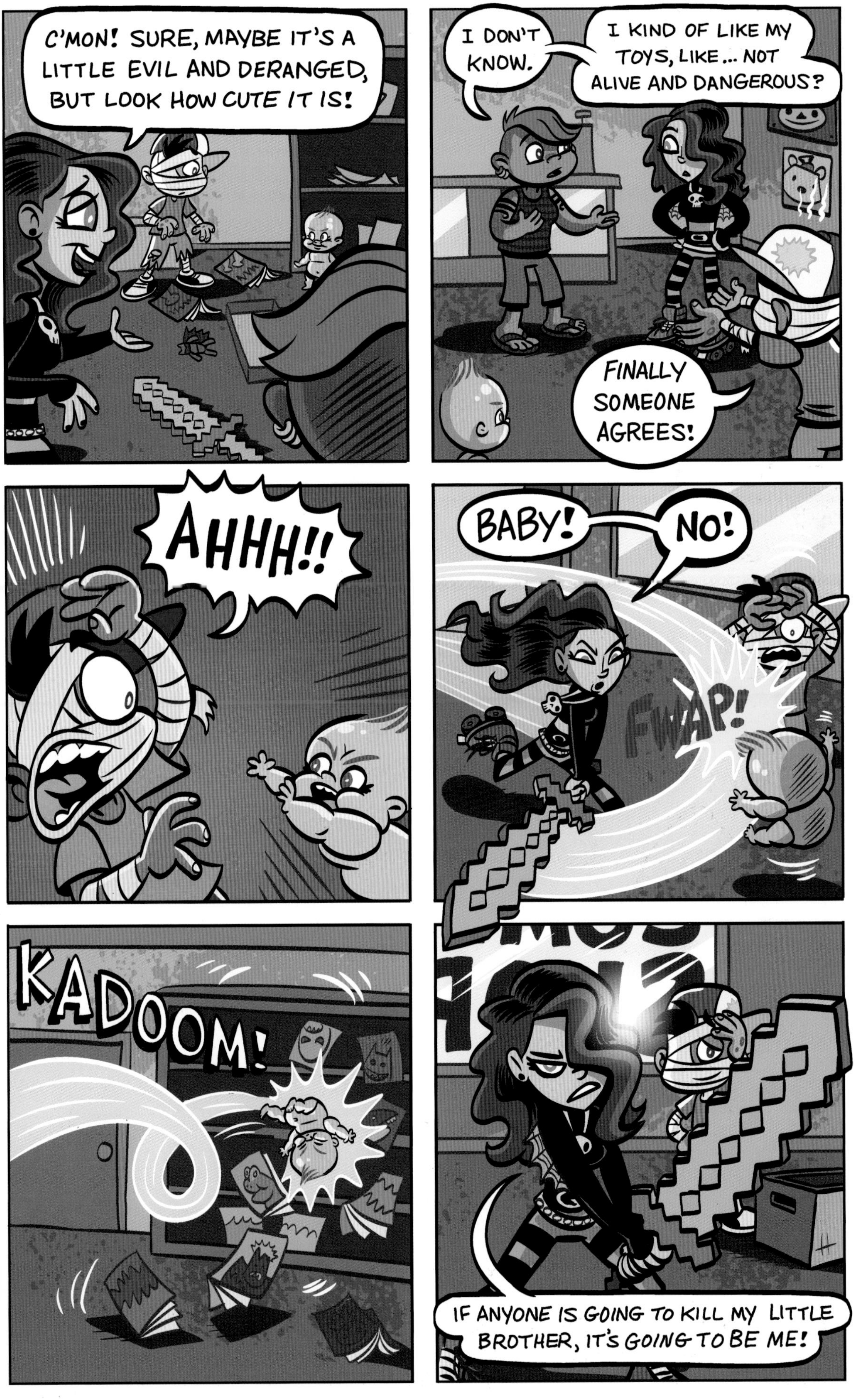
C'MON! SURE, MAYBE IT'S A LITTLE EVIL AND DERANGED, BUT LOOK HOW CUTE IT IS!
I DON'T KNOW.
I KIND OF LIKE MY TOYS, LIKE... NOT ALIVE AND DANGEROUS?
FINALLY SOMEONE AGREES!
AHHH!!
BABY!
NO!
FWAP!
KADOOM!
IF ANYONE IS GOING TO KILL MY LITTLE BROTHER, IT'S GOING TO BE ME!

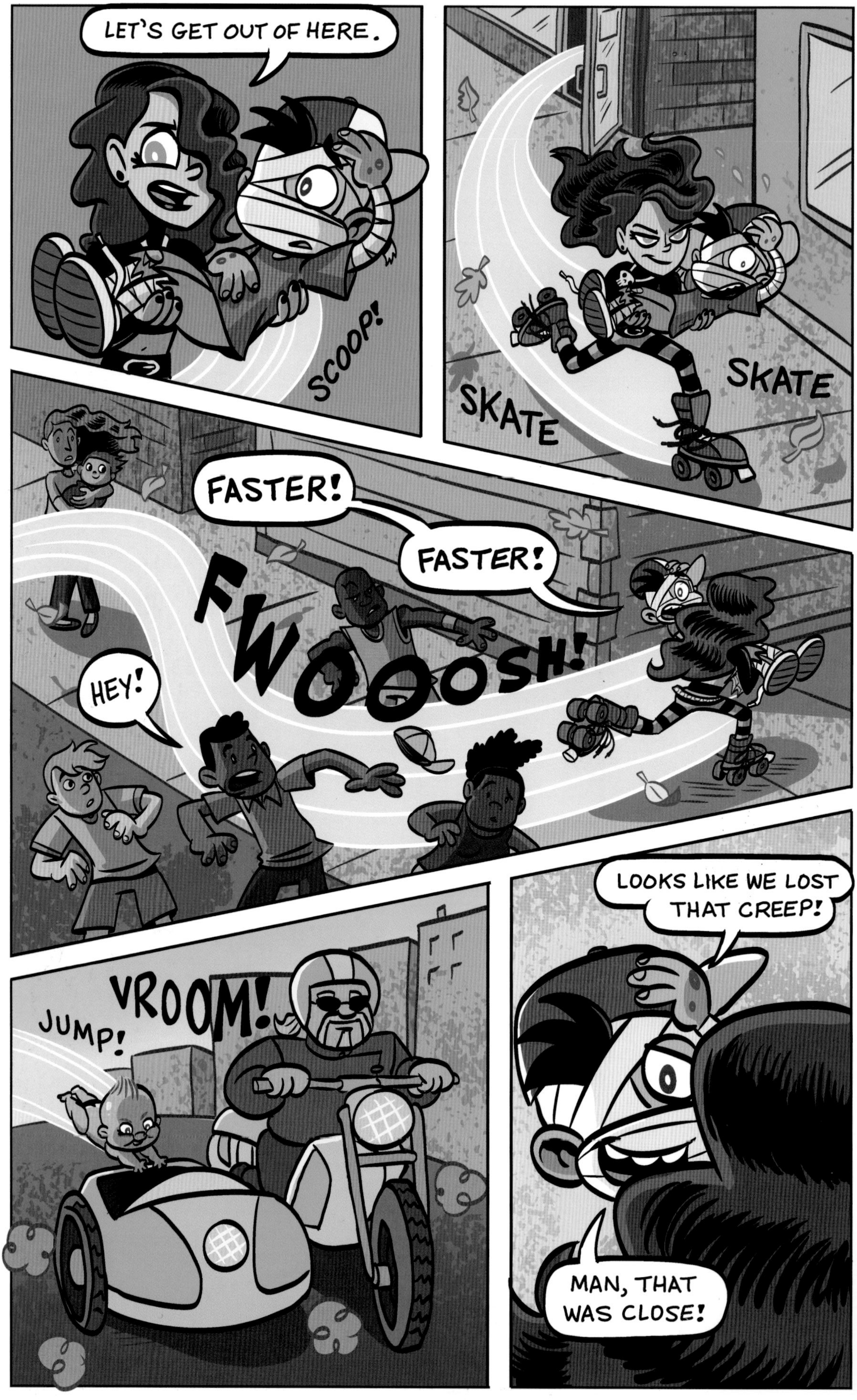
LET'S GET OUT OF HERE.
SCOOP!
SKATE
SKATE
FASTER!
FASTER!
FWOOOSH!
HEY!
VROOM!
JUMP!
LOOKS LIKE WE LOST THAT CREEP!
MAN, THAT WAS CLOSE!

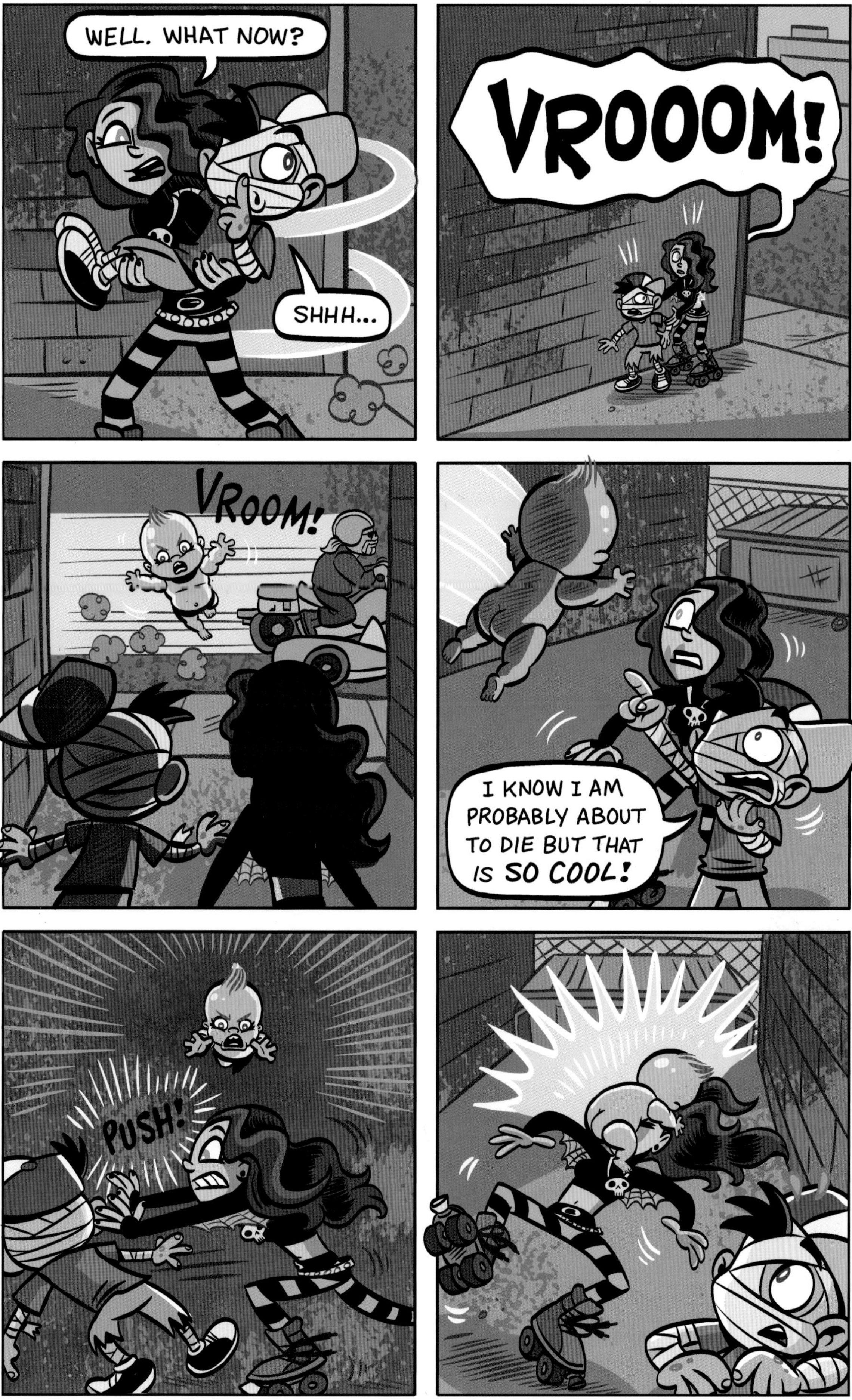
WELL. WHAT NOW?
SHHH...
VROOOM!
VROOM!
I KNOW I AM PROBABLY ABOUT TO DIE BUT THAT IS SO COOL!
PUSH!

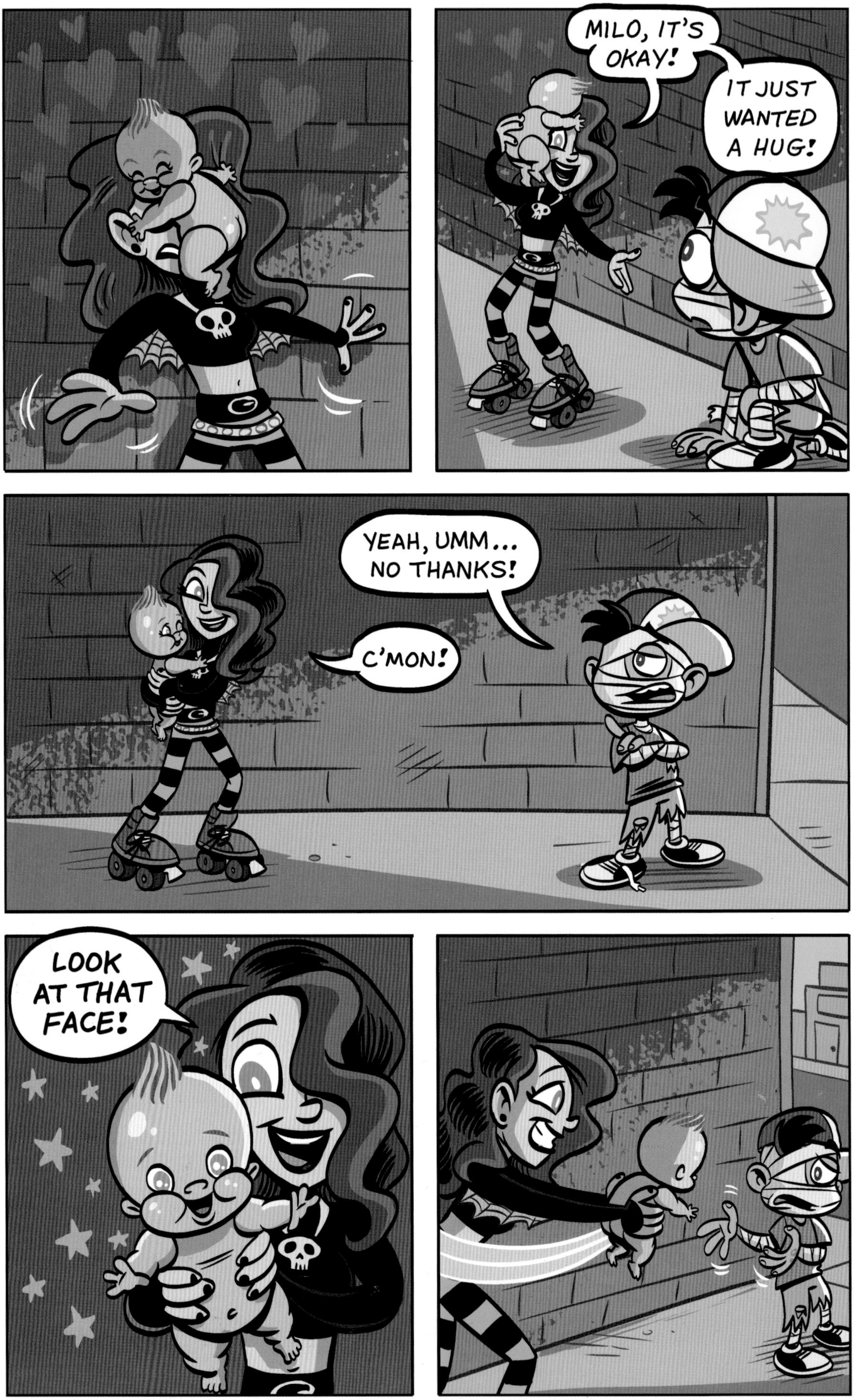
MILO, IT'S OKAY!
IT JUST WANTED A HUG!
YEAH, UMM... NO THANKS!
C'MON!
LOOK AT THAT FACE!

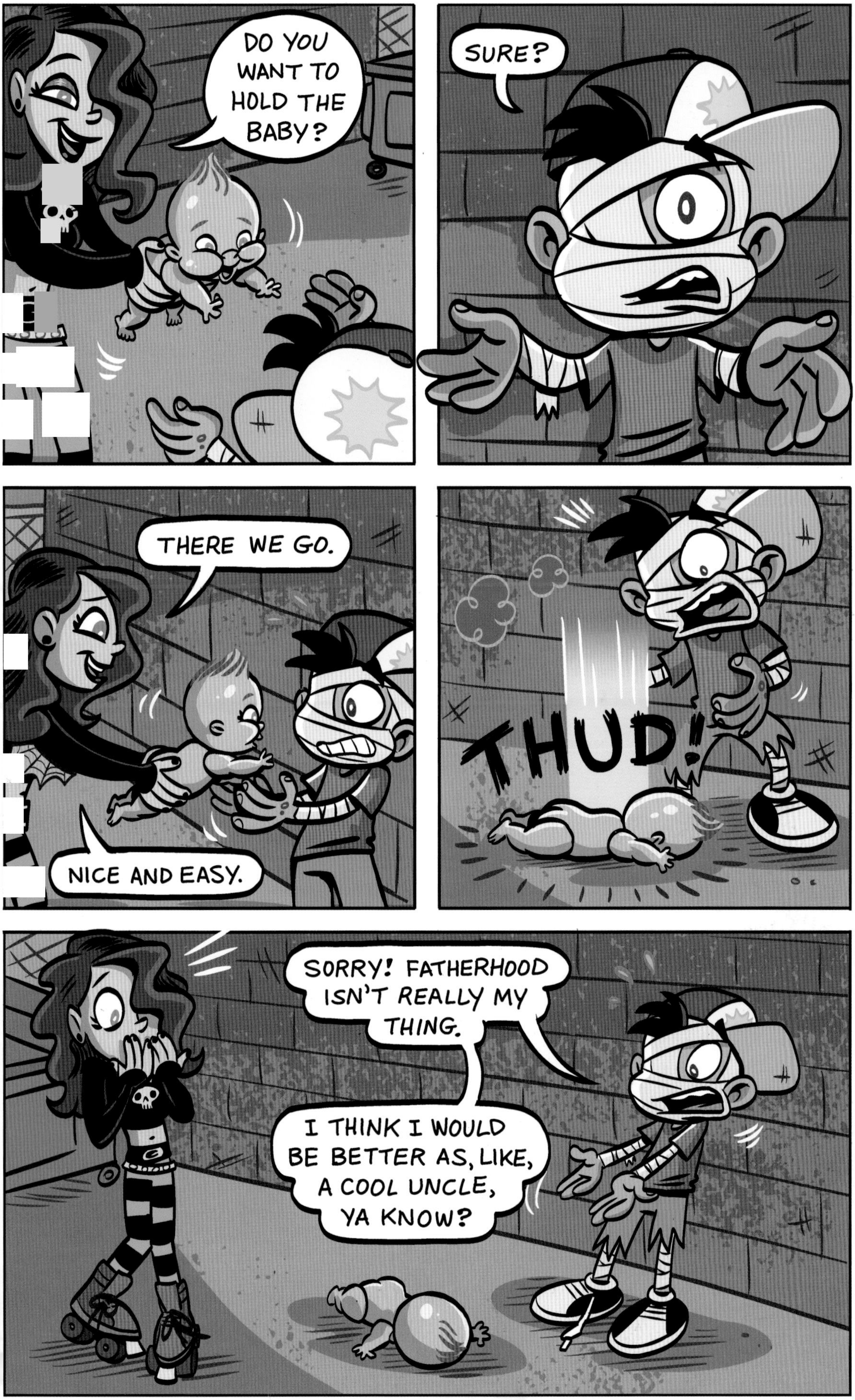
DO YOU WANT TO HOLD THE BABY?
SURE?
THERE WE GO.
NICE AND EASY.
THUD!!
SORRY! FATHERHOOD ISN'T REALLY MY THING.
I THINK I WOULD BE BETTER AS, LIKE, A COOL UNCLE, YA KNOW?

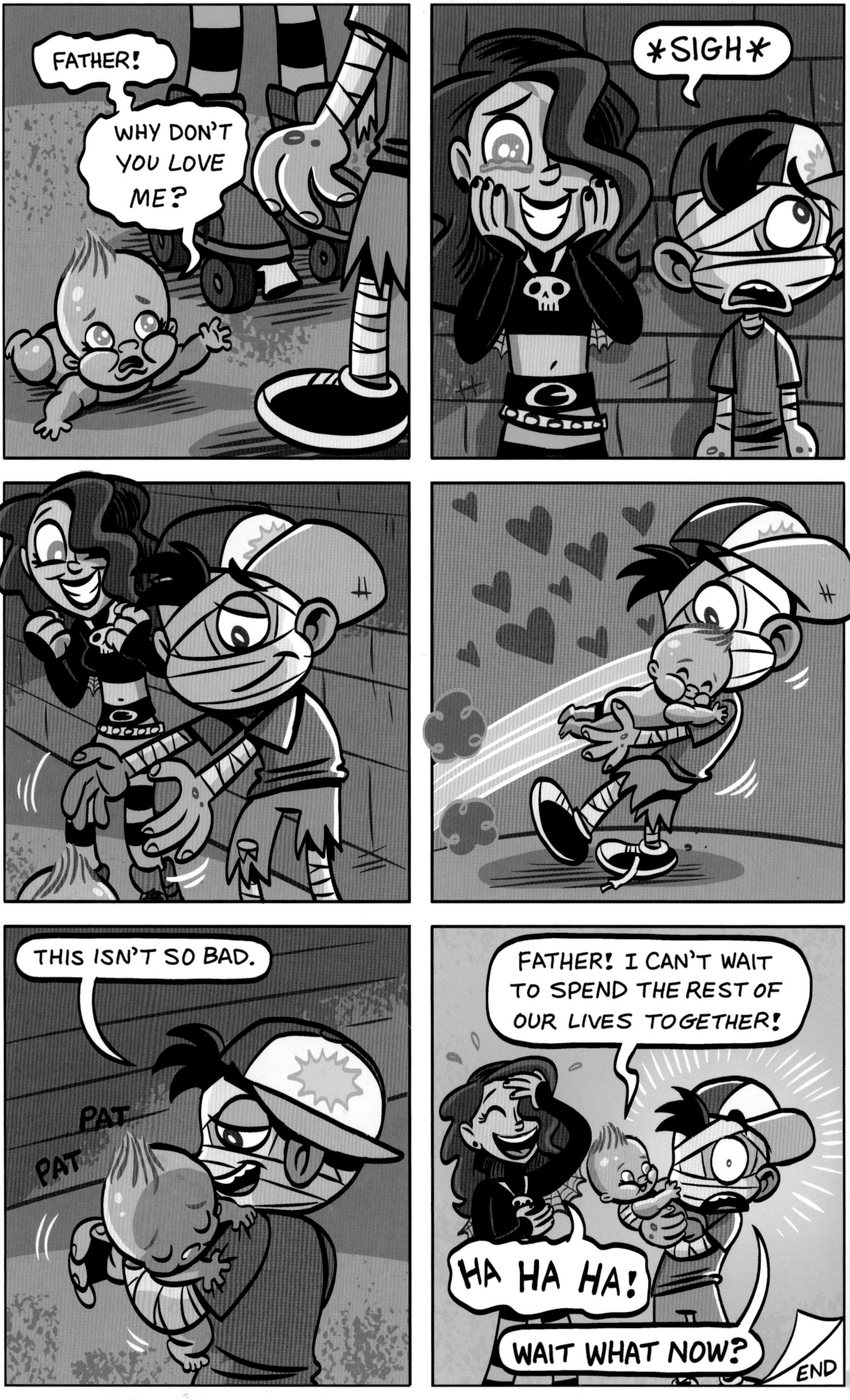
FATHER!
WHY DON'T YOU LOVE ME?
SIGH
THIS ISN'T SO BAD.
PAT
PAT
FATHER! I CAN'T WAIT TO SPEND THE REST OF OUR LIVES TOGETHER!
HA HA HA!
WAIT WHAT NOW?
END

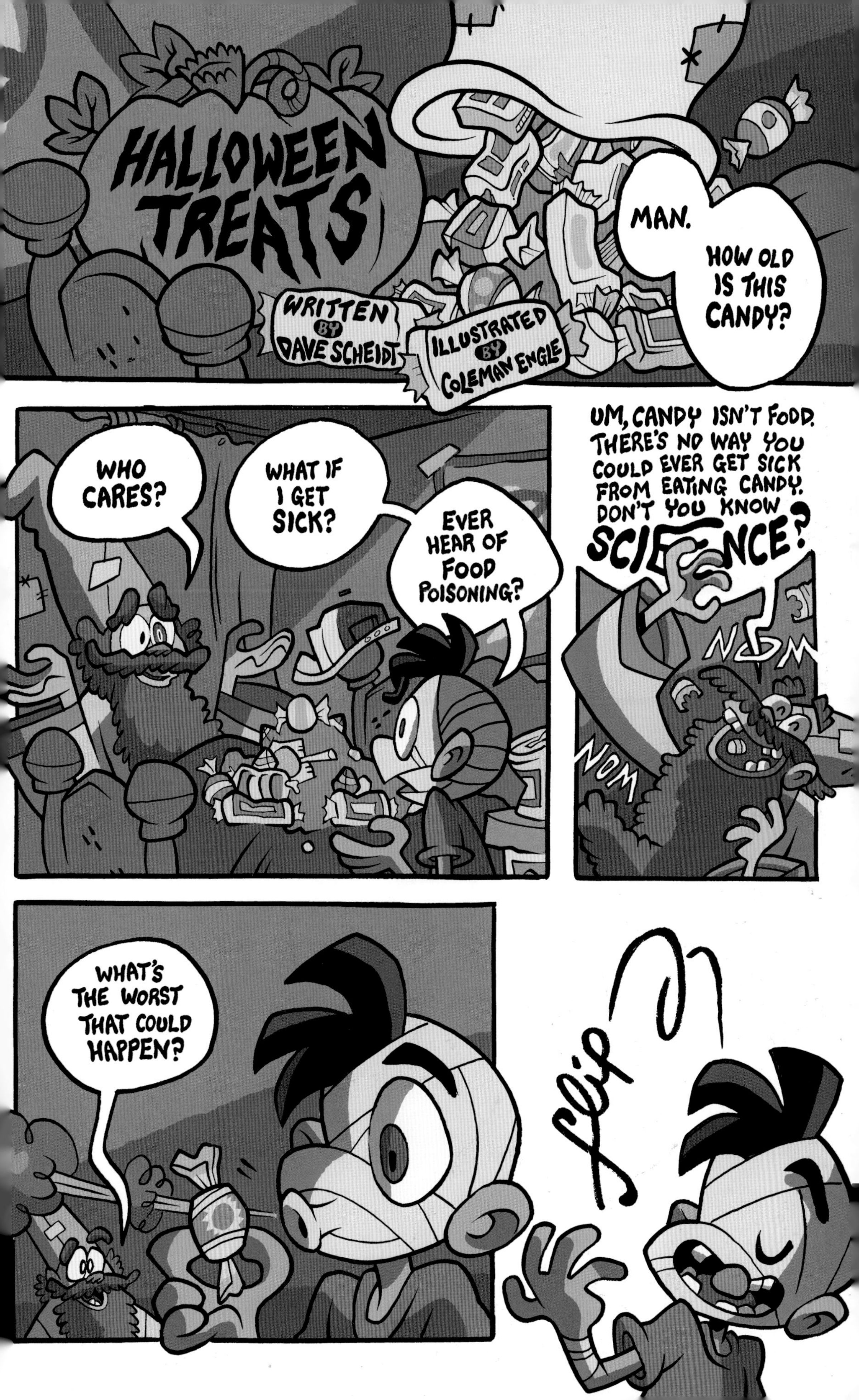
HALLOWEEN TREATS
WRITTEN BY DAVE SCHEIDT
ILLUSTRATED BY COLEMAN ENGLE
MAN.
HOW OLD IS THIS CANDY?
WHO CARES?
WHAT IF I GET SICK?
EVER HEAR OF FOOD POISONING?
UM, CANDY ISN'T FOOD. THERE'S NO WAY YOU COULD EVER GET SICK FROM EATING CANDY. DON'T YOU KNOW SCIENCE?
NOM
NOM
WHAT'S THE WORST THAT COULD HAPPEN?
flip

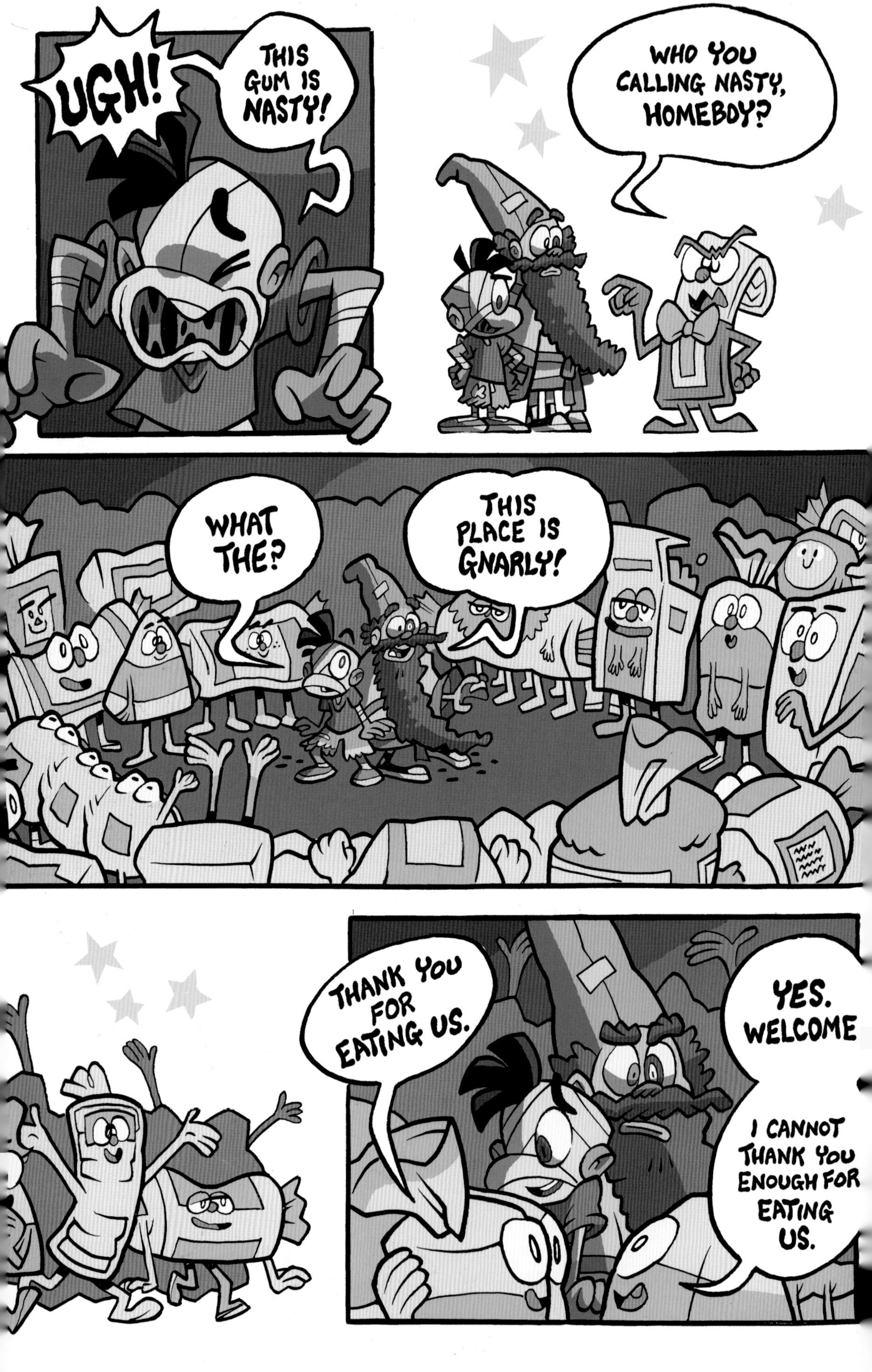
UGH!
THIS GUM IS NASTY!
WHO YOU CALLING NASTY, HOMEBOY?
WHAT THE?
THIS PLACE IS GNARLY!
THANK YOU FOR EATING US.
YES. WELCOME
I CANNOT THANK YOU ENOUGH FOR EATING US.

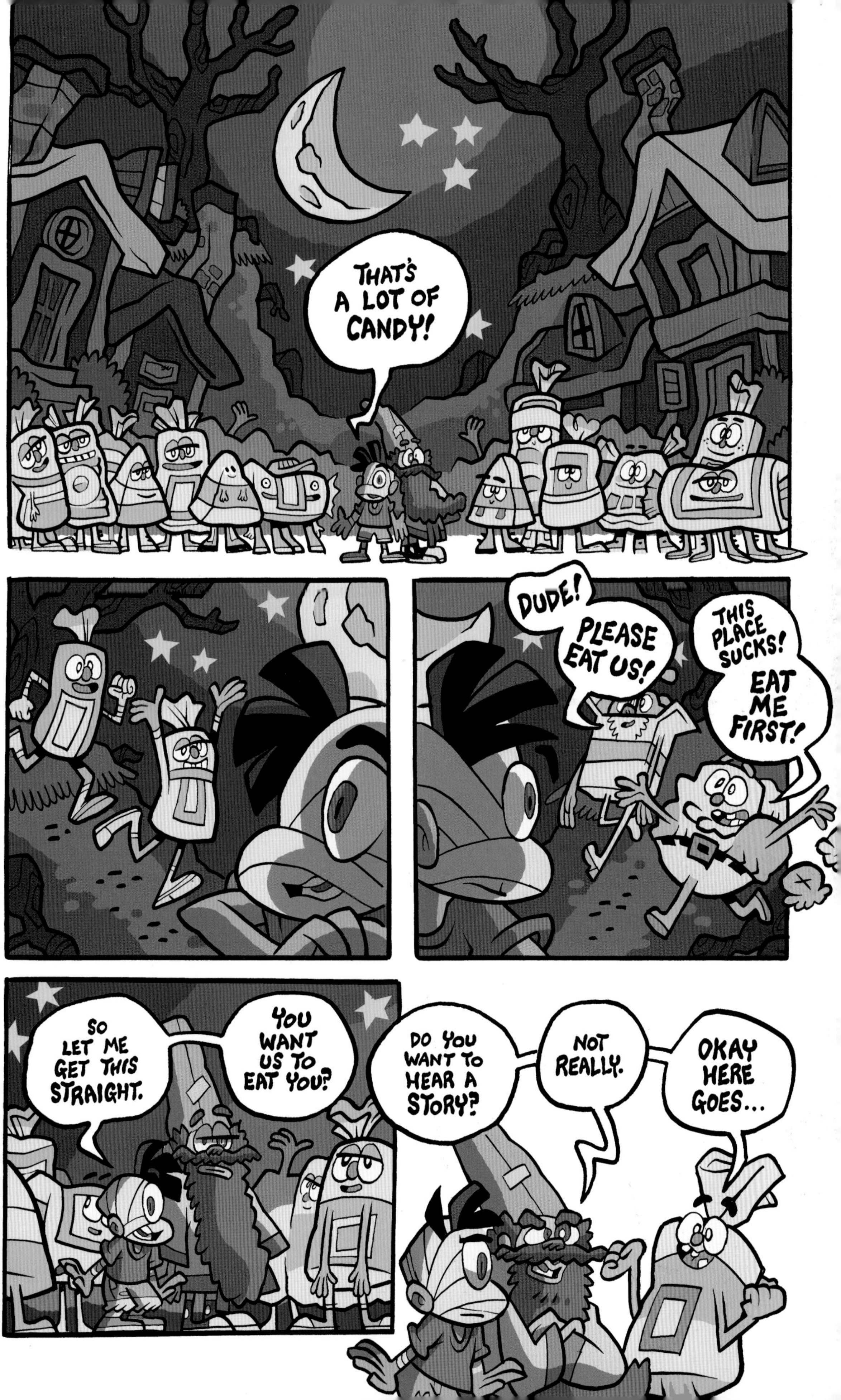
THAT'S A LOT OF CANDY!
DUDE!
PLEASE EAT US!
THIS PLACE SUCKS!
EAT ME FIRST!
SO LET ME GET THIS STRAIGHT.
YOU WANT US TO EAT YOU?
DO YOU WANT TO HEAR A STORY?
NOT REALLY.
OKAY HERE GOES...

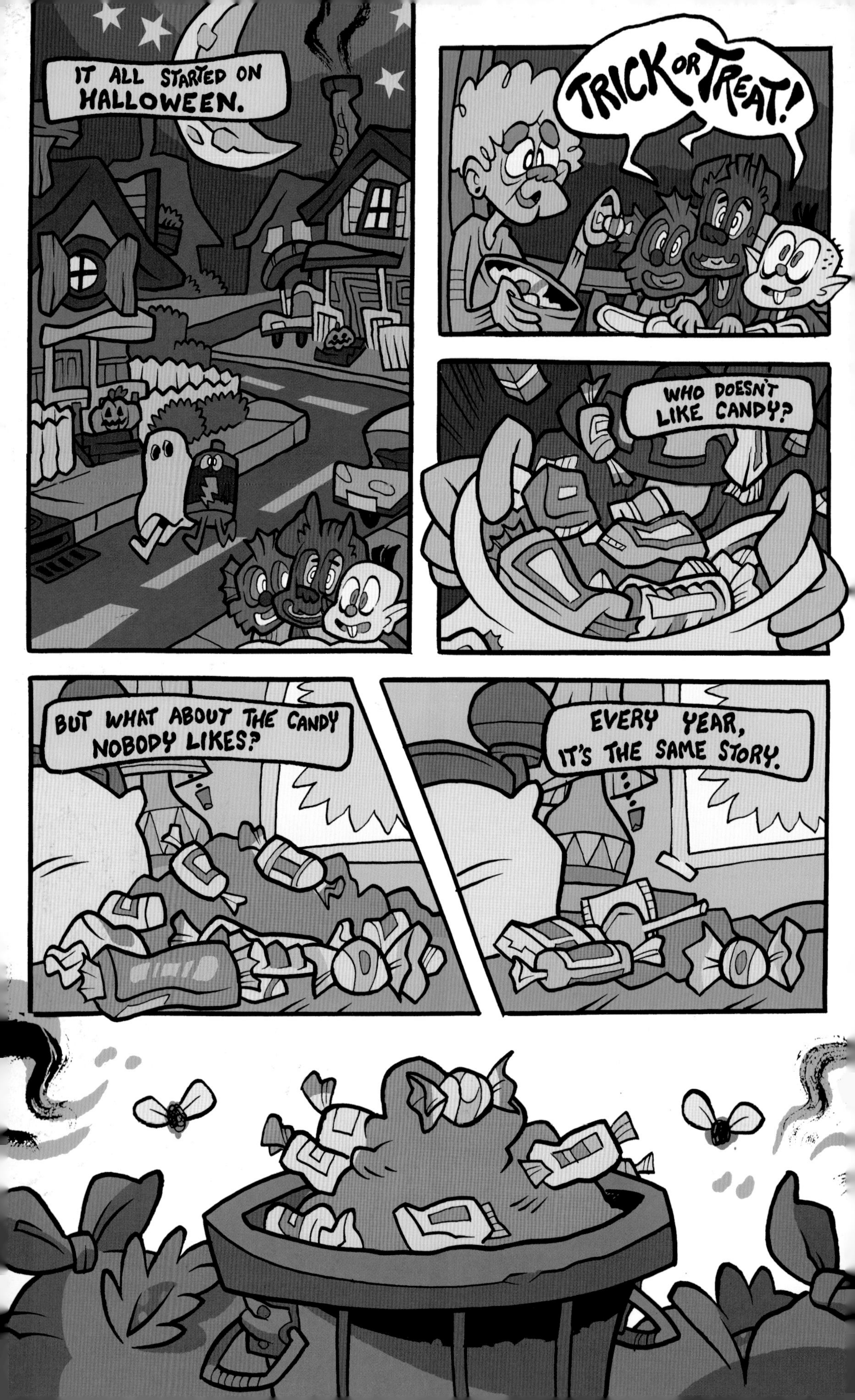
IT ALL STARTED ON HALLOWEEN.
TRICK OR TREAT!
WHO DOESN'T LIKE CANDY?
BUT WHAT ABOUT THE CANDY NOBODY LIKES?
EVERY YEAR, IT'S THE SAME STORY.

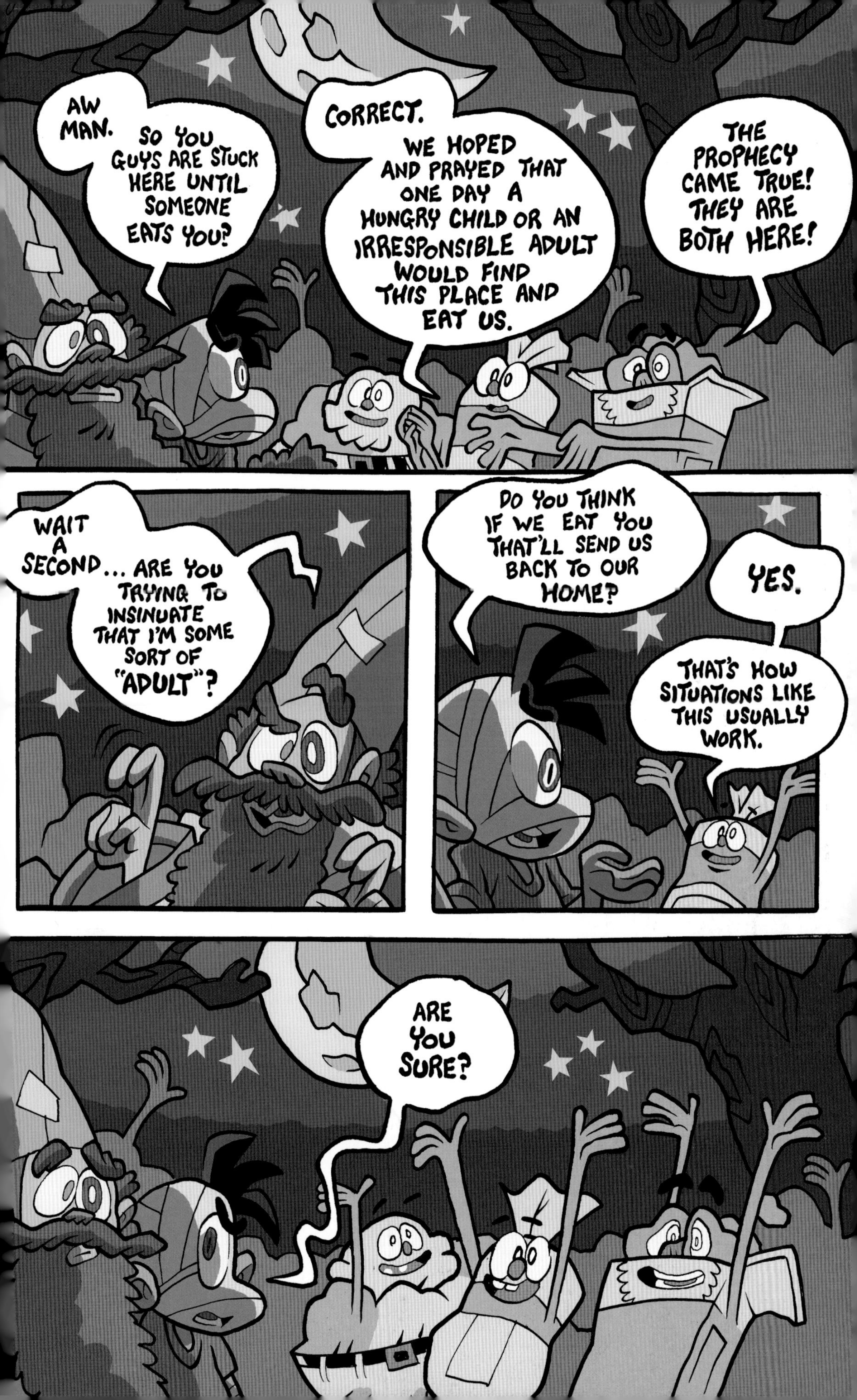
AW MAN.
SO YOU GUYS ARE STUCK HERE UNTIL SOMEONE EATS YOU?
CORRECT.
WE HOPED AND PRAYED THAT ONE DAY A HUNGRY CHILD OR AN IRRESPONSIBLE ADULT WOULD FIND THIS PLACE AND EAT US.
THE PROPHECY CAME TRUE! THEY ARE BOTH HERE!
WAIT A SECOND... ARE YOU TRYING TO INSINUATE THAT I'M SOME SORT OF "ADULT"?
DO YOU THINK IF WE EAT YOU THAT'LL SEND US BACK TO OUR HOME?
YES.
THAT'S HOW SITUATIONS LIKE THIS USUALLY WORK.
ARE YOU SURE?

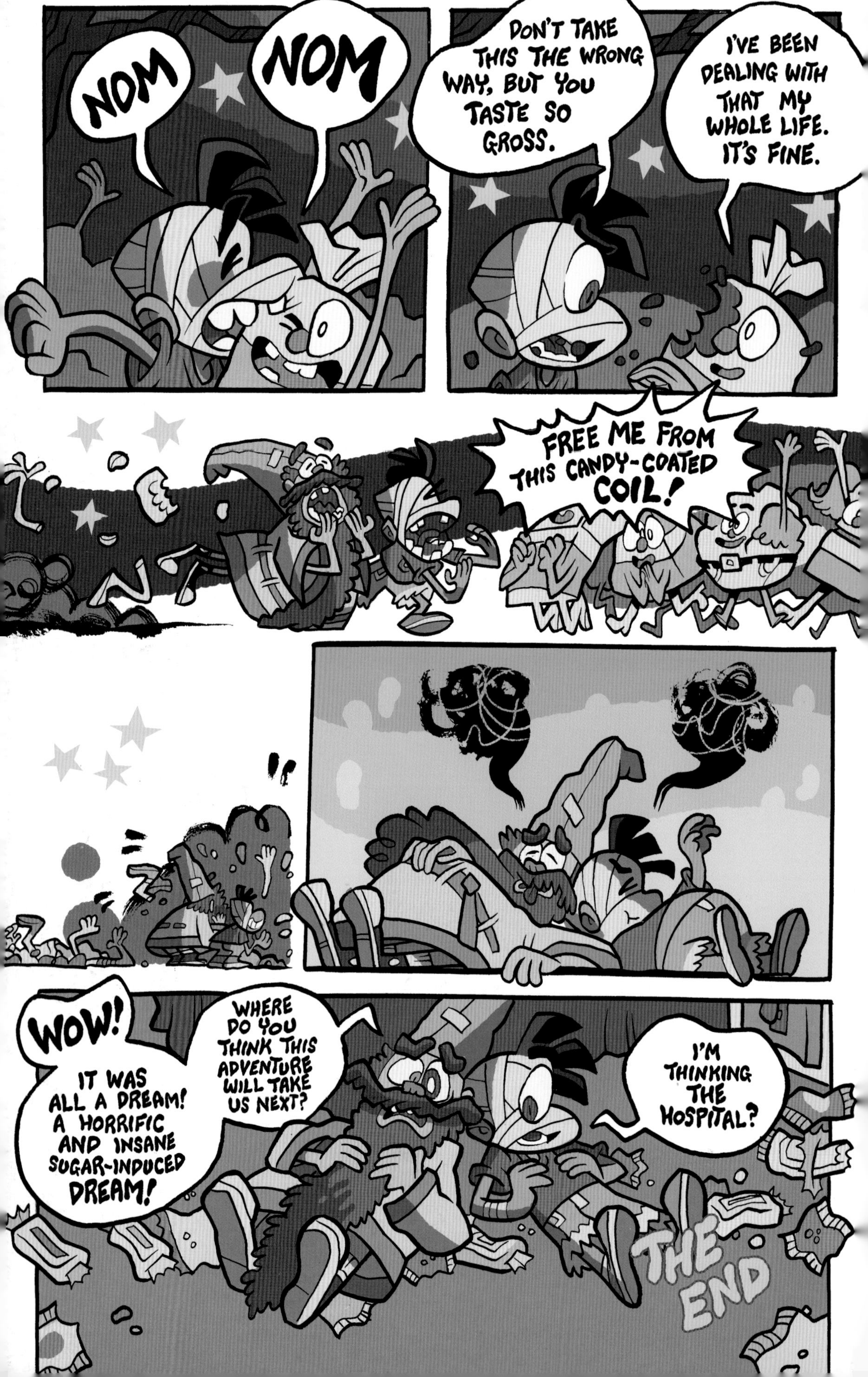
NOM
NOM
DON'T TAKE THIS THE WRONG WAY, BUT YOU TASTE SO GROSS.
I'VE BEEN DEALING WITH THAT MY WHOLE LIFE. IT'S FINE.
FREE ME FROM THIS CANDY-COATED COIL!
WOW!
IT WAS ALL A DREAM! A HORRIFIC AND INSANE SUGAR-INDUCED DREAM!
WHERE DO YOU THINK THIS ADVENTURE WILL TAKE US NEXT?
I'M THINKING THE HOSPITAL?
THE END

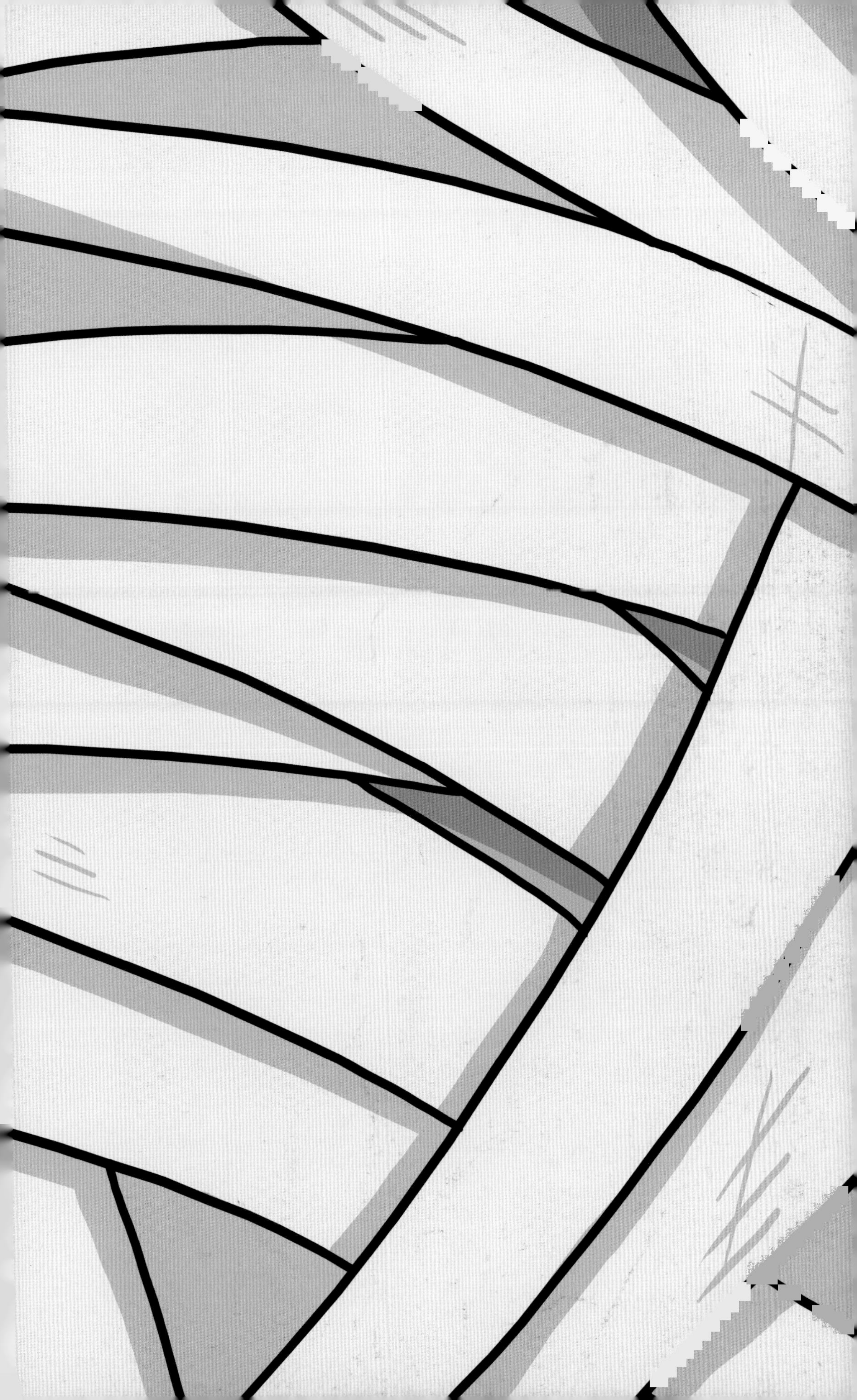

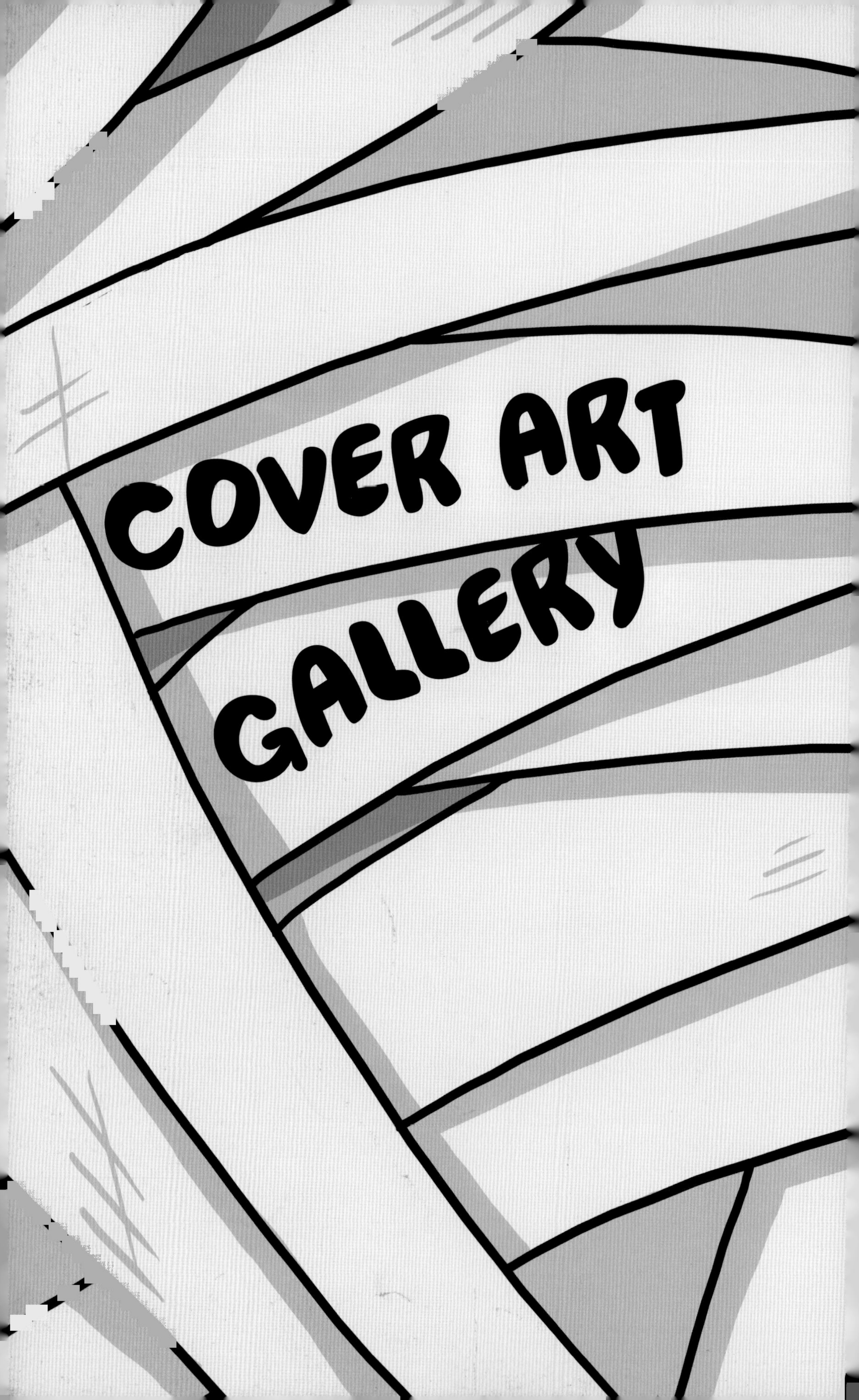
COVER ART
GALLERY

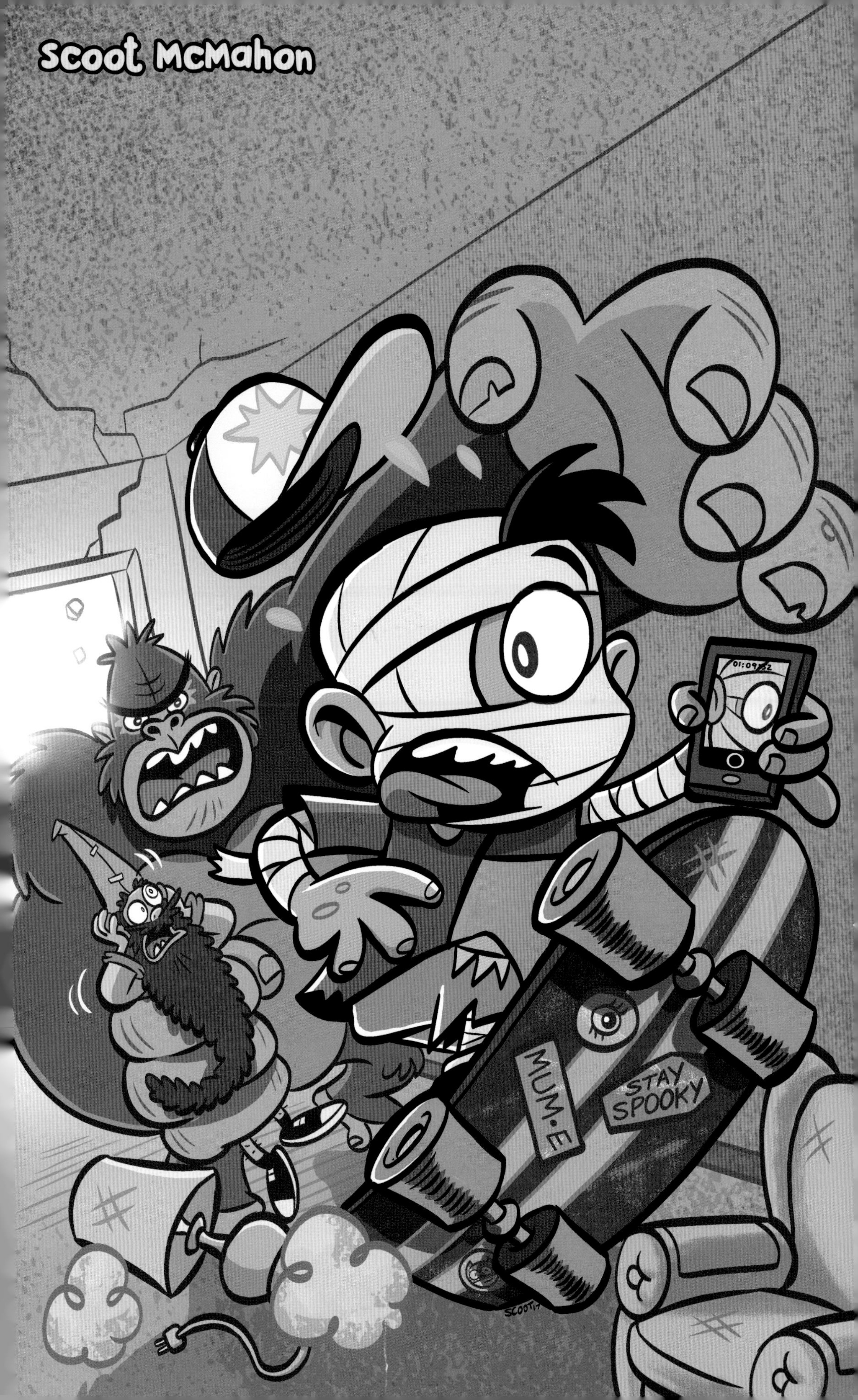
Scoot McMahon
MUM•E
STAY SPOOKY

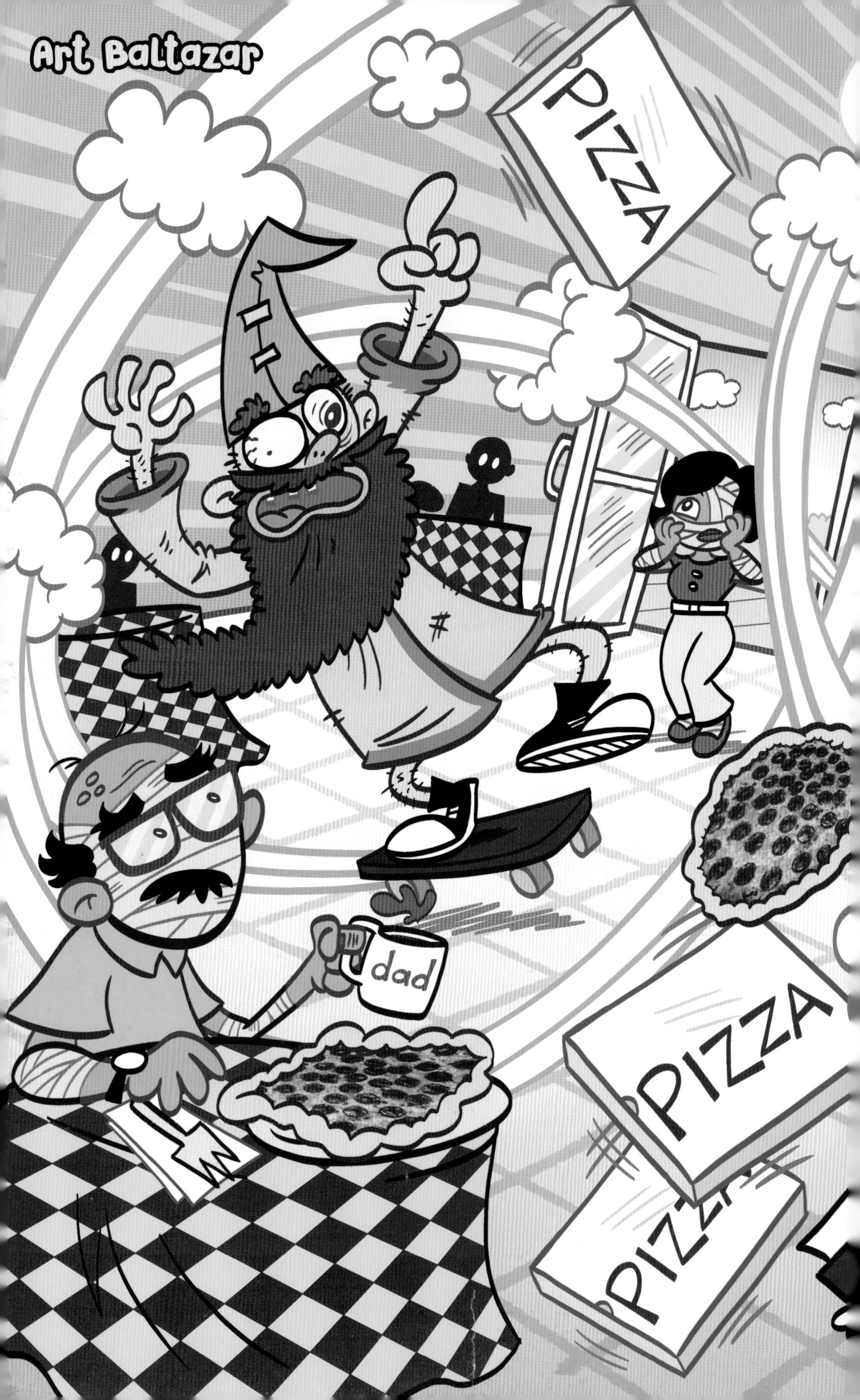
Art Baltazar
PIZZA
dad
PIZZA

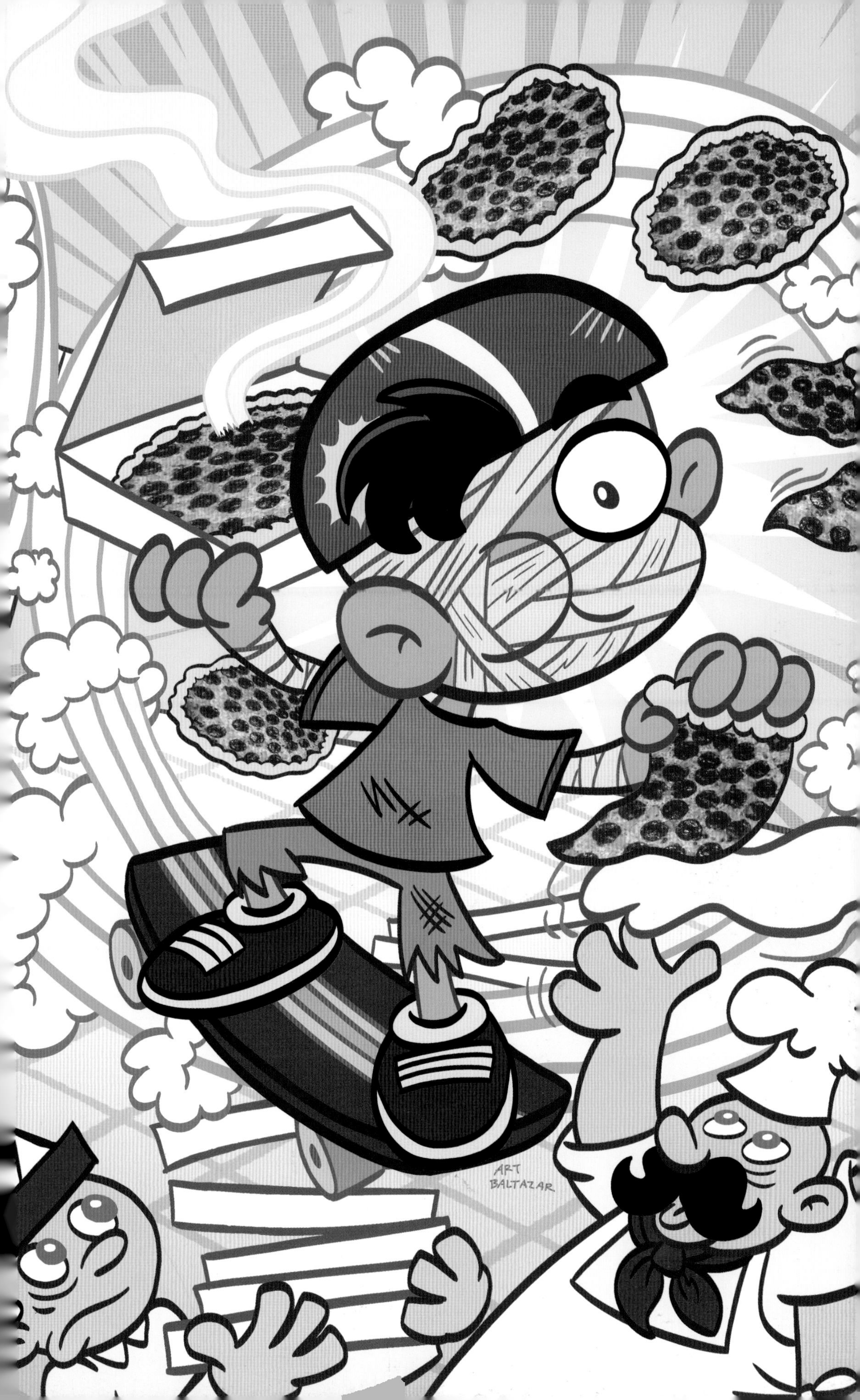
ART
BALTAZAR

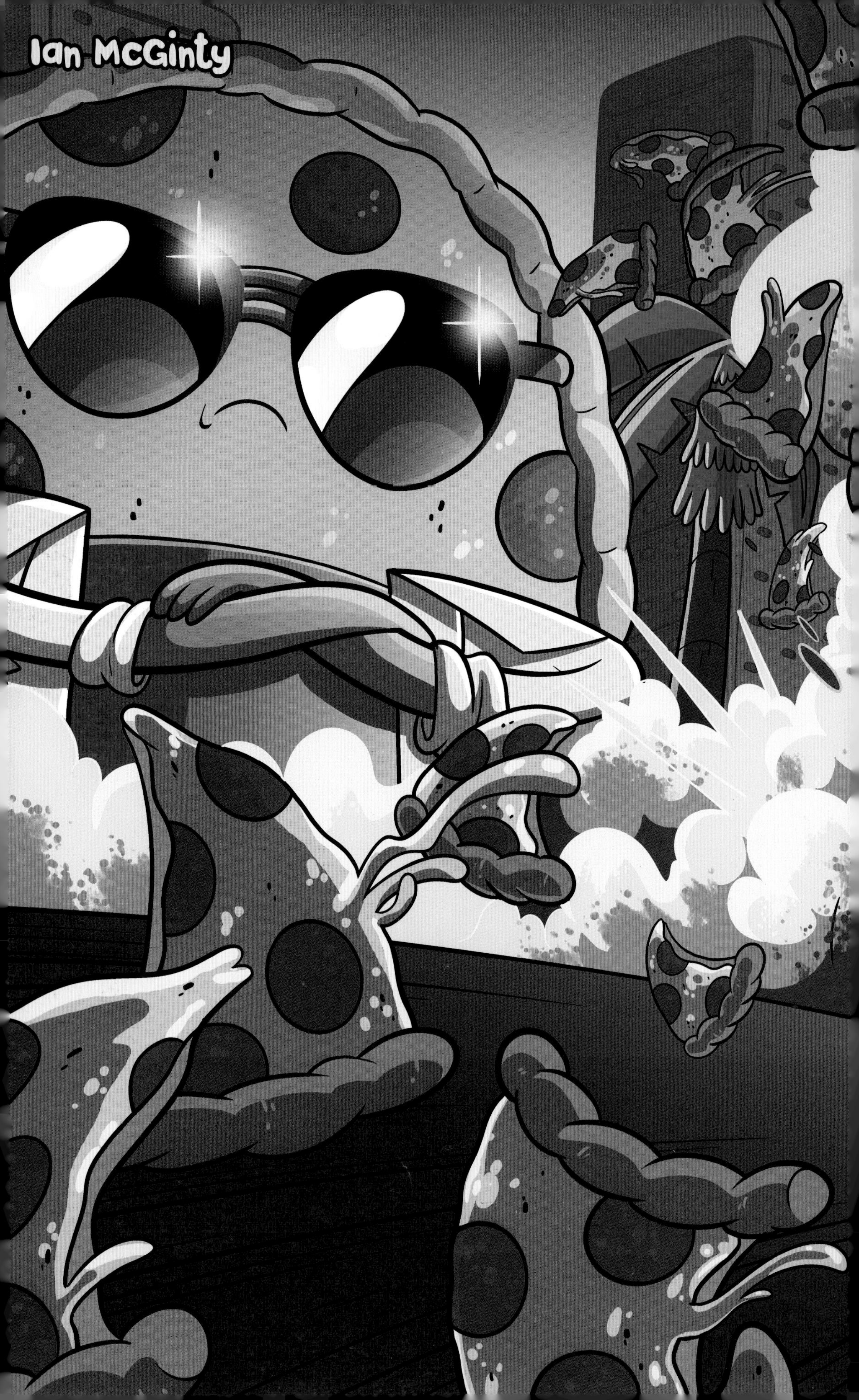
Ian McGinty

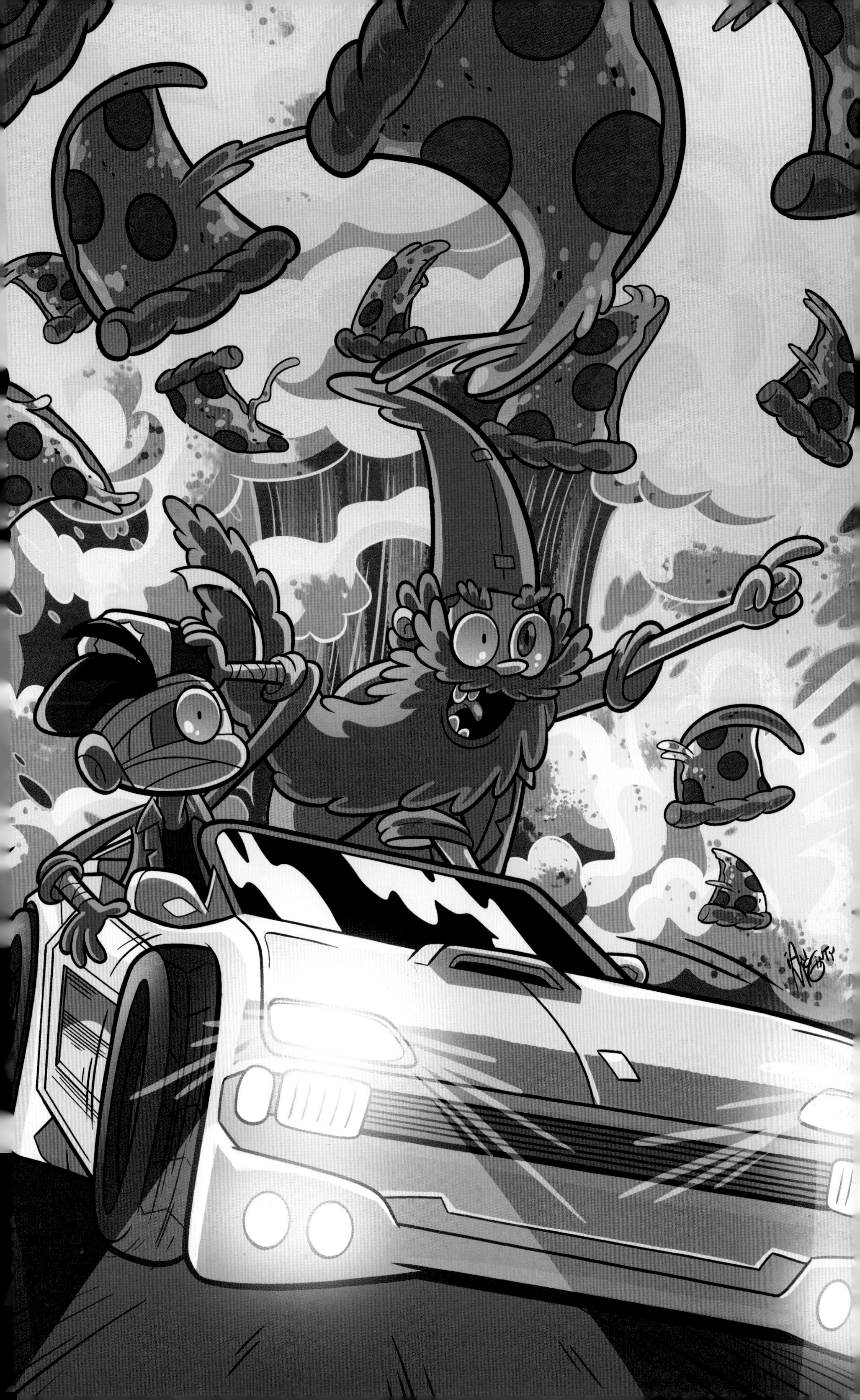

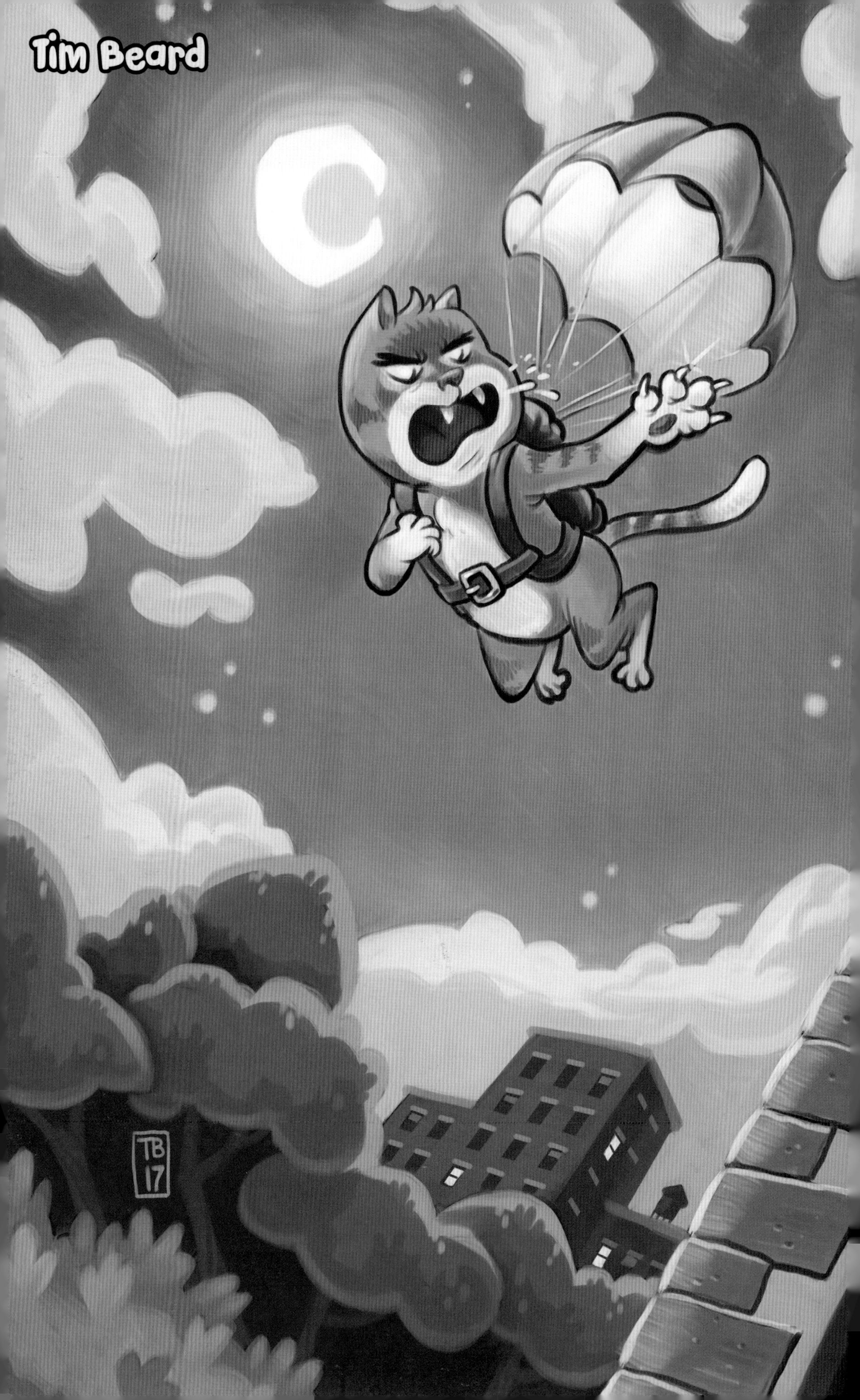
Tim Beard
TB 17

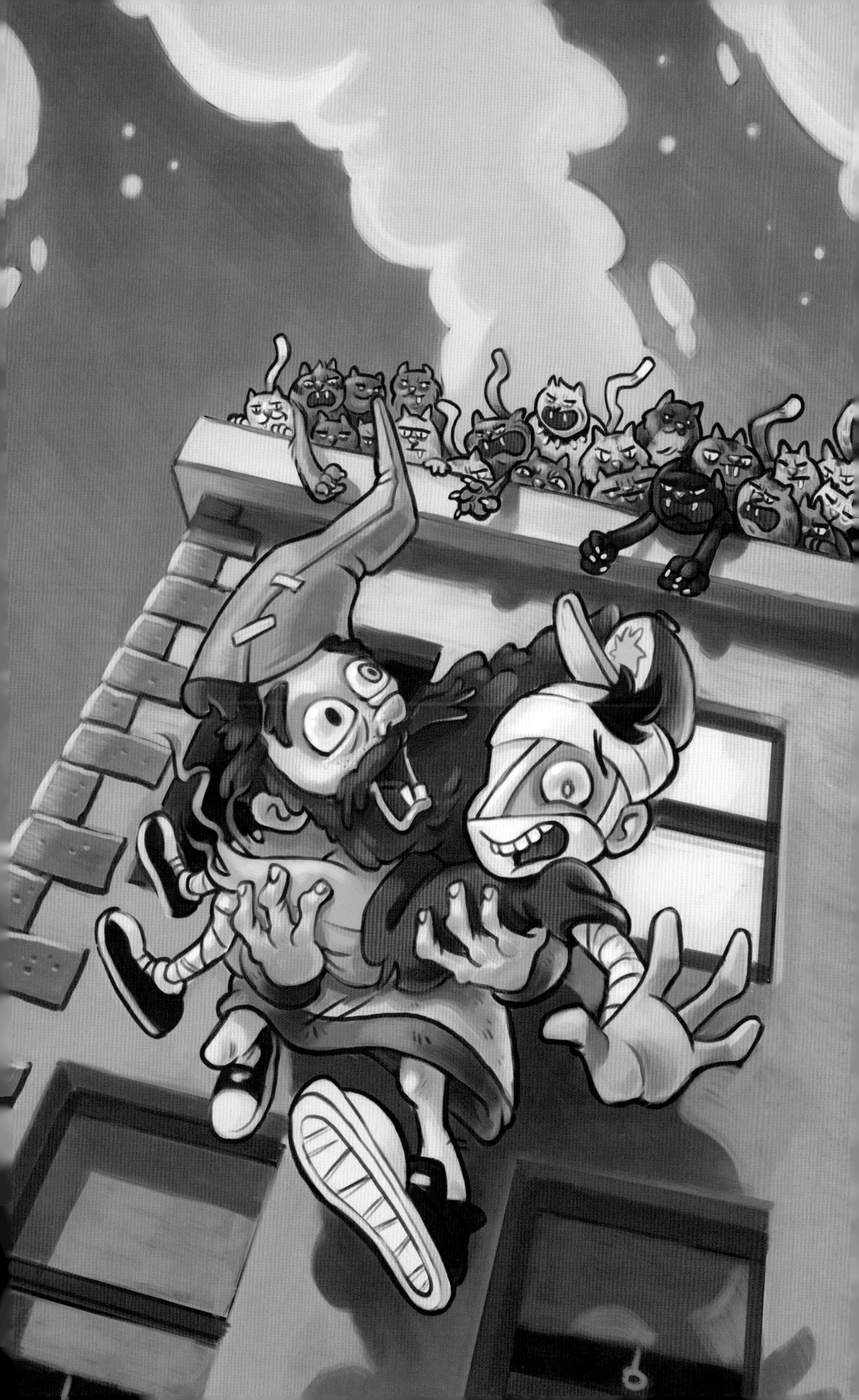

James Stanton

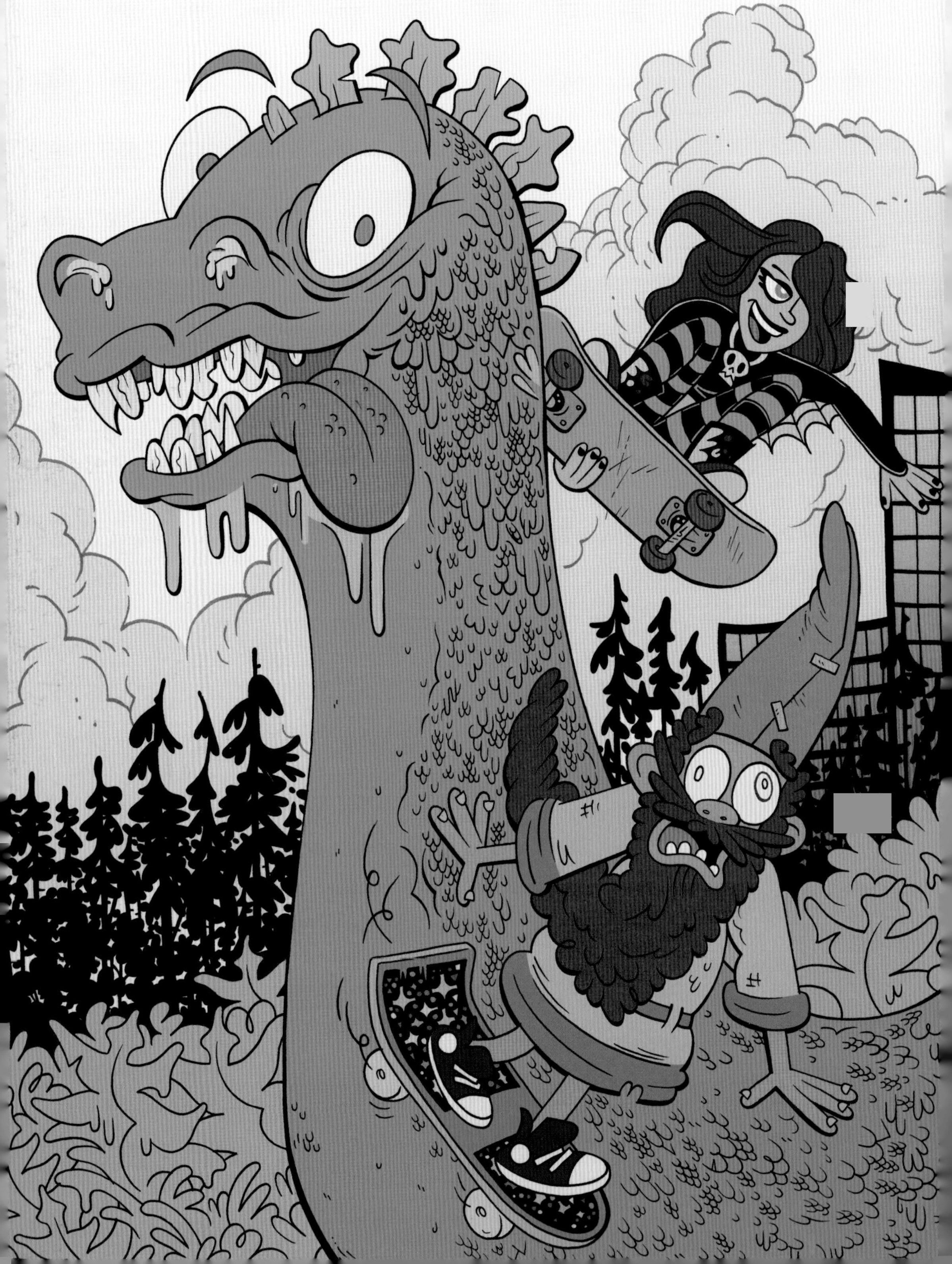

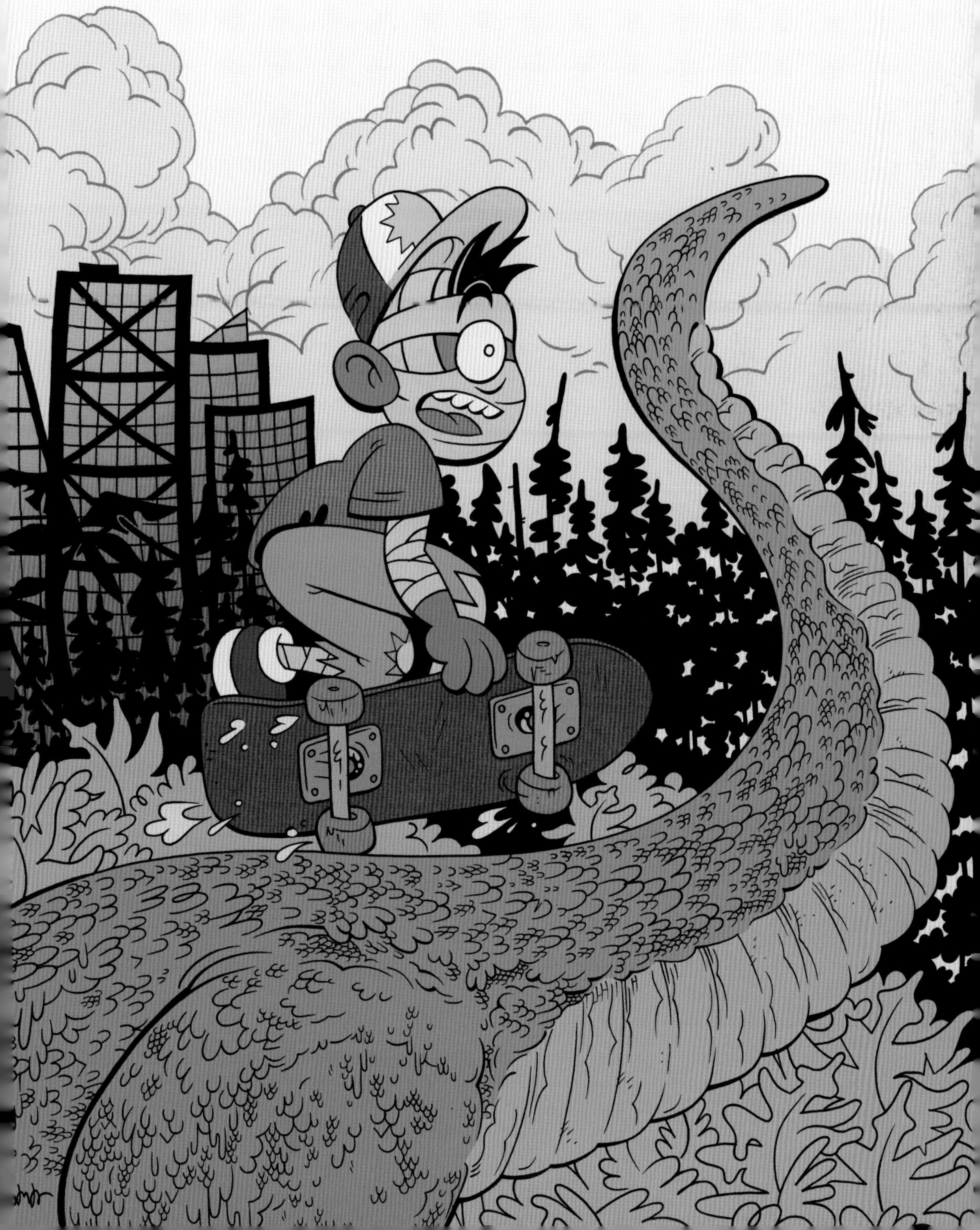

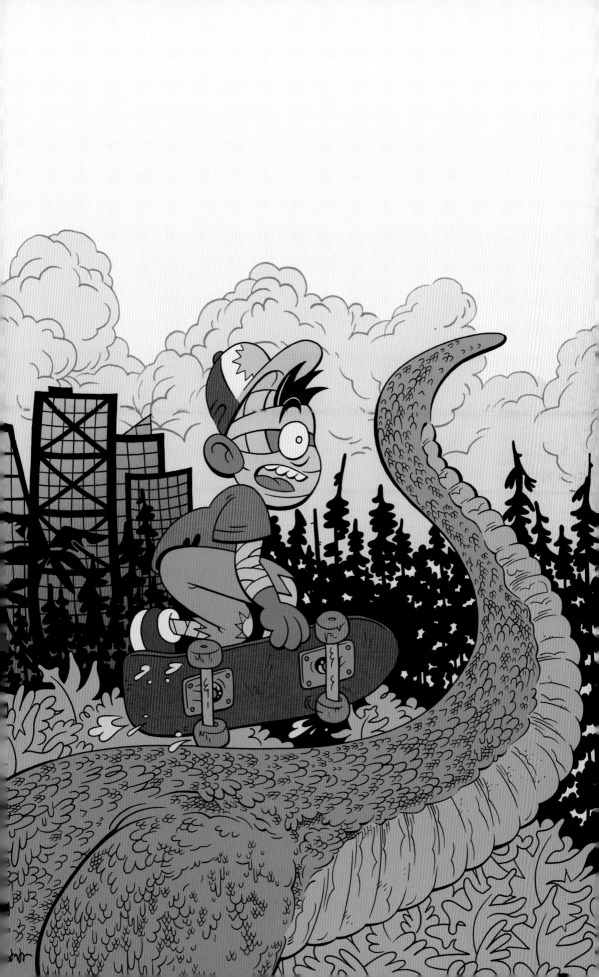

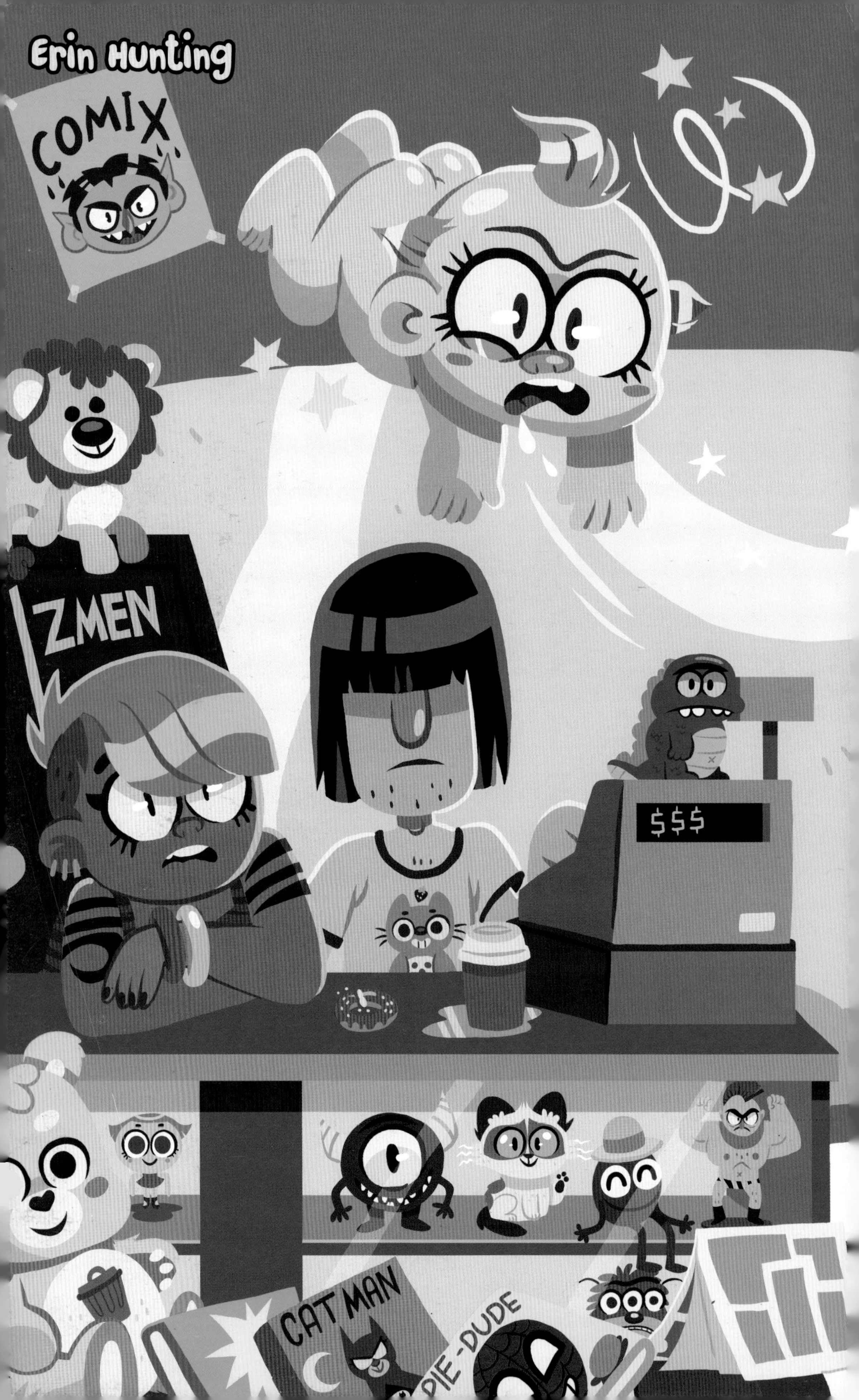
Erin Hunting
COMIX
ZMEN
$$$
CAT MAN
DIE-DUDE

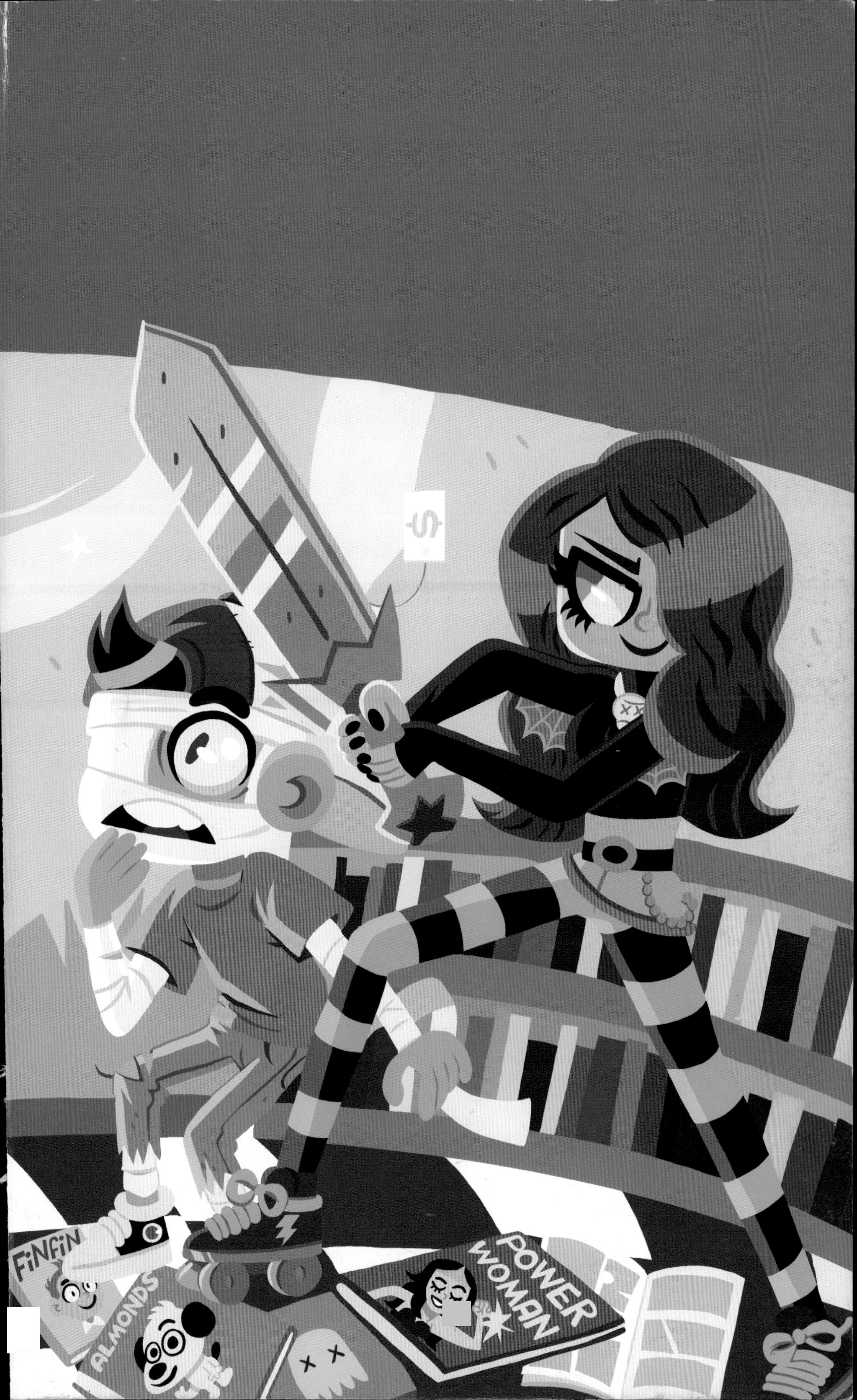
$
FINFIN
ALMONDS
POWER WOMAN

DAVE SCHEIDT is a radical dude from Chicago, Illinois. When he's not writing comic books, he enjoys eating pizza.

SCOOT MCMAHON is the creator behind the all-ages comics sami the samurai squirrel, spot on Adventure, and a regular collaborator for Aw Yeah Comics. scoot loves ninjas, superheroes, running, and pizza. find scoot at scootcomics.com.

SEAN DOVE Lives and works in Chicago, Illinois, where he self-published The Last Days of Danger, worked on Madballs, and cocreated Brobots. His favorite halloween candy includes those weird Tootsie fruit Rolls and fun-size 100 Grand bars.